Breaking Free

by
Teresa J. Reasor

This is a work of fiction. Names, characters, places and incidents are the product of the author's imagination or are used fictitiously, and any resemblance to actual persons living or dead, business establishments, events, or locales is entirely coincidental.

Breaking Free

Contact Information: teresareasor@msn.com

Cover Art by *Tracy Stewart*

Teresa J. Reasor
PO Box 124
Corbin, KY 40702

Publishing History
First Edition 2011

ISBN 10: 0615502431
ISBN 13: 978-0-615-50243-4

DEDICATION

To my partner in crime, Tracy Stewart. Thanks so much for the beautiful cover. And to all the members of Lethal Ladies. You are the bomb.

PROLOGUE

Damn thing fits like a coffin lid. Lieutenant "Hawk" Yazzie eyed the edge of what had once been the outer wall of a building balanced above him. Sweat trickled across his shoulder blade down his side. He thrust aside the claustrophobic pressure and focused on the two lookouts on the roof through night vision binoculars. They weren't moving. Good.

Come on, come on.

A silhouette appeared in the second story window. The light behind the man gave the impression of broad shoulders and a stocky frame. The rifle slung over his arm, the firearm's barrel pointed skyward, identified him as another hostile. Hawk squinted but couldn't make out his features. He'd counted six men upstairs earlier. Was this one of them or someone new?

Three clicks came over the radio. "Doc", Zack O'Connor signaled he was finished and in position.

Hawk pushed the call button on his radio in answer.

Where the hell were Cutter and Strong Man?

Derrick Armstrong, "Strong Man" broke radio silence. "We have a problem, over."

Hawk's muscles tensed.

"C's a no show, over," Strong Man whispered.

Fuck. The last assignment of their tour, and fucking Murphy's Law decides to kick in.

Hawk pressed the switch on his belt triggering his throat mike. "Cutter, come in, over."

Damn it, Cutter, respond.

Silence.

"Last location, over?" Hawk asked.

"Ground floor. I thought he was right behind me, over."

Hawk blinked the sweat from his eye.

"Five minutes, over." Oliver Shaker, "Greenback", their rear security, came across calm, level, reminding them they needed to get the hell out of here.

God damn it.

He'd never lost a man and Cutter wasn't going to be the first.

"I'm going back in for him, over." Hawk shook free of his pack and slithered like a lizard from beneath the slab, pushing his submachine gun ahead of him and kicking up dust.

There was always dust in this dry desert country. God, he was sick of it.

He belly crawled to the cracked wall fifteen feet to his right. The rush of adrenaline pumping through his system thrust his heart into overdrive.

He pushed to his feet behind a half wall still standing and glanced up at the second floor. Everything appeared still. All hell would have broken loose if they'd discovered Cutter. He was either trapped somewhere inside and waiting for an opportunity to escape or something worse.

Shit.

Hawk drew a deep breath and assessed the situation. He'd have to go up the street out of sight of the lookouts, go across, and work his way back. Keeping to the shadows next to the crumbled wall, he moved east down the strip of abandoned buildings.

Gravel crunched just ahead. He dodged into a doorway and flattened himself against the wall. Shadows closed around him like a cocoon.

A man strode by, a rifle held in the bend of his arm. He clasped a flashlight and projected a small golden circle on the broken sidewalk before him.

Hawk withdrew his SOG knife and fell in behind the tango. Concrete debris crunched beneath his feet. The man started to turn. Hawk slit his throat and any sound he might have made strangled to a gurgle. Hawk caught him as he sagged, dragged the body to a doorway, and rolled it into the shadows.

He took off his helmet, tossed it aside, and peeled off his tack vest. The cloying, coppery scent of blood hit him as he jerked the tango's shirt free and put it on over his body armor. With his dark hair and skin, he'd pass for one of them.

Maybe.

Hanging the MP-5 down his spine, he retrieved the MK-47 rifle and flashlight.

Seconds ticked by in his head like a metronome. Two minutes thirty seconds. His muscles jerked with his efforts to keep his pace to a stroll when everything in him urged him to run.

A voice called from the second story window asking if he'd seen anything. His heart rate surged.

Think.

Answer him.

He formulated an answer in the local Kurdish dialect. Sweat ran in itchy rivulets down his spine beneath the Kevlar vest that hugged his torso.

The man said something about a cold. Hawk grunted an agreement.

He thumbed off the rifle's safety and putting his finger on the trigger, dodged into the building through the front door. The room opened into a dark, empty hallway. After a moment's pause, he flipped on the flashlight and trotted down the hall to the fourth doorway on the left.

A voice called from upstairs asking what he was doing.

"Getting my ass blown up," he murmured beneath his breath. He darted into the back storage room. Crates stacked nearly to the ceiling lined the walls. One crate stood open, straw spilt onto the floor around it. AK-47 rifles lay nestled inside.

Intel was right. They had to get out of here.

Hawk flicked the flashlight back and forth as he worked his way through Cutter's route.

A black piece of fabric sticking out from behind some furniture caught his attention and he jogged to it. Cutter lay crumpled into a ball behind a heavily carved cabinet, his helmet beside him. Blood coated the side of his head near his temple and pooled on the floor.

Jesus. What the fuck happened? Hawk bent to check for a pulse. It beat weak and thready beneath his fingertips.

He glanced at his watch. One minute. Fear ripped through him. His breathing grew labored. He laid the flashlight and rifle atop some crates and swung his MP-5 into position under his arm. Bending, he heaved Cutter's limp frame up and over his shoulder.

Forty-five seconds. Hawk's stomach and back muscles grew taut as he adjusted to the one hundred and seventy pounds of limp weight with an effort.

He poked his head out. The hall light flashed on. A tango blinked at Hawk in surprise. He shouted an alarm as he raised a pistol and closed the distance between them at a run.

The forty-five automatic's muzzle looked like a cannon. And sounded like one as the tango fired.

Wood splintered from the door facing close to Hawk's face. He swung the submachine gun up and pulled the trigger in a controlled burst. Red blossomed across the tango's chest, the force of the bullets throwing him back against the wall. His body bounced off the surface then crumpled to the floor. Footsteps pounded above.

What a clusterfuck. They were sitting ducks in the hallway. Hawk sprayed the hall light with bullets killing it, then sprinted down the hallway to the front door. The timer in his head counted off the seconds, thirty-five—. He leveled a short burst of fire at the doorknob and it flew open. He struggled through the opening.

Bullets peppered the road and dogged his steps from above, ricocheting off the asphalt around him. Muzzle flashes exploded like sunspots in front of him as his men laid down suppressing fire.

Another shot of adrenaline coursed through his veins making Cutter's body seem like a featherweight as he zigzagged towards the cover of the crumpled wall he'd left five minutes before.

A foot away from safety, the sky lit and his ears popped. The ground heaved throwing him up and forward. Cutter's body flew through the air like a rag doll.

The world came crashing down.

CHAPTER 1

"Hawk."

Zoe Weaver's heart lurched at the masculine voice behind her. She looked over her shoulder, her gaze searching the group of casually dressed naval personnel who took up most of the backyard and deck. Several men called out greetings and converged on the tall man balanced on crutches just inside the wooden gate.

Hawk's midnight dark hair stood out against the lighter toned heads that surrounded him. His high forehead, sculpted cheekbones, and angular jaw were a study in pride and control as well as his Native American heritage. She had only a moment to admire the bone deep masculine beauty of his features before his pale gray gaze homed in on her. Shock reverberated from her midsection to the bottoms of her feet. Her heart rate kicked into a gallop.

Realizing her prolonged stare could be misconstrued; she turned her attention back to the tray of hamburgers she was replenishing. Had she known he would be coming to the Marks' barbecue, she'd have made some excuse to avoid the gathering.

Just his presence made her hands tremble and her stomach to somersault. A burst of resentment tightened her shoulders. She took a deep breath, drawing in the scents of chlorine, suntan lotion, and grilling meat as her rapid-fire heartbeat continued to thump against her ribs.

The man was six foot, four inches of Navy Brass through and through. He'd probably bleed Brasso if he scraped his elbow. The analogy wasn't true, but it served to remind her of whom and what he was. A Navy SEAL. Through and through.

Since meeting him six days earlier, she'd found it hard to push aside the impression he had made, or the anger she experienced because of it.

"I screwed up," had been the way Hawk had put it. Without any details. She understood injuries happened in combat, but he made no bones about taking the blame for her brother's condition. Like a good team leader.

To hell with that.

She wanted answers, not military platitudes.

She couldn't direct her rage at a situation, only at the man claiming responsibility. A likely military ploy.

Every time she went to the hospital and saw her brother hooked up to tubes and wires, she experienced another surge of emotion, grief and fear.

The strongest of them, fear.

She needed to know what had happened to Brett.

She scanned the small clumps of people scattered around the yard eating and drinking. Langley Marks, her host, had finally abandoned his position at the grill and joined some of the men at the volleyball net set up in the corner of the yard. Others sat at one end of the deck in the shade, watching the game and calling out encouragement to the players.

Under any other circumstances, this trip to California would have been a treat. The weather remained beautiful, the temperatures a moderate seventy degrees. Palm trees loomed over the wooden privacy fence encircling the yard. Hibiscus shrubs, hugged the deck, their big fuchsia blossoms a splash of color against the lightly stained wood that matched the sand-hued stucco on the house's exterior walls.

High-pitched squeals coming from the pool drew her attention. Her mother and sister sat poolside with Trish Marks, encircled by a ring of female supporters, wives and girlfriends of the men present.

The deep worry lines etched into her mother's face were a testament to her own beliefs. Getting involved with a man in uniform was just asking for pain. A father and possibly a brother were enough to give for her country.

The muted tones of a child's voice broke into her reverie. She looked around the food-laden picnic table in search of the source. Limping around the corner of the table, she spied a small discarded sandal peeking out from under the tablecloth. She kneeled and pulled up the edge of the plastic to look beneath.

Pale blond ringlets obscured the child's face as she danced a bathing suit clad Barbie doll, minus its shoes, across the decking and inserted her, legs first, into a pink, plastic convertible.

"Katie Beth what are you doing under there?"

"Playin'." The simple logic of the child's answer had her shaking her head. *Ask a dumb question.*

"Come out, baby."

Katie Beth looked up briefly before going back to her make-believe car journey. Pale blue eyes and a rounded jaw, much like her own, held the Weaver stubbornness she recognized all too well. "Don't want to."

"Why not, sweetheart?"

A pale pink lip protruded. "Grandma and mommy keep crying. I don't like it."

With a weary sigh, she rested her forehead against the edge of the table. "May I come in with you?"

Katie Beth cocked her head as though considering the request. "Okay."

She crawled beneath the table with her niece. With a four year old's trusting affection, Katie Beth climbed into her lap and cuddled back against her. Zoe rested her chin against the blond curls and breathed in the baby powder and sun block scent that clung to her.

"Grandma and mommy are very sad," she explained as she adjusted one strap of the hot pink bathing suit over the fragile curve of the child's shoulder.

Katie Beth's voice dwindled to a whisper. "Uncle Brett is sick."

"Uncle Brett was hurt while doing something very important, sweetheart." Her voice sounded husky and soft around the lump in her throat. "He wanted us to be safe. He wanted other little girls and boys like you to be safe, too."

"Mommy said I can't go see him."

"That's right. But—" her voice wobbled, and she cleared her throat. "Once he gets better, he'll come home and you'll get to see him then."

A beat of silence followed, then with her normal precocious bluntness Katie Beth asked, "Is Uncle Brett going to visit God like Grandma Rose?"

"No." Her arms tightened around the child as she fought back her own fear and uncertainty. "He's going to come home to us." She sought something to distract the child. "Would you like to be my helper, Katie Beth?"

"Okay."

"We have to help Mommy and Grandma feel better. You know what helps me feel better?"

Katie Beth shook her head.

"Getting your hugs makes me feel better. Why don't you go give Grandma and Mommy a hug, so they can feel better, too?"

"Okay. I'll take Barbie so she can hug them, too."

"I think that would be a good idea, sweetheart."

Katie Beth wiggled free and crawled from beneath the table, the doll clutched in her hand.

Some of the tension that drummed at Zoe's temples relaxed and she rested her forehead against her bent knee.

"Hello there, little bit."

She stiffened at the sound of Hawk's distinctive deep voice.

"What happened to your leg?" Katie Beth asked.

"I hurt it, but the doctor's are making it all better."

Zoe crawled forward to peek from beneath the table just as the child lunged forward and hugged Hawk's good leg.

His eyes widened in surprise, and after a minute hesitation, cupped the back of her head. Her blond ringlets curled between his long fingers. A smile touched his lips. Katie Beth jerked away as quickly as she had hugged him and ran through the guests toward her grandmother.

Hawk's attention settled on Zoe as she crawled from beneath the table and settled back on her heels. She took in the crutches and the bulk of the knee brace clamped around his leg. The denim of his cutoffs hugged his muscular thighs. A white t-shirt stretched across the broad width of his chest, delineating the shape of a well-toned torso. A strip of gauze covered a four-inch section of his arm just above his elbow. Bruises already turning yellow peppered his legs and arms.

How had he gotten those injuries? The rest of the team seemed free from any.

"If you'll have a seat I'll fill you a plate and bring it to you, Lieutenant."

One black brow quirked at her stiffly formal tone. "No thanks, though I wouldn't say no to a cup of coffee."

She nodded and flipped her long ponytail over her shoulder. Conscious of his regard, her limp had never seemed more conspicuous as she traversed the distance to the coffee pot and back, returning with a Styrofoam cup. "You prefer it black, don't you?"

"Yes."

Instead of going to sit at one of the tables with the other men, he hiked a hip on the deck railing, propped his crutches beside him, and reached for the cup.

"That knee will swell if you stay on it too long," she warned him.

"I know. Brett told me you were a physical therapist. How long have you been practicing?" He sipped the coffee.

"Two years. I can get you a chair."

His smile flashed white against the swarthiness of his skin. "If I allow you to get me a chair, you'll disappear as soon as I sit down."

His words fired her cheeks with heat and her temper at the same time. She held her tongue to keep the peace in front of the other guests.

"Your mother said your sister was returning home with Katie Beth tomorrow."

She nodded. Where was he going with this topic of conversation?

"I want to help, if you'll let me."

"How?"

"I know you and your mother are staying at a motel, which is pretty expensive. I also know that Brett's one bedroom will be pretty cramped. I live off post and can offer you both a place to stay until Brett is well."

Surprised, she studied his expression. "Why would you want to do that?"

"Because Brett is a member of the team and part of our family. When you place your life in another man's hands you get pretty close."

Her brother had placed his life in this man's hands and had nearly been killed. Looking into the steady gray gaze she couldn't level that accusation at him, though the thought bounced around in her head. She didn't wish Hawk ill. She just wanted her brother well again.

Part of what he said was true, though. Many of Brett's letters home held news of Hawk and the other men in his SEAL team. He spoke of them as though they were brothers—especially Hawk.

"I've spoken with your mother about it and she's agreed, but only under the condition that you agree as well."

Her attention swung back to her mother. The financial strain of staying at a motel had been worrying her. But what about the strain of living under the same roof as Hawk? With this *sorry ma'am it's classified* crap hanging between them and the attraction she fought to suppress—

Hawk would probably be embarrassed if he knew. She didn't want to dwell on the humiliation she'd face if he discovered it. She'd been through that before.

"You could make sure I don't overdo my PT. With our training we're used to pushing ourselves. As I understand it, I can't do that with a soft tissue injury."

"No, you can't." More at ease in a professional capacity than a personal one, the tension in her neck and shoulders eased. "If you push too hard before you have a chance to heal, you'll be back to square one."

"Then it's good I'll have you there to offer me advice. What do you say, Zoe?"

How was she supposed to hide her attraction for him, when he seemed determined to draw her out?

"When you're accustomed to living alone, even one extra person can be too many, Lieutenant. Perhaps you should give this idea a little more thought. You don't really know us very well. You'd be taking strangers into your home."

"And though your mother has met me before, I'm a stranger to you."

She hated the cowardice that had her jumping on any excuse to avoid getting closer to him. "Yes, you are."

A smile laced with charm quirked one side of his mouth upward. "Uncle Sam trusts me. Don't you think you could trust me too?"

She folded her arms against her waist. "You don't really expect to get anywhere with that line, do you, Lieutenant?" she asked, her tone dry.

He chuckled, the sound deep and masculine. "I couldn't resist. My motives aren't entirely altruistic. I'll be at PT once a day. I can adjust my schedule to coincide with the times you and your mother visit with Brett at the hospital. I can't drive and I know you've rented a car. We could ride in together and you could share my car and turn the rental back in. It'll save me from taking a bus or taxi or calling one of the men for a ride."

She took his empty cup, careful not to touch him. "More?"

****

Hawk shook his head. Damn she was stubborn.

Was she as determined to hold onto her antagonism toward him as she was in denying the magnetic sparks that arced between them? He watched the swing of her long hazelnut ponytail as she went to the garbage can and tossed the cup away. That heavy swath of tawny hair naturally streaked with blond seemed to beckon provocatively "follow me".

The trim, tight curve of her hips and buttocks drew his attention. A vision of him cupping her rounded derriere in his hands lanced through his thoughts with the impact of a cruise missile. His mouth went dry and his breathing grew short.

Why was he leaving himself open to frustration and rejection? She obviously wanted no part of him, and being Brett's sister, he couldn't pursue her anyway. Brett would expect him to protect her, not try to coax her into bed. The only reason he'd offered them a place to stay was to look after them. Wasn't it?

The slight hitch in her stride didn't bother him. Brett had told him about the accident that had nearly cost her a leg. She was a fighter, stubborn and strong. He recognized those qualities in her already. But Brett hadn't said anything about her obvious distrust of men. He hadn't told him how delicate and lovely she was, either. The slender self-assured young woman who stood before him looked very little like the gangly twelve year old child with freckles across her nose in the photograph Brett carried in his wallet.

To give her time to think about his offer, he changed the subject. "You're very good with your niece."

A small smile, the first he had seen thus far, peeked out. "She's been around for a while, so I've had a little practice.

She's unhappy because she hasn't been allowed to see Brett. Sharon thinks it would be too upsetting for her even if she could."

He read the strain in the faint, bluish shadows beneath her eyes and the lines around her mouth. The numerous hours she spent with her brother at the hospital were already wearing her down.

"When are you going back to the hospital?'"

"At seven-thirty. They'll let us stay till nine, but won't let us stay the night."

"You have to rest sometime, Zoe. Brett will need you once he wakes up."

If he woke up.

He could see the words punch through her thoughts as they did his.

"I'd like to go with you," he added, drawing her unusual pale blue gaze back up.

He noticed the dark blue ring around the lighter blue of the iris, the sweep of dark brown lashes, and the unblemished texture of her complexion. Would her skin be as smooth on other parts of her body?

Wayward parts of his anatomy responded to the thought.

Hawk cursed beneath his breath. Focus. Complete the mission. Get Zoe and Mrs. Weaver settled in his house and look out for them until Brett recovered and could do it himself. That's what Cutter would do if something happened to him—if he'd had any family left to look out for. An ache settled beneath his breastbone for a moment. He twisted his thoughts back to the task at hand.

"I'll have to drop Mom, Sharon, and Katie Beth off at the motel. Sharon needs to rest and so does Mother."

"What about you, Zoe?"

"I'm doing Okay."

The stubborn tilt to her chin brought a smile to his lips. He hadn't seen much resemblance to Brett until then.

A squeal and splash from the pool caught her attention. She straightened and looked toward the water.

"Doc's in the pool with Katie Beth and Langley's children. He won't let anything happen to them," he said.

He thought she might be beginning to relax with him when another smile tilted her lips.

"Katie Beth swims like a fish. She's also fearless. He may find he's bitten off more than he can chew."

"It must be a family trait. I've never seen Brett back off of anything, either. And from what he's told me, you can hold your own."

Her smile died as quickly as it had blossomed and her expression grew shuttered. "I hope you're right, Lieutenant. Brett's going to need everything he's got to come back from this. So will the rest of us. Please excuse me, I'd better check on my sister."

He swore beneath his breath as she limped across the deck and down the steps.

"How about a beer to drown those flames," Chief Petty Officer Langley Marks said as he held out a bottle dripping with condensation. His quick grin slid into a smirk. "Don't take it to heart, Hawk. The lady hasn't been any more receptive to any of the other men."

"It isn't like that, Lang. She's Brett's sister, she's off limits."

Langley's thick brows rose. "You'd better fill the other men in on that, then. More than one of them has been urging her to test the waters."

He experienced a quick twinge of irritation. "And?"

"She never even got her toes wet."

He fought the smile that tugged at his lips. "Good. If just one of them gets involved with her, there'll be hell to pay when Cutter wakes up."

Words of doubt weren't voiced, but hung between them. They both tipped their beers upward.

"I've offered them a place to stay until Brett recovers."

"Jesus, Hawk." Langley's lantern jaw hung open a moment. "I don't think you have a clue what you're taking on here."

"Probably not, but I'll get by." He rolled the half empty bottle between his palms, mindful of mixing alcohol and the pain medication he'd taken. "There's room for them and I'm not there much."

"You will be until that knee heals," Langley pointed out.

"I'll be taking another language class while I'm recovering, and once the swelling goes down, I'll have PT about an hour a day."

"Damn son, don't you ever relax?"

Hawk smiled.

Langley rolled his eyes. "You'll have to make sure you don't throw your underwear around, take out the trash after dinner each night, and put the toilet seat down."

"If that's all you do around here, it's no wonder Trish does so well while you're gone," he said.

Langley grinned. "There are a few other things I take care of that I didn't mention. If the situation changes between you and Ms. Weaver, I could offer you a few pointers."

Hawk took a swallow of beer. He wasn't interested in a permanent relationship, and Zoe Weaver had permanent written all over her. Permanent meant being there when you were needed, and as long as he was with the Teams he couldn't be. "It's not happening. She's Cutter's sister. I'm not laying a hand on her. Besides, her mother will be there to chaperone."

"I can see how that would put a cramp in your style, which leads us to another problem. If you're not laying hands on her, you won't be laying hands on any other female on the premises while they're staying there."

He shrugged. "I can lay hands somewhere else then."

Langley grew thoughtful. "You're really serious about this."

"Yeah."

"It could be months, Hawk, it could be never."

Pain twisted his gut into knots. "So could my knee. It doesn't hurt anything to keep a positive attitude, to hold onto hope. I figure if they can," he pointed the neck of the bottle he held in Zoe and her mother's direction, "I can."

"It wasn't your fault, Hawk. None of us knew Brett was in trouble. If you're doing this out of some misplaced feelings of guilt—"

"It was my responsibility to keep track of my men."

"You saved his life, man, and damn near got killed doing it. No one could ask any more from you than that."

But it didn't change the fact that Brett was hurt. He viewed the operation as a personal failure, though they had succeeded in destroying the building. The whole point of the mission was to get in and out without shots being fired, without injuries being sustained.

What had happened to Brett in that building? Who was responsible for his injuries? Until he knew the answer, it would continue to drive him crazy.

His gaze strayed to Zoe as she sat next to the pool in a lawn chair and watched the children paddling in the water. Doc O'Connor, the corpsman of the team, sat beside her on the concrete. She smiled at something he said then shook her head. The man took her hand and pressed it over his heart. She laughed then withdrew her hand and wagged a finger at him in a negative motion.

The tension drained from his shoulders and back when she rose to call Katie Beth out of the pool. Keeping Zoe Weaver from becoming involved with one of the team members was going to be a challenge. He could handle it.

Finding out what had happened to Brett Weaver would prove more difficult. But he'd do it.

He had to know.

CHAPTER 2

Out of the corner of her eye, Zoe caught Hawk's gaze focused on her as she maneuvered the car through a busy intersection. His presence in the seat next to her bred a hypersensitivity to her driving skills.

Surreptitiously, she glanced at him. He appeared at ease, his hands resting on his thighs. His right leg encased in a brace looked a mile long as it stretched beneath the dashboard; the left one appeared tan and muscular. His large frame filled the compact's passenger seat, leaving little space between them. The clean scent of his cologne mixed with the sun block her mother, Sharon, and Katie Beth had smeared on at the pool.

Katie Beth, having decided to take up with him in a big way, chattered away behind them. "Swan Lake Barbie is the bestest one. She has a beautiful dress."

"What about Frogman Barbie? Excuse me, Frog Lady Barbie?" he teased, shifting to look over his shoulder.

Katie Beth giggled. "There ain't no Frog Lady Barbie, Hawk."

"There isn't a Frog Lady Barbie," Clara Weaver corrected quietly. "Ain't isn't a word, baby."

"Sure it is, Grandma, I just said it," Katie Beth returned.

His grin flashed white. Zoe's stomach flip-flopped.

"A frogman is a man who swims under water with special tanks on his back filled with air," he said to Katie Beth.

"Uncle Brett did that in the swimming pool," she said.

"The last time he was home, he gave the neighbor's two teenage boys a demonstration in the pool," Clara said. "Katie Beth was fascinated. I can't believe she still remembers that. It was over a year ago and she wasn't quite three."

"I'm a big girl now, I'm four." Zoe caught a glimpse of Katie Beth's curls bouncing with the adamant nod of her head in the rearview mirror.

"I'm sure you're going to be a big help to your mama, now that you're going to have a baby brother or sister."

"It's going to be another girl," Sharon said from the back seat. "Right now it feels like there may be two in there."

"You'll be more comfortable once you're home," he said, his tone soothing.

"I want to stay but my doctor has suggested I come home. My due date's only eight weeks away, and he doesn't want me to take any chances."

The strain in Sharon's voice had Zoe's stomach tightening.

Hawk said, "Brett would want you to do what's best for the baby. He has the whole team, and your sister and mother, looking out for him. I'll be around the hospital checking in on him, too. I'm sure your husband wants you home where he can keep an eye on you."

Zoe agreed. Since being notified of Brett's injuries, they'd been on constant red alert. The strain was beginning to get to them all. Hawk's steady strength and air of command seemed a comfort to her mother and sister. And even she experienced a lessening of the pressure while around him.

"We can keep you posted on Brett's progress and you can keep us posted on yours. Turner will call us the minute you go into labor, if we're still here by then," her mother said.

Zoe brushed at the fine strands of hair that had escaped the ponytail holder. She loved her family, but she was eager to get to the hospital to see Brett. They had discussed this before and covering the same ground over and over seemed counterproductive. She could offer her sister only so much reassurance.

"Brett will understand that you have other responsibilities you have to deal with, Sharon," she said. "We've always understood how his responsibilities have precluded things in the past."

"I suppose you're right," Sharon agreed.

"Having a brother in the military, especially a SEAL isn't easy for anyone's family," Hawk said.

She fastened her attention on maneuvering through the parking lot and avoided glancing in his direction though she was aware of his gaze resting on her.

Had he recognized the resentment in her tone? Rationalizing that her brother's job was important and that he loved it didn't make it any easier. Never knowing where he might be, or how much danger he was in, made it doubly difficult. Fearing he was going to follow in their father's footsteps, literally, made it impossible.

The motel, a generic five-story structure with balconies all the way around, squatted in the center of a large parking lot. Because of Katie Beth's proclivity for adventure, they had opted to take a ground floor room and forego the effort it would take to keep her off the balcony.

"I'll be right back," she said. She exited the vehicle, leaving the engine running and the air conditioning blowing.

Katie Beth jumped out behind her grandmother. She grabbed Zoe's hand and held on like a Chinese finger puzzle.

Once they were inside the room, she settled Katie before the television to watch cartoons, and then turned to find Sharon in tears.

"There'll be time for you to see Brett tomorrow morning before your flight," she soothed. "Who knows, maybe he'll wake up tonight and tell you good-bye."

"Damn him, I wish he would." Sharon clung to her for a moment, her pregnant belly snug against Zoe's flat one.

"You're exhausted, Sharon. You need to rest. Mom does, too." Regret for her earlier impatience pinged away inside her, and she held her sister close. "Mom's right next door if you need anything. Cuddle Katie Beth and maybe you'll both sleep a little. I'll check on you when I get back after visiting hours are over."

"All right." Sharon drew back, her nose and eyes red, her face wet. She reached for a tissue on the nightstand and mopped her face.

"Call home and talk to Turner," Zoe suggested. "It will make you feel better to hear his voice."

Sharon nodded. "I will."

Zoe tapped the adjoining door and poked in her head. Her mother looked pale as she lay across the garish blue flowered spread. Her mascara, smeared from rubbing her eyes, crying, or both, underlined the exhaustion that etched her face.

"I'll be back in a while. Do you need me to pick up anything?"

Clara shook her head. "Give Brett my love."

Zoe's throat ached. She gave a brief nod and closed the door.

She hastily checked her own sun-worn appearance in the dresser mirror. Tugging loose the elastic loop holding her hair, and giving the heavy strands a quick brushing, she secured it back into a ponytail. Conscious of Hawk waiting in the car, she ignored the rest of her appearance and hastened to join him.

The pain and frustration seemed easier to deal with if she stayed in motion, if she had a plan of action, a goal. Eventually Brett would wake up, if she hounded him enough. He hadn't let her give up when it looked as though she might lose her leg. She wouldn't allow him to either.

She slammed the car door shut and reached for the seatbelt.

Hawk laid a hand on her forearm. "Something happen?"

His fingers, warm and calloused, rested against her bare skin sending a tingling sensation along her nerve endings. "No, why?" She rammed the buckle closed and tried to block off her response.

"You've got the same look on your face Brett gets when we're going into action."

She gripped the gearshift, but didn't put it into reverse.

"I know how frustrating it must be not to be able to do something," he said after a moment of silence.

"I don't think you do, Lieutenant." She recognized the edge that had crept into her voice and drew a deep breath.

"He's not just one of the men under my command, Zoe. He's also my friend."

The letters Brett had written to her had been witness to that. "If you're his friend, then you need to understand something."

"What's that?"

She met his pale gray gaze straight on. "I'm not going to let my brother die. He isn't going to lay there like a vegetable either. Whatever it takes, however long it takes, he's going to come back from this. If you won't or can't believe that, you needn't bother visiting him."

He gave a brief nod. "I'll help in any way I can."

"Good." Some of the tension inside her relaxed. "You can start by telling me what happened." She put the car in reverse, and turned to look over her shoulder.

"I can't discuss the mission, Zoe."

"I'm not asking you to. I don't care what, where, or when, I just want to know how my brother ended up in harm's way." She stopped at a stoplight.

"It's a war. We were all in danger. That's our job."

Those few words, so succinct, so blunt, caught at her heart and gave her a hollow feeling in the pit of her stomach. The light changed, and she stepped on the gas.

"I realize it's your job to put yourself in dangerous situations. I'm asking if Brett was hit by flying debris or attacked by someone. How did he end up in a coma?"

His features looked honed from wood. "I'd like to be able to tell you, Zoe, but I can't. An investigation is underway. I'm not at liberty to talk about it, not even to you."

A dropping sensation hit her stomach. "No one told us about an investigation."

"There's always an investigation when something goes wrong. I'm sure you'll be notified, now that you're here."

She fought the urge to pound the steering wheel in annoyance. "How do the other men's families feel about this closed lip policy?"

"I'm sure they find it just as aggravating as you do."

She took her eyes off the road long enough to flash him a look that had a wry quirk turning his lips upward.

"We go where no other unit can. We try to get in and out without anyone knowing we've been there. Most of the time, things go according to plan. This time, it didn't."

"When Brett first decided to become a SEAL, I did hours of research. I know how you train and I know how you operate. But knowing that doesn't help me a bit, now that he's hurt."

They drove in silence for several minutes. She tried to concentrate on the road and block out the rush of emotion that made her eyes sting and her throat to ache. She was being a bitch, but she couldn't contain her anger and grief. And he happened to be a handy target.

By the time she wheeled the vehicle into the parking structure at the hospital, tension had tightened her muscles to the point her leg ached from the strain. She knew she'd have to do some stretching exercises later to relieve the cramps. She had been on it too much today.

Because her own wreaked such havoc, she thought of Hawk's leg. "How's the knee?"

"A little swollen but holding up. How about your leg?" he asked.

Obviously, he had noticed her grimace of pain. "It's there—which beats the alternative." With the help of the door, she swung out of the car and gained her feet. By the time she'd come around the vehicle to help him, he had climbed out of the car and balanced on one foot. She retrieved the crutches from the trunk.

"Thanks." He hooked the crutches beneath his arms, and maneuvered around the car door and slammed it.

"How long did they say you'd be on crutches?"

He adjusted his speed to accommodate her slower pace.

"A couple of weeks. I didn't tear my ACL or do any permanent damage to the joint, just strained it badly enough for it to puff up like a basketball. I won't start PT for another week or so. I should be good to go in six or eight weeks max."

She nodded. "A whirlpool or hot tub would do wonders."

"So I've found. There's one at the house we can share."

Heat raced across her skin and settled in areas she tried hard to ignore. She pretended an interest in the flowering trees planted at equal intervals within the walk and hid the color in her cheeks.

The universal smell of antiseptic and pine scented cleaner permeated the air as they entered the hospital. She led the way into an elevator, and held the door for Hawk.

"Brett looks just as he always has," she said as they exited the elevator, and started down the hall to the right. "He has an IV and a catheter, but other than that he isn't on any kind of life support. If he doesn't regain consciousness soon, they'll have to put in a feeding tube."

"What does the doc say is the reason he won't wake up?"

"He's had a severe trauma to his brain. A subdural hematoma. They had to drill a hole in his skull to relieve the pressure. His coma was induced by drugs at first, but now—" She shook her head.

"He could wake up tomorrow and be fine. Or he could wake up and have brain damage."

She pushed open the wide wooden door. Silence rushed out to meet them. They stepped into the room. Each time, she saw her brother, so still upon the hospital bed, his head swathed in bandages, her heart ached as though it had been run over three or four times by an eighteen-wheeler.

A hard knot of emotion lodged in her throat. Had Hawk not been there, she might have indulged in a few tears to ease it. His hand slid down her back and came to rest against her waist. She pulled away. Her composure would desert her completely if she accepted the comfort he offered.

When she'd regained control of her emotions, she hazarded a glance at Hawk. His features were set in a grim forbidding expression, his lips compressed into a hard line. His pale eyes, darkened to steel gray, held a pain with which she was all too familiar.

****

Hawk dragged air into his lungs. Sucker punched. That's what it felt like to see Brett like this.

The man lay still on the bed, his skin nearly as pale as the sheets. The slow even rise and fall of his chest was the only sign he was alive. Hawk struggled to draw some reassurance from the fact his buddy seemed to be breathing on his own without difficulty. Wires ran beneath the pale blue hospital gown that only partially covered his chest. Electrodes were attached to his chest and a machine monitored his heart rate and blood pressure, another, his oxygen level.

Hawk cleared his throat before he could speak. "Let's go talk to him. Hey, Cutter, don't you think you've goldbricked enough?" he asked loudly as he approached the bed. "It's time to rise and shine, sailor."

Zoe brushed a kiss across Brett's forehead, and drew the sheet up over his bare chest.

It seemed surreal seeing the man so unresponsive when he had always been so active. Because he ran every day and lifted weights, as did most of the other team members, he was in prime condition. The slow rise and fall of his chest made it appear as though he'd just nodded off for a brief power nap, not a two week long excursion into a dark nether world.

Hawk lowered his tall frame into a chair next to the bed and propped his foot on the bottom railing of the bed. He kept up the one sided conversation with Brett, while Zoe exercised her brother's arms and legs so the muscles wouldn't atrophy.

Not being much of a talker, he found it difficult to keep the unreciprocated flow going. He talked about the team, about the barbeque, and about the remodeling project he worked on at his house.

"I could really use your help, Cutter. It's hard as hell hanging sheetrock by myself."

"Why do you call him that?" she asked.

"Most of the men have nicknames. Cutter got his during his first mission after graduating SEAL training."

Zoe looked so young, with her hair pulled back and the sun kissed blush upon her cheeks and nose. Reluctant to tell her anything that might put her brother, or his profession, in an adverse light he wracked his brain for an innocuous comment to explain. She beat him to it.

"Brett was always toying with sharp instruments. Knives. Screwdrivers. Axes. I imagine that comes in handy when you're in dangerous situations."

"Yeah, it does." Damn, she was tough. She faced off the hard things without flinching.

"Brett used to practice at targets in the back yard with a bow and arrow. He was on the archery team in high school. He won several competitions."

"And what were you like in high school?"

"Very shy and self-conscious."

"You outgrew it."

She bent Brett's knee, pushed his foot all the way up to his buttocks, then straightened the limb again. "I know my limitations and accept them."

His gaze dropped to the pant leg that covered her injury and he frowned.

A cursory knock sounded on the door and it opened. A nurse entered the room. Her thick dark brown hair, though pinned up according to regulations, still managed to look attractive. The green scrubs she wore didn't entirely hide the curves beneath.

Cutter was going to love waking up to her. She was just his type.

She nodded in acknowledgement of Hawk's presence. As he started to shove himself to a standing position, with the use of the chair arms, she waved him back down. "At ease, sir."

Her gaze swung to Zoe. "Hello, Zoe. Captain Connelly will be by in about half an hour."

Zoe nodded. "How have Brett's vitals been today, Angela?"

Angela checked the chart she carried. "Steady and strong."

She came forward to unwind the hose of a blood pressure cuff and wrap it around Brett's arm. She pumped the bulb and took the reading, then recorded it in the chart. She went through a routine of checking his pulse then looked over the reading on each machine, each time entering the data into the chart.

Zoe resumed the exercises.

"You might check into the hospital administration office. We subcontract some of our PT," Angela said as she watched.

"Thanks for the tip, but I'm not going to be here long enough to settle into a job. As soon as Brett's on his feet again, I'll have to return home to Kentucky."

Angela looked down at the chart for a moment. "It's early days yet. He may wake up tomorrow."

"I'm counting on it," Zoe said.

The doctor showed up a few minutes later. Hawk rose to his feet, and with the help of his crutches, balanced on his good leg. Though she had demonstrated more than once she didn't want his comfort or support, he stood beside Zoe while the doctor examined Brett.

He could sense her worry in the stiff way she held herself and in the way her eyes followed the doctor's every move.

"He's responsive to painful stimuli, his pupils are equally reactive, and his EEG shows normal brain activity." Captain Connelly said as he turned to face them both. "He just hasn't decided to join us, yet."

"I've been doing some PT with him, hoping the exertion will stimulate him and he'll wake up," Zoe said.

"It certainly can't hurt him. Talk to him as much as you can while you're here."

"I wanted to talk to you about that." Zoe squared her shoulders. Her battle-ready look slipping into place. Her jaw was set and her eyes homed in on Connelly like lasers. "I want permission to spend as much time with Brett as possible, even in between visiting hours. I'll read to him, talk to him, do PT, whatever it takes to get his attention."

Dr. Connelly's square jawed features softened in sympathy. "Miss Weaver—"

"Zoe," she interrupted.

A brief smile curved his lips. "Zoe. I know you want what's best for your brother."

"What's best for Brett is for him to wake up."

"Yes, it is," Dr. Connelly conceded. "But he's also sustained a trauma to his brain. He needs time to heal. I've spoken to one of the best neurosurgeons in the country, and have faxed him copies of everything in your brother's file. Let's wait and see what he says before you launch your campaign, all right?"

"And if he gives the go ahead?" she pressed, the determination in her expression unwavering.

"Yes, I'll give you a green light and you can camp out with your brother as much as you like—within reason." He laid a comforting hand on her shoulder. "It will ultimately be up to your brother, though. I know how frightening it is to see him lying there seemingly unresponsive. There is something going on in his brain. The readings of his electroencephalogram register brain activity. His brain pressure is normal now. His MRI shows no extensive brain damage. I don't know why he won't wake up."

"So there is hope," Hawk said.

Zoe frowned.

"Yes, there is. I haven't given up on Ensign Weaver. You shouldn't either," Connelly said.

Hawk nodded, a deep sense of relief easing the taut feeling of guilt that knotted his insides. He had to hold on to the belief that Brett would wake up, just as Zoe did.

As he looked down at his friend, his thoughts turned to other questions too hard to speak aloud. What if he woke up crippled, brain damaged, unable to care for himself? What then would Brett or his family do?

His attention focused on Zoe's face. The delicate curve of her cheek and jaw, the wing-like sweep of her brows, the straight narrow line of her nose, gave her features a fragile femininity that underlined her vulnerability, despite her expression of stubborn resolve. He suddenly realized that was her way of warding off the fear and uncertainty. Just as it was Brett's.

With the men in his command, he could give them a slap on the back, a nod, a thumb's up, a hooyah. Hawk did the only thing he could do with Zoe. He laced his fingers through hers in a show of support and comfort and immediately a thrum of electricity passed between them.

Zoe's attention shifted to their laced hands then refocused on the neurologist.

Doctor Connelly spoke as he crossed to the door. "I'll be speaking with you again tomorrow. I hope to hear something from the specialist I've contacted by then."

"We'll both be here, Doc," Hawk answered.

The door thumped shut quietly behind Connelly. The silence stretched taut as the strings on a parachute.

She stepped away, withdrawing her hand from his. She avoided his gaze as she moved back to Brett's side. For the hundredth time, she adjusted the sheet over him.

"I'm just trying to be a friend, Zoe."

"I didn't think anything else, Lieutenant."

"Hawk."

Her gaze rose to his face. "Hawk."

He grinned. "Now that we've settled that, when do you want to move in with me?

CHAPTER 3

"Hold on there little darlin'," Ensign Dan Rivera said as he came out of the attic stairwell. He caught Zoe around the waist and swung her out of the way as his two companions muscled a chest of drawers through the door and down the hall to the bedroom.

"Bowie—unhand that woman and grab the nightstand," 'Doc,' Ensign Zack O'Connor said as they disappeared into the bedroom with the chest. Neither he, nor Lieutenant Junior Grade Harold Carney, Flash, Adam's Executive Officer, seemed to find the bulky chest too burdensome.

"What if I don't want to unhand you, Zoe? How would you feel about that?" Bowie's brown eyes held a warmth she hadn't encouraged.

When he flashed his dimples at her, she thought he might just have some idea how potent his smile was, and how to use it to his advantage. What was wrong with her that her heart didn't leap at all the male sex appeal he exuded? The electric thrill seemed to be reserved for Adam "Hawk" Yazzie. He could walk into the room and every nerve in her body came to life.

"The only man I'm interested in right now is the Sandman, Bowie. I intend to take a long, long nap, as soon as you get the bed up. I'm beat." She knew she looked it, too.

Since getting the go ahead from the neurologist, she'd spent every moment, from dawn to midnight, at the hospital.

Bowie's masculine tones held a hint of west Texas. "I'll ask again, when you're not so wore out." He stepped away then looked over his shoulder at her. "I like long, slow kisses, cuddling, and I've been told I have a light touch. You might want to keep that in mind, while you're deciding whether or not to give me a chance."

The heat of a blush flared in her face. She found it impossible to come up with any kind of answer.

Bowie's smile widened. "We'll get the bedroom squared away for you right away." He went up the stairs to retrieve the nightstand.

She stood at the doorway of the bedroom, but didn't go in. "There's lasagna, salad, and garlic bread in the kitchen, when you want to take a break."

Doc looked up, his eyes as green as his Irish ancestor's homeland. His short auburn hair stood on end where he had raked his hands through it. "We'll be there ASAP, as soon as we get this bed frame together, and the mattress and box springs from upstairs."

"Lasagna is my favorite," Flash commented as he tightened a bolt, while Doc held the metal frame in place against the footboard. "Is it a family recipe?" A slight Boston undertone flavored Flash's voice with New England charm.

His quiet soft-spoken manner seemed more restful than the others and his blond, blue-eyed good looks were very appealing.

"My mother's."

"Do you cook?" he asked.

"Not a lick," she fibbed, a smile tugging at her lips.

Flash glanced up. "That's all right, I do." He winked at her.

She smiled. "Do they give a class in flirting, along with weapon maintenance and hand to hand combat, when you train to become a SEAL?"

"Naw," Flash shook his head. "We just pretty much know what we want, keep our eye on the prize, and don't give up. It's a characteristic of the breed."

She'd lived with two people growing up who fit that bill. Her father and her brother. She figured she could handle that.

"I wonder how you two would react if you met up with a female with those same characteristics?"

The two men looked at one another. "Run," they said together.

She laughed. It seemed like months since she had done so. It felt good.

"What's going on?" Hawk asked from directly behind her.

She turned and looked over her shoulder at him. He held a wooden lamp he had been repairing, a slight frown on his face. He had discarded his crutches for just the brace and she hadn't heard his approach.

"Nothing, we're just talking."

"Food's getting cold," he said as he slipped past her. His hand lightly brushed the small of her back, with just enough pressure that her nerve endings zinged, and her heart picked up its rhythm.

Bowie dodged around her with the nightstand. "Don't have to tell me twice when chow's on. Let Flash and Hawk take care of that, Doc. You and I can bring down the box springs and mattress."

"Sounds like a plan to me." Doc straightened and stepped out of the bed frame. The two went upstairs.

Zoe returned to the kitchen and helped herself to a small bowl of salad. She wandered out to the screened-in back porch and sat down in the old metal glider Hawk had renovated and placed against one wall. Green striped lounge pillows cushioned the seat. Propping her feet up on the brown wicker coffee table, she set the glider in motion. The sunset deepened to rose, maroon, and then purple painting the laminate floor with color. Through the screened windows, the sweet scent of honeysuckle wafted on the breeze. The cadence of the crickets thrummed in a synchronized ebb and flow, the sound draining the tension from her shoulders and neck.

The porch was fast becoming her favorite spot. She gravitated there to unwind when she arrived home from the hospital. Her bowl empty, she set it aside on the wicker end table beside the glider and eyed the sunken hot tub a few feet away. Maybe she could fill it after dinner when everyone left. With the aid of a few potted plants, and the canvas shades that could be lowered over the windows, she could find some privacy. Perhaps it would ease the pain in her calf from standing too long.

Imagining Hawk in the hot tub with any number of buxom, blonde beauties cost her more than a twinge or two of jealousy. A jealousy she tried to deny. Along with the feelings that inspired it. Every time she experienced the rush of excitement when he entered the room, or the hypersensitive tingle of heat when he touched her, a lingering ache centered just beneath her breastbone.

Better the ache of regret than the pain of caring for him more deeply and something happening to him. The sound of her mother's soft sobs coming from her bedroom late at night when she'd thought they were all asleep echoed through her head and gave her heart a sharp pinch.

Waiting for letters, emails, telegrams, had only played a small part of their life in the military. Praying they never got a visit from an official two-man detail to notify them that their loved one was dead had played a bigger one. And damn, if it didn't overshadow the rest. It made remembering any of the good times harder.

Drawing her bare feet up on the seat, she hugged her knees and rested her head atop them. She rubbed the sharp pain that lanced from her knee to her ankle as the damaged muscle stretched. She tried to forget about her leg, tried to function as normally as possible. There were days she succeeded, when the pain remained slight. When her calf burned and throbbed from standing or walking too much, she resented pandering to it but was forced to wear the brace she hated.

"Zoe," Clara Weaver spoke from the open doorway.

She straightened and turned her head to look up at her. The kitchen light lanced across her mother's face, setting alight the coppery tones in her hair. Some of the strain, apparent from the week before, had drained from Clara's features, easing the fine lines around her eyes and mouth. She had housework and shopping to attend to, which offered her a distraction and a sense of normalcy.

Her own discomfort at being so close to Hawk would be worth it, if living here gave her mother some respite from her worry over Brett.

"The men are finished. Come eat."

She lowered her feet to the floor and rocked forward to rise then stood stationary for a moment to make sure of her balance.

"You brought your brace, didn't you?" Clara asked.

"I don't need it."

Clara brushed a few strands of hair from Zoe's forehead, the gesture familiar as the look of concern on her face. "You're pushing yourself too hard."

"I just haven't done my exercises in a couple of days. I'll do them tonight after dinner."

Clara nodded and stepped back to allow her to enter the kitchen.

Hawk and Doc looked up from serving themselves from a large pan of lasagna on the stove. She fell in behind them.

He took her empty plate and traded it for the one he had just filled.

"Cut me a smaller piece, Hawk."

His gray gaze fixed on her a moment before he scooped the lasagna onto her plate and traded with her. "It wouldn't hurt for you to eat a little more," he said, his deep voice only a rumble. She wondered what it would be like to hear that tone whispered in her ear as his long, lean body covered hers. Her mouth went dry and she bit her lip.

She had to quit doing this to herself. Fantasies aside, she would never be brave enough to leave herself open to that kind of rejection again. Though he was doing all he could to make up for the situation, he had still uttered the words that guaranteed she would never let him close, "It's my fault Brett was hurt."

Why did she have to keep reminding herself of that? Her loyalty belonged to her brother, not to a man she barely knew.

Bowie pulled out her chair for her as they joined the rest at the dining room table. Doc poured her a glass of ice tea when he noticed she had forgotten a drink. Was the men's solicitous behavior motivated by friendliness? Or was it pity? She flinched from the idea.

She hadn't encouraged any of their advances, and if she did? The poor man would eventually run once he saw her scars anyway. It was good she needed all her energy for Brett. She'd return home, once her brother was back on his feet, in exactly the same condition she'd arrived in California. With her heart in one piece.

"After dinner, want to go out for ice cream?" Flash whispered from beside her.

"No fair making time with my woman, Flash," Doc said.

"All things are fair in love and war, Doc."

She shook her head at their good-natured competitiveness.

Her mother winked at her. "Unless you're ready to walk down the aisle tomorrow, my daughter won't be making time with anyone," she said in her best schoolteacher voice.

The men looked at one another. Flash laid an arm along the top of Zoe's chair. "Where should we have the rehearsal dinner, sweetheart?"

She laid a hand on flash's knee and leaned close. "There's something I have to tell you, Harold."

"What's that honey?" He covered her hand and focused on her with the eagerness of a bird dog spotting a pheasant.

"I always keep my eye on the prize, and I never give up."

His look of surprise had Doc bursting into laughter.

"You don't really want to see a grown man run in fear, do you?" Flash asked.

She shook her head, a smile playing about her lips. Her eyes rose to Hawk's face to find a frown just short of a scowl drawing his dark brows together. He had been uncharacteristically quiet for most of the day. With all the upheaval of giving up his office to offer her a room, was he regretting asking them to move in? If so, they could be out of there in next to no time.

Her reasons for being so eager to find an excuse to move out sobered her. She was running scared, the intensity of her feelings, when he was around, beyond her experience.

Flash touched her arm, drawing her attention back to his face. He spoke softly, for her ears only. "That new husky sound you have when you speak is sexy as hell. And as much as I'd like for you to whisper in my ear, I feel like I need to be teaching you some of the hand signals we use so you can rest your voice." His blue eyes held a serious light. "You need to pace yourself, Zoe, and let us take up some of the slack. Okay?"

Too touched by his concern to speak, she nodded. "I'll try."

He flashed a smile and turned to answer something Hawk asked from the other end of the table.

The men seemed determined to keep the dinner conversation light and as entertaining as possible. Though she enjoyed their company, exhaustion had her fighting off the repetitive urge to yawn by the time the meal came to an end. Flash's hand rested beneath her elbow as she struggled to her feet. She murmured her thanks as she found her balance.

She carried her plate into the kitchen and started to load the dishwasher.

"You and Clara prepared dinner. We'll clean up," Hawk said as he joined her.

"It's all right. It'll only take a minute to load the dishwasher and wash up."

He caught her wrist as she reached for another plate to rinse. "You're all in, Zoe. Go rest. And as sexy as a hoarse female voice sounds, you need to rest your voice as well."

Sexy? She placed her hand against her throat. "I'm fine." Her gaze rose to his face. Where Flash's earlier concern had touched her, the concern she read in Hawk's expression made her defensive. She didn't stop to think why. "You don't have to make concessions for me because of my leg. I can still pull my weight around here."

His eyes narrowed and his cheekbones flushed with color. As Doc and Bowie entered the kitchen carrying plates and glasses, he pulled her out onto the porch and closed the door.

"It has nothing to do with your leg, Zoe. You're up at dawn and don't go to bed until one or two every night. You don't have an endless supply of energy. No one does. If you're going to be in this thing for the long haul, you're going to have to pace yourself."

She recognized the truth in what he said, but resented he was the one to say it. "I can take care of myself. I've been doing it for a while now."

"Then you know what you need to do, so do it."

She stiffened at his tone. "Look, I'm not one of the men you can call onto the carpet and dress down."

His gray gaze raked down her slender form. "That's something I'm not likely to forget."

Her heartbeat accelerated. She experienced the stomach quivering sensation of riding a roller coaster car to the top of a tall-tall peak.

"Brett would be telling you to take care of yourself, wouldn't he?"

"Yes," she agreed. The word came out soft and breathy around the airless feeling beneath her ribs.

"If he were here, he'd be warning you about his fellow teammates. Flirting is fine, but should you start to date one of them, it's going to cause some hard feelings between them."

"They're only kidding around, Hawk. None of them are really interested in me. They're just competing for attention. They'd be behaving like that with any single female of datable age within a five mile radius."

"I disagree. I'm not going to have the three of them going at each other's throats over a woman."

The heart dropping sensation felt worse than any roller coaster plunge down a steep track. Pain whipped through her. That he had viewed her banter with Flash as something more than just light-hearted teasing was unimaginable.

"Well—I've never been viewed as a femme fatale before, or a manipulative tease." Her throat tightened with tears. "You're right about one thing though. I've had enough for one day. I'm going to bed." She shoved past him.

"Zoe—wait a minute—"

She jerked her arm from his grasp, and pushed open the kitchen door.

Flash, Doc, and Bowie working to set the place to rights, gave the large kitchen the feeling of being crowded.

She pulled up short, and tried to gather her composure. The screen door closed as Hawk entered the room behind her.

"Guys, I really appreciate all your help getting the bed set up and everything."

"No problem, Zoe," Bowie spoke for the group.

"I hope you'll understand if I excuse myself and go on to bed."

"No problem," Doc said. His green gaze traveled from her to Hawk, then back again, speculation in his expression.

Suddenly, the full weight of exhaustion pressed down upon her shoulders and she drew a tremulous breath.

"If you or your mom need anything, Zo, don't hesitate to call," Flash said, his features set in a frown.

She nodded and offered them all a hasty thanks, and a goodnight. As she closed the bedroom door behind her, she wished she were anywhere on earth, but in Hawk Yazzie's house.

CHAPTER 4

"Son of a—" Hawk swore the words several times beneath his breath as he removed the cover from the hot tub one handed and braced his weight on a crutch with the other.

"Need some help?" Clara asked from the kitchen doorway.

He turned to offer her an apologetic smile. "Sorry. I was just venting a little frustration."

"I've heard the tone and the words before, Hawk," she said. A smile laced with understanding curved her lips. She stepped over the threshold and helped him slide the lightweight vinyl cover behind the lounge.

"I keep the tub covered when it's not in use in case one of the team comes over with the kids."

"Good idea. Children are drawn to water like ducks to a pond. They'd be in it fully clothed in a heartbeat."

"Yeah." He flipped the switches engaging the heater and the pump. "It only takes a little while to heat." He lowered himself to the lounge and set aside the crutch. "Think Zoe would want to soak for a few minutes, if she's still awake?"

She laughed and shook her head at him.

"Sorry, I didn't think how that would sound. I just noticed she was in pain last night when she went to her room. I thought it might ease off if she relaxed in the tub for a little while."

Clara remained silent for a moment. She took a seat beside him. "I think she'll turn the use of the hot tub down, though she probably needs to take advantage of it," she said, her words measured. "Zoe is self-conscious of her leg. When she was young she just went right on as though nothing were wrong with it, but her first year in college, something happened. She won't willingly let you or anyone else see it."

He frowned. He hadn't seen this coming. Uneasiness took root in the pit of his stomach.

Clara ran a restless hand over the auburn curls that framed a face only a little fuller than her daughter's. "I'm only telling you this so you won't take her refusals personally."

He forced a nonchalant shrug. "We'll just have to arrange a daily time so she can have some privacy then."

She smiled. "You know, even when your children are adults, a parent can't really control the desire to shield them. Zoe likes to think she's tough."

"She is in some ways," he said.

"But not about this." Her blue eyes, so similar to her daughters, held a sadness that went soul deep.

He nodded. "Understood."

"You and your men were wonderful today," she said, changing the subject.

He smiled. "Awe shucks, ma'am— it weren't nothin'."

"I really appreciate everything you're doing for us."

He shrugged and focused on her face. "It's a big house. Big enough for the three of us, and then some."

"If we start encroaching on your space more than we should, don't hesitate to speak up about it." She got to her feet.

"It's not going to happen."

She shook her head at him. "You're used to baching it, Hawk. It may grow tedious having two women under foot."

"It'll be okay, Clara. If I start to feel crowded, I can always bug out for a few days."

"This is your home. If you need some space, we can do the bugging out." She turned as she reached the kitchen door. "If you have difficulty getting in or out of the tub, don't hesitate to yell."

He smiled at the comical image that came to mind of the two slightly built women trying to get his two hundred and ten pound frame out of the water. "I think I can handle it, but I'll keep it in mind."

His smile listed as Clara left. Zoe would probably leave him afloat and tell him to soak his head, as well as his knee.

His jaw tensed. It wasn't just his team's welfare he had in mind. He didn't want to see her hurt. For all their joking about marriage and rehearsal dinners, he couldn't picture any of his men being ready to take the plunge.

Zoe wasn't the kind of woman a man looked to for no-strings sex. Her shy flirtatiousness fired his protective instincts, but it also fired everything south of his belt as well. Knowing it probably did the same to his men drove him crazy, and damned if he knew what to do about it.

And what if one of them were responsible for Cutter's injuries?

The only one he could be sure of was himself. He had to protect her.

****

Zoe heard her mother's door close down the hall and struggled to rise from the bed. She couldn't sleep until things were settled between Hawk and her. She wouldn't be able to stay under his roof, if they didn't try to reach some kind of understanding.

Her leg ached as she made her way back down the hall to the kitchen. The exterior door stood open to the porch and she stopped at the threshold and scanned the room.

His arms stretched along the edge of the hot tub and his head was tilted back against a cushion. Ropy, well-defined muscles stood out in his neck, shoulders, upper arms, and chest. Though she knew every muscle, had anyone asked her to recite the names at this moment, she wouldn't have been able to identify a single one. Black hair dusted his chest just above the waterline. The size and strength of him awed her. The beauty of him stole her breath and made it hard for her to swallow. She forced air into her lungs and tried to block off the physical response that made it difficult for her to focus.

She took two decisive steps into the room. "I didn't want to go to bed without settling things between us."

His lids rose, his pale gray gaze fastening on her face for a moment before they slid downward over the faded sweat pants and cropped t-shirt she wore. He homed in on the two-inch band of bare skin just above her waistband, and a tempting tingle arrowed downward. Her knees grew weak. How could he make her hot and wet with just a look?

"I wondered when you'd be back to bust my chops." He sat up from his reclining position. "I was out of line earlier."

Surprise kept her silent for a moment. "I'm not here looking for a boyfriend. I'm here for Brett."

"I know that."

"I'm not a flirt or a tease either."

"If what I said led you to believe I thought that, Zoe, you're mistaken. I'm sorry."

He hooked his hands upon the rim of the tub and hiked himself up on the wide tile edge around it.

After the first glimpse of a rock hard six-pack bisected by a thin line of hair that disappeared beneath a brief black swimsuit, she averted her gaze. She wandered to the screen door to focus her attention outside, until she could get her breathing under control.

"My concern wasn't just about the cohesive condition of my team, Zoe. I was concerned about you, too."

Sure. The only blip she made on his radar screen was as a possible problem for him or his team.

"The men have been pressuring you."

"They'd be that way with any woman who came within their scope. It's the male way of being friendly. Because I'm Brett's sister, they'll tease and flirt, but they're not really serious about pursuing me." She forced herself to face him, just to prove to herself she could do it and still breathe.

Hawk probed her expression. "I heard Bowie ask you out, and it didn't sound like he was just interested in flirting."

Her cheeks grew hot. "I'm sure he's used that same line, and his killer dimples, with great success on any number of women. I didn't take him seriously."

His frown set his features in lines of masculine aggression. "Why not?"

She'd learned the hard way that men were only interested in girls who could keep up with them. To him and his men, a five-mile run was probably a cakewalk. There were days, walking across the room was like running a marathon for her.

"I'm not interested in a temporary relationship."

"Who's to say it would be?"

If she'd harbored any hopes he was the least bit interested in her, he'd just doused them. That was a good thing. He was doing her a favor. Being involved with a military man wasn't what she needed anyway. Seeing Brett in his condition offered her enough heartache already.

She leaned back against the door facing and studied his expression. "Are you encouraging me to go out with Bowie?"

"No." A frown drew his brows into a V above the bridge of his nose setting his features into intimidating lines. She wondered what he would be like truly angry. Probably scary as hell.

"I'm glad you're not trying to tell me what to do, because we both know I'll do as I please."

A warning glint lit his pale gray gaze as their eyes met. Just when she began to grow concerned they were about to have words again, a smile broke across his features and he laughed.

"How's the knee?" she asked, changing the subject. "You've been on it a lot today."

"It's feeling better after a few minutes in the hot tub. Why don't you join me?"

Even knowing he meant nothing by the invitation, her pulse hammered at her throat and wrists. A fantasy of all that smooth skin and hard muscle, wet and warm beneath her hands, flashed through her mind. "I haven't got a bathing suit." She hoped her voice sounded normal.

"Then come in, in what you have on now," he suggested. "You could cut your sweats off into shorts so the water can circulate around your legs."

Though tempted, too many painful past experiences triggered a feeling of panic that made it hard for her to swallow.

She forced a smile to her lips. "And ruin the fashion statement I'm trying to make," she teased.

"We'll pick a bathing suit up tomorrow at the PX then."

"I have other things to spend my money on right now, Hawk."

"I'll spring for it. You can't come to California and not have a bathing suit. This is the surf, sand, and sun state."

She couldn't meet the challenge she read in his gaze; she'd learned that the hard way. "I appreciate the offer, Hawk, but I probably won't have any time to enjoy the surf and sun and I'm certainly not too fond of sand."

"It isn't one of my favorite things, either, since BUDS training." He pushed off the rim of the hot tub back into the water. "You could lie down on the lounge and talk to me while I soak."

She hesitated, torn between the inexplicable attraction he held for her, and her need to keep him at a distance. The more time she spent with him, the more difficult it would be to ignore her response to him. And what if he discovered how she felt? Her stomach rolled and she placed a hand against it.

She turned to find him watching her and her legs grew weak.

"It could be dangerous for you to stay in the hot tub alone," she said as she stretched out on the lounge and drew a pillow beneath her head. "There have been instances of people being overcome by the heat of the water and drowning."

"That would certainly be an ironic end to my SEAL career. You'd better stick around."

His droll tone made her laugh. She wiggled and turned on her side. She intercepted a smile that softened his features and brought an answering one to her lips.

As hard as he tried not to look, Hawk's attention rested on that thin strip of pale skin visible beneath the bottom of her cropped t-shirt. He ached to reach out and follow the hollow dip of her belly to her navel with his fingers, then his lips. The drawstring dangling just below her belly button seemed to be giving directions. His gaze followed the round curve of one breast clearly defined beneath her t-shirt as she tucked her hands beneath her cheek.

He found the combination of sensual young woman and innocence tempting as hell. He drew a deep breath and, closing his eyes, tilted his head back against the cushion again. Maybe it was a good thing she wasn't in the water with him. He'd grown hard as a torpedo and the possibilities were just too explosive.

"Where are you from?" she asked.

She'd seemed so determined to keep him at arm's length, he raised a brow in surprise.

"I was born here in San Diego. My father worked construction and my mom was a legal secretary. My dad died in a fall on a building site when I was young. My mom raised me on her own. She died five years ago. Breast cancer." He controlled his expression with an effort though the ache of loss and the guilt was still there. Why had she not told him how ill she was? Why had she waited for him to come home? She'd waited too long and she'd died alone.

"I'm sorry."

The soft, husky sincerity he heard in her tone tugged his thoughts back. He turned his head to look at her. "I am, too."

"What was she like?"

Despite the anger a smile tugged at his lips. "A hard ass, but loving with it. I got mixed up with the wrong crowd as a teenager. Nearly got into a gang. She threatened to quit her job and hound my every step until I straightened up my act."

"It must have worked."

"Yeah, it did. She talked me into taking ROTC. Said if I was going to join a gang it might as well be one that would teach me the right kind of discipline. I stayed with it and earned an academic scholarship for college."

"Do you have any other family?"

"Some distant cousins on my father's side who live in New Mexico. My mother's father is still alive. He lives in LA."

"Brett said your father was Navaho."

"Yeah, half, which makes me a quarter."

"Because of your skin and hair color, I imagine it's easier to get around undetected in foreign ports."

"Sometimes." The defensive feelings caught him by surprise. "That isn't why you feel so uneasy with me, is it?"

Her face went blank with shock, then she sat up. "No! Why would you even think that? I mean, that I feel uneasy with you."

"You're on edge with me."

For a moment she stared at him then looked away. "It isn't you. I mean—." She rocked forward to rise to her feet. It took a moment for her to establish her balance, and for the first time, he realized what a struggle her injury proved for her.

He waded from the hot tub by way of the steps and grasped a towel from the end table. Turning aside to cover the lingering effects of his arousal, he wrapped it around his waist.

He hadn't meant to bring things to a head between them—those puns were killing him but he just couldn't leave it alone. He had to know.

Her features tense, she faced him. "I'm not prejudiced against you because of your Indian heritage, Hawk."

"Is it because I'm responsible for what happened to Brett?'"

"Are you?"

"I didn't hit him in the head. No. But it was my mission, this is my team. Every man in it is my responsibility."

Some of the tension left her features. "As much as I'd like a target to vent my frustration and anger at, I can't really hold you responsible for Brett's condition."

"Then what is it?"

"I don't want to be drawn back into the life again."

"Military life?"

"Yes." Zoe folded her arms against her midriff as though cold. "You don't have to enlist to be a part of it. I used to love it, the travel, new places, new people, the troops in uniform, their shoes spit shined, their brass polished until it gleamed. The singsong sound of a drill instructor calling out orders on the parade ground. Seeing them march in formation across the base. I loved it all. Then Desert Storm happened-"

"And your father was killed." He sucked in his breath as though he'd been hit in the solar plexus. Just when he thought he had things figured out something else cropped up.

She nodded, her body taut, her features carefully blank. "Brett being hurt was like—" Her throat worked as she swallowed and she shook her head. "I met you and your men. I've broken bread with you, laughed with you, been embraced by your families. I'm just having some trouble dealing with all these emotions, all these memories—"

He rested a hand upon her shoulder as she edged toward the door. The tension of her muscles as she struggled to retain her composure thrummed beneath his touch.

"You have to believe that we're better trained, better prepared, than they are, Zoe. We're going to be all right."

"I hope so, I really do."

She turned to face him and raised a hand to cup his cheek, her thumb moving along his cheekbone in a caress that caught him by surprise. His heart rate shot up as he met the clarity of her gaze.

"I didn't mean anything derogatory about your heritage. I'm sorry if it came out wrong."

He caught her hand when she started to withdraw. "It's all right, Zoe." He braced an arm against the door facing above her and shifted closer. The desire to feel her body against his made his breathing unsteady. He caught a whiff of her vanilla shampoo and a hint of some other floral scent on her skin.

She leaned back against the door facing, aligning her body to his stance. With a foot of space between them, they seemed to generate enough heat to singe the hair off his chest. Her fingers curled around his thumb as it pressed into her palm bringing to mind her fingers closing around other parts of his anatomy.

"I just meant that you should use whatever you had to stay safe." Her voice softened, her Kentucky accent, growing thick as honey.

"Yeah, I got that," He managed, though he felt starved for breath, as though he'd just finished a ten K run on a sandy beach.

She bit her bottom lip, leaving a glossy sheen of moisture behind. He bit back a groan. Blood shot to his groin. Jesus—Beads of moisture tracked an itchy path down his spine. It hurt to drag his gaze from her mouth.

Her mother was only a few yards down the hall. She trusted him. Zoe trusted him. It would be a breach of both their trusts for him to take advantage. He couldn't have an affair with his best friend's sister. He couldn't offer her any emotional security. He wasn't the permanent kind.

All those rationalizations didn't ease the tight heavy feeling of his arousal, or the ache of need that clenched inside him. He forced himself to relinquish Zoe's hand and take a step back. "It's getting late and you should be in bed." His voice sounded husky, almost a growl.

For a moment she remained still. Slowly, she straightened away from the door facing, and he curved a steadying hand around her upper arm. Her head down, she brushed passed him, her voice almost a whisper as she said, "Good night, Hawk."

He listened to her progress through the house until a door closed. Hawk drew a deep breath to ease his pounding heart and realized he was trembling.

Zoe leaned back against the bedroom door. Her heart beat so she could barely breathe, her legs felt weak, and her skin tight and hypersensitive. She caught back a groan. Dear God. All this and all he had done was look at her and hold her hand. If he ever kissed her, touched her, she'd probably burst into flames. She'd thought for a moment that he would kiss her, and she had been half wild for him to do so. Had he been able to read her desire in her face? God, she hoped not.

Forcing her legs to move, she limped to the bed and lay down. Feeling as though she might fly apart, she wrapped her arms tightly around herself and curled into a ball. Frustrated desire writhed and twisted inside her. Several minutes passed before her pulse settled to a steadier rhythm. As the adrenaline leached from her system, a wave of melancholy brought tears to her eyes.

She should have never stayed to talk to him, should have never allowed him to pressure her into sharing her feelings about the Corps and all the memories being here had generated. It had left her too vulnerable to other emotions. She had never experienced anything like this driving desire to open herself physically and emotionally to another human being. It was wonderful and powerful and terrifying.

The only other time she had been tempted to lower the barriers had been disastrous for her. Tyler had shaken her confidence in herself. It had taken months to deal with the feelings of inadequacy and pain the experience had generated. She'd doubted, for a long time, whether any man could look past her scars and see her as a desirable woman.

With Hawk, she wanted to be desirable, but knew she wasn't. If by some miracle she inspired a response in him, she'd have to act on it. God, how terrifying.

Her feelings for Tyler had been lukewarm in comparison to her response to Hawk. Because of that, he wouldn't just have the ability to hurt her, he could annihilate her.

A sound half despair, half longing bubbled up from deep inside her. She dragged a pillow from the other side of the bed and buried her face in it.

If she trusted him, and he reciprocated, and was shipped out, what then? The hollow desolate feeling the idea generated didn't bear thinking about. She didn't want a boyfriend in the military. She couldn't get involved with Hawk, she just couldn't.

CHAPTER 5

Hawk took a quick look in the mirror. He hadn't been in uniform since returning to the states. His commanding officer had interviewed him in the hospital in Iraq and a couple of officers from headquarters had visited him in the hospital stateside, and now they were probing again into the mission.

What the hell had happened to Brett? Who had tried to cave his skull in? Not a tango. They'd have raised an alarm and been swarming all over the building searching for the rest of them. That left someone on the team.

A hollow ache hit his stomach more painful than a bullet wound.

Flash had been outside the building the whole time monitoring the tangos on the roof. His periodic clicks over the radio had kept them posted on their movements.

But he could have slipped in just as they had.

Derrick had raised the alarm that Cutter hadn't come out. Doc had clicked his mic just before.

Bowie had set his package and taken cover outside the building before that, just as he had.

Any one of the others could have set his explosives package and been out of the building in time. They were all fast enough.

But how long had Cutter been unconscious?

Greenback had been two blocks down keeping an eye on their rear security. He'd had his hands full taking out two tangos blocking their route.

Hawk raked both hands through his hair and pushed the heels of his hands against his temples. He'd been over and over it a million times.

How could one of his men turn on his own teammate? Fuck!

Why had this happened? There had to be a reason behind it.

That was the key.

But how the hell was he supposed to find out if he couldn't talk to his men. They couldn't talk to each other about the mission.

But what had triggered Brett's attack might have happened before the mission. And that was fair game.

Hawk grabbed his bonnet from the dresser and shoved it under his arm.

Zoe's and Clara's voices came from the kitchen as he limped down the hall. As he entered the room, the two grew silent. Zoe gazed at him for a long moment her expression guarded.

"You look very handsome in your uniform, Hawk," Clara said with a smile.

Hawk returned the gesture. "Thanks. I have a meeting at O-eight-thirty at HQ. I thought you could drop me off and I'd catch a ride over to the hospital afterward."

Zoe rose to her feet. "Would you like some coffee before we go?"

"No. I'm fine."

Clara rose. "We're ready. I'll get my purse." Her sandals clicked against the hard wood floors as she walked down the hall.

Zoe turned to put the milk away, cleared the cups from the table, and loaded the dishwasher.

Her usual quick movements appeared jerky.

Hawk sidled up close behind her and rested a hand against the small of her back. "What is it, Zoe?"

"Is it about Brett?"

How had she known? Had she read his body language, his expression? "You know I can't tell you that."

"Don't you think we're entitled to know what happened?"

Hawk remained silent for a moment. "I was there and I'm not sure what happened, Zoe. We may never know."

Her jaw grew taut. "I won't accept that." She raised her gaze to his and was as close to tears as he'd ever seen her.

Every instinct screamed for him to hold her and offer her comfort.

As though she read his intentions she shook her head and slipped away from him to pick up the purse hanging on one of the chairs.

****

Zoe climbed behind the wheel and fastened her seatbelt. Had her mother been more at ease with the busy traffic in route to the base, she'd have asked her to drive to make it easier to avoid Hawk's gaze.

Though he tried to hide it, tension had settled in his shoulders and the hands he rested on his thighs.

They stopped at the gate and waited while the MPs checked their passes then signaled them through. Following

Hawk's directions, she pulled into a parking slot in front of a single story brick building.

"If you need a ride, just call mom's cell and I'll come pick you up," Zoe said as he unbuckled his seat belt.

He nodded. "I think I'll be able to catch a ride, but I'll keep it in mind just in case." He rested a hand on her arm, and for a moment his gaze rested on her face before he got out of the car. He retrieved a gym bag from the back seat, and closing the door, walked away down the path.

Clara transferred to the seat Hawk vacated. For a moment, both their attention rested on his back as he walked up the crisply edged sidewalk to the door of the building. "There's something about a man in uniform," Clara said on a sigh, her gaze followed Hawk, but something in her expression focused inward.

Zoe fought against the pain to draw a full breath, as memories of her own rose up to haunt her.

****

"That has to be the ugliest apartment complex in San Diego," Clara said.

Zoe turned the key in the ignition killing the engine and leaned forward to look up at the blocky building with its regimented lines. "Brett's only here to sleep and eat. All he needs is a place to hang his hat."

"I suppose so. Once he finds the right woman, he'll have to move," Clara said, a note of forced determination in her voice.

Would that happen for her brother in his current occupation? Would it happen—? Zoe flinched from the thought, shoved her sunglasses onto her face, and grabbing her purse, exited the car.

She popped the trunk and looked down at the olive drab sea-bag taking up nearly the whole compartment.

"I think we need a dolly," Clara said. "Stay here and I'll go in and ask management if they have one."

Zoe lowered the trunk lid, limped around to the passenger side of the car and leaned against the quarter panel to rest her leg.

She had to deal with these feelings about seeing Hawk back in uniform. He wore it so naturally. It suited his physique. Oh hell! Who was she kidding? It wasn't the uniform that bothered her. It was caring for the man wearing it.

Seeking a distraction from her thoughts, she turned to look down the street. Across the street two cars down a man stared at her from his vehicle. She took in blond hair and a strong jaw, though dark sunglasses obscured the rest of his face. His concentrated intensity, the stillness of his posture as he studied her punched her heart into an anxious race. A car whipped past between them. She took the opportunity to turn her back to him.

"Hello pretty lady."

Zoe started at the familiar voice, then smiled, relief easing the tension from her body. "Where on earth did you get that shirt?"

Flash laughed, his blue eyes alight with humor. "Nice, huh?" He twisted around to show off the bizarre print. His back and torso appeared to have been attacked by a paintball gun, a flowerbed, or both. "I got it in Hawaii. It's my lucky shirt."

Zoe looked over the top of her sunglasses at him. "Does it work?"

"I was hoping it would," he said, his grin oozing charm.

"Why Harold, I thought we already had an understanding."

He chuckled. "The other guys will be jealous." He leaned against the car beside her and folded his arms.

Why wasn't she more drawn to this man? He exuded charisma, was funny and sweet. But just didn't do it for her like—

"Are you just hanging out here or are you waiting for someone?" he asked.

"Mom went in to see if the manager had a dolly."

"What for?"

Zoe glanced across the street in search of the car and man. Both were gone. She shrugged off the residue of apprehension.

"We were going to unpack Brett's duffle, but it's too heavy for either of us to lift."

He straightened away from the car. "I can take care of that for you."

She smiled. "Do you live here?"

"No, I just recognized Hawk's vehicle and saw you standing here. I stopped to say hey and see how things were going."

She ignored the 'how things were going' part to avoid disrupting the carefree tone of the moment. "So, you're not busy right now?"

He looked at his watch. "I got a few minutes before I have to be somewhere. I can do this for you."

"Thank you, Flash."

"I like it better when you call me Harold," he said as he moved around the back of the vehicle and flipped open the trunk. He managed to wiggle the canvas bag free from the tight space and, grasping the handle on the side, swung it up onto his shoulder.

Zoe rushed to slam the trunk closed and proceeded him to the apartment complex door. A man with dark hair exited the building just as they reached the entrance. He held it open for them with a nod.

"May I borrow your cell phone? Mom won't know where I am and might worry if she shows back up at the car and I'm not there."

"It's hooked to my belt," he said, raising an elbow to give her access to his waist.

Zoe dialed her mother's number and arranged to meet her at the apartment with the key. "You could put that down until we get upstairs," Zoe said when he continued to balance the bag even after they entered the elevator.

"I'd just have to pick it up again. And besides it gives me the opportunity to impress you."

Eyeing the duffle that had to weigh more than fifty pounds, and how the taut muscles stood out in his arms, Zoe smiled. "Consider me impressed, Harold."

He shot her a cocky grin. "Have you ever been to Brett's apartment?" he asked.

"No, he'd just moved in when he deployed."

"Well, despite how the place looks from the outside, the apartments are okay. I think he got a break on the rent because the units were slow to fill."

"It's really not fair for any of you to have to pay rent when you aren't here," Zoe said.

"Well, it never hurts knowing you have a home to return to. And renting a room by the week can really suck."

"Are you saying that from experience?"

"When I first came out to California, I had to stay in a dump across town. There's something to be said for having your own bed and your own stuff, not to mention privacy."

Zoe paused a moment in thought. "You don't have any family out here either?"

"No. I don't have any family. Just the guys."

Zoe pressed a hand to her stomach as a dropping sensation struck it that had nothing to do with the elevator. So he was alone in the world like Hawk.

The elevator door opened and they stepped out into a long hallway. Clara stood just a few doors down.

"I'm sorry, Harold."

For the first time his easygoing expression grew serious. "Yeah, so am I."

"It's good to see you, Flash," Clara said as they reached her. "Thank you so much for helping us."

"I'm glad to do it, Clara." Flash squeezed through the doorway with only inches to spare. He continued through a Spartan living room, with the bare necessities of a couch, two chairs, a couple of end tables and lamps, down a hallway.

Zoe followed behind, taking in the bare walls with boxes still packed and shoved against them.

"We'll have to unpack for him and set things to rights," Clara said from behind her.

Her mother's comment brought the ache of tears to Zoe's throat. "Not today, Mom. I want to get to the hospital as soon as we unpack his things."

"All right, hon."

Flash lowered the seabag to the floor on its end in front of the bed.

A bed hastily made. As though Brett were returning in just a few minutes instead of the nine months he'd been deployed. Zoe's eyes burned with tears.

The room smelled musty from remaining sealed.

"I'll go open the sliding glass doors in the living room," Clara said, her voice uneven. She pressed a hand to her trembling lips as she hastened from the room.

"I can deal with this if you need to go see about her," Flash said, motioning toward the duffle.

Zoe shook her head. "If I do, we'll both go on a crying jag that will be counterproductive. We just need to keep moving forward."

Flash nodded. "All his uniforms and stuff should be clean. We kind of pulled together to get his gear squared away." He unfastened the heavy snap hook at the top of the bag. "I can take the uniforms to the base cleaners to be pressed if you like."

His kindness undermined her control, and dropping her purse onto the dresser, Zoe turned her attention to straightening the bed until she could regain her composure. "I'll have plenty of time to do that later. He won't need them right away. But I appreciate the offer."

"I'm sorry, Zoe. I didn't mean to—"

She straightened. "You didn't do anything wrong, Harold. It's just an emotional time for us right now."

"Yeah, I see that. If there's nothing else I can do to help, I'll take off." He edged toward the door.

"Come by the house tomorrow night. We'll be grilling out. I think some of the others will be there." She hazarded a glance at him and read his discomfort in the stiffness of his shoulders and the taut set of his jaw.

"Sure, will do. If you need anything just call my cell. The number will be on your mother's phone."

"I promise we'll be better company then," Zoe said and forced a smile.

"No problem, Zoe. I'll see you then."

She drew a deep breath as the sound of his steps retreated down the hall. He exchanged a quick goodbye with her mother. A door closed.

Zoe tugged open the top of the seabag and drew out the first layer of clothing. Desert camouflage. Every tag had Brett's name written on it. Pain stabbed her as sharp as a K-bar. She swallowed back the sob that thrust into her throat and opened the closet door. Grabbing the bare hangers there, she started unpacking for her brother.

When her mother returned to the bedroom, Zoe had a third of the bag unpacked and struggled to dump the rest onto the bed. Clara rushed forward to help her lift the heavy canvas duffle and give it a shake.

A mess kit, canteen, and ditty kit tumbled out with a crushed mass of t-shirts and underwear. Clara began sorting socks and pairing them while Zoe refolded the t-shirts and placed them in a dresser drawer.

Zoe paused in folding a shirt as her mother dragged a sock heavy with something across the bed. Clara shook the white boot sock and a sheathed knife dropped onto the bed.

"We probably need to put that in Hawk's gun safe, just in case," Zoe suggested.

"Probably so," Clara agreed and set the weapon on the nightstand.

Hearing a sound like dice in a cup a few minutes later, Zoe turned from hanging uniforms in the closet.

Clara held up a small circular stone. "Wonder what these are?"

Zoe limped to the bed and picked up one of the small cylinder shaped stones. She studied the pictographs on it. "They look like stamps."

"Would they be souvenirs?" Clara asked.

"Most likely. They'd be pretty placed in a shadow box frame. Maybe I can do that for Brett."

"We'll pick up a frame this week. I'll put them in my purse so we won't forget them." She scooped them up and placed them back in the sock.

"We can come back another day and unpack the boxes, Mom. I know you're eager to do that."

"I just want Brett to have a home to come to after he's discharged from the hospital."

Her mother's vulnerability, the hope she tried so hard to hold on to, seemed dulled today by grief. The emotional rollercoaster they both endured on a daily basis had taken a sudden plunge for Clara.

Zoe grabbed the seabag from the bed and, folding it up, took it to the closet. "We'll have this place whipped into shape before he gets out," she said as she shoved it onto a shelf. She flinched at her own forced positive tone.

Clara rose from the bed and brushed a distracted hand through her auburn hair. "I'm a little tired, Zoe. You wouldn't mind going to the hospital without me for a few hours."

"No, of course not, mom."

She scanned Clara's expression. The fine lines around her mother's eyes seemed to have grown deeper just since they'd arrived at the apartment.

It was so hard to hold on to hope when there was never any positive news to encourage it. Had her mother hit an emotional wall?

"Do you want to stay and unpack a few boxes?" Zoe asked.

"No, I just need a little while to myself."

Zoe slid her arms around her mother, her hold fierce.

Clara clung to her, her arms tight, her body taut. After several moments, her muscles relaxed and she stepped back. She brushed at the tears that glazed her cheeks. Weariness invaded her expression. "Maybe I just need a nap. Let's go."

"Is there somewhere you need to stop before I drop you off at the house?" Zoe asked during the short elevator trip to the lobby.

"No, I don't think so."

As the elevator door opened Clara murmured, "Shit—I forgot the knife and Brett's souvenirs."

Zoe laid a hand against the door to hold it open. "No problem. I can run back up and get them. It won't take a minute. Why don't you go on to the car and wait for me." She leaned against the door to keep it open while she dug in her purse for the keys. She handed them to Clara, accepted the ones her mother offered her, and then stepped back inside the elevator, allowing the door to close.

Was there any way at all she could make things easier for her mother? She shook her head and raked her fingers through the long ponytail that hung over her shoulder. Frustration clogged her throat and she drew a deep breath. If only they weren't so damn helpless in all this.

The elevator door opened and she limped out into the hall. She thumbed through the keys her mother had handed her and selected one.

The air inside the apartment smelled fresher for having the sliding glass doors open for a time, but there was also an elusive scent hanging in the room. Shaving cream? Suntan lotion? No.

Zoe strode down the hall into the bedroom. The sheathed knife and sock lay together on the nightstand. She picked up the knife and swinging her shoulder bag forward, unzipped it and shoved it inside.

Her eyes fell on the chest in which she'd placed Brett's underwear and socks. The top drawer hung open. Hung open when she'd closed it just moments before.

Time stopped.

One beat of her heart shoved into another. Every breath drew the indistinct scent into her lungs.

Her body seemed frozen, numb, her limbs liquid.

Silence stretched as loud as a scream.

Her attention swung to the closet and froze. Was someone inside hiding? Were eyes looking through the slats at her? The louvered doors seemed to bow forward though they didn't move.

Her fingertips rested on the sheathed knife. She'd never get the knife out and if she did he'd take it away from her and—

Feeling light headed, she pressed a hand to the nightstand. The sock filled with stones lay beneath her palm. She wrapped the top of the cotton garment around her hand. As the weighted toe swung upward, the stones rattled, like marbles clicking together. Her lungs seized. Her body shook.

Move! Move god damn it! Her legs felt spongy and weak as she hedged sideways giving the closet a wide birth. If he came out of the closet would she have the strength to swing the sock? Her shoulder blades brushed hard against the doorframe as she strained away from it and backed into the hall.

Her joints felt loose, her steps clumsy as, reaching the end of the hall, she turned and ran out of the apartment.

A few moments later, she hugged the elevator wall, as her lungs worked like bellows. Her leg ached and burned as though the damaged muscle had been ripped apart.

Had there been someone there? Or was it all in her imagination?

There had to be someone there? She'd closed the drawer. She knew she had. She wasn't crazy.

Had there really been a scent left behind. Or could it have just been Flash's aftershave? Had she noticed him wearing aftershave? Would it have lingered in the air with the balcony door open? Not likely.

She had to get the manager to go back up with her and check the apartment.

They'd be gone by then. Thank God. But how had they gotten in?

The sock hung heavily against her side. Thank God she hadn't had to use it.

CHAPTER 6

Lieutenant Commander Jackson eyed Hawk over the report he held, his features taut with a frown. Silence, tense and oppressive, stretched between them.

"So you're certain of Flash's position outside the building?"

Jackson asked.

Hawk forced his clenched fists open and rested his hands on his thighs. "Yes, sir. He was monitoring the movements of the tangos from the exterior and signaling us on the radio."

"Where was Ensign O'Connor?"

"His duty was to set charges at the North corner of the build, bottom floor. He finished, exited the building and signaled."

"But you didn't see him exit the building."

"No, sir."

"And Ensign Rivera?"

"Bottom floor, back room, South corner."

"Ensign Armstrong?"

"Bottom floor, back room, South East corner. And EnsignWeaver had the North West corner. I had the middle two rooms and the stairs."

"And you finished ahead of the others?"

"I got inside ahead of the others by a few minutes. I exited the building out a side window and took up a position across the street beneath the wall of a bombed out building there."

"Ensign Carney backs that up."

Hawk nodded. "Flash was acting radio man and was positioned on the roof of one of the buildings diagonal to the target."

"He observed the operation—including Ensign Weaver's rescue."

"Yes, sir."

"From his testimony, and the other men's, you should receive a commendation for saving Ensign Weaver's life."

Hawk raised one brow. A commendation hadn't played into his actions. It wouldn't help Cutter walk out of the hospital a whole man.

"Was there any bad blood between Weaver and any of the men in the team?" Jackson continued.

"Not that I'm aware of, sir."

"Armstrong and O'Connor were the last two out and Rivera just minutes before."

"Yes, sir. Armstrong raised the alarm, and O'Connor worked like a mad man to keep Weaver alive until we could reach the extraction point. Rivera and Carney helped me walk every step of the way there. Shaker guarded our back door. He'd taken out two tangos before we withdrew and two more during the extraction. We worked as a team, sir."

"Then what happened to Weaver inside that room, Lieutenant?" Jackson's voice took on an impatient tone.

There had been no debris around him. No sign of the weapon used to bash in his skull. There'd been no time to look. And they couldn't exactly return to the scene and investigate the evidence now that the building was toast. "I don't know, sir."

Jackson closed the report and tossed the manila folder aside. He rose and folded his arms.

Hawk followed suit coming to parade rest.

"Officially we're going to list this as an accident. But unofficially this will hang over every man's head in your team until we find out what happened, Lieutenant. Because you were the leader of the mission, it will hang over yours as well."

Having it spoken straight out had the knot in Hawk's gut tightening. In other words it could affect his promotion possibilities. For himself. For his team. "I understand, sir."

"These men know you, trust you. I'm expecting you to find out what the hell's going on with them. I want this shit squared away. Am I clear?"

"Yes, sir." Hawk kept his expression under control as a quick spike of renewed anger roiled inside his gut. Who ever had hurt Cutter had succeeded in injuring the whole team in the process.

For a few moments Jackson's gaze continued to bore into him.

With an impatient twitch of his shoulders he breathed, "Dismissed."

****

Hawk straightened his knee, pushing against the pressure the therapist put on the bottom of his foot. The joint remained a little tender but he completed the exercises the therapist put him through with ease. He breathed a sigh of relief. Maybe he'd be able to start some light training in a few weeks to work off some of this frustration. Not that it would do much good if he couldn't discover what had happened to Cutter.

God damn, Jackson. He fought to shove back the anger and resentment the man had triggered.

"You're doing very well," the therapist said.

He'd probably do better if it were Zoe massaging his knee, instead of a guy with black hair on the back of his hands. The instant reaction the thought provoked had him sucking air through his teeth. He needed a distraction and she certainly provided it.

"You're not overusing the joint, are you?"

"No." He shook his head. Zoe and her mother took care of the household chores and shopping. The inactivity was driving him crazy. With nothing else to focus on, he remained hyper alert to everything Zoe did. Zoe reading. Zoe snacking on an apple and licking the juice from her lips. Zoe sleeping on the lounge on the back porch her cheeks flushed, her features relaxed, and vulnerable, and so damned beautiful. Watching her do the most mundane things could spark off that hot gut wrenching need.

He twisted his attention back to the exercise the therapist led him through. Once his knee was back in shape he'd be able to drive again and find distractions outside the house. He had to pursue the answers he needed from his men.

With his therapy concluded, he caught the elevator to the third floor. Exiting the elevator, he saw Zoe as she walked just ahead of him down the hallway to Brett's room. The brace she had strapped around the lower half of her leg this morning offered her support, but made her gait stiffer and more awkward. It didn't detract from the rounded curve of her buttocks, though. She had the most perfectly shaped ass he'd ever seen—among other things.

He called to her and she turned, a canned soft drink clutched in her hand.

The strain he read in her expression had him quickening his pace.

"How did your therapy go?" she asked.

"Fine."

"Good. One of your men is here."

Seeing nothing unusual in the occurrence he raised a brow in inquiry.

"Ensign Armstrong."

"Yeah. Derrick's been on leave ever since we hit stateside. Some kind of family emergency."

She reached for the handle of the door, but he grasped it first and opened it for her.

When he saw the two of them, Derrick paused in mid-sentence as he spoke to Angela, Brett's day nurse, and rose to his feet.

"Strong Man, how'd the trip go? Everything all right?" he inquired as he extended a hand.

Dressed in his winter blues, the man's muscular bulk was evident as he shifted his body to shake hands. Derrick's obsession with weight lifting was well known among the team. He had obviously been pumping iron to recover the definition he'd lost while out of the country.

"Yeah, everything worked out. My sister had her baby, prematurely. She's going to be all right, but the baby will have to stay in the neonatal unit for a while. They think he'll be okay though."

"You're a new uncle. Where's my cigar?"

Derrick smiled. "Hey, good idea. I'll have to pick up a box to give out to the team."

"They didn't have any bottled water." Zoe extended the soft drink to Derrick and he smiled.

"That's all right." He focused on Hawk. "I just got off the plane from Louisiana and came straight here. Couldn't get an attendant's attention long enough to get a drink before touchdown." He popped the top on the drink. "Got a cup?"

Zoe crossed to the bedside and returned with a plastic cup wrapped in cellophane. She unwrapped it, careful not to touch the lip.

"I don't normally drink anything with caffeine or sugar," Strong Man said as he poured the liquid into the cup. "I'll share with you," he extended the can to Zoe.

"No thank you." Her stilted tone had Hawk studying her expression.

Though shorter by several inches, Derrick gave the impression of being taller than he was because of the width of his shoulders and the thickness of his arms. His blond haired, blue-eyed good looks usually drew flirtatious smiles from the fairer sex, not the wariness Zoe exhibited.

"I have to get back to my other patients," Angela said. "May I speak with you for a moment out in the hall, Zoe?"

Surprising him, Zoe slipped an arm around his waist and leaned against his side. It seemed natural to curve an arm about her waist in response.

"Why don't you have a seat and rest your knee? You and Ensign Armstrong can catch up while I stretch my legs," she said as she rested a palm against his chest.

With the softness of her breast pressing into his ribs, and the graceful curve of her waist beneath his hand, he experienced more than a little regret when she pulled away and left the room.

His attention focused back on Derrick. The words, "What the hell did you say to her?" were on the tip of his tongue as Armstrong handed him the pop can and said, "Cutter didn't mention he had a sister that hot."

A surge of irritation had him wanting to grind his teeth. "Brothers don't normally think of their sisters in those terms."

"I guess not. Something weird's going down here, LT. Ms. Weaver's been looking at me like I've got horns and a forked tail ever since I got here. Had she not said you'd show up soon, I'd have already bugged out."

"What do you think is going on?" He asked.

"Something's going on with Cutter. They kept checking him."

Concerned, Hawk rose to his feet to stand next to Brett's bed. It gave him a queasy feeling each time he saw the other man lying so still. He studied Brett's features carefully and scanned the monitors, but didn't recognize a change in their readings.

Derrick joined him there. "All the way back, I kept telling myself he'd be awake by the time I got here. Jesus—I can't believe he's still out of it." He raked a hand through his hair, his features creased with worry and frustration.

A red spot on the unconscious man's cheek drew Hawk's attention and he turned Brett's face to the light. A handprint stood out in stark relief.

An instant feeling of outrage and anger surged through him. "Son of a Bitch! Someone's slapped him."

Derrick stared at him, his lips parted in shock. "They think it was me." His voice had a flat quality. "That's why they were both looking at me like that." He shook his head adamantly. "No way, LT. I've been Brett's swim buddy since BUDS. I've covered his back ever since. I wouldn't smack him around, especially now. God! Look at him, he's completely helpless." Derrick's features took on a pinched look.

Hawk found it hard not to believe he was telling the truth.

"Hold on. I'll go get Zoe and Angela and we'll talk this out."

"They should have said something to me, so I could set them straight," Derrick said, anger beginning to overtake his defensive tone.

Hawk stepped outside the room. Angela and Zoe stood at the end of the hall their heads close together. They started walking toward him when they saw him.

"Derrick and I need to talk with you and Angela," he said, holding the door wide. The two women filed back into the room. "We've just noticed that someone has left a handprint on Brett's face."

"I'd only arrived five minutes before you got here," Derrick jumped in; his attention homed in on Zoe like a heat seeking missile. "I know that would be enough time for me to have done it, but I didn't. I swear to you, I didn't. Cutter is my swim buddy. We cover each other's backs. We always have. We may grab ass around, and punch each other, and do the male bonding thing, but I wouldn't lay a hand on him now that's he's—like he is." Two bright spots of color burnt in his cheeks and he nearly vibrated with outrage.

"Was there anyone out in the hall when you first arrived, Derrick?" Hawk asked.

"No. The nurses were down at the nurses' station, doing whatever they do there. I didn't see anyone else around. I just came in and went up to the bed. Cutter didn't respond when I talked to him, so I knew he was either drugged, or he still hadn't come around. I was about to go out and ask the nurses at the station about him, when Ms. Weaver came in and filled me in on what was going on." Derrick's attention swung from Zoe to Angela and back again. "I didn't touch him."

"Chill out, Derrick," Hawk said as he laid a hand on the other man's shoulder. He had to calm him down or he'd allow his defensiveness to cloud the issue. This situation pertained to Brett not him.

"There are security cameras on this floor aren't there?" he asked Angela.

"Sure."

"Show me where they're placed."

Hawk and Angela went out into the hall.

Zoe remained beside Brett. The anger and disbelief she had first experienced on discovering her brother had been assaulted had passed. Fear now lay like a cold stone in the pit of her stomach.

Had the man outside of Brett's apartment really been watching her? Was it possible that man had been Derrick Armstrong? All she'd seen was blonde hair. Had someone really been in the apartment or had it been her imagination? There'd been no sign of anyone when she'd returned with a security guard to check the apartment. No sign of any disturbance.

If it wasn't Ensign Armstrong who had left the mark on Brett's face, it had to be someone else who had access to the base. That left the rest of his SEAL team buddies, and anyone else who applied for a visitor's pass.

It was a slap this time, what might be done next? Anyone who would abuse a comatose patient was capable of anything.

Leaning over the railing of the bed, she laid her head down on the pillow next to her brother's and soothed the red marks on his cheek with her fingertips. Tears ran across her nose into the pillow as the feelings of pain and grief she had been suppressing welled up to overwhelm her. What was going on here? Who would want to hurt her brother?

"Hey, Ms. Weaver. We're going to take care of this. No one's going to mess with Cutter again," Derrick said from behind her, a panicky edge to his voice. "We'll find out who it was, and then, he'll be toast, I promise."

She kissed Brett's cheek and moved to hold him. His forehead lay warm against her cheek, his beard coarse beneath her fingers as she stroked his face. The life and vitality he exuded when conscious made it painful to see him as he appeared now. He had taken on the lifelessness of the cardboard cutouts candidates sometimes posted during elections.

"Please wake up, Brett, please," she pleaded.

The door behind her opened and closed softly.

Drawing on her shaky reserves, Zoe fought to suppress her emotions and stemmed the flow of tears. She had wiped her eyes and blown her nose by the time Hawk returned with Ensign Armstrong and Angela in tow.

His limp didn't dilute the air of command Hawk wore so effortlessly. She drew comfort from knowing he had taken charge of the situation.

He gave her a searching once over then said, "Angela has alerted security. One security camera has a straight shot at anyone getting off the elevator. The one at the end of the hall will have caught anyone coming from the stairwell from the other direction. The stairs stay locked, so they more than likely got off the elevator, but we'll have to wait and see."

"I've seen the stairwell door propped open several times late at night. I assumed it was one of the staff slipping downstairs for a smoke." She folded her arms against her waist to cover her trembling. "I'd like Brett to have a thorough examination to make sure the welt on his cheek is the only injury he's sustained."

"I've notified Captain Connelly, and he's on his way," Angela said.

She nodded. "I appreciate it." She turned her attention to Derrick Armstrong. He had seen her at her most vulnerable. She had been eyeing him like a criminal. She supposed that balanced things out in some way.

"You never said what your sister's baby was."

"A boy," he answered, his features tense.

"How much did he weigh?"

"Four pounds."

"He was tiny." She forced a smile to her lips she hoped looked natural. "What did they name him?"

"Adam."

Her attention shifted to Hawk. "You have a namesake."

"Yeah, how 'bout that."

She moistened her lips. "I don't believe you hurt my brother, Ensign Armstrong." Her throat tightened with more tears and she swallowed.

"Thanks." Derrick shifted from one foot to the other. "I suppose, if I'd been in your shoes, I'd have been suspicious too."

"As soon as we get a look at the security tapes, we'll know who was in Brett's room before Derrick arrived," Hawk said." Then we'll deal with them."

"I doubt security will let you see the tapes, Lieutenant," Angela said.

"We'll see."

His tone had Zoe taking a good look at him. His pale gray eyes looked flat and cold. The leashed fury she read beneath his features sent a shiver down Zoe's spine. She had thought he'd be scary when angered. She hadn't guessed the half of it.

CHAPTER 7

Clara met them at the door as they entered the house, her features tense with worry. "Turner called half an hour ago. Sharon started hemorrhaging. He rushed her to the hospital. They're doing a C-section. They don't know about the baby yet." she raked her fingers through her bangs. Two suitcases sat next to the front door.

The news hit Zoe like a physical blow. She closed her eyes for a moment as instant tears threatened. The hits just kept coming.

"I've got a flight out in an hour. I've called a cab because I wasn't sure you'd be back in time to take me to the airport."

"I can take you now, Mom."

"No, I've called a cab. You've been with your brother for most of the day and you're tired." At the sound of a car horn outside, her mother turned and looked out the window. "That's my ride."

Clara's composure started to crumble as she reached for the suitcases.

"I'll get them, Clara," Hawk said and swung a bag up in each hand.

Zoe opened the door for him then turned to embrace her mother. She fought back her tears as Clara withdrew to look into her face. "It's going to be all right, Mom. Sharon's young and healthy. And the baby will be fine."

Clara searched her pockets for a tissue to wipe her face. "I don't want to go. I don't want to leave Brett. I shouldn't have to choose between them."

The events that had taken place at the hospital and Brett's apartment ran through Zoe's mind. "Sharon needs you more right now than Brett does. He has me and Hawk to look out for him. He'll be fine."

"I know. You're right." She stuffed the tissue back in the pocket of her slacks. She focused on Zoe her look sharp, intent. "Don't go back to the apartment until the locks are changed. Promise me you won't."

"I promise."

"You have to pace yourself. You can't go all out like you've been doing. You can't try and take my place. Promise you'll try and rest some. If you get sick too, I won't be able to deal with it."

"I'll take it easier, I promise."

"I'll make sure she does, Clara," Hawk said as he entered the house. "The team will take up the slack."

A horn blew from outside again. "I have to go." Clara gathered her purse and a carryon bag.

Zoe hugged her once more. "Call me as soon as you get there."

"Turner may call before I make it there. Call me on my cell if he does," Clara said.

Zoe nodded.

Clara embraced Hawk. "I know you'll take care of both of them while I'm gone."

"I'll do my best."

Clara broke away from him and went out the door, closing it behind her.

The ticking of the clock in the kitchen sounded loud in the silence that followed her departure.

"You didn't tell her, did you?" he asked.

She shook her head. "I couldn't. She was already torn between them. Had I told her what had happened it would have just made it impossible."

"You did the right thing." He ran his hand down his jaw where dark stubble had begun to show. "Look, I'm going to fire up the grill and burn us some meat. We both need some food."

She had never been less interested in eating, but she recognized the need to feed her body. She hadn't eaten since before noon and it now hovered close to seven. She forced a smile to her lips. "I put some chicken in a marinade this morning before going to the hospital. I'll fix a salad and nuke a couple of potatoes while you incinerate the meat." She headed for the kitchen.

He gave a short bark of laughter. "It was only a little crispy around the edges last time."

She glanced over her shoulder. "Uh-huh."

"I got distracted for a minute."

"By what?"

His gray gaze swung away from her. "I refuse to answer on the grounds that I may incriminate myself."

An ache built in the pit of her stomach that had nothing to do with hunger. She forced a light teasing tone, "That means it was some Baywatch beauty within seeing distance of the yard. Maybe Mandy next door." Wishing it had been her he found distracting was like trying to touch the moon. The need to be held, comforted, loved, for just a few minutes, for forever, rose up in her like a physical pain.

****

Hawk shook his head. How could she be so completely oblivious to her own beauty? He'd been distracted by Zoe sitting out on the back stoop looking into the sun as it disappeared over the horizon. Bathed in pale peach light, her skin had taken on such an iridescent softness he'd had to fight hard not to reach for her. Just thinking about it brought a heavy feeling to his groin.

"It wasn't Mandy," he said. He couldn't say more. They were going to be alone together for two or three weeks, if not longer. He had to be careful.

He frowned. Zoe attributed his distraction to someone else too easily. She didn't see herself as a desirable woman because of her leg. Even though the single men in the team continued to flirt with her, it never occurred to her they could be serious. Her attitude made things easier for him from the standpoint that if she didn't take any of them seriously, she wouldn't get involved with one of them. And if she didn't get involved, it wouldn't kill him to see her with someone else. God, he had it bad.

Why couldn't he learn? He couldn't give her what she needed any more than he could Veronica. Not until he left the team. He didn't need to get involved with a woman who already fought against being drawn back into the "the life". It would be a recipe for disaster for them both.

Zoe bent to get the salad fixings from the vegetable bin at the bottom of the refrigerator. He studied her rounded derriere and his palm tingled with the urge to run his hand over the shapely curve. Her mother had just walked out the door. He had promised to look out for her. If he moved in on her now, it would be a betrayal of her trust. He had told the men that getting involved with Zoe was not a good idea and here he was aching to do just that.

They needed to get out of the house.

"We could go out, if you don't feel like cooking," he suggested.

Zoe straightened the vegetable bags clenched in her hands. She looked over her shoulder at him. "I don't mind fixing a salad and nuking some potatoes. But if you'd rather—"

"What about pizza or Chinese?" he suggested.

She bit her lip, "I don't want to leave in case Turner calls."

"I have my cell and can have the call forwarded, but on second thought—" He retrieved a pad and pencil from the counter close to the phone. "Tell me what you want and I'll order. You can go lie down until it gets here."

She shrugged. "Curry Beef, fried rice, and an egg roll," she said as she put the vegetables back in the refrigerator.

Surprised, he said, "I didn't know you liked spicy stuff."

"I love hot food, particularly curry."

"Next time I barbecue I'll fix my hot sauce to put on the meat."

"Hot sauce on a charcoal briquette does not sound appetizing." She flashed a smile, but worry dulled the affect.

He frowned at her in mock anger and tried to hide the concern that tightened the muscles of his shoulders and neck. If something horrible happened to her sister and the baby, how would Zoe handle it? How would he handle her? His stomach churned. He didn't want just to be a shoulder to lean or cry on. Another brother. Hell no!

But he couldn't be anything else either. It was too opportunistic. Once they knew Sharon and the baby were all right—There couldn't be a once. He couldn't get involved with Zoe. She didn't want it, he didn't want it. Damn this was hard.

He forced a bantering tone as he said, "You have to give me one more shot at the barbeque to redeem myself. Flamethrower chicken, tomorrow night, hot off the grill at six o'clock."

"All right."

He flipped open his cell phone and ordered the food. After ending the call he said, "It'll be about thirty minutes. You can lie down for a while if you'd like."

"I'll make some iced tea to drink with dinner first."

He wandered into the living room and turned on the television. Kicking off his shoes, he propped his feet on the coffee table and slouched down into the cushions. He tried to watch baseball, but the game became background noise as he tracked Zoe's location in the house as she walked from kitchen, bedroom, bathroom, kitchen again, and then traveled the distance of the hall, her uneven gate a distinctive cadence.

She entered the living room carrying two glasses of iced tea. She handed one to him and took a seat at the other end of the couch. She had changed into low-slung sweat pants and the old t-shirt he was beginning to love because it left a narrow band of skin visible at the bottom of the shirt and one shoulder bare.

"You can stretch out, there's plenty of room," he said.

"I'm all right." She found a coaster for her drink and curled her legs up on the cushion beside her, then folded her arms against her waist again. "This waiting is hard."

His attention swung to her face taking in the tension in her expression. "Yes, it is. Your brother-in-law will call in a few minutes."

"I hope so."

"We have to do a lot of waiting in the SEALS. Wait until we get to the location. Wait until we're in position. Sometimes we have to wait hours, or even days, depending on the mission. The rescues are better. With those you're trained to make sure everything goes like clockwork and you don't lose anyone." Or at least as few as possible.

"You rescued Brett," she said, her voice soft.

His attention swung from the television to her face. As long as the mission was between them there wasn't a chance in hell she'd lower those barriers and let him in. Maybe that was a good thing. Or was it? "Who told you that?"

"Doc said something in passing this afternoon at the hospital."

He couldn't tell her specifics about the mission but— "Brett didn't show up where he was supposed to be. It still isn't clear to me, or anyone else, why. I got to him just before detonation. He was already down when I found him."

"And now someone's slapping him while he's in a coma, just to make sure he isn't waking up."

"Yeah."

She blinked several times fighting back tears. He drew a breath of relief when she retained her composure.

"I think there was someone in the apartment today after mom and I left."

Hawk sat up, his body tense. Jesus Christ!

"Mom forgot something in the bedroom, so I left her downstairs in the lobby and went back up to get it. I can't prove it, but I just got the feeling—it was weird. The drawer in the bedroom was hanging open and I'd just closed it." She shook her head, confusion and fear working its way across her features. "I got the knife and other things and got out of there."

"Jesus, Zoe." His heart wedged it's way between his ribs, its beat so harsh.

"The security guard went back upstairs with me and checked it out, but there wasn't anyone there. But there was a smell, like shaving cream or something—I couldn't really place it."

She raked her fingers through her hair. "It sounds crazy when I say it out loud. I just sensed there was someone there. It scared the daylights out of me."

"God, Zoe. Why didn't you call me?"

"You were at your meeting with your commander, and there wasn't anything you could do." She drew a deep breath. "It may have just been my imagination." She dragged her hair over one shoulder. "In any case, we're having the locks changed. And the security guard offered to check the apartment a couple times a day until Brett gets home."

Hawk laid a hand over hers. "If anything at all like this happens again, no matter what the hell's going on, call me."

Her smile was half hearted though her hand covered his. "I don't want to think it but it feels as though someone on your team may have it in for my brother."

"Yeah, I know." What the fuck was going on? Anger and betrayal clenched inside him and his stomach rolled.

She uncurled her legs and turned toward him. "What do we do about it?"

Her instant drive to be proactive, to solve the problem had anxiety spiking.

"How can you be sure it wasn't me, Zoe?"

Her gaze remained steady on his face. "It wasn't you. You wouldn't have risked your life to save him otherwise."

Relief raced through him and some of the tension eased from his shoulders and back. "The nurses are on red alert now. Whoever it is will wait until things calm down before they try anything else."

She nodded. "You saw the tapes today from the hall cameras."

"Yeah. I viewed it along with half a dozen MPs and their commander. A guy dressed in scrubs came up the stairwell, entered the hallway, and went directly into Brett's room. No one else was in the hallway at the time. He stayed five minutes then left by the same route. The scrubs were large and baggy, and we couldn't get a read on his build. The cap he wore covered his hair. He didn't wear a mask, but he knew where the cameras were and how to keep his face averted from them. He even had rubber gloves covering his hands so you couldn't tell about his skin color. They're making me a copy to give to Lang. Next to Flash he's our best computer expert. We'll see if he can freeze-frame it and enhance some of the images to try and get a better look at the guy. But it could take some time."

"In the meantime, what do we do?" she asked.

"Exactly what we are doing. Keep the staff on high alert and make sure none of the guys on the mission at the time of Cutter's injury are alone with him. I requested a guard put on Cutter's room, but it's doubtful it will go through since it was just a slap and not an open attempt on his life. And we don't have any proof there was an attempt during the mission."

"Which ones?"

He hesitated. She had to know otherwise she'd be paranoid about all the guys. "Greenback was guarding our backdoor. I think he had his hands too full to have been involved."

"I haven't met him yet."

"No, his wife just had a baby before we went wheels up and he requested some time. That leaves Flash, Strong Man, Bowie, and Doc."

She closed her eyes and he could almost see her taking in the fact that someone she had broken bread with, flirted with, laughed with, might have tried to kill her brother. Her throat worked as she swallowed. When she opened her eyes she looked directly at him. "This must be very hard for you."

He gave a wry grimace. "You could say that. My life has been in all these guys' hands more than once, Zoe. The thought that any one of them could betray a fellow team member is just un-fucking-believable." The betrayal of it rolled around inside him making him sick. He shook his head, clenching and unclenching his hands as he fought the urge to hit something.

She shifted closer to him and laid a hand on his arm. "I'm sorry, Hawk."

He covered her hand with his, holding it against his skin, and absorbing the warmth of her touch. The need to drag her closer, to bury his face in the softly scented bend of her throat and take comfort from her was nearly overwhelming. Only family could give that special kind of comfort. It had been a long time since he'd had any family. The realization he was looking to Zoe for that, hit him with the punch of an AK-47.

He was getting in too deep, already. That nagging need to be close, to be connected to her, left him vulnerable. And what if he reached out to her? He couldn't give her the security she deserved. Where would that leave him?

He dragged his attention back to the discussion at hand. "There's something else. There could be more than one of them involved. The guys in my team are—tight. Or at least I thought we were. We look out for one another. Doc and Bowie are especially close. If one thought the other was being threatened, he'd cover for him. I thought Cutter and Strong Man were close too." He raked his fingers through his close - cropped hair, pressing his palms against his scalp to hold back the anger. "God, I used to think we really *knew* each other, but after today, I'm not so sure anymore."

"You can live with someone and not really know them, Hawk. No one shares everything about themselves with anyone, even their family. It could be one of them working alone and the other knows nothing about it. First, I think we have to look closely at Brett's relationship with them all. Do you know if he owed anyone money?"

"No. But that's not something he would talk about, is it?"

"Did he like to play poker, make bets, that kind of thing? I've never known him to be that interested in that sort of thing, but with him way out here, and us on the other coast I thought he might have changed."

"The guys all make little side bets about who'll be the first to complete an underwater demolition or reach the ground after we rappel out of a helo."

"Jesus." She shook her head. "I'm talking football games and you're talking war games."

"It's a way of shaking off tension before we do something dangerous. You can't just go into something like that cold without your mind and body gearing up for it." He suddenly wondered if he were telling her too much about what they did. He didn't want to scare her off and make her any more gun shy than she already was.

"Don't, Hawk."

"Don't?"

"I can tell from your expression you're getting ready to shut down on me." She touched his arm again. "I'm not some tender Tillie who can't handle the truth."

A soft huff of laughter escaped him. She read him better than he did her. She was more complex than the other women in whom he'd been interested. Or maybe he just hadn't wanted to understand the others like he did her. The back and forth transition from tough one minute to soft and vulnerable the next was a little hard to figure when it changed so quickly from moment to moment.

The phone rang at the same time a knock sounded at the door. For a moment Zoe froze, a look of anxious dread flitting across her face before she reached for the phone. Hawk rose to answer the door but focused on her features hoping to read something from her expression. He grabbed the takeout food from the delivery boy and shoved some money at him with an abruptness just short of rude.

"Need any change, man?" the kid asked.

"No."

Zoe sank back down on the couch, the receiver pressed to her ear. Her features appeared taut, and her fingers gripped the phone so tightly each joint stood out.

He swore beneath his breath unable to tell anything from her body language. He set the bag of food down on the coffee table. Every muscle grew tight as he waited for her to hang up. "Yes" and "no" and "Mom is on her way", didn't give him much to go on, but the fact that she remained calm eased some of his anxiety.

"The baby is all right," she said as soon as she hung up. "She was in distress and they had to get her out pretty quickly, but the pediatrician said she's doing fine now." She swallowed and her composure wobbled, but she held on. "They had to do an emergency hysterectomy on Sharon. They couldn't get the bleeding stopped. She's had to have transfusions." She rubbed her arms as though cold. "They nearly lost her."

He had to hold her. All the reasons why he shouldn't didn't matter in that moment.

He sat down next to her and put his arms around her. The way her head found the perfect spot between his chest and shoulder to rest in, the way her breasts pushed against his ribs had a rightness to it. There was no reserve in the way she wrapped her arms around him and held on. It seemed he'd waited months, not weeks, for a reason to hold her.

If only she were allowing him to do so under different circumstances.

She shook with reaction but she didn't cry. Driven to offer her comfort he said, "They *didn't* lose her or the baby. No matter what other sacrifices had to be made, Zoe, that's the important thing."

She nodded. "I have to call Mom."

Without releasing her, he stretched back to tug the cell phone from his belt and flipped it open. He scrolled down to Clara's number and pressed it, then waited for her to pick up. When she didn't answer, he said, "She must be on the flight already. The tower may allow the pilot to get a message to her though. I'll get the phone book and call the airport."

She drew back releasing him, but her hand rested on his chest for a moment, and she looked up at him. "I'm sorry, Hawk."

Confused, he asked, "For what?"

"It's been one family drama after another ever since we moved in here. It's not normally like this with us. If it gets to be too much for you—"

"Not a chance," he cut her off. "I'm sticking around for when something good happens to balance things out. Hey, it already has—you're an aunt again."

"Yes, I am." She offered him an unsteady smile and her shoulders fell in a release of tension.

"Congratulations, Aunt Zoe." He brushed her lips with a kiss he told himself was a friendly gesture, but his lips clung to hers. The soft, lush texture of her mouth begged to be explored. He wanted to taste her, test her response. He forced himself to pull back before teeth and tongue came into play.

Her eyes looked huge, and a pale vibrant blue. He read surprise in her expression and something else that grabbed him right below the belt.

"I'll get the phone book." He grasped the bag of food and carried it into the kitchen. He had to get away from her before he did something stupid. Like kiss her again

.

CHAPTER 8

Langley Marks swung the station wagon into a parking space at the firing range. Sporadic gunfire echoed from just over the man-made rise. "Flash, Doc, and Bowie should be here instructing." He didn't put the vehicle in park but continued to eye Hawk. "Are you going to tell me what's going on?"

Hawk shook his head. How had Lang known something was happening? Had he read his body language? Had something he'd said alerted him? He studied his expression. Lang was his oldest and closest friend since joining the unit. He trusted him implicitly. Besides he'd had only a peripheral part in planning and implementing the mission.

"Officially, Cutter's injuries have been ruled an accident. Unofficially, the brass has decided that until they know for certain what happened, those of us who took part in the mission, have a cap on our promotions."

"Jesus." Langley leaned back against the seat and shoved the gearshift into park. His expression remained blank with shock for several moments then he looked up. "Something else is going on here."

"Something happened while we were in Iraq, something Cutter saw or did." Hawk rubbed a hand along his jaw. "I don't know."

"They believe one of the team caved his head in and left him to die," Langley said as though trying to absorb it.

"Yeah."

Lang turned toward him. "They can't think it was you."

"No. But they expect me to get to the bottom of it. And the only way I can do that is talk to the guys and see what they know."

"Doc and Bowie are tight. They won't give each other up, if they're involved."

"Yeah."

"Derrick's a hot head, but he and Cutter have been tight since BUDS. And Flash was never inside the building."

"As far as we know," Hawk said.

Langley's brows rose. "Do you have any reason to believe differently."

"No, but I'm not limiting any possibilities. Shaker had his hands full with a tango but I'm not ruling him out either. I need to find out what Cutter was up to before the mission. If he had any disagreements with any of the men, owed them any money, that kind of thing."

"I can't see any of them going ape shit over money, so it has to be something else."

"Yeah, something worse. Something that could affect their careers. But what?"

Langley shook his head. "Jesus." He rubbed a hand over his closely cut hair. "And what if all this is bullshit, and Cutter just fell or something? It will affect all your careers—for nothing."

"No shit. But if it was just bullshit, why would someone be slapping him around to make sure he wasn't waking up?"

"Damn."

The disheartened tone of Langley's voice mirrored Hawk's own feelings.

Hawk shoved his hand into his pack and came out with a DVD of the hospital footage. "I need you to freeze frame the images on this disc and see if you can see who it is that came out of Cutter's room that morning."

"Consider it done. Flash is better at this than I am, but I suppose under the circumstances, you don't want to take it to him."

Hawk ignored the comment. "Zoe's staying at the hospital practically twelve hours a day afraid to leave Cutter alone."

"Shit," Lang breathed. "She can't keep that up."

"No she can't. That's why I'm here. Doc, Flash, and Bowie are here and I'm going to see what I can find out from them."

"Do you need me to watch your back?" Lang thumped the steering wheel with the heel of his hand, his features twisting with a grimace part anger, part frustration. "I can't believe I just asked that. Jesus—These men are members of our team."

Team. That word had taken on a different connotation to Hawk as soon as he'd discovered Brett unconscious inside the building. Would he ever be able to trust anyone as completely again? Realizing Lang was waiting for an answer he looked up. "I'll be all right. Keep your distance, Lang. You don't want to get tangled up in this."

"I'm here for you, Hawk, and for the team. Whatever you need."

Langley's show of loyalty loosened the knot of tension twisting his insides. "Thanks, man. I may need to use you as a sounding board, but I think it's smart to keep it between just the six of us."

"And what about, Zoe?"

"She's agreed to stay quiet until I figure things out."

"How'd you manage that?"

"We're Cutter's team too. Zoe's a Marine Corps brat. She knows how important it is to all of our careers. She knows the score." Maybe too well.

"Is she protecting everyone's career or just Cutters?"

Was it just her brother she was protecting? "I don't know."

Lang's brows rose.

"We're not—We haven't—" Hawk drew a deep breath. "Her mother asked me to look after her. I won't break that trust."

Lang's smile held a wry twist. "That's an admirable position, but I've seen the way you look at her, my friend. And I've seen how she looks at you, too."

He couldn't deny the attraction that ricocheted back and forth between them, but Zoe wasn't going to act on it. He had a gut feeling about that. "She doesn't want to get drawn back into the life. Her Dad was killed in Desert Storm and now Cutter's—" He swallowed. "And there are other issues."

Lang raised one thick brow. "Her leg?"

"Yeah." Hawk rubbed his jaw and tried to relax the urge to grit his teeth in frustration.

Lang's gaze grew sharp. "I wouldn't have thought that would matter to you."

"It doesn't matter to me," Hawk said his tone certain.

Lang frowned. "Shit."

That just about said it all.

Hawk grabbed his pack. "I've got to go."

"Call when you're ready to head back to the hospital. I'll be at the administration building."

"Thanks."

Hawk limped across the parking lot. A knoll of ground separated the cars from the range. He followed the path to the top of the shallow hill. BUDS trainees lay on the ground shooting at distant targets with AK47s. The cacophony of sound assaulted his ears as they fired.

Doc O'Conner paced back and forth behind the men watching as they practiced. As Hawk drew close, Doc's haggard look became evident. Blood vessels lined the whites of his eyes like tributaries and lines of stress dug crevices around his mouth.

At Hawk's greeting, Doc's smile appeared strained.

"How's it going?" Hawk asked.

"This batch seems better than most," Doc said during a lull in the noise. "Ensign Jeffers, the guy at the end, has sniper training. He's lethal every time."

Hawk watched the trainee for a moment. "Did you have a party and not invite me, Doc? You look a little rough around the edges."

Doc grinned. "No party. Well at least not one more than two people attended."

Was it really just a late night with a woman? Or something else?

"How's, Zoe?" Doc asked.

"Still spending twelve hour days at the hospital. We need to talk about Cutter. When will you be through here?"

"Something happen?"

"Yeah."

Doc glanced at his watch. "It'll be about an hour before we're relieved."

"Is Bowie around?"

"Yeah, he's walked down to the head and will be back in a minute."

"Bring him along. I thought Flash was here too."

"He's down at the administration building keying in a report."

Hawk nodded. "I'll give him a call on my cell."

Doc's brow furrowed and dread took up residence in his eyes. "Is Cutter worse? Is he—"

"No. But I need to speak with you about him. I'll be on the pistol range when you're done here."

Hawk sauntered down the field past multiple long distance training ranges to the sheltered pistol range and spoke to the range master to set up his target. Between the barrages of fire, he made a quick call to Flash on his cell and promised to meet him at the administrative building in an hour. He lifted his pack upon the narrow shelf that marked his firing position and separated him from the field.

What if they were all somehow involved in what had happened? His team. He flinched inwardly. Whether they were or weren't, he already looked at them differently. He'd viewed these men as part of his family.

God, he hated this.

He removed his nine-millimeter Sig Sauer and several clips of ammunition and placed them on the shelf. He slid the bolt back to check the weapon's chamber and finding it clear, slapped in a clip. He slid on his protective headgear, thumbed off the safety, raised the handgun, and waited for the next signaled burst of fire.

Squeezing the trigger and boring holes in the distant target helped relieve some of his frustration. Temporarily.

After he finished his practice, he stood atop the shallow plateau above the range and watched other personnel cycle in and out.

Thirty minutes later, Doc and Bowie arrived in a military Humvee. As they exited the vehicle, he studied each man's expression. Would it have been better if he'd talk to each alone? They'd faced BUDS together. If they had a choice, they'd faced the charges, the disruption to their careers together. Hawk rolled his head to loosen the taut muscles in his neck.

"Hey, LT. What's up?" Bowie asked.

"They're still looking into Cutter's accident and I wanted to touch base with you on it. Do either of you remember Cutter behaving differently before we were called up on the mission?"

Bowie shook his head. "No. He was joking and jacking around just before the drop. We were talking about going out with twin sisters he'd met when we got back home. If they were still available."

Hawk remembered the conversation. "He hadn't been complaining about headaches or any other physical problems?"

Doc and Bowie each shook their head.

"He'd been working out some with Derrick, not as obsessively as Strong Man, but just enough to get some definition," Doc volunteered.

"How was he with Strong Man and Flash? Did you pick up on any tension between him and either of them?"

"No," Doc said.

Hawk studied Bowie's frown. "Is there something you remember?"

"It was nothing. Flash said something to him about minding his own business the day before the drop."

"What about?"

"I don't know. It sounded like he was just giving him some advice about something."

"Anything else you can think of?"

"Why would Cutter go back into the building after he'd already gotten out?" Doc asked.

Hawk frowned. "What do you mean?"

"I saw him climbing back through the window after he should have completed his run."

He'd gotten out of the building, then turned around and gone back in. Why would he do that? Had he heard or seen something? Forgotten something? Not a chance with their training.

There were three blonds on the team. Cutter, Strong Man, and Flash. Had it been one of the others? Strong Man had radioed Cutter's absence. Flash had been positioned on the roof diagonally from the target location. If it hadn't been Cutter climbing inside the building, then who? Could Strong Man have radioed from inside the building?

"Are you sure it was him, Doc? Could you see the guy's hair?"

"No, it was too dark. Who else would it have been?"

"They don't think it was an accident." Bowie's tone was as flat as his gaze.

"No, they don't."

Doc's eyes widened. "Jesus—"

Bowie's features grew taut. "We're all under suspicion, aren't we?" He stepped close into Hawk's space. "What the hell did you put in your report, Hawk?"

Hawk braced a hand on Bowie's shoulder and met his gaze. "I wrote exactly what I found when I entered the building. Cutter was out cold and stuffed behind a cabinet, the side of his head bloody. The position of his body suggested that someone had put him there so he wouldn't be seen."

Bowie's features slackened in surprise and he stepped back. He and Doc exchanged a look.

"It wasn't either one of us, Hawk. Neither of us had a reason to hurt Cutter. He was—"Bowie paused, "*is* our buddy. We'd never even had words about anything."

Hawk studied Doc. Something was going on with the man. He seemed distant, dazed. "Is that true for both of you, Doc?"

"It's true." The man's gaze met his. "I'd never do anything to hurt Cutter. Never. I did my best to keep him alive until we got back to base."

The man's sincerity had him taking a relieved breath. His gut told him they were both telling the truth, but could he still trust his instincts. And what the hell was going on with Doc?

"All right. I want both of you to think back on the days before the mission. Every conversation, every observation, anything at all that you noticed about Cutter. And Doc, think back on the guy you saw going in through the window. Anything you observed about him."

"You don't think it was, Cutter?" he asked.

"I don't know. Why would Cutter turn around and go back in once he was clear? And if it wasn't him—" He left it hanging. "Write it all down, it may help you to think it through. If either of you remember anything at all you feel is relevant, call me. We have to figure this thing out." He looked from one to the other. "I'm not going to let team loyalty stand in the way of finding out what happened. Neither of you should either."

Bowie's hands clenched and released in an open characteristic of stress, but his anger seemed to have passed. "Aye-eye, LT."

Hawk glanced at his watch and bent to pick up his pack. "I need a ride to the admin. You guys ready to go?"

Doc nodded, the action subdued, tired. "Yeah, we're ready."

Silence, oppressive and painful, pressed down on Hawk as they drove from one location to the other. As Doc wheeled into the parking area, Hawk spotted Flash leaning against a car in the parking lot of the admin building waiting for him.

"Stay icy. We'll figure this thing out," Hawk said as he opened the door and got out.

"Damn straight," Bowie said, his tone hard.

Doc threw up a hand as he pulled away.

Hawk returned to the gesture and he turned to face Flash.

"How's the knee?" he asked before Hawk reached him.

"It's coming along."

"Good. What's up? Has something happened to Cutter?" Flash's brows rose then converged in a show of concern.

"No, he's about the same." Hawk studied Flash's narrow face.

"You had a bird's eye view on the whole mission. Did you see Cutter come out of the building then go back in?"

"No. All I saw was you going in after him right through the front door. That was the god damnedest thing I've seen since I've been a SEAL. Then a few minutes later when you burst out the front door and the muzzle flashes started flaring as all the tangos fired at you—" He shook his head at the memory. "You were born under a lucky star or something man. I still don't know how you kept from getting hit."

Uncomfortable with the memories Flash's observations dragged up, Hawk shrugged. "Just plain lucky I guess." He shifted his pack over his shoulder to a more comfortable position. "Did you change position at any time?"

"Not once I settled in."

"I want you to write down everything you saw that night, Flash."

He frowned. "I already wrote my report for Lieutenant Commander Jackson."

"Well I want you to do it again. But this time I want you to write down everything you can remember Cutter saying or doing in the days before the mission. There are some questions about what happened to him that have to be answered before Jackson will let it go."

Flash frowned and his jaw tensed. "All right. What's Jackson looking for?"

"Cutter was down before I found him. He wants an explanation."

"Shit, Hawk. Anything could have happened to him. He could have tripped and hit his head or fallen. We're never going to know what happened."

Was Flash hoping they wouldn't find out? "You can go in and tell Jackson that the next time you're at HQ."

Flash swore beneath his breath. "I'll try and remember what we talked about before the mission. But it's been over a month."

The strain of reading into what his men said, and looking at every word with suspicion, had his gut tightening painfully. Hawk swallowed against the sensation. "Do what you can."

"All right."

Flash's sullenness sparked Hawk's resentment. He drew a deep breath in a bid for patience and reached inside his pack for a copy of the CD the hospital had given him. The small subterfuge he had planned gave him a twinge or two of guilt. If Flash's findings were different than Lang's, would it prove anything?

"You're good with images. I'd like you to have a look at these and see if you can figure out who this guy is. He came out of Cutter's hospital room just before Derrick arrived."

Flash grasped the disk case. "Will do. I'll get right on it and call you later tonight."

"Thanks, I appreciate it." Would he be so eager to get on this if he were the one on the tape? If he was, would he try and cover it up somehow? "Have you seen Lang around?"

"Yeah, he was inside talking with Lieutenant Russell."

"I'll catch you later." Hawk turned.

"What happens if we never figure out what happened to Cutter?" Flash asked.

Hawk looked over his shoulder at him. Feelings of betrayal, guilt, and frustration rose up to color his words with emotion. "We're fucked."

CHAPTER 9

Zoe laughed as she watched Langley Marks, wearing
an apron that read "Fireman in Training", flip burgers at the
grill. His wife, Trish, stood beside him with a small cup of
water to dowse the flames thrown up by grease on the
charcoal.

Zoe drew in a deep breath of the chlorine-laced air and
tried to relax the tension in her shoulders. God, she and
Hawk had both needed to get out of the house and away
from the hospital for a few hours. Since he'd gone to the
shooting range the day before he'd been quiet and distracted.
Who had he talked to? What had they said? Damn the Navy
and damn this closed mouth policy. She was going to get him
to talk to her as soon as they got home.

Zoe's attention wandered back to Trish as she pointed
at something on the grill with her left hand while the fingers
of her right lingered against her husband's nape. Langley
turned to look at her, a smile playing across his wide
expressive mouth. An intimate look passed between the
couple.

"Incoming!"

Hawk's shout had her looking around just as he hit the
surface of the water, his body tucked in a cannonball. A
fountain of water splattered the three children sitting on the

side of the pool. They squealed and immediately leaped in to splash him.

Watching him play with the children, her smile reemerged. He was more than good with them. She didn't want to think about that either.

Trish Marks placed a glass of ice tea on the table in front of her with a slice of lemon floating in it. "You're awfully deep in thought, Zoe."

"I'm just watching the children."

Trish sat down across from her and folded a napkin to act as a coaster. "What's the news on your sister and the new baby?"

"They released my sister and the baby to go home a couple of days ago. The baby is doing well. She weighs seven pounds ten ounces, and according to my brother-in-law, Turner, eats like a pig."

Trish smiled, her freckled face wholesome and pretty. "That's great. And your sister?"

"She's very sore and moving slowly, but she's going to be all right."

Trish nodded. "That's good."

Zoe's gaze traveled to the three tow-headed children in the pool as Hawk passed a beach ball with them. "Hawk's really good with the kids."

"Yes, he is. He even babysat with Anna and Jessica one night when we had to take Tad to the emergency room with a stomach virus."

Zoe grinned and patted the area over her heart as though it were fluttering.

Trish laughed. "He's going to make someone a dandy husband one day."

With an effort, she kept her tone and expression carefully neutral. "Yes, he will."

"How are you and he getting along without Clara?"

She swung her attention back to Trish. "Fine."

"But—"

Zoe bit her lip to keep from smiling. "No buts."

"But—"

She laughed. "I bet you're really good at work."

Trish smiled, her eyes crinkling at the corners. "I've been told I can get the most hardened gang member to talk. That's part of being a good social worker, getting people to reveal what's bothering them." Her expression grew serious as she leaned her elbows on the table. "I was only teasing. I wasn't trying to pump you for information."

"Sure you were." Zoe shot her a look of understanding. "You're obviously close to Hawk and are trying to look out for him. Getting people to talk is part of my job, too. Sometimes it's easier to get other people to talk, than it is to talk about yourself."

"But—"

She was silent for a moment as she studied the other woman's face. "I'm waiting for someone who'll look at me like Langley does you."

Trish's blond brows rose. "The fellow in the pool might be a candidate."

Zoe looked back at the pool and caught Hawk looking at them, his pale gray eyes light against his tanned skin. His hair, slicked to his skull with water, looked as dark as a seal's pelt. He flashed a smile. A beach ball bounced off his head and he keeled over in the water as though the ball had knocked him out.

High-pitched squeals of glee rang out as the children descended on him. For a moment it was questionable whether the youngsters were trying to rescue him or drown him until they started to tug him to the side of the pool.

Trish rose, her attention on Langley at the grill. "Why don't you join Hawk and the kids in the pool while I see if I can avoid a culinary disaster at the grill? I'll loan you a suit. It's hot as Hades out here."

Anxiety shot through Zoe and she shook her head, though sweat rolled down between her breasts and along her sides. "I'm all right. Can I do anything to help?" She started to her feet.

Trish shook her head and waved her back down. "Everything's taken care of since you two brought most of the meal already prepared."

Once again she wondered about the invitation. Had Langley called Hawk during his therapy? Or had Hawk called him?

Every evening since he'd kissed her, she swung back and forth between anxiety and excitement as she anticipated being alone with Hawk. And each evening she'd tried hard to ignore the disappointment and hurt that lingered at his eagerness to spend the evening with friends, and now Langley and Trish.

God, she was pathetic. Lusting, longing, for a guy completely wrong for her. He wore a uniform, was an expert at hand to hand combat, weapons, explosives, and several other things she didn't have a clue about. And he could be shipped out of the country at a moment's notice. And he'd probably run the other direction if he ever once caught a glimpse of her scars or her leg.

Or would he? If he didn't run like every other man, what then? Would she become a clinging, love-starved ninny willing to put up with months of separation and uncertainty for the intermediate bouts of celebratory sex that would follow every time he came home? And how long would it last once he saw some other woman who had two beautiful undamaged legs and no scars?

Fear gripped her by the throat, as powerful as the longing twisting her stomach into knots. She flinched at the familiar pain that pulled at her leg as she hugged it to her chest. She couldn't even outrun the threat of so many possibilities. But she couldn't embrace them either. She closed her eyes trying to suppress the painful ache her thoughts triggered.

She was probably reading more into the kiss than he'd intended. She was agonizing over things her overblown imagination was creating. Otherwise he would want to spend evenings alone with her instead of inviting over friends or beating a quick retreat to the Marks' backyard.

Had he read what she was thinking in the way she had acted? Had she totally misread the entire situation? Was that why he had found a way to avoid being alone with her? God, how embarrassing to be the recipient of someone's unwanted interest and have to live in the same house where you couldn't avoid them.

She opened her eyes as she became aware of the lessening glare of the sun through her eyelids.

Langley stood beside her. "You okay, Zoe?"

She forced a smile to her lips though bile rose in her throat. "Yes, I'm fine."

"Just thought I'd warn you, a couple of the guys and their dates will be joining us. I've slapped a couple more burgers on the grill."

"The more the merrier." With more people around them perhaps she'd have some time to figure out how she was supposed to behave around Hawk, so he'd know she wasn't going to inflict her unwanted attentions on him.

"Yeah, that's what Trish always says."

She rose. "I'll go help her add some more lettuce to the salad and see if she needs me to run to the store for anything." She could use a few minutes alone.

Langley grinned. "Thanks, Zoe."

A few minutes later, gripping a shopping list with attached directions to the store in one hand, and her keys in the other, she opened the front door. Derrick Armstrong stood on the porch a slender, dark haired young woman, at his side.

"Hi." she stood to one side and held the door open for them. "Trish is in the kitchen and Langley and Hawk are in the backyard with the children."

"Thanks." Derrick and the woman stepped inside. "This is Marjorie, my girlfriend. Marjorie, this is Zoe, Cutter's sister, and Hawk's girlfriend."

Zoe opened her mouth to contest the statement.

"Are you leaving?" Derrick asked.

"I'm just running to the store. I'll be right back."

"We'll see you later then." Derrick turned, and with his girlfriend in tow, disappeared down the hallway.

She paused next to the car as a Toyota Camry pulled up behind her.

Bowie stepped out of his vehicle and smiled, flashing his dimples. "Need a ride, sweetheart?"

Was he the one who had hurt her brother? She forced a smile to her lips, though instant feelings of hurt laced with suspicion seemed lodged like a knife beneath her ribs. "Said the big bad wolf."

He pointed at himself with a thumb. "Who, me?"

Zoe smiled at his expression of exaggerated amazement. "I'm just going to the store for Trish. I'll be back in just a moment."

"Hop in and I'll take you. I'll push the buggy."

Was it wise to get into the car with him? Unable to think of a polite way to turn him down, she limped to the passenger side of the car and opened the door.

"Alone at last." Bowie smiled again and taking her hand in his, waggled his eyebrows at her.

She shook her head at him. Being on the receiving end of his flirtatious teasing, Zoe found it difficult to imagine him hurting her. But then, all the men were trained to kill, even Hawk. "Heel, Wolfman. If we don't get back pronto with the groceries, we may find ourselves going hungry." She withdrew her hand to fasten her seatbelt.

"I promise I'll feed you if we do."

"Thank you, Bowie. I can't promise to protect you from Trish though." She waved the grocery list back and forth.

"Can't say I blame you. Trish is tough. I'd put her up against any officer in the division." He started the car and backed out of the driveway.

"So how's Cutter doing?" he asked.

"He's about the same. He turns over in his sleep but he just doesn't open his eyes."

Bowie shook his head his features growing solemn. "He'll pull out of it. He's tough," he said after a moment's silence, but his tone lacked conviction.

He eased the vehicle to a stop at a busy intersection and signaled a right turn. "So when are you going to go out with me?"

She studied his attractive even features and killer dimples. Would she have been attracted to him had Hawk not caught her interest first? Possibly. Could she find out if he was the one who had hurt Brett if they did go out? Probably not. It would be dangerous if she did. If Brett couldn't defend himself against whoever had hurt him, she didn't stand a chance.

I'm not very good at the dating thing, Bowie."

"What's to be good at? We eat, watch a movie, talk. And other things if you feel comfortable with it."

Her face grew hot and she studied the houses they passed with desperate interest.

"There wouldn't be any pressure, Zoe."

She struggled to unglue her tongue from the roof of her mouth. "You're a really nice guy."

"God, don't say that."

"Why not?"

"Because every guy knows when a woman calls you a nice guy she's going to turn you down."

She laughed. "Isn't it better to be turned down as a nice guy than a jerk?"

"It's better not to be turned down at all."

She smiled. "I'm sorry. It isn't you."

"Then who is it?"

Her cheeks burnt.

"LT tried to warn us off, you being Cutter's sister and all. Maybe you better let him in on the fact that you've hooked up with someone."

The words struck her with the force of a medicine ball to the chest. "He warned you off?"

His brows shot up and he turned his head to look at her. "Well, it was worded as a suggestion, but the gist was clear."

"I see." Her earlier hurt slid right into a deep anger flushing her cheeks with heat and making her feel as though her ears might blow off her head. The idea of accepting a date with Bowie flitted through her mind, but it would just complicate things. Pay back seemed so petty, too.

"If you haven't hooked up with anyone—"

Despite her anger, she forced a smile. "You keep your eye on the prize and you never give up."

"Hooyah."

She shook her head. "It wouldn't be fair to you. You deserve to be a first choice, not a substitute."

"Who is this fool?"

A bark of laughter escaped before she suppressed it. "I'd rather not say. I'm not even sure he knows I'm interested, and I'd like an opportunity to work my way up to cluing him in."

His warm, chocolate brown eyes held a smile. "I have to tell you this shy stuff you got going on brings out all my big, bad, male protective urges. If this guy doesn't do right by you, you just let me know."

Could this all be a con? Could he be that good at hiding another personality behind all his charm? "Thanks. I'll keep it in mind."

Making a right hand turn, he pulled into the grocery store parking lot and whipped into an empty slot. He removed the key from the ignition and turned to look at her. "After I've cleaned his clock, you can give me a shot at that date."

The need to come straight out and ask him about his involvement was right on the end of her tongue. Was she looking into the face of a man who could betray one of his teammates?

Studying his open gaze, she just couldn't believe it. She had nothing to go on but instinct, and every instinct she had said Bowie wasn't involved. But could she trust her intuition when Hawk couldn't trust his?

"We'd better get this shopping done and get back."

He nodded and flashed his sexy grin. "Let's do it."

She shook her head at his continued flirtation and exited the car.

"Hooyah." She heard the word from inside the car.

CHAPTER 10

All the way back from the store the questions burned on the tip of Zoe's tongue. She had to ask him. Her heart beat high in her chest and she couldn't seem to get enough air into her lungs.

Bowie parked the car in front of the Marks' house and released his seat belt, but didn't move to get out of the car. "It isn't Derrick, is it?" He rested his hands on the steering wheel, then ran his fingers over the rubber casing that covered it.

Zoe eyed him, confused.

"Derrick's not the one you've hooked up with, is he?"

"No. It isn't Derrick. He's already got a girlfriend. I just met her a few minutes ago." Zoe gestured toward the house.

The tension in his expression relaxed. "I didn't have anything to do with Brett's injury, Zoe." He leaned back in the bucket seat and rested his hands on his thighs. "Maybe you should ask Derrick about Cutter."

Zoe studied Bowie's face. Was he saying he'd witnessed something between Brett and Derrick?

He gripped the steering wheel and turned it. "If anyone knows anything about Cutter, it will be Derrick."

The rumble of a powerful engine growled and Zoe glanced over her shoulder. A bright red Porsche glided into the slot behind Bowie's Toyota.

"Jesus! That's Flash," he breathed.

Zoe swung out of the bucket seat with a practiced grip on the doorframe. Bowie, his cheeks flushed with excitement, popped out of the car and started circling the Porsche like a shark circling prey.

"What did you do man, rob a bank?" Bowie asked as Flash unfolded his lean frame from the car.

"Naw. I got a really sweet deal and I wiped out my savings. Hey, Zoe."

"Hi."

Flash's blond hair reflected in the car's bright cherry red exterior as he braced a hand on the front quarter-panel. He looked tan and fit as though he'd been spending a great deal of time out in the sun. And he aimed a sexy smile at her and said, "Want to go for a ride?"

Zoe laughed and shook her head. "There are three hungry children and several adults waiting by the pool to eat. Maybe later."

Flash seemed a nice guy, they all did, but— How did Hawk stand this constant doubt? She leaned back against the rear of Bowie's car and watched the two men as they studied the sleek lines of the vehicle and discussed every virtue of the engine.

"You got to show the guys," Bowie said as he slammed the hood closed.

"Later." Flash patted the hood. "I've worked up an appetite just driving around town. I'm starving."

"We've just gotten back from the store. You can help carry the groceries in," Bowie said.

Bowie strung the plastic bags of groceries on his arms like oversized Christmas ornaments.

"I can carry some," Zoe said.

"We've got it covered," Flash said as he stretched to retrieve the last bag from high up in the trunk. A light thump had Zoe leaning forward to see if something had fallen out of a bag. A small cylindrical stone lay in the trunk near one of the rear lights. A stone just like the ones Brett had brought home. Zoe reached for it, but Flash scooped it up with a speed worthy of his call sign.

"That's my lucky charm. I'd hate to lose it," he said with a grin. "You can close the trunk and get the door."

Instead of making a comment about the stone, she slammed the trunk and went ahead of the two men.

As they came into the kitchen, Hawk stood at the counter pouring drinks for the three children clustered around him. A pair of cut offs hugged his legs and a t-shirt hung over his shoulder.

"Looks like you arrived just in time, guys," he said.

The door slammed behind the three children as they trooped back outside.

Bowie smiled as he lowered the bags to the floor. "What can I say, my timing's always been perfect. You know that, LT."

Zoe started unloading the bags. Flash placed his on the bar.

"I bought a car, Hawk. A really sweet ride. You'll have to check it out after we eat," Flash said.

While the two men talked about the vehicle, Bowie came to stand next to Zoe and lifted one of the bags on the counter. He took out a basket of fresh tomatoes.

"Thanks for making the grocery run with me, Bowie."

"Any time, Zo." He rested a hand against her waist and brushed a kiss on her cheek.

Startled by the gesture she looked up at him.

His brown gaze looked down into hers. "Remember what I said in the car." He ran the back of his fingers against her cheek in a brief caress. "You need any help here?"

Struck speechless, she shook her head.

As he and Flash sauntered out onto the deck, her numbed brain kicked into overdrive. Which bit of advice had Bowie meant? About talking to Derrick?

Or was it that she should be straight forward with Hawk about her interest in him? Was she really ready to leave herself open to hurt again by doing so? Should she keep Bowie in mind if things didn't work out between them as he'd suggested?

"What was that all about?" Hawk moved to stand next to her.

Surprised he had noticed the exchange, she glanced up at him. "Nothing. Did you really warn all of the men to stay away from me?"

His expression grew guarded. "Not exactly."

She folded her arms and leaned back against the counter. "Then why don't you explain to me exactly what you did say."

His features tightened. "I told them I didn't think Cutter would appreciate one of his fellow teammates trying to nail his sister. And I told them to keep in mind, if they were thinking about asking you out, that you weren't the type for a one night stand."

She shook her head, unable to decide whether to be angry at his interference or touched by his protectiveness. Was he keeping his distance for the same reason, or because he just wasn't interested?

"My brother doesn't live my life for me, Hawk. I'll sleep with whomever I want, when I want." She pointed a finger at him. "And Brett's approval or disapproval won't have a damn thing to do with it when it happens."

He caught the waving finger, and his lips quirked with amusement. "Understood." His gray eyes focused on her face and his smile died.

Zoe's stomach quivered at the sudden intensity of his expression. "I'm not looking for your approval either," she said. Her voice sounded weak and breathless.

"All right."

His acquiescence fired her temper and hurt her feelings. She tugged at her finger, breaking his grip. He stepped close and surprised, she tilted her head back to look up at him.

Placing an arm on either side, he hemmed her in against the counter, his body a breath away from hers. Her pulse leaped and she pressed a hand against his chest. The heat of his skin seeped into her palm like liquid fire.

Hawk's gray eyes narrowed. "I'm stuck between a rock and a hard place here. I promised your mom I'd look out for you." His throat worked as he swallowed and his voice grew husky. "I don't think fantasizing about taking her daughter to bed was exactly what she had in mind."

The knot of tension in the pit of her stomach dissolved as excitement raced through her to settle, tingling and hot, between her legs. Was it possible to have an orgasm just thinking about making love? If he plastered that long, lean, masculine body up against hers, she might just achieve her very first one without his ever having to touch her.

"I'm trying to take things slow here, Zoe."

She bit back a groan. If he went any slower, she might just dwell on all the reasons she shouldn't get involved with him, and chicken out all together. Her eyes fastened on the hard, fast beating pulse just beneath the skin of his throat.

She rose on tiptoe and pressed an open mouthed kiss there. His skin tasted of chlorine and heat.

He caught his breath, and his hand splayed against the small of her back and pulled her against him. The firm ridge of his arousal pushed against her stomach. When she leaned back to look up at him, he kissed her, the hungry pressure of his lips hot and insistent.

The tempting touch of his tongue against hers intensified the empty ache inside her. Zoe slid one arm around his neck and strained upward to fit herself against his tall frame more fully. She ran the other hand up his back, caressing his smooth, muscled flesh.

He cupped her buttocks guiding her closer, urging her legs apart as he thrust one long thigh between hers. Though she ached with need, she fought the compulsion to rub against the steady pressure of his leg. Hawk had no such reservation. He rocked against her, and Zoe groaned as the movement titillated the over-sensitized area between her thighs driving her closer to the edge.

"Daddy does that to Mommy, sometimes." The sound of a child's voice had them both freezing.

Hawk broke the kiss, his breathing ragged, his cheeks flushed. He looked toward the door leading out onto the deck. "I bet." He shifted putting some space between his lower body and hers.

Zoe stifled a sound somewhere between a laugh and a groan. At least the counter had blocked from view what else had been going on. She turned to look over her shoulder at seven-year-old Tad, the oldest of the Marks children. His red-blond hair, still wet from the pool, stood on end, but there was nothing in his expression that warranted concern.

"Mommy said the burgers were ready when you were."

Ready? Her face and ears burned with embarrassment.

Hawk's gaze dropped to hers, amusement in his expression. "Tell your mom, we'll be right there, Tad."

The door shut behind the boy.

Feeling exposed and vulnerable, Zoe turned her back to Hawk. "I was supposed to be slicing tomatoes and onions for the burgers." He pressed against her from behind, and her legs went rubbery. The soft warmth of his lips against the back of her neck sent delightful shivers down her spine.

"I'll slice the tomatoes, while you do the onions." He gathered three tomatoes in one hand and moved to the sink.

His touch lingered on her skin and she had to concentrate on slowing her breathing. She wrinkled her nose at him. "Let me guess, aside from the smell, you just don't want me to see you cry."

"Sweetheart, I almost did when Tad opened that door."

****

With two plates of food, one for him and the other for Zoe, Hawk settled in one of the deck chairs next to Marjorie Allen, Derrick Armstrong's girlfriend. Derrick leaned forward to look around the woman at Hawk. "How's the knee, LT?"

"Healing. The doc's given me permission to do a little lifting with it. I thought I'd start tomorrow."

Derrick nodded. "If you need someone to spot you, I'm available in the mornings. I usually start my routine around five."

Hawk nodded, his gaze wandering to Zoe as she dried off one of the children at the pool. Her leg might benefit from lifting weights, too, but not if Derrick were around to watch her. "I appreciate the offer Strong Man, but I'll have to take it easy at first. Sometimes having a partner tempts you into competing. I don't want to overdo it, and then have to start healing all over again."

Derrick waved a hand. "Understood."

Zoe limped over to join them, and Hawk rose to move a lawn chair next to his. He watched the quick rise of color in her cheeks as she sat down. God, all that shy, suppressed sexuality was driving him crazy. Especially when every time he looked at her, her eyes were saying everything she was thinking. And everything she was thinking seemed pretty hot. Had Tad not interrupted them, how much further would she have allowed him to go?

Bowie pulled a chair up next to Zoe and sat down.

What had he meant by the cryptic remark he had made to Zoe in the kitchen? He had obviously been trying to get her to go out with him.

Again.

It had taken all Hawk's control to keep from ripping into him. Until he drew a firm line in the sand, the other guys in the team would continue to put the move on her.

Hawk ran a hand down Zoe's back, and she looked up at him. He was suddenly aware of how often he had avoided touching her. That was going to stop right now. He tucked a short wisp of hair that curled against her cheek behind her ear. "I forgot to get us some drinks. I'll be right back."

When he returned Bowie was leaning close to Zoe, saying something. Hawk placed the drinks on the table and draped a casual arm over her shoulders as he leaned forward to listen to their conversation.

"How's Cutter doing?" Strongman asked.

Damn the man had no sense of timing at all. He'd hoped Zoe could have one afternoon away from the stress of her brother's condition. Hawk's gaze narrowed on him, but Derrick seemed oblivious to the look.

"He's about the same."

Derrick nodded. "I was thinking about the time we did our first blast. He was the best at skydiving. He had nerves of steel. I swear he could jump out of a plane a foot off the deck and still have time to pull the rip-cord and float to the ground."

"He's going to come back to it," Zoe said, her features stiff, her gaze locked on Derrick.

Derrick's cheeks grew red. His eyes took on a flat look as stony as his features. "Yeah, he is."

Tension blanketed the atmosphere at the table like smoke. Bowie jumped into the lull and began describing his first parachute jump.

"Anyway, my knees are knocking and I've got bats in my belly, and I get to the door of the plane. LT's standing there ready to follow us out once the last man jumps. I'm thinking of everything that can go wrong and going over every moment of my training, hoping I can remember it all if something does. I look out the door, and all I can see is open space, and it looks beautiful. The air is clear and the ground looks like a patchwork quilt. LT motions for me to go, and before I can think of any reason not to, I yell Geronimo and jump."

Flash leaned forward to speak down the table. "I thought I was at a remake of Butch Cassidy and the Sundance Kid. You know the scene where they jump off the cliff. I heard you yelling all the way down, or at least until you deployed your chute. And it didn't sound anything like Geronimo to me."

Laughter broke out around the table. Bowie narrowed his eyes at the man, though he laughed good-naturedly at his ribbing. "Those were whoops of excitement, you were hearing, Flash. Besides, I'm surprised you could hear anything above your own whimpering. You weren't exactly icy."

A deep flush darkened Flash's tanned complexion, and for a moment, his features tightened, then he smiled. "Damn straight. Jumping out of a plane three thousand feet in the air still isn't one of my favorite things to do. Give me a tank of air and drop my ass in the ocean, and I'm ready."

"Hooyah." The word traveled around the table.

Bowie turned back to Zoe. "On the way down, it was great. Like nothing I've ever experienced before. You could see for miles and there was just this high, excitement high, as you deployed your chute and glided down."

"I think I'd like to try it one day." Zoe took a bite of potato salad.

Surprised by the conviction in her tone, Hawk studied her expression.

Bowie's gaze moved from Hawk's hand resting on her shoulder to his face. "LT would be the one to take you up. He's probably got more jumps under his belt than the rest of us put together."

Zoe's attention swung to him.

His insides clenched at the idea of her jumping out of a plane. He had experienced some harrowing moments in the past, not that he'd ever share them with her. "I jump out of planes because it's part of my job, Zoe. I've never thought of doing it for pleasure."

"It's really expensive unless you're part of a sky diving group," Marjorie said. "One of the girls I work with is a member of a club. She and her boyfriend do it on the weekends. They spend every dime they can get their hands on to pay for it. Hang gliding might be an option though. You can rent the gliders while you train, and find out if you like it well enough to buy your own."

"Or what about parasailing?" Trish said. "You can do that any time and it's only about eighty dollars."

Hawk jumped at the idea. "What do you say, Zoe? We could do that this weekend."

Her expression grew shuttered, and she bit her bottom lip.

The muscles at the back of his neck tightened. He could almost read what was going through her head. She'd have to wear a swimsuit, and he'd be able to see her leg. How would they ever make love if she was afraid of his reaction to the injury? He didn't give a damn what it looked like. Her leg only made up a small part of who she was. *Come on, trust me, Zoe.* He wanted to say the words out loud.

"I'd love to do it."

The wistfulness in her tone gave him hope. "You haven't taken in any of the sights or gone to the beach. We can make a day of it."

"I can't leave Brett all day."

"Half a day, then."

She smiled.

Yes! He had her now.

"All right. Half a day."

She'd have five whole days to think about it. Five days to change her mind. Five days to worry about her leg and his reaction to it. Damn! He had to get Zoe out of her pants.

****

From her perch atop the picnic table on the deck, Zoe observed Derrick Armstrong as, resting a hand against Marjorie's waist; he guided her to his car. For most of the evening following her comment at dinner, he'd remained sullen and silent. She should have left it alone and not said anything. But the men were giving up on Brett. Derrick had already done so. She could tell by the way he always referred to him in the past tense.

Bowie, Flash, and Doc were better about it, but the way their eyes met whenever Brett's name came up in conversation—They didn't believe he'd come out of the coma.

Did Hawk feel the same?

She'd never ask him. She couldn't. She was holding onto her own positive outlook by her fingernails. She couldn't allow anyone's negativity to tear chunks out of her hope.

She turned her gaze back to the friendly backyard volleyball game. Flash served the volleyball and Langley went up for a return as it spun toward him.

Hawk's hand brushing downward over her back to her waist snapped her attention to him. His muscular thigh pressed along hers making her think about how he had thrust it between her legs and encouraged her to rock against it.

He'd touched her more during dinner than he had the entire time she'd been staying at his house. With every stroke of his palm he primed her hunger for more and her anxiety.

"Ready to go home?" Hawk asked.

Twenty minutes later, Zoe's nerves kicked in with a vengeance as they reached the midway point to Hawk's house. She cast surreptitious glances at him from beneath her lashes and tried to calm her uncontrollable heartbeat and unsteady breathing. What had she said to him about making love? Oh yeah—she'd do it when she wanted to. But he would too. She wanted it—wanted it so-o-o-o bad, but she was scared too. If he saw her leg, her scars—

Hawk's hand closed around hers. "Relax, Zoe."

She swallowed though her mouth was dust dry. She clung to his hand with both of hers and wished the bucket seats would allow her to slide closer.

"We don't have to rush anything," Hawk said.

He had been so patient, had taken things so slowly thus far— "It isn't that," she said, her tone weak.

"What is it then?"

"Have you ever wanted something you—" her voice dwindled away. If she said she was scared to death he'd misunderstand.

"That last step is hard. I know. I wanted to be a SEAL before I signed the scholarship papers for college. But once I graduated, knowing what a commitment it was—it was hard to take that last step." He glanced at her. "I'm ready when you decide you are. But we don't have to be in a rush. Part of the excitement of being a couple is learning about each other."

Her throat tightened. Why had she ever been afraid? "I wanted to be a dancer before the accident. I was taking tap and ballet and had fallen in love with it. I had movies of Baryshnikov, Natalia Makarova, and several others. Daddy had put up a bar and mirror for me in the garage." She smiled at the bittersweet memory. He had danced with her. He'd be Fred Astaire and she'd be Ginger Rodgers. At the time, she hadn't known who they were, but the fact that he had tried to share a little of her dream—

Hawk's fingers tightened around hers and she looked up. His features had gone completely still with control.

"It's all right. It was just a little girl's dream. The chances that I'd have been good enough to dance with a ballet troop were slim. I love my job. I love seeing someone walk when they don't believed they ever will. I help people rebuild a part of the life they've lost. I think that's more important than being on stage."

"Hooyah!"

That one word said it all.

Her nerves had receded completely when they pulled into the driveway at the house. Hawk held her hand as they went up the front steps. He released it to unlock the front door. He held it open and motioned for her to enter first. Just over the threshold her shoe snagged something and she stumbled. A loud whomp filled the enclosed space with a force that pounded her eardrums. At the same time, a flash of intense light seared her retina'. Startled, she cried out. Hawk shoved her down and his large body covered hers driving the air from her lungs. The acrid smell of smoke filled the first breath she drew.

"Stay down," he ordered, his tone harsh with command. He jumped up, his movements cautious and quick, and disappeared down the dark hall.

Zoe raised her head to look between the couch and chair and scan the room. White spots filled her vision but cleared quickly. A small blaze flickered in the center of the area rug in the living room. With every second that passed it grew brighter. She staggered to her feet and looked about for something with which to smother the flames. She jerked free one of the window curtains, threw it over the fire, and stomped on it. Puffs of smoke rose from beneath the fabric. The heat of the blaze penetrated her thin shoes.

Hawk appeared from the back of the house, a gun in one hand a fire extinguisher in the other. "The house is clear." He tucked the gun in the back waistband of his shorts, flipped the curtain aside, and sprayed it with the foam. His expression appeared calm but the quick way his gaze scanned the room, watchful and keen, gave her an idea of how he might behave in battle.

"What was this?" she asked.

"A stun grenade. We call them flash bangs. This one's been modified otherwise all my windows would have been blown out." He pushed aside the scorched fabric of the curtain baring a two foot wide burn in the center of the rug that went all the way to the hard wood floor beneath. He bent to run his hand under a thin wire and followed it to the door. "This is a trip wire. It was set up to go off as soon as someone hit it."

Zoe sucked in a harsh breath. "Why would anyone do this?"

He remained silent a moment. He pointed to a watercolor seascape over the couch. The black words printed on the glass stood out against the muted background like slashes. It read 'leave it alone'. The words sent prickles of shock and fear along her skin. She began to tremble.

The sound of police sirens screamed from down the street. Hawk removed the gun from his waistband and, pulling open a drawer of the table by the door, placed it inside. He reached up and swung the picture down to lay it behind a chair.

"We have to convince the San Diego police this was a prank, Zoe. There are too many things I can't tell them. I think they'll want to call in NCIS if they discover this involved real explosives."

"Then let them. Maybe we'll finally discover what's going on." The idea brought a wave of relief so strong it eased some of her trembling.

"And what if it's something Brett's gotten tangled up in?"

Zoe studied his expression for a long moment. Was he really willing to overlook having his house set on fire? What if whoever it was escalated to blowing the place up? Was his loyalty to his Naval *family* so strong? God, did she even need to ask that? "Why are you protecting them?"

"Because we need to keep this in the family, and deal with it in house. For all we know, I'm protecting your brother, too."

She caught her breath as anger flashed through her. Brett wouldn't be involved in anything illegal. She was certain of it. "What do you think he could have seen or done to cause this?"

"I don't know. But I intend to find out."

He was blocking her out again. First with his refusal to discuss his meeting at the shooting range, and now with this. Resentment burned through her patience. "We, Hawk. We, not I. If my brother's involved, so am I."

A police cruiser screeched to a halt outside. Out of the corner of Zoe's eye, she caught the flash of the lights atop the vehicle. She ignored it. "If I'm going to lie to protect them, you're letting me in. Or I'm going to tell the police everything and let the fur fly."

His features tightened and his gray eyes went flat with anger. "I don't respond well to threats."

"And I don't respond well to being shut out when it affects someone I love." Was she talking about Brett or him? God, she was wading through emotional quicksand and was sinking fast.

Footsteps sounded on the porch and a harsh rap came at the door. "All right," Hawk said, his tone grudging, sharp. "We'll talk later."

"Good. And by the way, Bowie says we need to talk to Derrick."

As he worked that out, she jerked open the door and prepared to lie.

CHAPTER 11

Hawk stretched on the bed and stifled a yawn. He glanced at the clock. It read O eight hundred. Water running somewhere in the house sounded like distant rain. Obviously, Zoe was already up.

His jaw tightened as the scene the night before played through his head. It had taken an hour to convince the two patrolmen that it had been a prank and not something more lethal. The experience had left him with an itchy feeling of guilt he hadn't done a damn thing to earn. The raw edgy mood of the night before came roaring back with a vengeance. Zoe'd had the same look the night before.

God damn it. Why did she have to be so insistent on knowing everything? She didn't understand that he owed his loyalty to his men. And did she *want* to understand the military point of view as to information about those men? No. Stubborn—

He drew a deep breath. The smell of smoke lingering throughout the house sent a spike of anger racing through him again. When he found out who was responsible for this, he was going to rip his head off and stuff it down his fucking throat. That it was one of his own men seemed impossible. A growl, part frustration, part anger tore loose.

He shifted his knee back onto the pillow and grimaced. The joint continued to be sore, despite his careful adherence to the therapist's orders. His experience with this minor injury was nothing compared to Zoe's long-term struggle. God, she was tough.

Last night, her limp had grown more pronounced. She needed to wear her brace more. She'd do well with a cane, but she'd never agree to use one. Would she still be as mobile in five years? Ten? Would she one day be in a wheel chair? Probably. His stomach clenched and he veered away from thinking about it.

As he listened to the shower running, an urge raced through him to go down the hall and join her. That would rip aside this wall of anger and distrust that had suddenly thrust up between them. He would soap his hands and slowly run them over every inch of her skin. And end the anxious dance they were doing. She would offer him the comfort—

God, what was he thinking? It would probably send her into a self-conscious panic, before he ever got that far. With a sigh, he ran his fingers through his close-cropped hair.

She had to lower the barriers when she was ready. If he pressured her too much, she might push him away. But damn, it was hard to wait. He'd never had to work this hard to earn a woman's trust.

Did the challenge she presented have anything to do with the strength of his attraction, or was it just, Zoe? If they did hook up, would his feelings change? Would his desire plane out like it usually did?

The shower stopped. She'd go back to Kentucky eventually. The thought, like a warning, nipped at his half-aroused state with the coldness of reason. Zoe was attached to her family, really attached. The chances she'd stay out here ran from, not very likely to no F-ing way.

She had a life in Kentucky, a profession she was licensed to practice there. So why was he getting involved with her? There were other women with a hell-of-a-lot less baggage, who would stick around. Why was he putting so much effort into wooing her?

Because he'd been hot for her since the first time he'd seen her.

But then what?

Was a short-term affair what she was looking for? A little experience under her belt? A little experience—Zoe was a virgin, he'd bet his SEAL insignia on it. And he'd be her first. The term virgin territory took on a whole new meaning as he allowed the implications to sink in.

"Jesus." He sat up, his heart pounding as though he'd done a five-K run full out. Zoe wouldn't give herself lightly. He was already finding that out—first hand. He was suddenly hot and hard as a cruise missile. He groaned aloud at how his own thoughts ran to cheesy puns that did nothing to relieve the pressure. But she'd still leave and he'd have to deal with it, if he got in too deep.

A loud thump sounded from somewhere down the hall and the water glass on his nightstand shook. He shoved off the bed to his feet, her name on his lips.

"Zoe?" he yelled louder, two long strides taking him out into the hall.

Her silence had him swearing as he broke into a trot, his knee protested. Her room was empty, and he passed on to the bathroom door. Resting his hands on the door facing, he called through it, "You okay, Zoe?"

"I'm okay. I just have a Charlie horse." Her tone sounded strained. "Just give me a minute."

A soft groan pumped his already galloping heartbeat up a notch. "I'm coming in," he warned as he turned the knob. She was sitting in the floor clothed in lightweight pants. He caught a glimpse of lush, well-shaped breasts before she grabbed the towel from around her hair and covered herself.

Ignoring the immediate punch to his arousal, he knelt on the ceramic tile at her feet

Her features were set in a pained grimace as she kneaded the muscle. "God, I hate these things."

He brushed aside her fingers and began to rub and massage the knotted muscle vigorously. At first hard as a baseball, it suddenly began to relax and give beneath his fingers.

Zoe bit her bottom lip and clenched her eyes shut. When her lids finally lifted and she looked at him, he relaxed a little. "Better?"

She nodded. "Yes. Much." She focused on his face, her expression serious. "This is kind of a thing with me." Her tone sounded weary.

"You mean after being on your feet a lot?" He shifted the movements of his fingers from rough to soothing and rubbed the pant leg up to her knee. Pinkish-white scars crisscrossed her calf like cracks in a hardboiled egg. Of course, both legs would have been injured in the accident. How much worse was the other one? He knew part of the calf muscle was missing.

"Yes." Her gaze traveled from the leg he was caressing to his face. And for a moment, her blue eyes probed his expression.

"I get them, too, after too much exertion." When she remained silent he asked, "Need a ride to your room or do you want to try and get up?"

She bit her lip. "I can get up on my own."

Knowing she was now out of pain, he allowed his eyes to skim over the curve of her breasts visible above the towel. She looked so delicate. He ran his fingertips along her shoulder, his thumb tracing the fragile length of her collarbone. His hand looked dark against her fair skin. Feelings of protectiveness, tenderness, and desire crashed together inside him, making his voice husky. "I'll help you up, just in case another one hits." Rising from his kneeling position, he offered her a hand.

Once on her feet, Zoe rested a hand against his chest and the heat of her touch penetrated his t-shirt as though it weren't there. When she tucked herself against him, he slipped an arm around her waist while he ran his hand down her back to the top of the low-slung pants. Her hair, still damp, smelled like vanilla. He curved a hand along her hip turning her into him, letting her feel his reaction to her. His heart took up the rapid tattoo of machine gun fire when she drew a deep breath and released it, her breasts pushing against his ribs.

"Sometimes, the way you look at me—" she said, her voice a husky whisper.

He knew what she meant. He'd caught a few of her unguarded looks that had grabbed him right by the libido, and left him breathless and aching.

"I'd like to do more than just look." He bent his head, and kissed her shoulder, his lips parted so he could taste the heat of her skin. She shivered in response and her hand curved around his neck, her fingers messaging his nape.

"Come to bed with me, Zoe. We'll neck, and touch each other, and make each other feel good."

She drew another breath and pressed closer to him. "God, I want to."

Her Kentucky accent, thickened with emotion, had him smiling.

"But?"

"It's daylight."

"So?"

"Hawk—You just saw some of my scars."

"Yeah, so?"

"The rest are worse. I had to have skin grafts to cover some of the really bad injuries. They had to take skin from other parts of my body to do it." She looked away. "I look like Frankenstein from the waist down."

"A few scars aren't going to make a difference to me, Zoe."

"I've heard that before. And it did."

Following some of his earlier thoughts, the idea of her being with some other guy hit him with the kick of a grenade launcher. He grasped her arm. "Who was this fool?"

Her eyes widened in shock.

He forced himself to release her and take a step back. "Sorry—I just—" Just went warrior at the thought of her giving herself to some other guy. Man he was getting in deeper and deeper. He needed to pull back.

Hadn't Clara said something about her suddenly growing more self-conscious about her leg in college? A surge of anger had heat rising in his face. *That damn creep.* "He was a fool, Zoe. A damn fool."

Her smile started out a small twitch of her lips and spread into a full-fledged grin. "Thanks." She rose on tiptoe to brush her lips against his cheek. "He was."

She turned her bare back to him, and reaching for the t-shirt draped over the towel bar, shimmied into it.

Hawk nearly groaned aloud.

When she faced him, her expression had grown serious. "We need to talk about last night." She hung the damp towel over the edge of the tub and took up her brush.

Hawk drew a deep breath. "Yeah we do."

She ran the wide spaced bristles through the heavy mass of hair she drew over one shoulder.

"I'm sorry you had to be grilled by the police."

Zoe shook her head. "I'm more concerned that someone we know actually set off an explosive device in your house. It just started a fire this time. They could blow the whole thing up next time."

"There isn't going to be a next time, Zoe."

"You don't know that." She laid the brush on the edge of the sink and drew a deep breath. "I've been up half the night thinking about this. You have to turn this thing over to NCIS."

"I can't do that before reporting what's happened to my CO."

She remained silent, but her jaw tightened. "Where do you think Flash got the money for the car?"

"I don't know." He ran his fingers over his hair. "Some of the guys work security jobs in their spare time. I know Flash has done that in the past for extra money."

"I know about military pay. And with the cost of living out here—" Zoe shook her head. "To buy a sixty thousand dollar car—it just takes my breath away to think about it."

"When you're young and single and the only one you have to support is you, you can afford to do something extravagant—I guess."

"You're young and single and I don't see you doing stuff like that. You've poured every dime into this house, I'm sure."

"My mom left me the house and she had insurance that paid the mortgage off when she died. So, I guess I'm more financially secure than most of the team. Hell, most of the platoon."

"So why haven't you been snapped up by some woman hungry for security and your killer body?"

Her casual tone sounded forced as though she was uncomfortable asking the question.

"It's the hazards of the job, Zoe. It takes a special woman to stick around for the long haul once they get a taste of what it's like to be alone for twelve or fourteen months out of a two-year span. And there's the fact that I wouldn't be there for someone if they got sick while I was out of the country, or had an emergency. I can't offer the emotional security a guy with a nine-to-five job can."

"Maybe you just haven't met the right kind of woman then. I don't expect my family to be there for me constantly. I take care of myself. But I know I could depend on them if something came up." she said, her voice soft, her features averted.

Was she saying she was the *right* kind of woman? Could she live with the separations, the worry that he might not come back every time he went wheels up? The secrecy. She wasn't doing so well with his refusal to call NCIS. How was she going to do when he refused to tell her anything about their deployments? The speculation had his emotional radar jangling with alarm.

"What will your commander do about what happened last night?"

Probably ride his back like a forty-pound pack. "I don't know."

A phone rang and Hawk turned and left the bathroom. Zoe followed.

"I have to go out," he said as he laid the receiver in its cradle.

"Yes." Her brows rose in question, her expression expectant.

"I can't tell you where I'm going," he said. "You can take the car and go on to the hospital and I'll meet you there later."

Her eyes searched his face then dropped away. The disappointment in her expression snagged his conscience and made him uncomfortable.

By way of an apology, he felt compelled to say, "I'll be at the hospital as soon as I can."

She gave a one-shouldered shrug. "I can handle whatever comes up at the hospital by myself. Take your time."

For the first time, he understood what the married members of the team went through. She viewed his not sharing as a lack of trust. He withheld information, not because he didn't trust her, but because if she didn't know about what he and Lang were up to, she couldn't be compelled to testify against them.

Damn this relationship stuff was hard.

****

"If your brother doesn't wake up within the next two weeks, we may have to think about transferring him to the long-term care facility for extra services, Ms. Weaver."

Dr. Connelly's words hit Zoe with the force of a wrecking ball. For a moment, her legs threatened to give way. She gripped the end of the bed in an attempt to retain her balance.

"You're giving up on him," her tone sounded hollow.

"No. But we do need the bed on this floor for more critical patients. Had there been a bed available we would have already transferred him to the brain injury care facility, where he could get more intensive services than we can provide here."

Anger pushed through the shock she attempted to absorb. "Those facilities are just warehouses, Dr. Connelly, and you know it."

The doctor's eyes focused on her face. "Not here, Zoe. We have a state of the art facility. They'll provide him with more of the physical therapy you've been doing with him yourself, as well as other services." He paused, then looked down at Brett's chart. "There are some medications I want to try on your brother to stimulate him, and see if we can wake him up. Some do have a few side effects, but for the most part the benefits would out-weigh the risks."

She studied the doctor's face searching for any kind of hope to hang onto, but his expression remained neutral. "When will you try them?"

"I'll get the paperwork started as soon as rounds end." He paused. "This is not like a TV movie. We'll begin with one medication, and may have to try several before one works."

"All right." As the sudden rush of adrenaline eased off, she began to tremble. She folded her arms against her waist to hide her reaction.

Connelly laid a comforting hand on her shoulder. "I have to warn you about all the possibilities, Zoe. To drop it on you later would be like dropping a bomb on you. You've thought about what it would be like—should things not progress as we'd like."

Despair threatened to smother her hope. "Brett is going to wake up." When the words came out flat and without her normal positive exuberance, she cleared her throat and said it again with more conviction. "Brett is going to wake up."

Connelly nodded his gray head briefly. "A nurse will be in to administer the first round of medication within the hour."

As he and the nurse left, a wave of dizziness tackled Zoe and she had to brace her hands on her knees. Brett had to wake up. This had to work. She wouldn't be able to bear it otherwise.

****

"I appreciate your giving me a ride to the base, Greenback," Hawk said as they stopped at a red light in traffic.

"No problem, LT. I've been meaning to come by and hang out but I've been doing some bonding with my daughter. I missed her birth, and I'm trying to catch up."

"How's that going?" Hawk asked as he studied the man. Oliver Shaker, "Greenback", maintained a solid reputation for being a squared away soldier. Though slighter built than most SEALS at five foot eight inches tall and a hundred and forty-five pounds, Hawk had seen the man lift an unconscious guy nearly half again his weight. With his dark hair and eyes, there had to be some Italian ancestry in his background and his Godfatherish New Jersey accent fit that image.

Greenback smiled. "Shelby's a doll. She's six months old and every time she sees me she smiles and laughs."

How was it a hardened warrior could look so sappy? An answering smile curved Hawk's lips.

Greenback ducked his head. "I know—I know." He waved a hand dismissively.

"It's great, man. Katie Beth, Zoe's niece, took up with me while she was here. She's a real sweetheart. I can see how you could learn to love one of your own real quick."

"I was going to re-up when my enlistment was over, but I'm giving serious thought to going back to school and finishing my degree so I can move on to something else. I mean, if something happened to me, Shelby would never know me."

Hawk nodded. It happened sometimes. A guy got married, his wife had a baby, and suddenly he started worrying about the people he'd leave behind if something happened to him, and he lost his edge. Dwelling too much on home and family could be a distraction. One that could get him killed.

"You think that's a mistake?" he asked.

Hawk shook his head. "No. I think you have to do what's right for you and your family. It's an easier decision when you have no ties and less—" he bit back the word baggage, "familial responsibilities." And what did that slip say about him? He frowned.

He dragged his attention back to Greenback. "I've asked all the guys to write down anything unusual they noticed about Cutter before we went on the mission. Can you think of anything that happened or was said that struck you as out of the ordinary?"

Greenback remained silent for several minutes. "I mind my own business, Hawk. And I don't repeat stuff that I hear."

He knew something. Hawk's heart drummed in his ears for a moment as his blood pressure shot up. He remained silent giving him time.

"Brett saved my bacon twice during the last few missions. I owe him." Greenback shifted behind the wheel as though uncomfortable. "I know as a breed, we're looked at as professionals, sure, but kind of wild-ass cowboys, too. You know Brett's pretty squared away. I mean he likes to have fun, just like the rest of us, and he's not above a prank or two, but he keeps his personal and professional life clean."

Greenback took his eyes off the road to glance at Hawk. "Whatever's going on, I don't see Brett being involved. I think he's just collateral damage."

Hawk nodded. "That said—"

"Derrick has had a couple of assault charges dropped in the last year. And Flash gambles quite a bit. I heard Brett trying to offer them both advice at different times just before the mission. Well, actually he was on Flash's ass hot and heavy about something."

"You don't know what it was about?"

Greenback shook his head. "They shut down when I got close, but the tension was pretty thick."

Hawk narrowed his eyes against the sudden glare as they turned into the sun. He reached into his pocket for his sunglasses and shoved them on.

"I know there's something going down—"

Hawk drew a deep breath. "I don't think you'll have to worry about it. There's no way you could have taken out two tangos, snuck into the house, knocked Cutter unconscious, gotten out, and gotten back to your position in time. We're talking minutes here. It had to be someone there."

"Fuck—"

He couldn't agree more. But the information didn't clear any of them, just gave him more to look at. "I appreciate you hanging yourself out there."

Greenback shrugged. "Brett deserves better than he got."

"Yeah, he does."

****

Time seemed to pass at a turtle's pace. With every glance at the clock, anxiety pulled at Zoe's muscles like weights, tightening her shoulders and neck. As her anxiety rose, so did her anger. Damn the man responsible for Brett's injuries. She wished every vile thing she could think of on him while stifling the urge to scream.

She paced the floor more out of a need to burn off some of her emotion than an inherent restlessness.

Hawk arrived bringing with him the scent of the ocean. Just seeing him brought every defense she had crashing down. Her fear for her brother spurred her toward him, and she pressed close.

"What is it?" he asked, his arms tight around her. It was a moment before she could trust her composure and explain what Dr. Connelly was going to try.

His features grew taut and his black brows fisted. "How dangerous is this?"

"Connelly said he believed the benefits outweighed the risks. There could be a few side effects, but that's all. Brett doesn't have much to lose at this point, Hawk."

His jaw tightened. "I suppose not."

She started to tell him the rest, but held back. If she repeated Dr. Connelly's words, it would give them credence. If she gave them credence, she'd begin to accept them. She wasn't ready to do that yet, not as long as there were other things they could try. Not while there was still hope Brett would wake up.

She moved to her brother's side. They had removed the bandages from his head and pale bristle-like fuzz was beginning to cover his scalp. The liquid nutrition, fed into a tube through his nose and down the back of his throat, was keeping him from losing weight, but his muscle tone was growing less pronounced. They had begun to turn him more often to make certain he didn't develop bedsores. She wanted to grab him and shake him. Her throat ached with her desire to scream at him to wake up.

Hawk's hands rested on her shoulders from behind offering comfort. The gesture brought her emotions close to the surface, and her eyes stung with tears. She wouldn't give into them. To give into them was like giving up.

"It's going to be all right, Zo."

She nodded. She folded her arms and leaned back against him, drawing strength from his closeness.

He slipped an arm around her waist. When Angela came in, he continued to hold Zoe. The nurse piggybacked a new IV onto the one Brett already had in his arm, and hung the bag of medication on the IV pole.

Hope, excitement, and fear crashed together inside Zoe making it difficult for her to breathe. She squeezed Hawk's arm. "How quickly will it work, if it's going to?" she asked, her voice sounding husky as it worked around the knot of emotion in her throat.

The nurse looked up as she adjusted the tubing. "It could be minutes, or a few hours, or even days. It just depends on him."

Zoe nodded, her eyes going to Brett's face.

Angela gave her arm an encouraging pat as she brushed by. "Call me if there's any change."

Zoe gave her a brief nod.

"If Cutter opens his eyes and sees me holding you like this, he's likely to climb out of bed and kick my butt," Hawk said as the door closed behind Angela.

It took real work, but she managed a smile as she looked over her shoulder at him. "Don't take this wrong, but I hope he tries."

He gave her a gentle squeeze and released her. "Try and relax, Zoe. Like Angela said, it may take a while."

She sat down beside Brett's bed and picked up a book she had been attempting to read but didn't open it.

Hawk settled in the other chair and turned the TV onto a sports channel, but he looked at her instead of the screen.

Brett took a deep breath and turned on his side. The book landed with a dull thud as Zoe leaped to her feet.

CHAPTER 12

Shit—shit—shit. The word kept going through Hawk's head as he drove through the busy streets toward home. He flexed his shoulders to try and ease some of the tension settling right between his shoulder blades. Watching Brett's every movement had kept them both on red-alert. Having to leave the hospital, with him still comatose, had been a crushing disappointment.

Watching Zoe had been nearly as painful as watching Brett. With every passing hour, her hope had slowly dimmed. She had grown quieter and shut herself off from him. He had never seen her so low.

"I think I'll go lie down for a few minutes," she said, as they entered the house.

He nodded. He needed a stiff drink to drown his disappointment, and a good workout to burn off his frustration.

"In case you need me, I'm going downstairs to work out," he said.

Laying a hand on his arm momentarily, she limped down the hall toward her room, but stopped midway to turn and look over her shoulder at him. "I appreciate your staying with me today."

He shrugged. "Where else would I be?"

She looked away.

He stifled the urge to go to her, something in her posture keeping him at a distance. "The doctor said they might have to try several meds, remember that."

She nodded, her eyes downcast.

"He's a SEAL, Zoe. Uncle Sam doesn't want all those hours of training, and the money it cost, to be wasted. They'll try everything to get Cutter back on his feet."

She started to say something, stopped, and nodding again, continued on to her room.

Hawk rubbed a hand over his face. He needed to hit the weights and work off the emotional overload. He went to his room, changed into shorts, and went downstairs to the unfinished room beneath the back porch. Bare sheetrock covered two walls, the other two sported wooden two by fours and insulation.

He needed to finish this job and doing something creative might be more beneficial than lifting weights. He closed the door, so as not to disturb Zoe. Positioning wood blocks along the bottom of the wall, he lifted a four by eight sheetrock panel onto the supports. Using a drill, he sank the screws to hold the board in place. He had just moved on to the next sheet when Zoe came down the stairs. She had changed into sweatpants and a t-shirt and was wearing her brace.

"I thought you were going to lie down."

"I couldn't. We've sat too long at the hospital and the inactivity is killing me. You can't do this by yourself. Well, obviously you can, but I'd like to help."

He nodded. "Grab the end of this board and hold it steady while I sink the screws."

As Zoe worked beside him, he debated how much to tell her. Because of his job, so much of his life had to remain secret. Had that behavior grown to be such a part of him that he didn't know how to share even the things he could? Was that why Veronica had walked away?

Within an hour they had covered the lower half of two walls. "The upper half can wait until one of the guys comes over."

"If you have the sheetrock mud and tape, we can start applying it to the walls you have finished."

Surprised, his brows rose. "I didn't know you'd worked construction."

"Every woman needs to know how to do basic repairs. Not all of us have a man around the house, and now-a-days, not all men go in for projects like this, even if they're around."

After her earlier depression, he was relieved to see her smile. He lifted a ten-pound bucket of joint compound onto the center of the tarp they stood on, and opened it. "I had to learn. There aren't many contractors around here interested in doing small jobs." He looked around for a piece of molding with which to stir it. "Besides, I like the feeling of accomplishment I get when I've completed something and it's just the way I want it." He mixed the compound with a discarded strip of wood.

Zoe gathered two paint trays and two trowels. "You've done a beautiful job upstairs. I especially like the back porch."

He looked up at her and smiled. "I've noticed." He drew a deep breath. "Today when I left—I checked out some things. Flash paid for the car with money he won in Vegas. Brett, Bowie, and Doc came up clean. And Derrick's finances are clean, but I found out something else I want to check out more thoroughly before I share it."

Zoe straightened from her bent position. Her smile, soft and warm, shot straight to his groin. "I'm not going to ask how you found out about this," she said. "Thanks for trusting me."

The curve of her lips drew his attention. The only thing he could think about was getting her as close as possible. He reached for her and guided her against him. He brushed away a streak of sheetrock dust from her cheek. "How about we finish this another time? We can order something to eat and climb in the hot tub."

Her smile faltered and she focused on his chest. She bit her bottom lip. When she finally spoke, her voice sounded weak as though she couldn't get her breath, "All right."

Hooyah!

His heartbeat leaped into a faster rhythm. He knew he was grinning like a fool. It seemed it was a night for letting down barriers.

The doorbell rang upstairs. He bit back an oath and glanced at his watch. "Maybe we can scare off whoever that is with the threat of work." He brushed her lips with a soft kiss.

****

While she waited for Hawk to return, Zoe spread a thin layer of compound along the seam where two boards of sheetrock met and applied the tape. *Lord, don't let me regret agreeing to get in the hot tub with him. Don't let him regret it either.* If he freaked out once he saw her leg, at least it wouldn't be in a public place in front of a beach full of people.

But Hawk wouldn't freak out. He had too much control for that. If he went all stiff with control, she'd just back away before they got any more involved. They shouldn't anyway. She knew they shouldn't. As soon as the doctors declared him fit he'd be shipping out again. She pressed a hand to her stomach where a hollow feeling settled.

"Strong Man and Marjorie have come by and brought Chinese," Hawk said from the stairs. His expression appeared subdued. "He's offered to help me hang the rest of the sheetrock as soon as we eat."

She sighed. Just when she was building her nerve up and Derrick Armstrong shows up. Something about the man rubbed her the wrong way. "I'll put the lid on the compound can."

As she entered the kitchen, Zoe heard him ask Hawk, "So, are you guys still planning on the parasailing thing?" He spooned rice onto a plate.

"Yes, we are," Hawk said.

"You'll love it, Zoe," Marjorie said as she offered her a container of Cashew Chicken.

"I think I will, too."

Derrick took a bite from his plate. "I hope they don't make some excuse that prevents you from going up because of your leg."

Resentment flared through Zoe, and she took a deep breath before she spoke. "My leg shouldn't be an issue. I won't need it to fly. I'm more at ease in the water than I am on land, so if I hit the water, I'll be just fine."

"I already discussed things with the guy in charge," Hawk said, his tone quiet and resolute. "There won't be any problem."

She glanced in his direction and caught his quick smile. If Hawk got any more thoughtful and understanding, she was lost. Her attention returned to Derrick. Was she more resentful of the comment because he had posed it? Or because she was suspicious of his involvement in Brett's accident?

Derrick shrugged. "Sounds as though you have everything covered. I just thought it would be a really big disappointment if you got there, and they wouldn't let you go up."

She forced a smile. "Thanks. I appreciate your concern."

The doorbell rang. Zoe motioned to Hawk to stay where he was. "I'll get it this time."

Zack O'Connor, Doc, stood on the porch. For a moment, she stared at him, feelings of suspicion and betrayal ricocheting through her. Had he been the one who had hurt Brett?

"Hey, I just thought I'd swing by a minute and see how you guys are doing."

His slow smile seemed so open. "Come in, Doc. Derrick and Marjorie are here. Everyone's in the kitchen." She shut the door behind him and led him toward the kitchen. "Have you eaten? There's Chinese takeout."

"I'm good. I've already eaten. I wouldn't mind a beer though."

"I think Hawk has some in the fridge."

"Hey, Doc," Derrick greeted him, "You arrived just in time. As soon as we eat we're going to help Hawk finish the walls in his rec room."

"That's cool. I haven't done anything more strenuous than lift my toothbrush for days. Had a bug that laid me low."

Zoe studied him as she handed him his beer. He did look a little pale and worn down. "We wondered where you were," Zoe said, handing him a beer. "Maybe you should just supervise with the construction, since you've been sick."

"Naw, I'm back in the game now." He smiled at Zoe. "So you've been talking and wondering about me, huh?" He ran a brief caress down her back.

Zoe fought the urge to roll her eyes at his flirting. "You were missed by everyone at the Marks' barbeque two nights ago."

"Zoe's being nice. I didn't miss your sorry ass at all," Derrick said with a grin.

Doc narrowed his eyes. "I'll remember that the next time I treat *your sorry ass* for jungle rot, out in the field. That next penicillin shot might be water."

Their good-natured banter continued throughout the meal. After cleaning up, the entire group moved downstairs. The three men merged into a team, as they started hanging the remaining pieces of sheetrock.

"They're something, aren't they?" Marjorie said from beside her as she held the paint tray for her. "All my girlfriends are crazy with envy that I'm dating Derrick, his being a SEAL and all. But they don't know the half of it. They have these kinds of reckless, wild man images, but they like—pull together when they're in a group, like family. Sometimes I'm even jealous of the time he spends with the guys because there's times, when we're together, I feel he's closer to these guys than he is to me. I mean how close would you have to be to lay down your life for someone?"

"They have to go into battle with one another, Marjorie. Their survival depends on their being able to work together. I suppose they have to know one another so well, they can communicate without words."

Marjorie shifted the tray full of sheet rock mud. "It really does something to them. Every time they ship out, Derrick comes back kind of aggressive and jumpy, like his skin doesn't fit him anymore. It takes him about a month to get back to normal, and then I'm still walking around on egg shells with him for a while."

She peeled her attention away from the men to look at Zoe, her expression serious. "He's been totally freaked about Cutter. They've been buddies since BUDS, and he just can't deal. That's why he doesn't come to the hospital. He'd like to call and ask you about him every once in awhile, but the whole scene that went down when he showed up at the hospital that first time has made him believe you wouldn't welcome him calling."

Strong Man hadn't thus far struck her as the sensitive soul Marjorie painted him, but Zoe hadn't been around him enough to judge. She'd welcome his calls if it guaranteed he wouldn't show up at the hospital again. It might keep her brother safe. "He's welcome to call me any time to check on Brett. I won't mind."

"I told him that, but he didn't believe me. Maybe you could tell him before we leave."

Zoe nodded. She scooped up more drywall mud with the trowel and spread it along a seam. "All right."

Marjorie helped her position a ladder close to the wall and held it steady, while Zoe climbed it. Zoe hooked the paint pan onto the ladder and scooped more mud.

"Where did you learn to do this?" Marjorie asked.

"My brother taught me. When he's home he likes to do things around the house, like Hawk. He says it helps him relax. My dad did, too."

"Was he in the military, too?"

"Yes, a career Marine. He was killed in Desert Storm by friendly fire."

"Jesus," Marjorie breathed. "I'm sorry."

"Thanks," She swallowed against the immediate thickness in her throat. Even after so long, it hurt.

"And now Cutter's hurt, and you're with Hawk. How do you deal with all that?"

She wasn't exactly with Hawk, and she wasn't certain she ever would be, but she wasn't sharing that with a stranger. "You love them, despite their need to risk themselves. You don't really have a choice. You can't pick and choose who you love, can you?"

Her own words resonated. Did she love Hawk? She looked over to where he and the men worked. She studied him. His brows were drawn together in concentration, his pale gray eyes focused on the task at hand. With his lips pressed together in a thin line he looked intent and determined. Would he approach an emotional attachment with as much fervor? How would a woman go about inspiring that kind of response from him? She pressed her hand against the hollow sensation the thoughts triggered.

"No, you can't." Marjorie's reply had her shifting her attention back to the woman in time to see an expression of sadness flicker across her face.

Finished with the strip from ceiling to mid-wall, Zoe climbed down the ladder. She stepped off the last rung and lost her balance. Grabbing at the ladder to stabilize herself, she caught Marjorie's bell-shaped sleeve along with it. The other woman sucked in her breath and grimaced in pain.

"I'm sorry, Marjorie." Releasing the fabric, Zoe caught her breath, a sickening, dropping sensation hitting her stomach. "Oh my God!"

CHAPTER 13

"Did I hurt you?" Zoe stared at the large bruise on the woman's arm just above her wrist.

Marjorie jerked away. "No." She shook her head as she smoothed her sleeve back over the injury. "It's nothing. I just banged my arm on something the other day and have a bruise now. It's a little sore."

It didn't look like an accidental injury. It looked like someone had grabbed her arm hard enough to leave the impression of every finger. Zoe studied the woman's face, a prickly, numbing shock traveling down her body. She gathered her composure with an effort and looked into the woman's face until Marjorie's eyes rose to meet hers. "Is there anything I can do?"

"No. I'm fine." Marjorie's fingers smoothed the sleeve again. "But it might be a good idea for you to stay off that ladder. You almost fell."

"Maybe you're right." She had to do something. If there was the slightest possibility Derrick Armstrong was abusive, she had to try and help Marjorie. She struggled to bring her scattered thoughts and emotions together. "Sometimes I don't want to recognize my limitations. I just keep ignoring them, until they slap me in the face."

"You seem to do pretty well," Marjorie said. "And Hawk doesn't seem to mind."

"He's very supportive, but there's a line where support can turn into pity. Once that happens, the balance is thrown off." Zoe's attention strayed to Hawk as he used the drill to sink sheet rock screws. A ridge of muscle along his shoulder blade stood out beneath his t-shirt. Her mouth went dry as she thought about running her hand over his strong back and feeling the movement of his muscles beneath her hands. "Relationships are all about balance, don't you think?"

Marjorie brushed her sun-streaked hair over her shoulder. "I hadn't ever thought about it like that, but yeah, I guess you're right."

"When one partner is too demanding or has unreasonable expectations, the relationship can escalate into something unhealthy and painful for both people."

Marjorie's features grew slack, then shuttered. "I suppose so."

Zoe stifled a sigh. She sensed she'd gone as far as she could. She didn't want the woman to shut down completely and push her away. She changed the subject. "What do you do, Marjorie?"

"I'm a software analyst for a corporation that makes computer games."

"That sounds way more interesting than being a physical therapist."

"It doesn't to me," Marjorie said with a smile. "All those jocks who come to you for treatment—" She fanned her face as though hot. "You and Hawk haven't slept together yet, have you?"

Having the tables turned triggered an instant urge to retreat. Yet how was she to expect Marjorie to open up to her, if she wasn't ready to do the same? She drew a deep breath and looked up from smoothing the compound at the bottom of the seam. "No we haven't. I had a really bad experience in college, and it made me a little wary."

"Hawk's a really good guy. He'd never hurt you."

The momentary possessive, predatory look of jealousy on his face as he had grasped her arm that morning in the bathroom came to mind. It had been jealousy, hadn't it? Or had it been something else? He had never been out of control though, and had immediately backed off. "No, I don't think he would ever hurt me, intentionally. I suppose all men have the potential, but it all boils down to control."

His behavior at the hospital after Brett had been slapped occurred to her. "I've seen him furious, but he never lost it. He turned his anger toward getting something accomplished, not trying to destroy anything." She had sensed his frustration tonight after returning from the hospital. He had done the same thing.

"I suppose it helps that they can go blow something up now and then and release their aggressions."

Zoe nodded toward the three men hanging sheetrock. "Or they can do something constructive with a hammer and nails."

When Marjorie remained silent Zoe looked up to find her studying Derrick's broad back, a look of sadness on her face.

Emotion settled in the pit of her stomach as heavy as the bucket of sheet rock mud she dipped into. For as much sympathy and concern as Marjorie inspired, Zoe dreaded having to share her suspicions with Hawk just as much.

****

Hawk tossed the damp towel into the hamper and tugged on a pair of sweat pants and a t-shirt. He needed to talk to Zoe. But the things he needed to say couldn't be said to anyone outside the team. God damn it! Every day something happened that hammered at his trust in his men. God he needed a drink, he needed something.

Leaving his room, he turned toward the kitchen, but noticed the light still on in the living room and changed direction.

He paused at the entrance and watched as Zoe rubbed a towel against the mass of hair she draped over her shoulder. She looked up as he took a step into the room.

I think Doc might be strung out on drugs. He nearly said the words aloud just to feel the weight of them. He couldn't be. The team was tested for drugs all the time. And even compounds like steroids showed up in the tests. Surely Zack wouldn't risk getting canned from the team. Not for drugs. Not for anything.

He'd been alone so long. Held his own council over things that had revisited him over and over. Things he couldn't share with her. But the pain of this was too much.

"There's something going on with Doc. When I asked him if he and Bowie had been fishing lately, he said he hadn't seen him in nearly two weeks. That's some kind of record, because those two are tight and, besides chasing women, fishing is one of their favorite pass-times."

Zoe set aside the towel and combed her fingers through her hair. "Maybe he's really been sick and Bowie's stayed away to keep from getting it."

"I don't know." He rubbed the back of his neck, the muscles there tight with frustration. "I'm going over to his apartment tomorrow and have a talk with him." He was tired of these suspicions. He was going to get to the bottom of this shit.

"Hawk—" Her tone sounded tentative and laced with something else he couldn't quite pinpoint. He focused on her. Her hesitancy had his stomach churning.

"I think Derrick might be abusing Marjorie."

The shock of it hit him like a punch.

"She had a bruise on her arm that looked suspicious. She said she'd hit it on something, but you could see the finger marks. I tried to talk to her, but she clammed up."

"Jesus! What the hell is going on with these guys?"

"They're just guys, Hawk, under tremendous pressure. All of you are." She rose to her feet and came to him. When she put her arms around his waist and pressed close, some of the pain eased.

"We send you to awful places and ask you to do things, terrible, painful, necessary things, and then we ask you not to think about it, remember it, or internalize any of it. We ask the impossible."

She leaned back to look up at him. "Maybe I'm wrong. Maybe the circumstances surrounding our first meeting has affected how I feel about Derrick, made me suspicious of him to begin with. Maybe I read the whole situation wrong. Maybe it really was an accident."

God, he hoped so. He ran his hands over her back and traced the slender shape of her through her t-shirt. Just touching her made him feel better. "I'll talk to him tomorrow. See if I can draw him out. If these guys are in trouble, I have to reach out to them and get them squared away. They're my men, Zoe."

"I understand."

Was that possible? Could she really understand how his loyalties were being pulled in a dozen directions? One of them might have attempted to murder a member of their team? The thought hit him in the solar plexus every time he thought it. It made him sick. But until he figured out who was responsible, they deserved the best he could do for them.

"I want whoever hurt Cutter to pay, Zoe. But unless he wakes up and tells us, we may never know."

"I know."

"He may already be paying for it. It would have to be eating at him." How could it not? "If it's one of them, and I find out which, he'll pay. I promise."

Her blue eyes settled on his face. "I know."

He brushed her lips with his and rested his forehead against hers. He wanted to lie in bed with her and hold her and be held in return. Acknowledging those feelings brought with it a surge of pain and desire he didn't know how to deal with.

She touched his cheek, her fingers caressing. "You don't always have to stand alone."

Hawk swallowed as need clamped around his throat and made it impossible for him to speak. They had both sustained emotional blows today. But was that a reason to make love?

"You're such a temptation to me." Her voice sounded husky and soft. She nestled closer and stood on her tiptoes to rub her cheek against his.

His heart took up a heavy rhythm and he fought the urge to cup her hips and drag her closer. So there was more there for her, too. Finding his voice he said, "Giving in to a little temptation now and then can be good for you."

She drew a deep breath. "Can it?" Her lips brushed his jaw.

This shy, playful, kittenish thing she had going was killing him. "Yeah, it can," he forced out between breaths. He

grasped her hand and tugged her down the hall. Pausing at
each switch for quick kisses, he turned the lights out.

The instant they crossed the bedroom threshold, he
read Zoe's feelings of awkwardness. Color deepened in her
cheeks, and she avoided looking directly at him. When she
pulled away, he thought she might beat a hasty retreat, but
instead she moved to the opposite side of the bed and he
realized she was removing her socks.

He shucked his t-shirt and tossed it atop the basket in
the closet. As he turned, her bundled socks shot past him,
ricocheted off the lid and fell into the hamper. He looked up.

Focusing on his face, Zoe stretched out on his bed; her
arms bent beneath her head, leaving her midriff visible, the
skin creamy and smooth. The lamp on the nightstand
played upon her features etching the curve of her cheek and
turning the reddish blond highlights in her hair to copper.
She smiled at him. Blood rushed south, and he grew harder.

Visions of him peeling off her sweat pants and thrusting
inside her played through his mind. He climbed onto the bed
beside her and buried his face in the pillow with a groan. He
just had to block out that smile until he knew he had himself
under control.

Zoe's hand ran over the back of his head and neck in a
caress, and he turned his head to look at her. The tenderness
he read in her expression intensified the ache.

"It's been a long day," she said.

"A week at least."

She smiled again, then grew serious. "Our living
together—it could become—awkward."

Was she looking for an excuse to back away again? Or
was she giving him an opportunity to do the same? He
turned on his side to face her and tamped down the old

feelings of pain and abandonment. "If you let every difficulty keep you from reaching for what you want, Zoe, you'll never truly live."

"I was thinking of you." She ran her fingertips along his shoulder, her eyes tracking the movement. Her light, caressing touch raced through him to the bottoms of his feet. She focused on his face, her eyes dark, her pupils nearly swallowing the pale blue irises. Her voice sounded husky as she said, "Turn out the light."

His heart stuttered then beat hard against his ribs. He leaned back and extinguished the bedside lamp. For a moment, the darkness was profound until his eyes adjusted to it.

She kissed him, her lips parted in invitation. All the nights he had lain awake, craving her, rolled over him like a tank. With a groan, part relief, part need, he crushed her close. Hungrily, greedily, he tasted her passion in the eager sweep of her tongue against his, and in the way she molded herself against him.

His hand shook as he ran it up beneath her t-shirt. Her skin felt like warm silk, her breast full and soft. Her nipple beaded beneath his palm and she groaned. He wished he could see her expression as he touched her. He strived to be gentle, but felt starved for her touch, for the feel of her body against his own.

He tugged her t-shirt upward and she wiggled free of it and pressed her breasts against his chest. Her bare skin brushing against his felt like heaven. When he rolled on top of her, positioning himself between her legs, she slid her hands down his back, cupped his buttocks, and rocked against his erection in a way that nearly sent him over the edge. He had to slow things down. But sweet Jesus, he didn't want to. He slid downward, latched onto her nipple, and sucked.

Zoe's breathing caught and she thrust her fingers into his hair. The sweet, empty ache inside her grew with every touch, every kiss, until she thought she might fly apart at any moment. She couldn't touch him enough, couldn't get close enough. His lips against her stomach, his breath on her skin, his tongue dipping into her navel, all had her nearly sobbing with need. When he dragged the sweat pants and panties down her legs, she couldn't wait to be free of them.

Then he was on top of her, kissing her, trembling against her as he touched her between her legs, his fingers so wonderfully, carefully gentle. That he trembled with wanting her fired her blood and made the empty, writhing need inside her grow in intensity.

She ran her hand down his chest, over the flat muscular plane of his stomach and beneath his shorts. The size and heat of his erection was both startling and arousing. He groaned her name, his voice a low rumble against her ear that vibrated along her nerve endings and raised goose bumps on her skin.

"Come inside me," she managed, the words a breathy, pleading whisper.

He shook free of his sweats, and leaned over her to reach in the nightstand. The wispy crackle as he tore open the condom sounded loud, underlining the huge, terrifying, wonderful step she was taking, they were taking. With his first push of entry, the sweet intimacy between them caught at Zoe's heart and she drew him down to her, her lips seeking his. The wanting, the needing, tangled into a surge of love and desire so strong she could barely breathe. The quick burning pain of his possession seemed nothing compared to the closeness she shared with him.

"God, Zoe, tell me I'm not hurting you." His lips skimmed her cheek, her brow, and came back to her lips.

"You're not." Not yet. She cut off the thought and ran her hands up and down his back urging him closer. He moved deep inside her, triggering an answering thread of renewed need. He groaned her name again, his voice ragged. His slow, gentle rocking movements quickened. She clung to him and turned her lips against his throat, tasting the heat of his skin. She lost herself in the play of his muscles beneath her hands, and the damp brush of his taut belly against hers. Her breathing grew labored as she gave herself to him, moved with him, moved against him. At the first pulsing wave of his release, pleasure erupted inside her, so sweetly satisfying, she gasped his name.

****

When his breathing had returned to normal, Hawk searched for and found Zoe's lips. "The next time we do this the light stays on," he said, his tone adamant as he slowly eased out of her though he was reluctant to move.

Her hands ran up and down his back in a caress. "Maybe."

"No maybes. I want to see you when I touch you next time, Zoe."

"Maybe we can work our way up to that, a little at a time."

"You just trusted me enough to make love with you. How can you do that, and not trust me enough to let me see you while I'm doing it?"

"In the dark, I can be as beautiful as any other woman for you."

Pain grabbed him by the throat. "Oh baby—" He rested his cheek against hers and swallowed against it. "You are beautiful, Zoe. Every time you walk into a room, I get hard. I've been going around for weeks in that condition."

"I have too, I mean, not hard, but, you know." Her voice was just above a whisper. Her lips parted and warm touched his shoulder.

An instant response shot through him and he turned his lips to hers. "Hold that thought. I'll be right back."

He eased away from her and off the bottom of the bed. Closing the bathroom door, he turned on the light and moved to the toilet to discard the condom. He froze. "Oh, shit." A dropping sensation hit his stomach worse than a three thousand foot parachute jump. As the prophylactic hit the water, he drew several steadying breaths, a thousand thoughts and emotions bombarding him as he watched the useless thing circle the toilet bowl and disappear down the drain.

He wrapped a towel around his waist and opened the door, leaving the light on. She had gotten under the covers, and as he crossed the threshold, she drew the sheet up over her breasts. Two long steps put him at the foot of the bed. The pale light from the bathroom etched one side of her face and shoulder, leaving the rest in shadow. She looked so young, so small. Responsibility lay like a weight upon his shoulders. "We have a problem, Zoe."

CHAPTER 14

"Are you on the pill?"

Hawk's face was in shadow and she couldn't read his expression, but his tone held a note of—forced calm.

"No, I'm not."

"The condom broke, Zoe."

She stared at him, trying to take in what he'd said. Shock hit her and her facial muscles stiffened. She struggled to control her scattered thoughts and count days. "I think it will be all right. But I guess, if we're going to do more of this, I'd better call in the morning and see about some kind of backup birth control."

"Jesus—" He rubbed both hands over his short hair. "I'm sorry, honey."

She swallowed as the bathroom light played upon his long lean body, highlighting the muscles of his stomach, and the precarious grip the towel held on his hips. Even with anxiety still curling her toes, she wanted him all over again.

Completely unself-conscious, He whipped the towel free and climbed into bed. "You don't have to worry about diseases or anything. We get checked out all the time. And I don't take chances." He gathered her close. "Nothing like this has ever happened before."

"You don't have to worry either."

"Yeah, I noticed."

Heat flared in her face when he continued to look at her. "I just haven't met anyone I've wanted to—" She searched for the right words.

Hawk had no such trouble. "Lower the barriers for?"

"I guess you could put it that way. There was only one other time."

"Wow, that's a lot of pressure and responsibility you just dumped on me, along with a pretty big compliment."

She chuckled. "I'm sure you can handle it."

"Will you tell me what the guy in college did?"

Her stomach muscles tightened. She wasn't ready to share one of the most degrading moments of her life. "Why? There's nothing that can be changed about it."

"Because it's important to the way you are with me now, Zoe."

Surprised by his pushing for more, instead of the reverse, she remained silent. Was she ready for the emotional intimacy he was shooting for? She didn't know. She turned on her side and guided his arm around her waist. Hawk slipped his arm beneath her neck and tucked his legs beneath hers, his body, adamantly male, molding to hers from behind. She caught her breath at the instant shock of desire that pulsed through her.

Silence settled between them. Unable to relax, she caressed his arm with her fingertips. She couldn't share the whole terrible, embarrassing, painful story. "Once he saw my scars, he couldn't—function." Her voice came out just above a whisper around the knot in her throat.

His lips moved against her shoulder. "If a few scars could make such a difference in the way he felt, he didn't deserve you, Zoe."

"You haven't seen them yet. You may feel the same."

"We can find out right now," he started to rise.

She grabbed his arm. "Not yet, Hawk."

He subsided. "It isn't going to happen. Trust me, Zoe."

She drew a deep breath. She had trusted him enough to make love with him. Why couldn't he be satisfied with that like other men would be?

"You're not going to chicken out on our date this weekend are you?"

"No." She'd resigned herself to his seeing everything this weekend. But, it was going to be hard. Really hard.

"It's only two days."

"Are you trying to pick a fight?"

"No."

"Then, give it a rest."

He chuckled and the sound vibrated against her back.

"All right. I'd rather make love with you than war." His hand cupped the lower half of her abdomen and he nuzzled her neck. "It feels good to hold you like this, Zoe."

Desire swept through her and she placed her hand over his. Her voice a husky whisper, she said," It feels good to be held."

She turned to face him. The pale yellow light touched the ridge of his brow, the slope of his nose, but she couldn't see his eyes clearly, or their expression. His hand swept down her back to cup her buttocks and guide her against him. His fingers lingered on the ridge of a scar on her backside and she held her breath as he traced its rectangular shape.

"Did you know in some African cultures they mark their bodies with scars because they believe it shows courage?"

"No, I didn't know that."

"They also believe it adds to their beauty, and in certain areas of the body, it enhances sexual pleasure."

His fingertip continued to caress the ridge sending prickles of awareness down over the curve of her bottom right to the very core of her. Her heart beat so fast she couldn't catch her breath. "Are you just shining me on, Lieutenant Yazzie?" she managed as she stroked his back.

"No, I'm not." He kissed her, the pressure of his lips soft, tempting. "I'll never lie to you, Zoe." His erection rested against the inside of her thigh as he pushed closer. "Does it feel like I'm lying to you?"

"No," she said in a tone strangled by renewed need. She molded the soft curve of her belly to the muscular tautness of his and drew his lips back to hers.

He turned pressing her back on the mattress and every inch of his long torso aligned with hers. She caught her breath as the course hair on his chest rubbed her breasts and the tempting length of his erection brushed against her intimately.

"I've been lying here every night since you moved in, wanting you and feeling guilty," he said as his lips caressed the underside of her jaw.

"Why guilty?" She ran her fingers over the short hair at his nape.

"It's a matter of trust, Zoe." He drew back to look down at her.

She traced one high cheekbone with her thumb. She wanted him. Now that she had finally taken this step, she refused to allow her family to interfere with that. "I trust you to take care of me, in every way."

He groaned and kissed her hard. "You know what I'm talking about," he said, his breathing unsteady.

"I'm not thinking about anything but you and me right now. My family has no place in this bed between us." She traced the curve of his ear with her tongue. He shuddered and rocked against her.

"Your mom will take one look at us and know, Zoe. Moms have a sixth sense about these things."

"My sex life is none of her business," she whispered and blew in his ear.

He turned his lips to hers, the sweep of his tongue hot and torrid. "I'll lock up the firearms, just in case." He breathed as his body once again took possession of hers.

****

"I'm fine, Mom," Zoe said as she cradled the phone between her shoulder and ear. She tugged at the knot in her shoe string. *I made love with Hawk and it was more than I ever expected.* That was probably more information than her mother would ever want to know. She dropped the shoe on the floor and sat down on the couch.

"And Brett?"

"They're trying another medication tomorrow or actually adding another medication to the one he's on. His heart rate is remaining steady and his blood pressure. He's turned over on his own once, so I'm hopeful he's close to waking up." *Please God!*

"And Hawk?"

"He's fine, Mom. He's taking me parasailing tomorrow."

"Don't you have to do that on the water?"

"Yes. I'll have to wear a bathing suit."

Her mother's silence stretched across the distance. "How do you feel about that, Zoe?"

She chose her words carefully. She wasn't ashamed of having a relationship with Hawk. But she didn't want her mother to think he had waited for her to leave to move in on her daughter either. That wasn't the way it was at all.

"I'm a little—nervous about him seeing my leg. I don't want him to pity me or go all super protective."

Clara chuckled. "He's taking his job to look out for you seriously, huh?"

She turned to look at Hawk as he entered the living room. "Yes, he is." God, she sounded sappy.

His white t-shirt stretched across his chest, delineating the contour of the muscles there. He paused at a table just inside the front door and picked up his wallet and change. Khaki shorts hugged his taut waist and sculpted buttocks in just the right way. Looking over his shoulder at her as he stuffed his wallet in his back pocket, he caught her watching him. His pale gray eyes focused on her with a look that left her tingling and breathless.

"He's been staying at the hospital with me." Just in case something bad or good happens. She swallowed against the sudden tightening of her throat. "And we've been doing some remodeling here at the house. We've almost finished the rec room walls. Some of the team came over and helped us hang the sheetrock."

"Zoe—" Her mother's tone stopped her breathless rush of words.

She placed a hand against her midriff where her heart had fallen. Her mother knew. She had never been able to hide anything from her. Something in her tone had made it all clear as glass. She swallowed. "Yes."

"Be careful, honey."

All the concern and unconditional love expressed in those three words had her eyes stinging. "I'm—I will, Mom."

"I'd like to speak to Hawk." Clara's tone changed just as quickly to protective mom mode. Zoe had heard it before.

Tempted to tell her he wasn't available, she stalled instead. "How are Sharon and Katie Beth? How are both of them doing with the new baby?"

"Sharon's doing well after the surgery. She's been a little weepy but she's doing well and Katie Beth's in little momma mode right now. How long that will last, none of us knows. She doesn't like diaper time at all."

Zoe laughed. "And Ali-Marie?"

"Growing like a weed and eating well. She gets up twice a night, so right now none of us are getting much sleep, but that will change soon enough. She's a beautiful baby. She looks a lot like you did. Now quit stalling and hand the phone to Hawk."

Zoe bit back an oath and motioned to Hawk. Biting her lip she handed him the receiver, then watched his expression. His yes and no answers gave her no clue what her mother was saying, nor did his expression. He hung up and his lips quirked upward.

"What did she say?"

"She just wanted to be certain I was going to look out for you on the water."

"She knows."

"If she does, she didn't say anything to me." He tugged her close and brushed her lips with his own. He smelled of soap, toothpaste, and a woodsy scented cologne mixed with his own clean scent.

His hair was still damp from his shower as she smoothed the dark strands with her fingertips.

"Besides, you said last night you weren't going to let your family interfere with our being together."

"I'm not."

"Then what are you all worked up about?"

What *was* she worked up about? Was she worried her mother would be disappointed in her for sleeping with Hawk? Or was she more worried about her saying something to him about it? The latter, definitely.

"My family is way too protective of me. I don't want them giving you a hard time if or when they find out we're sleeping together. I'm not really worried about anything they might say to me."

"I'm a big boy, Zoe. You don't have to run interference for me." His hand caressed the rounded curve of her buttocks.

She tiptoed to better mold her small frame against him.

"But it sure feels good when you're covering me," He murmured against her ear, his warm breath making her shiver. He dipped his head to kiss her again and for a moment she forgot everything but the pleasure he gave her each time he kissed her.

"I have to meet Derrick in fifteen minutes. When's your doctor's appointment?" he asked, his tone husky, his gray eyes alight with feelings.

"Noon."

"I'll be back at eleven to pick you up."

She nodded and released him.

She studied the door as it closed behind him. With his kiss still burning on her lips and her heart still beating in her ears, she hadn't had time to think about Derrick Armstrong. If Hawk questioned Strong Man too directly would he blow up and try and hurt Hawk? Zoe rushed to the door and pulled it open.

CHAPTER 15

"What's going on, Strong Man?" Hawk said as he ducked beneath the hood of the bright Canary yellow Jeep to stand next to Derrick.

"Ah—Marjorie didn't start my car while I was gone and the battery's dead." The man sounded out of sorts. "I have to have a jump to start it."

"No problem, I have cables and I can pull my car around."

"Thanks, LT. I appreciate it."

Hawk got back in his Saturn Vue and did a U-turn in the apartment complex's parking lot to arrange the cars nose to nose. Pulling the lever inside his car to open the hood, he paused to turn off the ringer on his cell phone, and tossed it onto the passenger seat. If he and Derrick were going to have a heart to heart, he didn't want any interruptions.

Getting out of the vehicle, he retrieved the jumper cables from his trunk and linked the two batteries. At his signal, Derrick started his Jeep. The vehicle emitted a high-pitched squeal like a prolonged scream.

"Sounds like you might need to spray that belt with some lubricant," Hawk yelled above the noise as he approached the man's window.

"Will do, as soon as I'm sure this sucker will hold a charge."

The sound died down to a persistent squeak as Hawk unhooked the cables and rolled them up. He tossed them into the trunk and turned off the Saturn.

Leaving his vehicle running, Derrick exited the car and joined him. "What's up, LT?"

"I thought I'd just touch base. You've been out of town with your sister, and this is the first time I've been able to drive the car since straining my knee."

"Sometimes you just have to get out of the house away from them, don't you?"

Them? That one word didn't sound good. There was aggression and impatience crammed in there, as well as a touch of condescension. He struggled to keep his expression neutral. "Well, Zoe's pretty easy to get along with. She likes her own space sometimes, too."

"What does she do? Go shopping?"

"No. She reads a lot. And she spends a lot of time at the hospital."

Derrick frowned. "That's tough duty."

"Yeah, it is."

Derrick leaned back against the car beside him, his expression subdued. "Cutter isn't going to wake up, is he?"

Hawk shook his head. "I don't know."

"He looks dead," Derrick said, an empty note in his tone.

Hawk glanced at him and found him studying his shoes.

"He's breathing on his own, and all his vitals are normal. He's going to come out of this."

Derrick looked up. "It freaks me out to see him like—he is."

"I know. It did me too at first. But we have to stay hopeful for his sake, and for Zoe's. And if you say anything negative about his prognosis, don't say it in front of her. She insists he's going to wake up."

"She's got her head buried in the sand. He looks bad."

"He's losing weight, Derrick. But we can't lose faith. He's tough."

Derrick nodded. "Yeah, he is."

"During the mission, did you hear anything unusual inside the building?" Hawk asked

"No. The tangos upstairs walking back and forth. I was focused on getting my package delivered and getting out of there. Cutter was down the hall doing the same. Or so I thought."

"His charges had been set, but he was down when I reached him."

Derrick shook his head and rubbed a hand over his brow. "It just doesn't make sense to me."

"Did Cutter know about the assault charges you've had leveled against you?"

Derrick's features blanked with shock. It took a moment before he recovered. "Who told you?" His voice sounded hoarse.

"Who, isn't important. It's that there were charges brought to begin with. You've dodged a bullet, Derrick. And if it's established that Cutter knew about them, you could be in real trouble."

Derrick clenched his fists "I didn't touch him. He's my best buddy. We're tight. We might do the bonding thing and punch each other but we cover each other's back. He'd never rat me out." His eyes narrowed. "Who did?"

His patience splintered and Hawk thrust his face close to his. "Who the fuck cares? The problem is that if I found out about it, the brass will too, and then you'll be knee deep in shit. Use your head, Strong Man. You know what I'm saying."

Derrick's features looked wooden. "I didn't hurt, Cutter. I'll take a lie detector test to that."

"I don't think the Navy's real impressed with those since they train us to lie so well." Hawk said, drilling his point home. "How's Marjorie?"

"She's all right. Why do you ask?"

"I noticed she had a bruise on her arm."

Derrick looked away. "She hit her arm on something. She's all right."

Hawk fell silent waiting for Derrick to look at him. "We've all been under the gun. Our last tour was tough. And with Cutter being hurt during the last mission—sometimes emotional stressors trigger problems. If you're having a problem with anger management—"

Derrick's cheeks grew flushed and his eyes narrowed. "Was this your idea or your girlfriend's?"

"Mine, Derrick." He met the other man's gaze straight on. " All it takes is one incident being reported by the MPs, or something going through the court system, and it can haunt your career. Upper brass wants men who can stay cool under pressure."

"Yeah, they want us to be bad-asses only when it's convenient for them." Bitterness laced the man's voice, and pain flickered across his face. "I felt as though we were shadow boxing, LT. You could never tell who the enemy was. And what's up with this bombing your own people shit? Why sacrifice a hundred of them just to get at two Americans?"

Hawk laid a hand on Derrick's shoulder. "They want the U.S. Military gone, Derrick. Out of their country. And they're willing to sacrifice whoever they have to, to see it happen. And as long as they're threatening people, we can't walk away. So we're stuck in a cycle." He shook his head. "The politicians' reasons for us being there don't mean shit. We're there trying to protect the regular people on the street. That's what we do, protect those too weak or defenseless to protect themselves. It's what we're about." He looked the man in the face. "And that includes the people we love here at home."

Derrick's gaze dropped away.

Hawk drew a deep breath and chose his words with care.

"Marjorie seems to be supportive, Derrick."

"Yeah." He rubbed his hands over his head brushing his close-cropped blond hair up.

"Do you think seeing someone, talking things out, would help you deal?"

"I can't, LT. If word get's back to the brass it will do just as much damage to my career as a police report."

"No, it won't. Because it looks like you're being responsible and dealing with the problem, not ignoring it. And besides that, you can see someone off post."

"Like that's going to happen without someone finding out about it. And what about your girlfriend?" Derrick's eyes narrowed again.

"Zoe knows how to keep a confidence."

"I've never known any female able to keep her mouth shut."

Hawk couldn't completely quash his anger. "Yeah, you have, Derrick. *Marjorie*. She didn't say a word. It was the bruise *you* left behind that has me here talking to you, *not anything she said or did*." He studied the other man's expression carefully. "She's not going to have trouble from you because of this talk, is she?"

"No."

There was a sullen tone to Derrick's voice. Hawk eyed him. The window of connection had closed, and the man was growing defensive. He'd have to back off and follow through again later. "While you think about it, if you feel like the pressure's building and you need someone to talk to, you call me."

"Sure."

Derrick's continued brevity, the tension in his body language, shouted a warning. "If I don't get it together, you'll turn it back on me."

"That's the trick, Strong Man. I won't have to. You'll get back what *you* put in. Like most things in life." Hawk straightened away from the car and crammed his hands in his pockets.

"All right. I get it."

At the dismissal in the man's tone, Hawk eyed him. Should he push any harder, it might come back on Marjorie. Jesus! All the psychological training he'd received and he couldn't figure out what to do. If he tried to use a threat to keep Derrick under control, it might push him into doing something regrettable. He'd gone as far as he could. For now.

"Stay icy, Strong Man ," he said as he got into his car.

"Yeah." Derrick nodded, his expression hard, unreadable.

As he pulled out of the parking lot, Hawk looked up into his rearview mirror. Derrick stood there watching him drive away, and something in the man's body language had alarms going off in his head. He'd have to stay in close touch with him, and if he stepped over the line again, he'd have no choice but to call in the MPs.

He'd have to report this to his commander and his own actions related to it. He couldn't hold back that information, it could come back to bite him. But Jesus, the idea made him feel like a snitch. And on top of the lack of progress in finding out who had hurt Cutter, it would make for a delightful meeting with Lt. Commander Jackson.

Reaching over to the cell phone beside him, he flipped it open to check for calls and recognized his home number on the device several times. Zoe had obviously been trying to reach him. He pushed the button to return her calls.

"Where are you? Are you all right?" her voice came across the connection in a strident tone he had never heard before.

"I just left Derrick and I'm on my way back home to pick you up. What's up?"

"Why didn't you answer my calls?"

"I turned the ringer off while we were talking. What's wrong?"

Silence hung over the line and he checked to see if the signal had broken.

"Hey, Zoe, talk to me."

"I was worried when you didn't answer. I thought maybe he'd hurt you. Damn it, Hawk—"

This time he knew the signal hadn't died. She'd hung up.

CHAPTER 16

As Hawk came in the front door, Zoe bit back the words threatening to erupt. How could he have turned off his ringer? He knew how distrustful she was of Derrick. He was abusing his girlfriend. She was certain of it.

What if Brett had found out about Marjorie's abuse and threatened to report it to Hawk? Or their commander? Derek could be discharged if he was arrested and the charges proven.

"Hey, you all right?" Hawk's greeting, so carefully measured, triggered an urge to gnash her teeth at him. She stifled the desire to stomp her feet and scream at him. Why was it, by their very attitude, men were able to project the belief that an angry woman was an unstable one?

"No, I'm not all right." She struggled to keep her voice at an even pitch though the emotion clogged her throat. "I was concerned that Derrick might do something to hurt you. And you turned your ringer off so I couldn't check on you."

He reached out to touch her arm, but she drew back. If he touched her, her anger would probably dissolve and she'd cry. Damn, she hated being such a girl.

Hawk's brows fisted in a frown. "I didn't want any interruptions. It was hard enough to talk to him without the phone going off."

Okay, she understood that. But Derrick Armstrong was an unstable man. "He could have attacked you."

"And what could you have done about it if he had, Zoe? You were here, and my having the phone on or off wouldn't have changed your ability to do anything about it."

Her heart drummed in her ears as her temper spiked. He sounded so damned rational. She fought the urge to shake him. Yeah, that could happen. "I tried to call you right after you left to talk you out of speaking to him. You didn't answer then either."

"I must have been in a dead spot. I'd have answered if I'd gotten the call."

He was handling her. Arrogant ass—She narrowed her eyes.

Reaction settled in and she folded her arms against her to suppress the shakes. "I don't trust him. I think he's the one who attacked my brother. All I could think of was that, if he felt threatened, he'd do the same to you."

"Well, he didn't. We didn't do the male bonding thing and punch fists, but he didn't go psycho on me either. He's pissed, but he realizes he either deals with this problem, or it's going to blow his career out of the water. And as for him being responsible for Cutter's injuries, it's a possibility, but we haven't got any firm proof. Until we do, my hands are tied, Zoe."

She understood, but she didn't want to be so in control right now. She'd been so afraid for him. If she experienced this strong a reaction over a confrontation between him and Derrick Armstrong, how would she deal with it when he shipped out again?

Tears burned her eyes, and she turned away, afraid he would read what she was feeling. God, how would she bear it?

"Are you going to let me hold you or are you going to stay mad?" he asked, his arms sliding around her from behind.

She wanted to jerk away from him and burrow into him all at the same time. His touch triggered such pain, and such comfort. She swallowed against the tearful surge that made her throat ache. "I was angry-afraid for you, Adam, not angry-angry. There's a difference—in case you don't know."

"I know." His voice sounded husky. His lips touched the back of her neck making her shiver. "You just called me Adam. Only my mom called me Adam after I went into the Navy. When she was mad or very serious about something she'd call me Adam Yazzie."

"Well, I'm very serious, Adam Yazzie. I don't want you counseling him again and trying to save his damn career. If he hurts Marjorie, he deserves to spend time in the brig."

"Well, I can't say I disagree." He nuzzled her neck as his hand cupped the underside of her breast, his long fingers kneading it.

Instantly, an empty ache settled between her legs and she reached behind her to run her hand down his long thigh. The need to pull him in as close as he could get, to hold him tight and keep him safe, twisted inside her.

Turning to face him, she cupped his face between her hands and studied his features with a desperation she couldn't quite suppress. "Tell me you'll be careful."

"I will, I promise." His gray gaze remained steady on her face. "You don't have to worry about me, Zoe. I can take care of myself." He ran a hand down over her backside.

She stretched upward, looped her arms around his neck, and sank into him, aligning her body to his. His instant response made her heart accelerate.

"Zoe—" His husky whisper sounded like a groan.

She turned her lips to his, parted, eager, and tasted his response. Passion fired between them like wildfire, hot and intense.

Hawk's hands ran under her blouse and caressed her back, molding her closer. "Appointment," he murmured when they broke for breath.

"Screw it." She dragged his mouth back to hers needing his kisses, his touch, his body inside hers.

Cupping her buttocks, he hiked her upward and she wrapped her legs around his waist. The hard thrust of his erection rubbed against her intimately with each step he took and she squirmed against it.

"Oh God, baby—" Hawk fell across the bed with her beneath him. His fingers clumsy with eagerness, he jerked her blouse up, peeled her bra upward, and his mouth hot and wet latched onto her nipple.

She cupped his head, holding him against her, then slid her hands down across his shoulders, her fingers kneading the muscles there as pleasure spiraled inside her, making her ache for more. She wanted him inside her, his weight pressing down on her, his muscles taut as their bodies worked toward completion together.

Zoe wiggled downward. She unbuckled his belt and unfastened his pants. Her palms cupped the curve of his buttocks as she shoved his pants and boxer briefs down. His erection sprang free and her fingers closed around him, pumped up and down once-twice.

"Zoe—" Hawk panted her name and pulled away to pull her pants down. She jerked one leg free and he came back to her, driving inside her with one quick thrust then rocked, pushing inside her as deep as he could get.

Her body tightened around him and she cried out as she climaxed, the intense sensation racing through her like an electric current leaving her fingers and toes tingling.

When her vision cleared, she caught the flash of his smile as he began moving inside her again in a gentler more leisurely rhythm. The feeling of pleasure began building inside her again. She pulled his shirt up and he wiggled free of it.

She nipped at his shoulder, smoothed the spot with her tongue, then sucked. He shuddered and his movements became rougher as his control slipped. She clung to him, driven by a need to be as close as possible, to feel him alive and safe inside her.

Tracing the straight line of his spine with her fingertips, his muscles flexed beneath her palms. She acknowledged his strength and his vulnerability and held him, opening her body, her heart to him. She pressed a feverish kiss to his collarbone and the furious beat of his pulse beat against her lips.

"Zoe—" Hawk's deep voice sounded a hoarse plea as the heavy torrent of his release throbbed deep inside her. It set off another quick, sweet sweep of sensation, less intense, yet no less satisfying. It echoed through her for long, slow moments.

She cupped the back of his head as he rested his head in the bend of her neck, his breath hot and moist on her skin.

"Jesus! I forgot to use a condom again," he said raising his head to look down at her.

She couldn't lay the responsibility on him. "It was my fault. I shouldn't have been so—impatient."

Hawk's frown dissolved and he shook his head. "You know you drive me crazy, too." He caressed her cheek. "If something comes of this, Zoe, you know you can depend on me to do the right thing."

She studied his expression, so serious, so direct. Would she want him to do the right thing because she'd gotten pregnant? Would that be enough? No way!

"We'll need to be more careful from now on. I'd prefer to have a choice, if, why, or when I get married. If you're talking financial support and weekend visits—"

Hawk kissed her, hard. "I grew up without a dad and my kids aren't going through that." He withdrew from her and sat up.

His sudden withdrawal leaving her bereft, Zoe worked her bra back in place and tugged her shirt down. He pulled his boxer briefs and pants up his calves and she eyed his tight muscular buttocks as he stood and pulled his clothing all the way up. She marveled at the beauty of his body even as her thoughts ran in a totally different direction.

Being a SEAL, he couldn't control a bomb dropping out of the sky or sniper getting in a lucky shot. Didn't he see that? "Are you saying that you're giving up the military should you become a father?"

Hawk went completely still, his gaze fastened on her bare legs first one, then the other.

Zoe froze, her stomach plummeting.

Don't look at them. The words were a shout in her head, but her tongue lay paralyzed. Time seemed to stop. The sound of her own breathing filled her ears. The stark emptiness of his expression caught and squeezed her heart.

Feelings of being naked and vulnerable crashed over her, and she jerked to a seated position and swung her legs off the bed. Her pants and panties, still wrapped around her foot, lay twisted on the floor. A hard, cold knot of panic gripped her throat as she yanked them free and tried to get them separated and turned right side out. Her hands shook and didn't want to work.

"Zoe—stop."

Hawk tried to grab her hands, but she pulled away. She had to get the pants on. She had to cover up.

"God damn it!" He twisted them from her grasp and threw them across the room. "Look at me." He dropped to his knees in front of her.

She didn't want to see his look of shock and revulsion. She didn't want to look at him, and know every connection they had made was over. He turned her and cupping her face looked into her eyes. She read shock and pain in his expression, but thank God, no sickness.

"Zoe—" His throat worked as he swallowed, and he dropped his hands to her hips. He dragged her off the bed to straddle his lap, her knees bent on either side of him. His arms tightened and he held her close. For long moments, he rested his forehead against her shoulder. His fingers cupped her buttocks, holding her as he drew several long, slow breaths, but the tension just kept building in his body, his shoulders growing taut.

She ran her hands up his back and he drew back to look into her face. "It doesn't change the way I feel about you, Zoe. Not one damn bit. They're just scars. They don't change who you are. You got that?"

Quick tears blurred her vision and she nodded, though afraid to believe he truly meant it. But the pain of not believing left her barely able to breathe.

His cheeks grew flushed, and a cold, hard rage built in his expression darkening his eyes to slate and sharpening his features. "Tell me that the son-of-a-bitch who did this spent some time in jail. Tell me he was beaten and tortured every day he was there."

"He's dead," she managed, her voice finally working.

"Good. I'm glad." His hard, level tone was almost scarier than his expression.

Realizing how deep his anger ran, Zoe touched his cheek in a tentative caress.

Hawk's gaze focused on her, and the intensity of his expression eased. He smoothed back a strand of hair from her chin. "I'm sorry. I didn't mean to go Alpha on you. It's just—I can see what was supposed to be." He ran his hand down her thigh. "What should have been. And to know he took that from you-and there's nothing I can do about it."

"It happened a long time ago." The frustration she read in his face eased the tight band of emotion constricting her lungs. "At the time I was too young and too focused on just learning to walk again to realize how much this would affect my life later."

"Don't let him and that asshole in college have that much power over you, baby. They're not worth it. Break free of all that and concentrate on who you are now, Zo." His fingers slid over the side of her damaged leg, bent along his thigh. "Am I hurting you holding you like this?"

Break free. If only she could. If only she had the courage to do so. She shook her head, even though the position pulled at her calf muscle. "But I might need some help getting up."

"Not yet, okay?" He rested his forehead against her shoulder again.

Zoe stroked the nape of his neck and eventually the angry tension drained from him. When his large hands ran up beneath her shirt molding her closer she caught her breath.

"I know you want to go to the hospital, but do you suppose we could take an hour or so before we go?" Hawk asked as he nibbled her earlobe. His hands cupped her buttocks again.

Her heart and her breathing stuttered. She sucked in air as the familiar tempting heat began to build inside her. "An hour would be good."

He drew back to look at her and a teasing smile laced with tenderness spread his lips. "It might take a little longer. I'll want to take my time, now that I can see you."

Tears threatened again, but she blinked them back. "Are you sure?"

He kissed her, his lips and tongue tempting and insistent. "Doesn't it feel as though I'm sure?"

His arousal, hard and ready, pressed against her, and her uncertainty melted away. "Yeah—it feels just right."

CHAPTER 17

Hawk leaned back against the car and folded his arms. He glanced toward the public restroom where Zoe had gone to change into her swimsuit. A man hauling a cooler trudged past, his beach bag laden wife following close behind, holding the hands of two little girls.

The woman paused to lift one of the children onto her hip, then grabbed the other child's hand and moved on.

The little girl reminded him of Katie Beth and he smiled. How had Zoe, with her leg injury, gotten along hauling Katie Beth like that? With the rapport she had with her niece, he'd lay odds she'd done it often. Even imagining her lifting the added weight of a toddler made him anxious. Why was he even thinking about this stuff?

He jerked his thoughts away from the question and glanced at his watch. The run-by at the hospital had made them a little late, but they were okay, he'd built in some crunch time.

How would Zoe react to other people seeing her leg? She'd been quiet on the way here and he'd read tension in her face, though she'd tried to shake it off. He had watched her mentally bracing herself in the car even before he'd pulled into the parking lot.

Closing his eyes, he rolled his neck to loosen the taut muscles there and tilted his face to the sun. She could do this. She was stronger than she thought. Besides it would do her good to check out Mission Beach and soak up some sun. They both needed a break from the hospital.

The injury, much worse than he had expected, had left the lower half of her leg looking fragile and thin, smaller than the other. But it wasn't nearly as unsightly as she imagined. Rectangular shaped skin grafts covered the injury like a patchwork quilt. The similarly shaped scars on her buttocks and thighs, where they had harvested tissue, were only a little lighter than the rest of her skin.

Every time he looked at her leg his stomach went hollow with pain. He wanted to punch something. Preferably the man responsible for every minute of suffering she'd had to experience. But the bastard was out of reach. Frustration brought a knot to his stomach.

He pushed it away as he heard the distinct cadence of Zoe's walk. He kept his eyes closed preparing himself for his first glimpse of her in a bathing suit. She'd be beautiful, scars and all.

"Hello, sailor, want to go for a boat ride?" Her voice held a husky note that had him smiling, though he could detect a slight nervous shake in her tone.

He opened his eyes and focused on her flushed face first before sliding his gaze downward. The bathing suit top, covered with hot pink flowers, cupped the generous swell of her breasts and dipped between. Her skin looked smooth as cream and a physical response to the sight raced downward instantly. "Hooyah—"

She laughed at his murmured response. "I'm so glad you're a breast man."

As his gaze dipped lower over the slender indention of her belly and the graceful swell of her hips, his arousal intensified. The sheer wrap-around skirt that matched the suit hung low on her hips covering her bad leg, but showing the other. "I think I must be an anything, anytime, anywhere man where you're concerned, sweetheart." He caught her around the waist and brought her close so she could feel it for herself. His lips skimmed her brow.

Zoe's cheeks colored and her eyes darkened. "That could get us arrested," she teased.

His hand ran down her back to the edge of her suit bottom. "It might be worth it." A smile tugged at his lips. "But then you'd miss the parasailing adventure I've booked for us, and I want you to experience it, Zoe." He hit the mechanism on his car keys to open the Saturn's trunk and put in her clothes.

****

As they walked down the block to the beach, Zoe focused on Hawk's response to the bathing suit to try and offset the tension building inside her. The look on his face as he had run his eyes down her body had gone a long way in doing just that. It was going to be all right. She had to get over being so self-conscious of her injury. If she hoped to continue seeing Hawk, she had to participate in some of the things he enjoyed doing. She would get through this, and it would be a great experience. She really wanted to do this.

"Have you decided whether or not you want to go up alone or with me?" Hawk asked.

"I think I want to do it alone."

"All right." He caught her hand in his. "It's much safer than jumping out of a plane."

"I think I'd enjoy that too, but I wasn't certain about the landing part." She studied his features.

"I'm glad you opted for this instead. The thought of you bailing out of a plane—" He shook his head. "I have to do things in my job that I don't want to watch you do."

His admission thrilled her, because it implied that he cared about her, but it also hinted at the danger in which he willingly put himself. "Why do you do what you do, Adam Yazzie?"

He turned his head to look at her. "Because I'm good at it." His fingers tightened over hers. "And at the end of the day, I know I've made a difference, even if no one else knows it."

"And because you like the excitement of it?"

He smiled. "Sometimes. Then there are times when it's hot and boring and a pain in the ass." He guided her around a family of five making their way away from the park, carrying coolers, beach bags, and toys. The smell of sun, sea, and suntan lotion lingered on them like the aroma of simmering spices.

"Brett said he liked it because there were always new challenges being thrown at you, and you had to think fast on your feet."

"Yeah, there's that too. I love the training and the focus and the sense of purpose."

"Does it make you happy?"

"I've had moments of pleasure and satisfaction and moments of excitement. And the adrenaline rushes that go along with it all, too."

She knew he was avoiding using the word danger. The adrenaline rushes would go along with risking his life.

They came out of the shaded side street onto the boardwalk and Zoe was hit by light and colors, sounds and smells, as the beach opened up before them. The cluster of colorful umbrellas, that dotted the horizon, looked like exotic mushrooms sprouting from the pale, yellow ochre sand.

A baby, about eighteen months old, her face framed by blond ringlets, shoveled the dry powdery stuff into a pail. A woman sat next to her watching her every move. A large man, his belly already turning red from too much sun, lay sleeping on a quilt.

A group of boys whipped by on roller blades, dressed in t-shirts and loosely hanging shorts. The smell of grilling meat hung in the air.

Hawk paused by a streetlight attached to a concrete divider separating the beach from the long strip of stores and restaurants. He reached into his back pocket and pulled out a tube of sun block. "I don't want to see you get burnt. Out on the water, you catch more rays than you're aware you're getting." A grin spread slowly across his lips. "I'll do you, if you'll do me."

Zoe fought the urge to roll her eyes. "That ranks right up there with that cheesy line you used on me the second time we met."

"What was that?" he asked, handing over the tube of sun block when she reached for it.

"Uncle Sam trusts me. Don't you think you can, too?"

"Well, it worked for the guy in the movie." He tugged his t-shirt off.

"Women don't want lines. They want to know you're truly interested in them."

He sat down on the railing, and his pale gray gaze settled on her with such intensity a dropping sensation struck her stomach. He drew her between his widespread feet. "I'm very interested in you, Zoe Weaver."

The look in his eyes sent an arrow of arousal zooming straight between her legs. "Thanks, I'm interested in you, too." She squirted out a thin stream of sun block, and rubbing her hands together to coat her fingers, spread it over his wide shoulders and down his chest. He felt so warm and alive. Zoe wanted nothing more than to capture this moment and hold it still so she could absorb every nuance.

The way he looked against the backdrop of an azure blue sky brushed with wisps of clouds, how dark his hair looked while his pale gray eyes appeared so startlingly light, and how he smelled of sun block, soap, and him, warm and musky. He turned so she could do his back.

She had touched him while making love, but it was different doing so in public. It was a possessive gesture for everyone to see.

Was he aware of that? Did he want that?

Was this all something physical that would burn itself out? Or would he begin to pity her and that would eat away at it until it ended?

His knee was only a few weeks from healing completely and he would go back on the active duty list. After that, he could be called back in at any time. Knowing that affected every experience she had with him. It was as though every moment she was with him, she was saying good-bye. Would she be strong enough to accept it when it really happened?

He turned to face her and squirted sun block out in his palm. "Turn around, Zoe."

She did as he asked and reached up to hold her ponytail out of the way. She had never been so aware of a man's touch as he rubbed the sunscreen over her shoulders and down her back. The texture of his hands was slightly rough, callused, their pressure gentle.

"I want to ask you something, but I don't want you to take it the wrong way."

His tone, so subdued, sent anxiety slicing through her and she turned to look over her shoulder at him. "All right."

"The injuries, other than your leg, there are no long term effects are there? I mean, down the road—"

The question, so unexpected both gave her hope and made her wary. "No. The rest of me is fine. And as long as I do my stretching exercises, I'll be able to walk."

The tension in his expression relaxed and he smiled. His fingers brushed back a long strand from her shoulder. "Your hair has gotten lighter in the sun since you got to California."

"Yes, I know." He touched her nose gently with the tip of his finger and spread sun block over the bridge. She smiled at him. For a moment his eyes settled on her lips with a heated look wiping away her tension.

He caught her hand. "Let's get something to drink and wander down the boardwalk for a few minutes. We have time."

They people-watched as they walked down the concrete strip running the length of Mission Beach. Teenage girls and boys basked in the sun, or played Frisbee, families clustered together on blankets and towels.

She had never seen so many voluptuous women and muscular young men all greased up and worshiping the sun. The air, sun-soaked and moist, caressed her bare skin. No one turned to stare or point and she began to relax.

"It's not nearly as tough as you were expecting, is it?" he asked.

Zoe shook her head. "No."

She fell silent for a moment. "Has there been anyone you wanted to settle down with?" she asked, her tone hesitant.

"I was tempted once. I couldn't be there for her like I should have been and she broke it off."

A dropping sensation struck Zoe's stomach. There had been someone special. She caught her breath against the rush of jealousy that made her face burn. Who was this woman?

Her voice came out husky and soft. "I'm sorry."

He was silent for a moment. "It's hard for a woman to stick it out alone. She's met someone else now and moved on." He turned to look at her. "I couldn't really blame her. We weren't engaged, but we'd been talking about living together, then my unit got called up. It gets lonely and it takes a special woman who can stay faithful and who can carry the weight while we're gone."

"Like Trish and my mother."

"Yeah." He nodded

"She has her job and the kids. It helps when you have family around. You stay focused on what's important."

Hawk glanced at her. "Sometimes I forget you're a Marine Corps brat."

"It's been a while since I was one, but the memories are still there." Some good. Some bad. Being with him these weeks had dulled the sharpness of the bad ones, and the pain. It was clearer to her now why her mother had hung in there and kept things together while her father was overseas.

She looked up as a group of boys rollerbladed past them.

Hawk caught her against his side as one teenager wheeled close with only inches to spare.

"We'd better head back," he said.

While they waited for the crew to show, Zoe eyed the powerboat from which they were going to parasail. The thirty-one foot vessel looked sleek and fast. "Have you ever wanted to own a boat?"

"Yeah, but they take some upkeep, and I pretty much spend most of my time working on the house. Maybe once I get the remodeling job finished—"

She looked down the dock and anxiety dropped into her stomach like a lead weight. Dressed in bathing suits and t-shirts, Derrick Armstrong and Marjorie walked down the dock toward them.

Something in her expression must have alerted Hawk, for he turned to follow her line of sight.

He gave her hand a squeeze. "Maybe they've just come to see us off."

After his talk with Derrick the other day, she doubted it.

Hawk focused on the other man his gaze narrow and intent. His expression sent a shiver up her spine.

CHAPTER 18

"I called two days ago and arranged for us to go out with you guys," Derrick said with a grin as he and Marjorie joined them.

"That's great," Zoe said.

Hearing the strain in her voice, Hawk gave her hand a squeeze. He wasn't going to allow Derrick Armstrong to spoil their day together. If he said one thing about Zoe's leg, he'd find himself backstroking back to the beach.

"How's it going, Derrick? Did you get the car up and running?" he asked.

"Yeah. I had to have a new battery. The old one wouldn't hold a charge."

Marjorie commented on Zoe's bathing suit and while the women talked, Hawk took the opportunity to ask, "What about the other problem we spoke about? Have you had time to check into things there?"

Derrick's jaw tensed. "Yeah, I'm taking care of things."

"Good, I'm glad to hear it." If he saw one hint he'd left another bruise on Marjorie, he was calling the MPs.

"Marjorie's wearing her bathing suit. You can check her out."

Marjorie turned to say something to Derrick, and upon seeing his sullen expression, her smile died and her features took on a tight anxious look.

Hawk's stomach tightened. He'd give Derrick time to decompress before they left them. That way he wouldn't have an excuse for taking his anger at Hawk out on her later. Damn, this balancing act was the pits. He could only imagine what Marjorie had been going through.

"We're here to shake off some stress and have a good time. No worries today, ladies," Hawk said, his tone light. "What do you say after our adventure on sea and air, we look for a good restaurant on land and pig out?"

"What do you think, Derrick?" Marjorie asked.

Derrick smiled, seeming to put his anger aside. "Sure, sounds like a plan to me."

The boat crew arrived, and after a brief introduction the three men did a safety check of the vessel, and handed out life jackets. Hawk guided Zoe to a seat on a wooden bench close by. Derrick and Marjorie sat down next to them.

One of the crewmembers approached, his hair streaked white by the sun. He flipped a baseball hat onto his head and adjusted his sunglasses. "We're waiting for a couple and their twelve-year-old. They called and said they'd be a few minutes late. If it's all right with you four, we'd like to give them ten minutes."

"Sure, we're not in any hurry," Hawk said.

"Thanks. As soon as they get here, we'll do a small run through of how everything works, and get underway." He wandered back to the boat.

"How's your brother?" Marjorie asked Zoe. The woman shoved her sunglasses further up her nose and tucked a long strand of brown hair behind her ear. Her windbreaker covered her modest one-piece bathing suit as well as her arms preventing Hawk from seeing how the bruise on her wrist was healing, or if she had any new ones.

"Brett is doing well. His vitals and brain activity are normal." The brevity of Zoe's answer had Hawk eyeing her.

If Derrick was the man responsible for Brett's condition, and he found out they were trying to revive him with drugs, would he try something more to prevent it? Did Brett know something about one of his teammates that could threaten one of them or his career? The questions just kept circling in his thoughts with no answers. Damn it, why wouldn't Cutter wake up?

"Has Lang got anything off the tape from the hospital?" Derrick asked.

Hawk said, "We're supposed to go over to his house tomorrow and view the images he's managed to freeze frame and enhance from the tape. There are none of the face, but we might be able to figure out who the attacker is by body type and movement."

Derrick nodded. "Sounds like a plan. If there's anything I can do, let me know."

Hawk studied the man. Would he offer that if he were guilty? Or would he do so just to mislead them? Could they be suspicious of Derrick because of his anger management problems, and ignoring someone else who could be the real threat? Anxiety sliced through him at the thought.

They couldn't guard Brett twenty-four hours a day. The nurses were still on alert. He'd be all right. And Derrick was here with them.

Tension tightened the muscles in Zoe's body resting against his, and he looked down at her. He read worry and guilt in her expression. "You're supposed to be relaxing today," he murmured softly. "Brett will be fine, and he wouldn't begrudge you one afternoon of pleasure, Zoe."

Her smile was a little forced, but she nodded.

Marjorie touched her arm briefly. "He'll wake up soon, Zoe."

Zoe smiled at her. "I hope so. How are you doing?"

"I'm fine, been busy at work. I have to go to San Francisco in a few days on a business trip. I'm hoping Derrick can get leave to join me. It's just overnight, but San Francisco is really interesting, and I think it would be fun."

How Marjorie could continue to try and build a relationship with someone who had physically abused her was beyond Hawk's understanding. Where was her family when all this was going down? Why weren't they trying to intercede?

"San Francisco sounds great." Zoe said. "I've heard it's a beautiful city."

"Before you go home, you and Hawk need to make a trip there. It really is a special place," Marjorie said, her tone enthusiastic.

"As soon as Brett's back on the road to recovery, maybe we will," Hawk said. "There are some fantastic restaurants there."

"Have you thought about relocating here, Zoe?" Derrick asked.

The pounding of running feet shook the dock and echoed across the water and back. Both the noise and the late couple's arrival delayed her reply.

Hawk studied her face. Would she want to relocate? Their relationship was so new they hadn't even begun to consider that possibility. They'd just been so into each other, physically, and discovering each other in other ways, they hadn't discussed anything serious. Did Zoe see him as someone she wanted to settle down with?

Every time his job came up, anxiety crept into her expression, her body language. After losing her father, and Brett being injured, he understood why. But could she love him despite what he did for a living? Did he want her to? Could he stick it out with her? What if something were to happen to her while he was "in the real world"? His stomach knotted.

The boat crew motioned them forward for a quick demonstration of how the parachute and harness worked and the safety procedures, and then they boarded the boat. Hawk kept his hand on her hip to steady her against the sway of the deck and guided her forward to a seat at the bow. Derrick and Marjorie followed with the other couple and the young girl.

A crewmember shoved off, and the captain turned the boat into the bay. They idled past several large multi-million dollar houses, their back yards facing the water. A pelican, perched atop a private dock piling, stretched with a ruffle and flap of feathers that only hinted at the length and breadth of his wingspan. He opened his beak as though suppressing a yawn.

Zoe laughed and pointed to him. "There's the life. Hanging out in the sun all day, all the fish you can eat, and your only responsibilities are taking naps and impressing the lady pelicans in the neighborhood."

Hawk smiled at the comment. "How do you know it's a male?"

"He has that macho "come over to my post, baby," look in his eyes."

Hawk laughed.

On a jutting finger of land, two sea lions barked a greeting as they passed. The animals dove into the water, their brownish-gray bodies shiny, slick, and limber as they streaked through the liquid.

"It seems the wild life is coming out just for you today. It's rare for them to come this far into the bay," Hawk said.

"What are those bushes growing close to the water?"

"They're sea grapes," Marjorie answered. "Their leaves are usually light green but they've turned dark purplish-red because we've had a recent frost."

"Marjorie knows all about plants," Derrick said. "She's been planting some flowers around the front of the house."

Hawk heard pride in Derrick's voice when he spoke about Marjorie. How could the man care for her and hurt her?

Hawk spread Zoe's windbreaker over her shoulders and she turned to look up at him. "We're getting ready to pick up speed. You might get a little chilly." A smile spread her lips and brought quick heat to his skin. He helped her don the jacket over-top the life preserver and slipped an arm around her pulling her against his side. She leaned into him.

The boat's nose rose as its speed increased and they headed through the channel. To the right, Mission Beach came into sight. Palms etched a distinctive silhouette against the horizon, their frilly green tops in frivolous opposition to the long straight buildings that stretched in a parallel strip behind the beach.

Turning to Hawk, Zoe raised her voice above the wind. "It really is a beautiful place."

"Yeah, it is. Just wait until you get up in the air."

"I've changed my mind. I want you to go up with me."

He studied her face. "All right. You're not afraid, are you?"

She shook her head. "I just want to share it with you."

He smiled and tightened his arm around her.

The beach grew distant and the boat slowed as it neared a buoy. The metal float bobbed and weaved in the vessel's wake. Perched atop the device, sea lions clung to it as though they were riding a carnival ride, and ignored the humans looking at them.

"They're so used to people they don't pay much attention to us, unless of course you're stupid enough to try and pet or catch one," Derrick said. "You'd get bitten for sure."

The boat headed further out to sea.

"Who wants to go first?" A crewman said from behind them.

"We will," Derrick said, raising a hand. He grasped Marjorie's arm and the couple moved aft.

"Have fun," Zoe said.

Zoe swiveled around to watch and laid an elbow on the back of the seat. Hawk turned as well. One at a time, Marjorie then Derrick stepped up on the slightly raised flight deck and were secured into a seat harness that clipped them to the parachute side by side. The two-toned blue and white chute already filling with air billowed behind the boat. As the vessel moved forward, a winch fed the rope out, and the couple rose slowly into the sky.

Hawk cradled her back against his chest. "This really is easier than jumping out of the belly of a plane," he said against her ear and fought the urge to nuzzle the tender spot beneath that he knew made her shiver.

She rested her hands on his arms. "Have you ever had trouble getting your chute to deploy?" she asked.

If he told her the truth, she'd freak out for certain. She might leave him...she might never give him a chance.

"No. If there's trouble with the main chute, there's a back up."

Even with the danger involved, what he did was as much a part of him as *who* he was,, he couldn't change that. If she couldn't accept his being a SEAL, he'd have to break it off. He'd have no choice. An ache settled just beneath his breastbone.

Maybe he should break things off now and save them both from heartache. Before either one of them got in any deeper. He studied her profile. He couldn't do it. He couldn't give up on her. Zoe wasn't a quitter. He had to believe that. Even if he was setting himself up for a harder fall than a three thousand foot parachute jump.

Her shoulders grew taut, the tension in her body mounting. She turned to look up at him and started to say something then changed her mind. After a pause she asked, "You're really careful aren't you?"

The desperation he read in her face gripped him by the throat. "Yeah. We're trained to be very, very careful and to stay calm during emergencies."

She nodded and rested her head in the hollow of his shoulder. Hawk's lips brushed her temple with a sigh of relief.

They had dodged a bullet, for now at least.

****

The low level whine of the winch being activated drew Zoe's attention to the back of the boat. She watched as Derrick and Marjorie were slowly reeled back in. The vessel came to a stop.

"Your turn," Derrick said as he joined them at the front of the boat.

"You're going to love it, Zoe," Marjorie enthused. "You can see all the way to Mexico from up there."

Zoe's legs were shaky, not from fear or excitement about the flight, but the sudden serious tension between her and Hawk. There had been a moment when she had wanted to say, "Why do you have to be a SEAL? Why do you have to do a dangerous job?" Something in his face had strangled the words. If she said them, if she challenged what he was, it would be over.

The military wasn't just a job. It was a way of life. It was a calling, like being a minister or a Peace Corps worker. It had to be, otherwise, why do the job? To ask him to give it up would be like asking him to stop breathing.

She got to her feet and shed her sandals and the wrap around skirt that matched her bathing suit. "Could you hold on to this for me, Marjorie?"

"Sure." Marjorie's eyes settled on her thigh where a rectangular scar, pale and shiny, defaced the top of her leg.

As Zoe walked forward, she imagined every eye on the boat homed in on her left calf. She avoided looking at the other passengers. It didn't matter what they thought. As long as Hawk could look at her and still want her, nothing else was important. His grasp on her hand never faltered as he followed her aft to the flight deck.

The young blond crewman offered her a hand up onto the platform. "Hold onto my shoulder while I help you with the harness," he instructed. "All you have to do is sit and enjoy. The parachute will do all the work." He clipped the harness to the rigging. A crewman stood behind them controlling the chute as the wind pulled and tugged on it. Hawk braced his feet as the man strapped his harness and secured it to the tandem bar. The boat started forward.

At the blonde crewman's nod, the other released his hold on the rigging. The chute, already filled with air, shot upward lifting them from the deck. The wind whipped about them as they rose. The ocean stretched away into the horizon disappearing into a bluish-white haze. Hawk's hand covered hers on the rigging and she turned her head to look at him.

He shouted above the wind. "You kick ass, baby." His grin projected equal parts amusement and pleasure. "You just strutted your stuff like a model and every guy on the boat was looking at your perfect backside."

"No they weren't."

"Yes, they were. I didn't know whether to be jealous or proud."

Zoe burst out laughing. "Only you could come up with something like that. You are shining me on, Lieutenant."

"I'm not. They weren't looking at your leg, they were checking you out."

"Great. Now I'll be worried about everyone looking at my behind."

"That's what guys do, Zoe. I checked it out the first time you walked away from me, and every time since."

She grinned and shook her head.

The sound of the wind grew the higher they floated, making talking impossible. The buoyancy of flying free intensified.

On the right, Mission Bay circled around, a maze of cerulean water. Red and white buildings on the boardwalk became a miniature shopping village. The roller coaster at Belmont Park looked like a toy as the cars rose then whipped around the tracks. San Diego stretched outward to the southeast beyond it.

Down the coast Ocean Beach and Point Loma, lightly textured strips of green and yellow-brown, stretched against the bluish-gray water. A distant pier shot like a compass needle pointing out to sea. Along the sand crusted coastline, white foam frosted the waves like powdered sugar.

Hawk pointed downward and Zoe looked below. A pod of dolphin streaked through the water then bobbed to the surface in staggered synchronization. Their strength and speed in the water was impressive even from so high up.

The look of interest on his face as he watched them brought a smile to her lips. Tenderness swelled inside her. This passion, this emotion he inspired, filled the emptiness inside her in a way she'd never experienced before.

Hawk pointed toward the city indicating several places of interest. Zoe was as much aware of his every look and gesture as she was the scenery. They were together, yet separate, and totally in communion with one another without words.

When the chute started being towed in from below, she sighed.

Back to the real world. Back to the hospital and her brother who still hadn't woken up. Back to Derrick and Marjorie and the special tension their association with them created.

Back to this tug of war that never stopped between her feelings for Hawk and what he did.

She was in love with Adam "Hawk" Yazzie.

But if he asked her to commit herself, she didn't know if she could live with this feeling of constant dread, in order to be with him. But could she live without him?

She had to make a choice.

CHAPTER 19

Hawk studied the shelves of books, CDs, and DVDs on either side of the TV. There was no rhyme or reason to their arrangement. A collection of framed drawings, obviously done by the children, set atop the shelf in an arrangement. It was the normal clutter of family that his house lacked. And it was part of what made the Marks house so welcoming. The place, enjoyed by the whole team, was a kind of hub where they all met, probably more often than Trish would like.

"This is what I've got, Hawk," Lang said as he hunched over the computer keys. With a click of the mouse, he enlarged the image of a man dressed in hospital scrubs on the computer screen. He then pushed a button on a signal splicer to project the image onto the large forty-eight inch television screen.

"He has a badge on his pocket but it's turned to one side, and I can't get the name. I've tried every angle in several images. Even if I could, it could be one already attached to the scrubs before he put them on."

"What about the face?" Hawk asked.

Lang changed the image on the screen. "He has his head down, and the camera only picked up his hat. He's carrying a basket just like every other lab tech."

Damn it, he wanted to know if one of his men was involved, yet dreaded it. Zoe laid a hand on his back in support, and he glanced in her direction.

"What about the body type?"

"Nothing stands out. He's about six feet. Could be any one of the guys. There's not enough of his hair showing to identify him."

Lang rolled back from the computer desk and looked up at him. "There ought to be a schedule for blood work being done. Has security checked it out?"

"Yeah, but there was some mix up as to who drew blood that day because one of the techs had a family emergency and had to leave. And they're not certain who filled in for her."

"Shit," Lang swore then glanced up at Zoe. "Sorry."

"I've heard the word before. Even said it a time or two myself, Langley," she said with a smile and a shrug.

"The initials of the tech should be on the samples. They have to date them and keep a record," he said.

"The dates are there but they're entered under the original lab techs ID." Hawk raked his hands over his close-cropped hair.

"It sounds like someone's going to get an ass chewing when they find out who really drew the blood."

"Possibly." Hawk rubbed a hand over his jaw. "But it doesn't shed any light on who hit Cutter. Have you thought of any moments of friction between Cutter and any other member of the team?"

Lang shook his head. "No."

"All right.

Hawk glanced in Zoe's direction. She wasn't going to like it, but he had to talk to Doc and try and rule him out once and for all. And he'd have to do it alone. He turned his attention back to Langley. "I have a few more things I have to check out today. Maybe that will clear everything up."

"I'm here if you need anything else."

Hawk nodded and slapped him on the shoulder.

"What's next?" Zoe asked as they left the Marks' house.

"I'm going to drop you by the hospital then go over to Doc's apartment. I need to talk to him."

Zoe's brows drew together in a frown and her expression grew anxious. "I understand why you have to go, but promise me you'll call me as soon as you get there, and as soon as you're finished."

He looped an arm around her waist. "You got it."

"You'll be careful?" She sounded more like she was trying to convince herself than ask a question.

Was she finally accepting that he could take care of himself? He hoped so. "Always, Zoe."

She tucked a long strand of hazelnut hair behind her ear. She looked younger with her hair down, more vulnerable. He tugged her close and kissed her. The kiss, and her response, built from softly comforting to passionate in only seconds.

"Are you trying to distract me, Lieutenant?" she asked, her tone breathless, her hands moving restlessly up and down his back.

He rubbed his cheek against hers. "Yeah, is it working?"

"A little."

"A little." He raised his brows. "I must be losing my touch." He gave her a gentle squeeze. "After I'm through talking to Doc, and you spend some time with Brett, we'll see exactly how distracting I can be."

A smile curved her lips but anxiety was still reflected in her eyes.

"It's going to be all right, Zoe."

She straightened her shoulders. "Doc doesn't strike me as the type to turn on a buddy. I mean—he swims around in the pool with the Marks' kids like he's one of them. I just can't picture him doing anything to hurt Brett, or you."

"I can't either, but something is going on with him." He guided her down the sidewalk again.

Zoe grabbed his arm stopping him. "And you know this how?"

"I called Bowie and asked if he'd heard from him. He said he talked to him nearly every day, but that Doc was sticking close to home. Something's wrong. I'm going over to find out what it is."

"I think you need to. If he's having some kind of health issues, you may need to get him to see a doctor. And if it's something Bowie's keeping close to his chest, and didn't feel comfortable sharing with you, Doc will have to tell you himself."

"My thoughts exactly."

****

Standing in front of the hospital, worry gripped Zoe's stomach like a clenched fist as she watched Hawk's car disappear around the corner. *Please keep him safe,* she breathed heavenward, then limped toward the main entrance of the hospital. Once through the glass doors, she withdrew her visitor's pass from her pocket and showed it to the guard, then moved on to the elevators.

On the way up, she watched the numbers change on the panel and braced herself before seeing Brett. Now he had a feeding tube to insure he had enough nutrition. Just seeing that tube going into his nose made her flinch each time. The day they'd put it in, she'd realized they were losing ground, and no matter how hard she'd fought to hold onto it, a little of her hope had bled away.

Pain welled inside her and she leaned against the elevator wall fighting back the tears as despair threatened to overwhelm her. How much longer would they continue to care for Brett here? How much more time would they give him to wake up?

When the doors opened before her, she forced herself to step out. She didn't want to be here. She didn't want her brother to be here. If only she could take him home.

Angela waved from the nurse's station. Zoe forced a smile to her lips and returned the gesture. As she continued down the hall her steps slowed then came to a stop just outside the door. It was so hard to face this day after day. With every day that passed, it got harder and harder to believe he would get better. Fear ate at her hope like acid.

Why wouldn't he wake up? How could his EEG's be normal when he wouldn't open his eyes? It had been a month, what was he waiting for? Why couldn't he find his way back to them? The ache the questions left in their wake was almost unbearable.

He didn't give up on you, she reminded herself. *Yeah, but at least I tried.* God damn it, why wouldn't he try?

Zoe shoved open the door with enough force it hit the wall. She froze. A man dressed in blue scrubs stabbed a needle into the I.V. running into Brett's arm and pushed the plunger.

Fear catapulted through her. Her calf burned in protest as she broke into a staggering run. "What are you doing?

Who are you?" she demanded. "What did you just give my brother?"

The man jerked the needle up narrowly averting stabbing her. He raised his eyebrows in surprise as he braced a hand against her shoulder holding her off. "I'm Ensign Earnest Cramer, R.N. I've been transferred from the second floor."

"It's alright, Zoe," Angela spoke from the door. "Ensign Cramer *is* who he says he is."

Relief as intense as the fear shot through Zoe's system. Tears burned her eyes. Suddenly light headed, she bent at the waist to steady herself and grasped the railing on the bed.

"Geez—Zo—Keep it down would you. What are you yelling about?"

She jerked. The sound of Brett's voice weak but distinct stole her breath.

He raised a shaky hand to rub the stubble on his jaw, his fingers following the feeding tube running into his nose before his hand collapsed onto his chest. "I feel like shit."

"Brett—" She shoved past the male nurse. "Oh God, Brett—" She leaned over the rail and looked into her brother's pale blue eyes. He focused on her face with a confused frown. Beard stubble dusted his jaw and his upper lip, and his eyes looked swollen as though he'd slept really hard, but she read recognition in his gaze as he looked at her. He'd never looked more wonderful to her. Tears of joy blurred her vision as she embraced him. "Thank, God. Thank, God." A sob clogged her throat cutting her words to a whisper. "I'm so glad you're back."

****

Hawk frowned at the collection of newspapers heaped on the apartment stoop. Maybe Doc had gone on leave for a few days. He turned to look for his jeep in the parking lot. It sat parked in front of the apartment, the SEAL trident symbol on the front license plate making it easy to recognize.

Hawk knocked on the door and waited. After the fourth attempt went without an answer, he reached for the knob. It turned easily and a twinge of concern had him pushing the door open.

He took in the scattered newspapers, and magazines, the empty beer cans and pizza boxes. The living room with its long leather sofa and two recliners wasn't usually inspection neat, but he had never seen it look as though a hand grenade had been tossed into it.

He took a step inside the apartment. "Yo, Doc," he called out.

"Just a minute," a voice came from down the hall straight ahead.

Hawk drew a relieved breath. For a minute—

"Hey." Doc appeared from the passageway. He was dressed in warm-ups and a t-shirt. The front of the shirt was stained wet with sweat and he was breathing hard. A heavy beard darkened his jaw and his eyes were red rimmed and blood shot."

Hawk stared at him for a second before he could get his thoughts together. "Am I interrupting something, man?"

"Naw, I was just working out in the back bedroom on my machine and didn't hear you knock. Come on in."

Hawk stepped further into the room.

Doc grabbed a stack of newspapers off the couch clearing a space for him. "I've been busy and not here much. Been working out a lot."

Hawk looked more closely at him. He did appear to be bulking up. That added layer of muscle looked in total opposition to the rest of his appearance. "Looks like you had a party last night. How come you didn't invite Zoe and me?"

"Naw, I just haven't cleaned up much. Can I get you something to drink?"

Hawk raised a hand in a negative gesture. "I'm good. We haven't seen you around and I was out, thought I'd come by."

"How's Cutter?" Doc asked.

"He's still the same."

Doc nodded. His expression became wooden and his throat worked as he swallowed.

Hawk leaned forward, rested his elbows on his knees, and laced his hands. "What's going on, Doc? You look like hell."

The man frowned as though in pain then wiped a hand over his face. "I got dumped as soon as I got back from Iraq."

Hawk drew a deep breath as relief eased the tightness of his shoulders and back. Thank God it wasn't drugs.

"I got hooked on this girl, Patricia, before we left the states. Bowie was still hound dogging, but I was keeping things exclusive with her. Had been for about six months. I really thought we had something special going. We emailed and wrote each other the whole time I was gone." He shook his head. "As soon as I got back, she broke it off." He leaned forward to rest his head in his hands then rubbed his fingers through his hair making the auburn strands stand out in all directions.

"I've been there myself, Doc, I know how it is." Hawk looked around the room. Depression could do a lot of things—but this looked like more. "I know it isn't easy. But you have to pull it together and put it behind you, man."

He couldn't believe he was saying those words. They were so damned meaningless. They were supposed to be the toughest of the tough, the ultimate warriors. But, damn it was hard not to be able to find someone who understood that they were people first, and just as vulnerable as everyone else.

He could save lives, protect those weaker than himself, lay his life down in the defense of his country. But he couldn't ask a woman to share his life when he wasn't there half the time. And he couldn't be there for her when she needed him. It was too much to expect.

Doc leaned back in the chair, his green eyes looked old and tired. "It was a hard tour, with Cutter and everything, then getting dumped right after sort of threw me."

"I know that feeling." He caught his breath.

Doc smiled, but the gesture looked forced. "I talked to Bowie this morning. He's mourning the fact that you stole his girl right out from under his nose."

"His girl, huh?"

"Yeah, he thinks Zoe's something special."

Hawk smiled. "Yeah, she is."

"Actually, all the guys seem pretty crazy about her. You mess up with her and you'd better watch your back."

Hawk waved a hand. "All right, enough already."

Doc smiled again, this time with a little more sincere amusement. "It'll be interesting to see what her mom says when she gets back from Kentucky. You do know that state is in the *Bible Belt?* They don't take too kindly to men bopping their daughters without some kind of proposal first."

Hawk chuckled, though a niggling feeling of panic caught at his throat. He suppressed the urge to swallow. "I've heard that somewhere. I've already locked up all the firearms, just in case." Clara was going to be royally pissed, no matter how Zoe tried to shrug it off. He dreaded the confrontation.

"Yeah, this coming from the guy who warned all of us about what kind of girl she is." Doc's smile dimmed, and he turned serious again. "Don't screw it up, Hawk. And if you're going to do the right thing—then do it quick, so she won't feel like you care less for her than you do the job."

Had that been what had caused Doc's break up? He didn't want to ask and poke at a wound already raw.

Doc's suggestion suddenly hit him right between the eyes. Did he care more about being a SEAL than he did for Zoe? He rubbed the back of his neck. Did she think that? Was it just worry he read in her face every time he mentioned his job? Or something else? He understood her reservations, but they were only going to be together while she remained in California. Weren't they? The niggling feeling of uncertainty in his gut raised his heart rate.

He dragged his attention back to Doc. "Why don't you get dressed and come to the hospital with me? Afterwards we'll grill out and have a beer and you can visit with Zoe and me. We can even call and invite some of the other guys over."

Doc hesitated then nodded. "I've been to the hospital, but only a couple of times. It's tough looking at one of our buds, knowing it could be one of us laying there."

"Yeah, it is."

Doc clenched his fist on the arm of his chair. "God damn, Cutter. What was he thinking? That sorry SOB—"

Shocked, Hawk frowned at the sudden explosion of raw anger. His cell phone went off, and he swore at the intrusion. When he looked at the screen a dropping sensation hit his stomach. It wasn't Zoe's cell, it was the hospital. He flipped the phone open and held it to his ear. His smile spread and spread until he knew he was grinning like a fool. By the time he closed it he had to swallow several times before he could speak.

"Let's go ask him. Cutter just woke up."

CHAPTER 20

Just listening to Brett's voice as he spoke to Hawk and Doc had Zoe's throat closing together. Her emotions seesawed between joy and fear.

The feeding tube remained in place, just in case. But Brett seemed completely fine. Though he was weak, he could move his arms and legs. His memory for people and faces appeared unaffected. He didn't recall what had happened that had put him in the hospital, but his recollection of the days preceding the accident seemed to be intact.

"Have you called your mom, Zoe?" Doc asked as they stood together next to Brett's bed.

"Yes. I held the phone so Brett could talk to her." She swallowed against the knot of reaction that rose in her throat. "She's going to come out on the first available flight, but has to go back to my sister's for a few more weeks."

Doc looked haggard, his eyes bloodshot. "Are you all right?" she asked. "We haven't seen you since the night you guys finished the sheetrock in Hawk's rec room."

"Yeah, I'm fine. Now that Cutter's awake maybe the team can get back in sync. We've been out of rhythm without him and Hawk. How did the parasailing thing go?"

"It was great."

"Good, I'm glad you enjoyed it. Looks as though you're getting a tan and your hair's sun streaked."

Zoe nodded. "We've been grilling out a lot, and I catch a few rays while Hawk's burning whatever meat we're having."

Doc laughed.

"I heard that remark," Hawk said from where he stood at Cutter's bedside. "You're not going to let me live that down are you?"

"I don't have anything else to razz you about. You do everything else so well."

Brett's gaze traveled from Hawk to her, and she could read the question in his face. Zoe stepped to the bed. She cupped his cheek, and brushed the hollow of his cheek with her thumb. "Mom and I were staying at Hawk's house when Sharon's baby came, and she had to leave and go back to Lexington."

"What about my apartment?" he asked.

"We've been by to check on it and air it out. Hawk thought it would be a bit cramped for me and Mom so he offered us a place to stay."

Brett's attention shifted to Hawk. "Thanks, man."

Hawk laid a hand on his shoulder. "No problem."

"You said you hurt your knee." Brett stopped to rest between sentences. "When are you going back on active duty?"

"Well, actually I start back Monday. The paperwork is piling up, and I'm starting another language class."

Zoe's stomach dropped at the news and she pressed her hand to her midriff. She knew it was coming. She just hadn't expected it so quickly.

Hawk continued, "I can't do any running until the doc signs off on me, but I've already been doing some light weight lifting. Instead of running, I'm doing the exercise bike to see how my knee stands up. Another two weeks and I should be back to normal."

"Good, I'm glad," Cutter said. "No one's told me what happened."

Hawk and Doc looked at one another.

"There's time to talk about it later, Cutter," Hawk said.

Angela, Brett's nurse, came into the room. "I know you're all excited about Ensign Weaver being awake, but you don't want to tire him too much. You need to give him some time to rest. You can come back for visiting hours at seven."

Reluctantly Zoe nodded and moved to the bed to embrace Brett.

If he went to sleep again, would he be able to wake up? What if as soon as they had weaned him from the medication, he just dropped off and never awoke again?

"I'm afraid to leave him," Zoe said, as they stepped out in the hall. Hawk reached for her, and she buried her face against his chest. The harder she tried not to cry, the faster the tears streamed down her face to wet his t-shirt. All the stress and grief she'd suppressed for weeks seemed to rise up inside her. Hawk guided her down the hall away from Brett's door to the nurse's station. She'd never needed his comfort and support as much as she did right now.

Moments passed before she regained control. When she finally drew back, Doc offered her some tissue and an awkward pat on the back.

Angela exited Brett's room and started toward them. She looked at Zoe and came directly to her. "He's going to be fine. He's even flirting with me, already."

"He won't go back to sleep and—"

"We're keeping him on the meds for a while to be certain, but the chances are very, very slim. Whatever injury his brain sustained, it's obviously healed itself. His EEG's look good. His blood work is normal. You've already heard what the doctor said when he did his neurological exam. We're going to do another CAT Scan and a few other tests, and we'll have the results tomorrow."

They couldn't ask for any more than that. Everything else was up to Brett.

"Come back at seven after you've had a chance to regroup. You need that as much as he does."

Zoe nodded and wiped her eyes then dragged a smile to her lips. "Thank you, Angela."

The woman grasped her forearm and gave it a squeeze. "I'll keep a close eye on him, and I'll call you if I think he needs you."

Zoe drew a bracing breath, feeling a little calmer. "All right."

****

Hawk closed the car door and put the key in the ignition.

"You guys can drop me back off at the apartment if you want," Doc said from the back seat. "Now that Cutter's awake, you'll have people you'll want to call, and stuff you'll need to do."

Hawk looked over his shoulder at him. "We have to eat first. You can share a meal with us, then I'll run you home."

Doc nodded.

Hawk gave Zoe's hand a reassuring squeeze. Her eyes and nose were red from crying and she still looked a little shaky, but she offered him a smile.

On the way home, he kept a running dialogue with Doc about the best restaurants in San Francisco, and their locations. Marjorie's suggestion of a romantic weekend trip had taken root. He wanted to have the whole thing planned before he sprang it on Zoe as a surprise. Now that Cutter was awake, they'd have no reason not to go.

The house smelled like the spices and cooking tomatoes, Zoe had put in the crock-pot that morning for some kind of pasta dish. Her being here had made the house feel more like a home. Though he had been trying to build one by himself, it still retained a little of the aura of a crash pad for when he was in the states, or doing more training.

"How's the rec room coming?" Doc asked.

"I've put primer on the walls, but I haven't gotten them painted yet."

Zoe turned and grasped Doc's arm, the unexpected movement catching Hawk's attention.

"Did you do something to hurt my brother, Doc?"

The question dropped like a bomb from the blue had Hawk's heart stuttering. She was standing too close if the man decided to go off. Hawk stepped forward and reached for her arm.

Doc's features went still with shock then paled. "No-no I didn't." He shook his head, but there was something resigned in the way he said it. And instead of the instant anger Hawk had expected, he slumped down on the couch and ran a hand over his face. "I didn't hurt him, but I didn't do all I could to save him either. Not like Hawk."

Zoe eased down in one of the chairs as though her legs had given out.

Hawk shook his head. What the man said wasn't exactly right. He was the team's best medic. Though they all knew how to render first aid and give pain meds in a pinch, Doc knew his stuff. "You kept him going until we got to the extraction point, Doc. You bound my knee and kept me going until then, too."

"But I didn't go into the building after him. I knew the damn thing was going to blow at any minute, and I couldn't get my ass moving to go after him. I couldn't even get my mouth to work long enough to tell you he'd gone back in." Doc's eyes were glassy with emotion as he looked up. "All I could think about was my girl and how much I wanted to be home with her. And I froze."

He grasped his head as though in pain. "I just froze." All the guilt and shame the man was feeling was right there on his face. "It was like it was all happening in slow motion. Then suddenly you were going back in and we waited for it to go up with both of you inside. Each second seemed like an hour. Then you were out, running with Cutter thrown over your shoulders and you had barely made it clear when the charges went off."

"You were down and covered in rubble. I still couldn't move. I thought you were both dead. Bowie dragged me over to where you were. When we uncovered you, you both looked like ghosts covered with gray dust. It wasn't until then that I could really move again, I could really even breathe."

"On the way back in the chopper, you gave us both pain meds and started an IV on Cutter, Doc." You did everything you were supposed to do," Hawk said. And he could have killed Cutter then if he'd really wanted him dead. Had they been suspicious for nothing? Was Cutter's injury an accident and no one's fault? If he'd been on his way out, why the hell had he gone back into the building?

"I could have gotten him out before the charges went off, long before you had to go back in for him. I just sat there and stared at my watch as the seconds ticked away. Thirty seconds—a minute—two. I don't know how long." He fisted his hands in his hair and pulled.

Hawk dragged a large ottoman over to sit on in front of him. "How many times have you dragged an injured man to safety, Doc? How many times have you kept one of us up and going, even when we were injured or sick? We're all called on to do extraordinary things."

Doc shook his head and made a chopping motion with his hand. "I'm a SEAL for God's sake. I'm not supposed to freeze up when things get tough. We train so that doesn't happen."

"But we're all human, not supermen. And we all have our fears, the fears that make you hear a hollow ringing in your ears and feel as though you're going to heave. Mine is jumping out of an airplane at three thousand feet. I bet I can guess what yours is."

Doc drew a deep breath, and his features began to relax by degrees.

Hawk leaned forward to rest his elbows on his knees. "What would have made Cutter go back into the building knowing the timers were running out?"

Doc clenched his hands on the arms of the chair. "I don't know. The crazy son-of-a-bitch." There was anger and guilt and pain all mixed up in the exclamation, but it sounded as though some of the anguish had leached out of Doc's voice now that he'd talked about it.

"Did you tell Captain Addison when he interviewed you?"

"Yeah, I told him Cutter went back into the building, but I didn't know the reason. And I told him how you went in after him."

"What was Brett's worst fear?" Zoe asked, her voice quiet. She had remained so still, so quiet, the entire time he had been talking to Doc, it drew both their attention.

"I don't know," Doc said.

"I just thought—I don't think my brother had a death wish. And he had to have a strong motivation for going back into the building."

Hawk met her gaze. If Doc's fear kept him out of the building, maybe Brett's had had something to do with his going back in.

Doc leaned back in his chair. He looked exhausted. "Since he doesn't remember that day at all, I don't know how we'll ever know."

"How long's it been since you slept, Doc?" Hawk asked.

"I don't know."

"After we eat maybe you can crash in my room for a while, before I take you home."

"Yeah, all right."

The fact that the man wasn't arguing, pointed out how vulnerable he was right now.

Zoe rose to her feet and offered him a hand. "If you feel up to it, I'd appreciate your taking over the grill. I don't trust Hawk not to burn the beautiful steaks I've had marinating all day."

Doc looked up at her and for a moment Hawk saw his eyes grow glassy as though tears weren't far off. With an effort he shook it off, took Zoe's hand, and got to his feet. "I'll make sure they don't burn."

"Good."

After he had the grill lit, and the steaks on, Hawk put Doc in charge of watching while he came back into the kitchen for a moment of privacy with Zoe.

"He would have no more hurt Brett than you," she said softly as she tore lettuce up in a bowl.

"No." He helped himself to a beer from the fridge. "If he'd really wanted to, he had too good an opportunity to do it before we made it back to the hospital."

"All that guilt because he didn't live up to his idea of what he was supposed to be. You guys carry a heavy weight with that SEAL code of honor."

He didn't know whether to read criticism into the remark or not. "Yeah, I guess we do."

She rested her hands on the table and swallowed as though it were difficult. "Thank you for going into that building and saving my brother's life." Her voice dwindled away toward the end as she struggled to maintain her composure.

Hawk rested an arm around her waist and brushed her temple with his lips. "He'd have done the same for me, Zoe."

She turned and slipped her arms around his waist and held on tight for several moments. She looked up at him. "Wonder if Brett will ever remember?"

"I don't know, baby. We'll have to wait and see."

"Do you think we were suspicious and worried for nothing?"

Hawk wished he could say yes. But that handprint on Brett's cheek still bothered him. It bothered him a lot.

CHAPTER 21

Zoe reached for her mother's hand as she stood beside her in the elevator. "They're going to take the feeding tube out tomorrow. He's complaining about not getting any solid food."

Her mother's eyes grew suspiciously bright. "We're so very fortunate. God has smiled on us, Zoe."

Zoe gave the hand she held a squeeze. "Yes, he has."

The elevator doors opened and Zoe bent to pick up the huge basket at her feet and they stepped out into the hall. Three nurses at the station smiled and called out words of congratulation.

Zoe placed the basket on the counter while her mother continued down the hall. She'd give her a few minutes alone with Brett before she joined them. "I baked some goodies just to celebrate and say thanks for all you've done for my brother. The guys downstairs had to have a few of the brownies, of course."

"If it was Roger Hastings, I'm surprised there's anything left. He looks like a string bean and eats like he's feeding leftovers down a garbage disposal," Valerie Harris, one of the nurses said, as she came over. "I'm so jealous. I could gain five pounds just looking at a picture of these." She shrugged as though saying who cares, and helped herself to a cookie.

Zoe laughed. "I hope you enjoy them." She nodded to Ensign Cramer.

Derrick Armstrong stood next to her mother at Brett's bedside. An electric current of fear raced through Zoe and her eyes went immediately to Brett to check his safety. Seeing Marjorie sitting in one of the few chairs in the room as well, Zoe breathed a sigh of relief. The chances the man would try something with his girlfriend in the room were slim.

"Hey, Sis. Strong Man and Marjorie just stopped by to visit a minute." He was sitting up in bed. The IV was disconnected but they had the feeding tube still in. Except for that small thing, Brett looked normal, as though nothing had ever happened.

"Good." She crossed to the other side of the bed and bent to kiss Brett's cheek. Her mom's eyes and nose were red from crying, but she offered Zoe a smile and turned her attention back to Brett.

Zoe fought hard to control her expression as she approached Derrick and Marjorie. She offered Marjorie a smile and touched her arm, then nodded to Derrick.

"Where's Hawk?" Derrick asked.

"He'll be here in a few minutes. He had to stop downstairs to get some paperwork filled out so he can return to duty Monday."

Derrick nodded and adjusted the hat he had tucked under his arm. Dressed in the blue camouflage working uniform he looked impressive. "I'm on lunch break, I have to get back to base." He turned to Brett and the two looped thumbs and grasped wrists in a handshake. "Glad you're back, man. Gotta go." He nodded to Clara. "Good to meet you, ma'am."

On the way out he brushed Marjorie's lips with a kiss. "See you tonight, babe."

Marjorie's stillness during the kiss, sent alarm jangling through Zoe and she frowned.

Marjorie stood and went to the foot of the bed. "I should be going too." She touched one of Brett's blanket covered feet, the movement tentative. "I'm glad you're better, Brett."

"Me, too. Thanks."

"I'll walk with you to the elevator and give Mom some time to visit with Brett, Marjorie," Zoe said, on impulse.

The woman nodded. "Sure."

"How did the trip to San Francisco go?" Zoe asked as they walked down the hall together.

"It was great. I think Derrick had as good a time as I did."

"Good."

Marjorie's eyes shifted away. "He can be really sweet."

"I'm sure he can, Hawk can make me melt in my shoes."

Marjorie laughed. "I can imagine." Her expression turned serious. "I know that Hawk talked to Derrick. I know you probably said something to him about my arm."

"Yes, I did. I was concerned for you."

Marjorie nodded. "I appreciate it. Derrick's seeing a counselor, and he seems to be really trying. He is doing better with his anger." Her tone wavered between defensive and hopeful.

"I'm glad. I hope he'll stick with it." For Marjorie's sake, Zoe really prayed he would.

"Me too." Marjorie fell silent for a moment then moved restlessly as the elevator doors opened. "I have to go."

The woman seemed so isolated, so alone. Zoe touched her arm. "I'm going to be staying with Brett for a month after he's discharged from the hospital. If you should need to talk, or want to just get out for a little while and go shopping, call me."

"Hawk won't mind?" The woman's eyes searched Zoe's face.

"No, of course not. Why should he?"

Marjorie shrugged. "I thought by now you two might have decided to live together, or something."

They already were. "We've been busy with Brett and a few other emergencies. We haven't really talked about what we're going to do once Brett is released."

Marjorie stepped into the elevator. "Hawk's going to ask you to stay. I know he will."

Her reassurance helped to ease Zoe's niggling feeling of doubt. Since her mother's arrival he'd been—different. She couldn't really put her finger on it. She raised her hand in farewell as the elevator doors closed.

Was Hawk going to ask her to stay with him on some permanent basis? And if he did, what would she say?

The second elevator door opened and the subject of her thoughts stepped out. He smiled, then frowned. "Something wrong?"

"No, I was just saying good-bye to Marjorie. She and Derrick stopped by for a few minutes."

Hawk's arm looped about her waist and she did the same to him.

"She says Derrick's doing better."

"Good. How's your mom?"

"She's a little teary, like I was the first day, but she's doing okay."

She looked up and studied his profile. "Do you think we need to say anything to her about us?"

He frowned. "Like what?"

Anxiety rolled over her like a tank leaving her breathless and weak. That's what was different. He'd backed off since her mother's arrival. He'd grown more careful with the easy gestures of affection she'd become accustomed to. Her voice sounded thin. "That we've grown close, and we want to see where it's going to take us."

"You've been giving it some thought," he said.

"Since the first time we made love. Haven't you?"

"Yeah." He smoothed back a strand of hair from her shoulder. "It might make your mom uncomfortable with me, if you come straight out and tell her we've been sleeping together."

She studied his expression. She tried to swallow but she didn't have enough moisture there to complete the action. She wanted to say talk to me, Hawk, but the words stuck in her throat, and her face felt numb.

She stepped closer to him to avoid a nurse pushing a mobile computer. "They're going to do a more thorough neurological exam later today to see how much brain damage Brett's sustained. I'll have to stay with him for a few weeks after he's discharged."

"He can stay with us at my house."

Zoe stopped. Would he be so quick to offer that if he were thinking of backing off from their relationship? Her heart pounded as though it might come out of her chest. God help her if he was getting cold feet, or tired of her. "We have to talk about this some more, before we bring it up with Mom and Brett."

"Are you worried about what they'll think?" he asked.

"Are you?"

Hawk turned to face her, his gray eyes intent. "No, I'm not. I just know moms are a little protective of their little girls and well—it puts me in the position of having broken my word to look out for you."

Was that all it was? She'd have given her good leg just to feel a little relief. A moment passed before she could catch her breath. She smiled. "You haven't done anything I didn't want you to."

"I think your mom might have a different perspective on that, honey."

The door opened behind them and they looked up. Clara stepped out in the hall. There was a frozen look to her features, and she appeared pale. "Something's wrong with Brett."

****

Dr. Connelly leaned against the adjustable table next to the bed, Brett's chart held in both his hands. "It's called expressive aphasia. It's caused by an injury to the area of the brain that controls verbal communication."

Zoe's stomach grew hollow with fear. Her gaze shifted to her mother. Her features looked wooden with control.

Brett's voice, still weak, held a taut note, "So that's why I feel as though the word is right there on the tip of my tongue, but I can't get it to come."

"That's very common with head injuries," Dr. Connelly said with a nod.

"Mom was showing me pictures and I couldn't remember—"His expression grew tense as he concentrated on getting the right word to come out. "C-Cat—"

"Katie Beth," Clara supplied the name for him.

Brett shot her a frown. "Yeah."

"Who is Katie Beth, Brett?" Dr. Connelly asked.

"My niece."

"You know who she is, but you can't say her name when you look at her picture."

"No, I couldn't get the word to come to my mind."

Dr. Connelly nodded. He looked down at the chart he held. "You don't seem to have trouble identifying the people in this room."

"No."

The doctors gray brows drew together. "Who's the woman standing next to your bed?"

"My mom, Clara."

"And this young lady." Connelly pointed with the chart.

"My sister, Zoe."

"And the fellow next to her?"

"Lieutenant Yazzie, Hawk, my commanding officer."

"You have all these people here supporting you, son. You're not alone in this."

"I'm going to contact the head of our speech pathology here on staff. As soon as we've finished our tests, they can do their own evaluation and get you started."

Brett nodded. "Thank you, sir."

"Your brain has sustained a trauma, Brett. I've already talked to you about the extent of that."

"Yes, sir."

"You're a living miracle. You woke up."

"Yes, sir, I know that."

"It's going to be tough," Connelly continued. "You've done tough before with your SEAL training."

Brett's jaw tightened and Zoe read his fear behind the careful blankness of his expression.

"As long as you go at it with as much determination as you did that, there's a good chance, you'll overcome this."

"I hope so, sir."

Zoe heard doubt in the word *hope* and laid a hand on his shoulder. "You will, Brett."

"We'll have more information in a few days and know better how to progress from there."

As soon as Dr. Connelly left the room, a taut silence followed.

"Guys, I think I'd like some time alone for a little while," Brett said.

Zoe's gaze met her mother's over Brett's head.

"All right, sweetheart." Clara bent to kiss Brett's cheek and his arms went around her.

"Love you, Mom."

"I love you too." Her eyes grew glazed with tears as she straightened, but she quickly blinked them back to offer him a smile. She left the room.

Zoe hugged him hard and met his blue gaze head on. She ran a comforting hand over his fine halo of hair that stuck straight up in the air. He looked so much like he had as a little boy with his hair cut so short. He was still her big brother, but she suddenly realized their roles had reversed. "I know this is a blow, but you'll be fine."

"Sure, Sis."

"Hawk, I need to speak to you privately for a minute," Brett said

"Sure."

****

Hawk approached the bed as soon as the door closed behind Zoe and her mother. He had seen that battle ready expression on Zoe's face so often he only briefly acknowledged it on Brett's features.

"I need you to take some pictures for me," Brett said. "The equipment we use, some of the people we work with. I have to know how wide spread this memory-language thing is."

That sounded like a reasonable suggestion to Hawk. "All right. How bad do you think it is?"

"If you can't remember your own niece's name, it's bad."

Hawk laid a hand on Brett's shoulder. "You knew who she was, you just had trouble with her name. You haven't forgotten her."

"No, but Jesus!" Brett's frustration and panic were plain in his expression, his voice.

"You need to relax, Brett. You've just woken up from a month long sleep. You haven't given yourself time to get acclimated to being awake again. It may just be a temporary thing."

"That isn't what it sounded like to me."

Hawk agreed. But getting worked up over it was going to be counterproductive.

"You know how it is when we get ready to go into action, how we shake off outside stressors. You need to home in, Brett. Focus on getting back on your feet first, then tackle this language—" He hesitated. Beating around the bush wasn't going to help. "problem."

"There wasn't a moment your mother or your sister ever doubted you'd wake up. Zoe's been here every day, talking to you, doing P.T. on you. If you have half as much faith in yourself as those two ladies do, you'll have this thing ironed out in no time."

The anxiety leached out of the man's features after a few moments. "Thanks, Hawk."

"No problem."

"So, are you sleeping with my sister, or what?" Brett asked.

CHAPTER 22

From her position on the back porch, Zoe listened to her mother and Hawk talk as they cleaned up the kitchen after dinner. "I've been doing some physical conditioning to get back up to speed, now that I can run again," he said.

He'd never stopped training, just running. She had grown accustomed to his daily schedule in the last few weeks. Even though he'd had to pamper his knee, he hadn't missed a morning in the rec room lifting weights or of late using the exercise bicycle.

He had more discipline, was more deeply committed to his job, than anyone else she knew. Could he commit himself to her with half as much resolve?

Everything grew quiet. Her mother came out onto the porch. She sat next to Zoe on the glider and sighed as she set it in motion.

"I've missed this," Clara said. "I think you're right, this is the best room in the whole house." She tilted her head back against the top of the glider and closed her eyes. "Are you and Hawk having an affair?"

Zoe's stomach lurched. She wasn't ready for this. She stared out at the large, orange, ball-shaped sun that hung on the horizon before turning to look at her mother. "We've gotten really close. He's been a rock for me, for Brett."

Her mother opened her eyes and looked at her. "And me. You don't have to sing his praises to me, Zoe. I know he's a good man."

"But?" Zoe heard the defensiveness in her own voice.

"No, buts." Clara met her gaze head on. "You're an adult, this is your business. I just want you to be careful."

Careful. It was too late for careful. "How did you do it, Mom? How did you watch Dad leave and not die inside every time? How did you not resent the fact that he wanted the Marine Corps more than he wanted us?"

"That isn't true, Zoe."

The shock in her mother's expression, her voice, had Zoe studying her features.

"Your father never *wanted* to leave us, Zoe. He loved us. He didn't *want* to go." Clara grasped her arm. "That last time—You weren't completely recovered, and he knew we needed him home. But he had a commitment to his men. They were depending on him."

Zoe pushed back that small part of her that urged her to ask, "Why weren't we first?"

"Your father believed in what he was doing, Zoe. I knew when I married him he was a Marine. It was important to him. As important as being a SEAL is to Hawk."

Zoe stopped the glider as she leaned forward to prop her head in her hands. "The team is Hawk's family. He's been in the Navy since graduating college. I think it's taken the place of the real family he didn't have." Who else did he have? Her stomach clenched at the thought. She looked up. "I know it's more than that. He thrives on the camaraderie, the connection he has with his men. He has to protect and serve his country. It's his life."

She sat back and ran restless fingers through her hair dragging it back from her face. Could she share him with his unit? If she stayed with Hawk, she had to find a way to deal with these feelings of abandonment. She couldn't project that resentment onto him. It would eventually destroy their relationship.

Her mother laid a hand on her arm, and Zoe looked up. "Now that Brett is awake, they'll discharge him from the hospital pretty quickly. You said you wanted to stay out here with him, but if you need time to think, you could go back to help Sharon for a few weeks."

An empty ache hollowed Zoe's stomach and squeezed her heart at the idea. How could she ever think she could leave him? God, she loved him so much.

"How many more weeks before Sharon can drive?" she asked.

"Three."

Zoe swallowed. "The doctor's already released Hawk to go back to full duty. A few weeks or months after that his unit could be called up." She closed her eyes against the urge to cry. "I want to spend as much time with him as I can."

Clara nodded. "I understand."

She really did. Zoe read it in her mother's expression, in her eyes. "This is really hard, Mom."

"We don't pick the people we love, Zoe. We just love wherever our heart takes us. I love Hawk too, you know."

"Yeah, I know." Zoe moved to lean her head against her mother's shoulder and Clara grasped her hand tightly in hers.

"You've done hard before. If it came easy, it wouldn't mean as much. Your father and I crammed as much loving into our lives, in the months he was home each year, as most people do in a lifetime, Zoe. I don't have any regrets. I always knew he loved me."

"Is that why there's never been anyone else?" Zoe asked.

"He was a hard act to follow. And I had you, Sharon, and Brett to think about. Brett's so like his father."

Zoe squeezed her mother's hand. "Yes, he is. He'll come back from his head injury and get back to his unit. I know he will."

Clara drew a deep breath. "Sharon's going through a depression because of the hysterectomy. She's going to bounce back, but it's going to take time." She pressed her cheek against Zoe's forehead. "We've all done hard," Clara said. "I just wish we could do easy a little more often."

"Me too, Mom. Me too."

****

Damn, it felt good to be back in action. After only a week he was recovering his stamina and muscle tone. Having finished his reconnaissance, Hawk squatted within the cover of the thick brush, and eyed the block building they were using for the close quarter drill.

The assignment was to surprise the pretend terrorists inside, capture them, and free the pretend hostages without a loss of life. He pondered several possible scenarios. Doc appeared next to him and Hawk signaled a withdrawal. They fell back to the road.

Hawk checked the safety of his nine -millimeter sig, even though it was only loaded with simunition, and holstered it. He removed a scrap of paper from his jacket pocket and sketched a map of the interior of the building. He spread it out on the hood of the armored Humvee and motioned for Strong Man, Doc, Flash, and Bowie to gather close.

"There are six tangos and two hostages. The hostages are being held in the kitchen on the west side. This is the plan."

Doc and Strong Man disappeared into the brush going west. Flash and Bowie followed a few minutes later. Hawk worked his way north, using the clusters of palm as cover. Scoping out the front door, he watched as one of the tangos inside paused before the window to look out, then moved away.

Crawling beneath the brush, Hawk worked his way to the corner of the yard. He removed the field binoculars from around his neck to check the position of the men inside. There were three in the front room but three others he couldn't see. He narrowed his eyes against the reflective glare of the setting sun and clicked his radio, "Three tangos here."

Derrick's voice came over the radio at a whisper. "One in sight here playing guard to the hostages."

"Two in the kitchen," Doc's voice said into his ear.

Hawk clicked his radio once to let them know he understood. Crawling to a spot diagonal to the front windows, he looked one last time, then tucked the binoculars inside his shirt. The coast clear, Hawk leaped to his feet and ran the distance from the brush to the front door.

Hugging the wall next to it, he removed his pack and retrieved the block of C-4 Bowie had given him and the hardware he needed to rig the detonation. Careful to visually measure the amount of explosive he intended to use, he pinched off small squares of the plastique, mashed them into the door hinges. He checked the wireless remote to make certain it was working, then hooked the detonator to the plastique and wired the rest of the circuit.

He eased off the front stoop and bobbed up to look through the window to check the position of the men inside. He meant to blow the door off its hinges, not take out the front of the house or injure anyone inside the room. In a real scenario, he wouldn't be so careful unless hostages were in the room.

Hawk crawled around the edge of the house to the east corner bedroom. Popping up, he checked to make sure the room was empty then stood up. He removed his K-bar and dug at the putty that held one of the windowpanes into the frame. He cut it away then pulled the pane free. Inserting his hand, he unlocked the window and pushed it up.

Muffled voices came through the bedroom door from the front room. He paused, checking to make sure none of the tangos were on their way to check out any sound he had made. Nothing.

He shrugged free of his pack and eased it inside the room to one side of the window, then boosted himself over the edge into the house. Even the rustle of his clothing sounded loud and his every muscle tensed as he waited to see if his entrance had been heard. He clicked his radio, letting the men know he was in position.

A few seconds passed then he heard the distinct reply from each of the other men. They were in position.

Hawk pulled down the protective goggles, flipped the detonator on and pushed the button. A loud "whomp" shook the bedroom door. He dropped the detonator, and jerked the door open and instantaneously shot the first man he saw. A bright yellow spot of soap compound painted the front of the tango's vest. "Down, get down." The three other men in the room hugged the deck. A fourth ran into the room, his weapon drawn and Hawk turned taking him down.

"Clear," Hawk said.

Doc's voice came from the right.

Hawk pushed the protective mask up then stumbled back at the impact as a simunition cartridge skimmed his cheek. His face stung like hell and he gritted his teeth against the pain. His vision obscured by the bright yellow compound, he ripped the safety helmet from his head. His eyes teared up. "Shit."

"All clear, the hostages are secure," Bowie's voice said in his ear.

"Hawk—" Doc appeared at his side and his expression going from amused to concerned in a nanosecond. "Christ! We have to get that shit out of your eyes."

"No, shit." Half blinded by the soap, Hawk allowed Doc to lead him into the kitchen. He hung over the sink and rinsed his face and eyes over and over with water. The burning sensation finally eased but the welt on his cheek had begun to swell and it hurt like a son-of-bitch. Someone handed him a towel and he dried his face and hair with a couple of quick swipes.

"Well, the good news is that you rescued the hostages, Lieutenant." Lieutenant Arnold, team leader of the hostage team, said. "The bad news is you've been shot by one of your own men." There was just enough smug amusement in the other man's voice that it torked Hawk's building anger to near explosion level. He shot Arnold a look that killed the asshole's smile.

He looked up to see his men clustered together in the kitchen, standing watch. He would not air his teams' dirty laundry in front of another unit. He didn't doubt for one minute he was being fucked with.

"The loss of one man is not acceptable, we'll be repeating a similar exercise at 0-eight-thirty tomorrow morning, until we get it right. And we're going down to the shooting range and running practice drills until fifteen hundred today."

Silent, somber, the men filed out the back door of the house. "Will your team be available?" Hawk asked Arnold.

"Yeah." Arnold's jocularity had done a one eighty and his features appeared somber. "Good thing it was a simunition round and not live ammo."

"Yeah. I got lucky." Hawk set aside the towel on the counter.

"We'll be back in the morning."

"We'll be ready," Arnold said.

Hawk nodded. He retrieved his pack from the bedroom and went out the door he'd blown open. His cheek throbbed like a toothache but his anger was worse.

He had just enough time to regain control of his temper before he made it back to the Humvee. Doc and Bowie each straightened from their leaning position against the vehicle as he came into sight. Derrick, resting in the shade of a scraggly elm, got to his feet. Squatting next to him, Flash straightened and turned to face him.

"You don't fucking see me standing here because I'm dead. Dead by the hand of one of my own men." He looked from one man to the other. "Who the fuck shot me?"

"It was me, LT," Flash stepped forward.

A red haze of rage partially obscured Hawk's vision. He lunged toward Flash, and it took every ounce of control he could muster not to beat the man into the ground. He thrust his face close to Flash's and his gaze bore into his. "What the fuck is wrong with you?"

"I tripped over Strong Man's foot and my weapon discharged."

"That's a fucking rookie mistake. A god damn rookie mistake."

Rage burned the back of his throat and had blood rushing to his ears. His cheek pounded as though someone were drilling into his face with a router.

"The next time one of you shoots me, it damn well better be with live ammo and you better kill me, because when I get up, I'm going to rip your fucking head off."

"Get in the Humvee. We're hitting the practice range. And tomorrow we'll be doing the drill again."

****

Zoe pulled into the first available space at the parking structure her thoughts on Hawk and his return to duty with his team. He seemed happier, energized being back to work. She didn't know whether to be happy for him or resentful. She missed having him at the house.

He'd looked dangerous and handsome that morning dressed in desert camouflage pants and a dark t-shirt that hugged his muscular torso. The sunglasses he had donned had hidden his eyes and given him a menacing air. When he'd looked over them at her, she'd nearly melted beneath the heat in his gaze and came closer to doing just that when he'd grabbed her and kissed her good-bye.

The late afternoon sunlight had dimmed to a dusky glow on the horizon as she entered the hospital. Her mother had returned to Lexington and with Hawk at work, the house had seemed empty all afternoon, but it had given her some time to think. She'd filled out the application to work at the hospital. It had felt like a leap off a tall cliff into open space, but she'd done it. She'd drop it off at the office before going upstairs to see Brett.

Since it was closing time at the office, she handed the application off to one of the personnel there and wound her way down the corridor to the emergency bay waiting room to the elevators. She pushed the button next to the doors and caught a glimpse of a serviceman dressed in body armor standing at the entrance to the waiting room. From the back, his wide shoulders and pale blond hair reminded her of Derrick Armstrong.

Thoughts of Marjorie had her stepping away from the bank of elevators and limping to the door. "Derrick?"

At the sound of his name he turned to face her. Standing behind him, Doc and Bowie looked up.

"Hey, guys. What are you doing here?"

The three exchanged looks. "There was a training accident and we brought one of the team in to be checked out," Bowie said. "We're sticking around to give him a ride home once he's released."

Zoe's attention went from one to the other. The way they kept avoiding her gaze had her breath catching in her throat. Her face felt numb. "Is it Hawk?" Her voice sounded as though from far away. "What happened?" If it wasn't serious they wouldn't be here.

Doc grasped her arm above the elbow. "He's okay, Zoe. The goggles protected his eyes."

His eyes. There was something wrong with his eyes. Her ears filled with a horrible ringing and spots swam before her gaze.

"Whoa," Bowie grabbed her upper arm as Doc's grasp tightened. They guided her to a seat. Doc forced her head down. A wave of nausea struck her, and she thought she might throw up.

"He's all right, Zoe. It's just a bruise, and a little eye irritation, but we thought it best to get it checked out just in case," Doc reassured her as he squatted close.

Someone slapped a wet cloth on the back of her neck, which helped. As the nausea passed, she eased up to test her ability to stay upright.

"I'm good to go guys," Hawk's voice came from behind Bowie and Derrick. His tone changed to one of impatience as he said. "My cheekbone's not broken just bruised. Damn paperwork took longer than the exam."

Just the sound of his voice had quick tears stinging her eyes. She pushed herself off the seat and someone's hand beneath her elbow offered her support.

A look of surprise flitted across Hawk's face when he saw her. A purple bruise discolored his cheek and the whites of his eyes looked painfully inflamed. "What are you doing here, Zoe?" His tone held a hint of accusation as his gaze swept the men around her.

"I was just dropping some paperwork off at the office before going up to see Brett," she explained. His tone, his look—he hadn't wanted her to know. She swallowed against the painful knot of emotion lodged in her throat. "I saw Derrick standing in the waiting room and came in to see what was going on."

He tossed his vest to Bowie and his hand curved over her shoulder and he drew her close. Zoe hid her face against his chest as she struggled against the soul pounding relief that raced through her. He smelled of sweat, him, and a foreign smell, like firecrackers. It took her a moment to process that it was gunpowder.

"I'm fine, Zo. It was just an accident." His hand cupped the back of her head.

Unable to speak, she nodded. Dear God, how precious he was to her. She clung to him, the urge to wail her fear and grief almost more than she could control. It was some moments before she trusted herself to step back from him. Her tears left two dark wet spots on his blue t-shirt mid-chest. She looked around for the other men, but they were gone. Hawk's body armor lay on the chair next to them.

"Let's go home. You can call Brett from your cell in the car."

She nodded.

****

Hawk stared at the computer screen. Writing the report for his commander hadn't purged his feelings of betrayal, but stirred them into a fever pitch. Had Flash's shot really been an accident? Or had it been a warning to back off? What the hell had been going on in Iraq before they came home?

Something criminal? Something that would impact a SEAL's career.

Drugs? No way. Treason? Not a chance.

How bad was Flash's gambling problem, and how much did he owe? Hell, *who* did he owe?

Had Derrick been abusing his girlfriend all along? Had Brett known?

Girlfriend. Zoe's expression of fear and shock as she'd stood in the emergency room waiting room had made him aware of how deep her feelings for him ran, and how vulnerable she was because of it. He'd never seen anyone so pale without them being down.

His idea of just keeping things superficial, just keeping them limited to the sex, had imploded the first time they'd made love. He just hadn't realized how completely he had given of himself, and how vulnerable he was because of it, until he'd seen her there. He'd never meant their relationship to cause her pain. But he'd been helpless to shield her from it.

For the first time, the realization that he wanted something permanent with her, wasn't just a thought that ricocheted through his mind to then be tucked away to look at later. The panicky tightness he'd experienced in his chest at Doc's apartment returned with a vengeance.

He wasn't just in love with her. *He loved her.* But if something happened to him, could she deal with it? From her reaction this afternoon, he didn't think so. But short of giving up his career—what could he do about it?

He could end it, and save her from all the dread, worry, and grief. Just the thought hit him with a punch as painful as the simunitions round that had grazed his cheek that afternoon.

Could he really do it? Could he be as selfless as that? He was certain he had never felt like this about any other woman, knew it in his bones. But in order to keep her, he'd have to make a career change. Could he give up being a SEAL?

Everything in him rebelled against the thought.

The guys in his company had been his family for so long. The men standing next to him were the one constant, the one thing he could depend on.

Until now.

What if his career continued to stall because of this situation? What would he do then?

It wouldn't. He'd see to it. Because without the team what would he have? And he'd been alone, except for them, since his mother had died. Five years now.

The guilt he kept carefully tucked away reared up, nearly choking him. He hadn't been there for her, anymore than he could be for Zoe if they went wheels up.

A tap sounded on the bedroom door behind him. He grasped at his composure and said, "Come in."

Zoe stood at the door, her hand on the jamb, and balanced on her good leg as she rested the foot of her damaged one atop the other. Her color had returned but she looked tired. Were they going to fight about what had happened? The phone rang down the hall and she sighed. "I'll get that, it's probably, Mom."

Hawk drew a deep breath. He had a few moments reprieve, a few slim moments to think things through.

When Zoe returned, he tried to behave as though he was immersed in what was on the computer screen.

"Are you too busy to talk?" she asked.

"No, I'm not too busy." He pushed the chair away from the computer, a sense of resignation weighting that feeling further.

Zoe leaned back against the edge of the desk. She reached for his hand. "You're sure you're all right?"

"Yeah, I'm fine." His fingers brushed the swollen area just beneath his eye. "Just a little sore. The drops they gave me have almost cleared my eyes."

She slid off the desk edge and perched on his thigh to rest against him. She rubbed her soft cheek against his and brushed her lips along his jaw.

With just that small caress he wanted her so much it tangled his insides into knots. "About today—"

She pressed her fingers against his lips and drew back to look him in the face. "Not yet, Adam. I just want to be close to you for a few minutes first. I wish things could be simple for us."

Hawk kissed her, smothering the rest of what she had to say. He just didn't want to hear it. Not yet. Instead of talking about all the reasons they shouldn't be together, he wanted to feel all the reasons why they should. His mouth clung to hers until he teased her tongue into play.

In the touch of her hands, the heated taste of her mouth, there was an eagerness in her response that bordered on desperation.

"Zoe." He urged her to her feet. He drew her close and ran his fingertips up and down her back in gentle brushing caresses. "I never wanted to cause you pain," he said softly.

He could feel the tension in her body as she struggled not to cry. She hid her face against his shoulder. "I know."

"It's always a possibility. We have to train hard. We sweat now so we don't bleed later. I've sworn to protect my country with my life, if I have to, Zoe."

"I know. But it wasn't the enemy who shot you today."

"It wasn't a real bullet. It was a simunition round packed with a soap compound."

"Does it matter that it wasn't a real bullet? *You were shot*. Who shot you?"

"I can't tell you that. It was a training accident and the only person I'm allowed to discuss it with is my commander."

She drew back as though he'd slapped her. "What did you do, sign a nondisclosure contract the moment you donned your uniform this morning?"

Guilt gave him a hard pinch at her look of betrayal. "Something like that. It's just the way it is."

"Why is it you put the Navy ahead of everything and everyone? It isn't your family."

Veronica had said much the same thing. She'd screamed at him that when he'd joined the Navy he'd married an institution, instead of a living, breathing woman. But it had never let him down, not until now. He closed off the thought.

If Zoe was this upset over a bit of secrecy, how would she feel when they went wheels up to places unknown? When he couldn't even contact her because they were under deep cover?

His throat worked as he swallowed. "I think we need to pull back." His chest hurt as he drew a deep breath. "I'm not ready to make a choice between you and the Navy."

"Is that how you see it, Hawk? That I'm asking you to give up your career for me?"

"It's all I've had for a long time, Zoe. It's all I've worked for, for years."

Her hand slashed through the air in sudden anger. "Is this job going to grieve for you when you come home in a body bag? Is it going to support you if you come back with an arm or leg missing? Is it going to give you children, or a real family? Is it going to hold you and offer you comfort when you feel betrayed by your friends."

So she had seen that, too. But he'd seen some things, too. What about her physical condition? What if she got sick and died on him while he was gone? Like his mother had. The guilt had hounded him for years. He couldn't go through that again.

"I can't ask you to stick it out. When we go wheels up and I'm shipped out for six months, a year, longer, you'll be back here in the states and you'll get tired of being alone, waiting on someone who might or might not return. You'll get tired of wondering if I'm hurt or dead. You'll resent my being gone just like you're resenting my not telling you everything right now. And if you got sick or were hurt, I couldn't be here for you and you'd resent that too."

She brushed at a fresh wave of tears that streaked down her face. "Not if you love me."

For a moment, some unseen force squeezed his heart in a tight fist. "I won't say that, Zoe."

She turned away, sparing him from seeing her reaction. But when she faced him again, anger etched a bitter light in her eyes. "What was the whole point then, Adam? Was it to show the poor little crippled girl that someone could fuck her despite the scars?"

He welcomed the anger. It helped him seal off the pain. He reached for her and gave her a shake before he could control the urge. "Stop it."

"I would have never pegged you as an emotional coward. You're ready and willing to lay your body, your life, on the line, but not your heart."

The accusation stung more than he wanted to acknowledge. "You don't know what you're talking about, Zoe."

She threw out a hand in a beseeching gesture. "Then explain it to me."

"I can't let anything distract me from what I have to do. You don't need the added grief of another person you care about being in harm's way. It's as simple as that. I'm trying to spare you that."

She jerked free of his grasp. "You're a little late, Adam. I already love you."

His heart beat as though he'd run a fast sprint across a beach. He bit back the words, "I love you too." If he said them, he'd make her happy—temporarily. But every time he had to leave, every time his job came between them— she'd end up miserable. As miserable as he'd be if something happened to her while he was gone.

"I'm sorry, Zoe."

She shook her head, her expression blank, stunned, and staggered back toward the door.

Hawk took a protective step forward, his hand extended to steady her. She flinched away from his touch and limped out into the hallway. A few minutes later he heard the front door open and close.

He had done what he had to do. He'd done what was right for them both. Hadn't he?

It hurt like hell.

CHAPTER 23

Zoe studied the exterior of the apartment building. The utilitarian architecture was blocky and unattractive, but it served Brett's needs and suited his life style. She climbed the front steps and inserted a key into the locked front door, twisted it, then pulled it open. Her soft soled shoes squeaked on the industrial gray tile as she limped to the elevator in the lobby. Stepping inside, she pushed the button for the third floor.

Her tear ravaged reflection stared back at her from the polished metal door. She bit her lip and looked away. It did no good to cry. What was done, was done. She refused to be one of those weak willed women with no pride, who begged for love.

She couldn't return to Hawk's house. If he didn't love her, wouldn't allow himself to love her, she couldn't stay there anymore. At least she had some place to go.

She should have seen it coming, had seen it coming that day at the hospital, she just hadn't wanted to face it.

The elevator door opened and she stepped out into the hall. The florescent lighting overhead appeared dim as she turned left and walked down to apartment three-fourteen.

Her hand shook and she shoved the key in with more force than necessary. The door swung inward and the hall light fell in a large rectangle on the floor. It touched the shiny surface of a row of picture frames on a bookcase. The pulled drapes blocked the outside streetlight's glow. The living room stretched like a black void before her. She ran her fingers along the wall just inside the door, searching for the light switch.

Fingers grasped her wrist and jerked. A high-pitched yelp tore from her as she stumbled forward. The door slammed shut cutting off the light. She breathed in the distinct smell of latex as a gloved palm cut off her scream. Fear rocketed through her. She kicked and squealed beneath the pressure as a muscular arm held her back against a tall male body.

She clawed at the hand covering her mouth. The words *don't hurt me, don't hurt me* jetted through her mind in a scream. Her feet struck a piece of furniture. She braced them and pushed. The man grunted as he staggered and hit the wall. His hand dislodged for a second.

Before she could draw breath to scream, he shoved her. Zoe hit the back of a waist high chair or couch, the momentum thrusting her over it in a flip. Her cheek skidded across the fabric of the cushions. She threw up an arm to protect her head as she rolled off into the floor. Her weak leg crashed into something wood. Pain shot through the limb, stealing her breath. White spots swam in her vision. The apartment door was jerked open. The florescent bulbs in the hall speared the room with light then the door slammed shut again.

Running feet pounded in the hall, then retreated into silence.

Nausea rolled over her with a force of a tsunami. A cold sweat misted her skin and she retched, one, two, three times. Nothing came up, her stomach too empty to produce anything but dry heaves. Her leg throbbed like an abscessed tooth making every movement agony. She curled into herself and shivered in reaction.

"Please God, don't let it be broken," she moaned as she pushed herself up to a sitting position and leaned back against the chair she had flipped over. She swallowed as a fresh wave of nausea made her stomach pitch.

The door shook as someone pounded on it from outside. "Hello—" A male voice came through the barrier. "Is everything all right in there?" The knob turned and the door swung open as though in slow motion. The hall lights illuminated a dark silhouette in the opening. A man.

Where was *he* when I needed him?

"Please call 911," she said, her voice shaky and weak.

"Jesus Christ!" The light flashed on and she blinked at the familiar face. Bracing a hand on the back of the couch Bowie leaped over it and came to kneel beside her.

****

"God damn it!" Hawk flipped his cell phone shut and tossed it on the couch. Zoe's refusal to answer hers was driving him crazy. It had been hours since she'd left. He needed to know she was all right. Needed in a stomach clenching, head pounding, throat aching bad way. A hollow feeling had settled in his chest that refused to let up. As he slumped on the couch and cradled his head in his hands, he had, for the first time in years, an urge to—no he wasn't going there. Men didn't go there.

His phone rang, and he snatched it. Disappointment punched through his system as he read the number on the screen. "Hello."

"You need to get over here to Scripps Mercy," Bowie said, his tone terse. "Zoe's been checked out, and they're trying to talk her into letting them admit her, but she's determined to leave."

Hawk leapt to his feet, every muscle tensing for action. "What's happened? Is she hurt?"

A beat of silence followed and when Bowie spoke his tone was subdued. "Yeah, she's hurt."

"I'm on my way. Keep talking." Hawk grabbed his keys from the dish in the hall, the phone pressed to his ear. He slammed the door behind him and stalked to the car. His heart beat in his ears so loud he had trouble hearing Bowie as he continued.

"Some asshole broke into Brett's apartment. She walked in on him. He flipped her over a chair, and she hit her leg, the one that's—you know. They've x-rayed it, and it's not broken, but they still want her to stay overnight, just to be sure there's no further damage."

"Did she get a look at the guy?"

"No. He'd pulled all the drapes, and it was a total blackout in the apartment. The cops were there when she left in the ambulance."

"Fuck!" Hawk backed out of the driveway. "Keep her there, I'm on my way."

****

"You need to stay, Zoe," Bowie said.

It was the tenth time he'd said it. Now that the pain in her leg had settled down to a dull throb, Zoe wasn't buying it. She'd had enough of hospitals to last her a lifetime. "I hit my leg, and it's not broken. I'll do fine with the crutches. I'll follow up with the doctor the ER guy recommended, and I'll be fine." Please God let the leg be fine.

She wiggled off the edge of the hospital bed and balanced on one foot while she looped her purse over her head to hang across her body to her hip. The strap hit the fabric burn on her cheek and she flinched. She touched it gingerly, checking the ointment the nurse had applied. "I need to get back and see what's happening at Brett's apartment." She adjusted the crutches beneath her arms.

Bowie frowned. "We're supposed to wait for you to ride down in a wheelchair."

"I'm good to go, and I'm not waiting."

Bowie threw up a hand in supplication. "I'm seeing a new side of you that reminds me of Cutter."

"Is that so surprising?"

He grinned. "No." The smile faded quickly. "Aren't you going to call Hawk, and let him know what's happened?"

She concentrated on putting the paperwork and pain medication the nurse had given her into her purse. "That would be redundant, since you've already done it."

He rested a hand on her shoulder. "Look, I don't know what's gone wrong between you, but he deserved to know you were here."

Zoe drew a deep breath as all the things she could say whipped through her mind. *What happened is he stomped all over my heart. He didn't want my love. He's gone from wanting to let my family know we're a couple, to telling me it was all a mistake.*

"It isn't important to anyone but me, Bowie. I don't intend to put you in the middle. What happened between Hawk and me stays between us." It hurt to draw breath, but her voice sounded only a little—strangled. "Now, I'd appreciate a ride to the apartment, and if that's inconvenient, I can call a cab."

Bowie sighed. "That won't be necessary. I've got it covered."

In her peripheral vision, she saw his hand hovering just within reach of her arm the first few swings she took with the crutches. "I've had years of practice with these. The only thing I don't like to do is go down stairs."

"Good thing they only have elevators here," Bowie said.

"Yeah."

They stood in front of the elevator.

Bowie snagged her arm when the door opened. "Look, Hawk is on his way. Stay just long enough for him to see for himself you're ambulatory."

All the things Hawk had said to her, all the pain he'd dealt her because of it, rose up to give her heart a painful squeeze. Tears blurred her vision. She concentrated on the tile beneath her feet instead. "I can't do that, Bowie. I'm not ready to see him again, yet. Please call him and tell him not to bother coming."

She caught the edge of the elevator door with the end of her crutch before it closed. It slid back open. She propelled herself inside.

Bowie breathed an expletive and stepped inside. "If you want him called, you're going to have to do it yourself."

Then he'd make an unnecessary trip. She wasn't calling him.

When she didn't make a move to get her cell phone from her purse, Bowie swore again. A half dozen people filtered into the conveyance from the next floor keeping him from making any comment.

The doors opened on the lobby level and they waited for the others to exit. "You at least owe him a phone call, Zoe."

"I'm not getting into who owes who. Stay out of it, Bowie."

She swung forward.

They caught another elevator to the parking structure attached to the hospital. "Stay here and I'll get the car," Bowie said. He strode up the paved incline.

Zoe's hands gripped the crutches. The air, moist and cool enveloped her. Standing alone, an exaggerated vulnerability swept over her. The distance between the floor and ceiling appeared to narrow. Her chest constricted, and it grew difficult to breathe. Her good leg struggled to hold her weight. Delayed reaction. Anxiety. That's all it was. She'd be okay.

The doors behind her opened and she bit back a yelp, startled by the sudden sound.

Hawk stepped out of the elevator, along with a man and woman. The couple hustled past and moved up the incline.

Relief drained Zoe's fear away, and for a moment she continued to stare at Hawk. The need to feel his arms around her struck her with such physical longing she began to shake.

Hawk's stare pinned her as his long strides closed the distance between them. As he crowded close, heat radiated from his body. "Come back to the house with me, Zoe."

She turned away from the look of grave concern on his face. Her hands tightened on the crutch handles. "No thanks." She looked up the row of cars to where Bowie had disappeared. Where was he?

"Please, Zoe. Your safety is more important than what's happened between us."

Nothing was more important than what had happened between them. Nothing. Every touch, every look, every word they had shared was everything. That's what he didn't get. "I don't need you to protect me. I can buy locks, and guns for that. I don't need you to provide a roof over my head. I have that covered. The one thing I needed from you, you say you can't give me, so please—just leave."

Hawk rested a hand on her shoulder and she jerked away.

"Zoe—I have to know you're safe," Hawk said in a tone, nearly hoarse with emotion.

Pain and anger gave her the courage to look up at him. "Why would that matter to you? If you go wheels up, and you're seven thousand miles away, will you know if I'm sick, or hurt? Will I know if you are?"

Hawk's expression blanked for a second, then he flinched. "I promised your mom—"

"To hell with that and to hell with you!" Had her hands been free, she'd have slapped him. "And to hell with Bowie for deserting me, just so you'd have time to ambush me." She swung around and clomped her way back to the elevator.

Bowie's breaks squeaked as he pulled up in the car. The elevator door opened before Zoe. She got on and hit the close door button with the heel of her hand.

****

Hawk rubbed a hand over his forehead where a dull ache throbbed just above his eyes. He had never told Zoe about his mother's death. But she couldn't have hit him with anything that hurt worse. He should have been there for his mother during her illness. He should have been with her when she died. He would have been, had he known she was so ill. Why hadn't she sent for him? Because he'd been unreachable. She had died alone. Emotions sliced and diced his insides like a blood-thirsty sushi chef.

Bowie approached him. He pulled his thoughts back to the current situation with an effort. "I'm parked out front of the hospital. She'll catch a cab. I'll follow her to the apartment. Can you give me a quick rundown of what happened?"

"You know Cutter's apartment is next to mine. My date and I had just finished dinner, when we heard a crash from inside there and some strange muffled noises. When the door slammed hard enough to shake the walls, and there was the sound of running in the hallway, so I thought I'd better check it out. That's when I found Zoe. She was down, and hurt. I was afraid to move her. Sheila, my date, called nine-one-one from the hall, and we stayed with her until the police and the ambulance came. Sheila's still at my apartment waiting for me to get back. I asked her to stick around. I asked her to listen in on the cops and see if she could pick up on anything."

So at least this time Bowie had an alibi. Some of the tension eased from Hawk's shoulders. "If you don't mind, I'd like to come up and see what she has to say myself," he said.

"Sure." Bowie searched his face. "Zoe has a mad on that doesn't quit, and a stubborn streak a mile wide. The ER doctor wanted to give her a shot, but she refused it. They gave her some oral pain meds, and she's supposed to follow up with a doctor tomorrow."

Hawk nodded. The adrenaline rush he'd experienced after Bowie's call had passed and his hands shook. He clenched them into fists. "I'll see you back at the apartment building."

Bowie nodded. "I don't suppose she'll give me a pass on trying to give the two of you time to work things out, will she?"

Now that he'd ended things with her, would Bowie try and make his move? And if he did, what right did Hawk have to say anything about it?

The pain he'd read in her expression only moments before made his sudden jealousy seemed petty and foolish. Though it killed him, he said, "She won't stay mad at you, Bowie."

"What about you, LT?"

Hawk shook his head. "I'd better catch up to her. See you back at the apartment complex."

As soon as he was in the elevator on his way downstairs, his thoughts swung back to Zoe. He'd put her in direct danger without knowing it. He'd expected her to come back to the house, not catch a cab to Brett's. He should have known when she didn't answer her phone—

By trying to do the right thing, he'd done the wrong thing? And now it was up to him to make it right.

****

Hawk punched in Zoe's number on his cell one more time, but it went to voice mail and he didn't bother leaving another message. She wasn't going to talk to him.

He hit Langley Marks' number.

"Marks here."

"Lang. Do you remember who packed up Cutter's stuff when we left Iraq?"

"Strong Man and Flash had that detail. Flash and I dropped it at the apartment. The super was going to let him in but, Zoe and her mom were there already, so he left his duffle with them."

Had Zoe unpacked it or her mother? Had there been anything unusual in it? Damn it. If he hadn't chosen just now to try and—

"What's up, Hawk?" Lang's voice in his ear dragged him back to the current situation.

"Someone broke into Cutter's apartment tonight and attacked Zoe."

"Jesus." Lang breathed. "Is she all right?"

"Her leg's been injured. But she's ambulatory. She's gone back to Cutter's apartment and she's alone. Bowie lives next door, and the chances that anything else will happen—" He drew a deep breath. "The short of it is, I fucked up, Lang. In a big way. And Zoe won't let me anywhere near her. Won't even talk to me."

"You broke it off." Lang's voice sounded flat. He swore beneath his breath. "We're going wheels up soon, and you broke it off rather than ride it out."

The accusation and disappointment he heard in Lang's tone punched him with guilt.

"I suppose I should send Trish, but I won't. There might be a slim chance of the fucker coming back. I'll see if I can bring Zoe back here with me. If she'll let me in."

"Thanks, man. I owe you."

"I really thought things would be different this time, Hawk. It isn't any of my business what you do, but—Zoe deserved better than this."

Hawk couldn't think of a thing he could say in his defense. His voice sounded hoarse as he spoke around the knot in his throat. "Will you call me and tell me how she is, let me know where she is?"

Lang fell silent for a moment. "Yeah, sure. Later. I'm going to get her now."

****

Half an hour later, Hawk watched as Langley gave a wave then entered the apartment building. It ate at him that it was Lang who was keeping her safe instead of him. By pushing Zoe away, he'd sent her right into the bastard's path. Zoe hadn't walked into an attempted robbery, as the police believed. It had to be the same guy. What the hell did Cutter have in his apartment the fucker would be searching for? And why had he waited until now?

Because Cutter had regained consciousness.

Hawk pulled out of his parking space and wove in and out of the traffic on his way to the Naval Medical Center in Balboa.

Though Brett didn't remember the last couple of weeks in Iraq, there was a slim possibility that he would eventually. And whatever he had in his possession, they'd have to retrieve before he returned home. It had to be something he'd brought back from Iraq. But he'd been comatose when flown home and his gear brought back with the rest of the men. Who had packed his stuff? Who had unpacked it?

At the hospital, the nurse's station stood deserted as Hawk came out of the elevator on Brett's floor. He strode down the hall. He heard feminine laughter as he approached Brett's room and paused outside the door. He tapped on the wood and pulled the door open. Angela, one of the nurses stood by the bed with an electronic blood pressure cuff. She and Brett both looked up as Hawk stepped into the room.

"Hawk—" Brett began.

"Lieutenant—visiting hours were over long ago," Angela said, a frown marring her smooth brow.

"Brett's sister had an accident this evening. I came to tell him," he said, his tone short.

Brett stiffened and he swung his legs over the bed.

Angela pressed a hand against his shoulder.

Brett shot her an impatient glance. "What's happened? Is she okay?" Brett asked.

"She's on crutches, hopefully just for a while." What if it wasn't just a temporary injury? What if the damage was worse than Bowie had understood it to be? How would he find out how she was if she wouldn't talk to him? How could he have been so stupid?

Brett's jaw tensed. "It's her leg?"

"Yeah." Hawk's gaze swung to Angela. "Could you give us a minute?"

Her gaze moved from Brett to Hawk and back again. "You're still weak from weeks of inactivity, Ensign Weaver. You're doing great in P.T. but you need to take things easy."

"Sure, I hadn't planned on jumping up and doing any calisthenics while you're gone," he said, his tone taut.

Angela frowned and her lips tightened. She gave a nod as she passed Hawk.

Hawk dragged a chair over to the bed and sat down. "I know you're having trouble remembering some things before the mission, but you need to try and remember the last two weeks we were there, Brett."

Brett's brows slammed together over eyes just a fraction less dark than his sister's. "What does that have to do with Zoe being hurt?"

"She was attacked when she went to your apartment. Someone was inside searching the place and she walked in on them."

"What do you mean attacked?"

Hawk fought his rising impatience. "I mean the fucker threw her over the back of a chair and she smashed her leg on a table."

"Jesus!" Brett shook his head then rubbed his temples as though in pain. "God damn mother—" His head came back up. "You said searching, not robbing."

"HQ has been waiting until you were stronger to question you about it. I'm not waiting any longer. Something happened in Iraq, Brett. You weren't taken down by a tango. One of the team bashed your head in and left you to be buried inside the building."

The shock of it seemed to hit Brett broadside and his features went slack. Hawk quashed the quick feelings of sympathy and continued. "I know about Strong man's assault charges and I know about Flash's gambling debts and I believe it's one of them. I need to know what you do about both of them. In short, I need you to get your fucking memory back, and tell me what went down that almost got you killed. Because that something just got Zoe attacked."

Brett drew a deep breath. "My memory is a black hole just before the mission, Hawk."

"What's the last thing you remember?"

"Doing the practice runs to get our timing down."

"What do you remember about Derrick's assault charges?"

"He beat up his girl friend and when the cops showed up they brought charges against him. When she wouldn't testify they dropped the charges. They cut him some slack because he's in the teams and he was getting ready to ship out."

Hawk ran his hand over his hair roughing it up as he beat back the urge to bite his fucking head off. "And you didn't say anything to me."

Brett grimaced. "I had hoped I'd be able to talk to him. I thought I'd convinced him to see someone when we got home."

"But?"

"I can't talk to you about this, Hawk. When someone takes you into their confidence—"

"He may have beat your head in and left you for dead."

"No." Brett shook his head. "Derrick would never do that."

"You knew something that could end his career as a SEAL. What about Flash?"

"I don't know. He and I aren't buddies, we're team mates."

"Who is he close to in the team?"

"I don't know. Maybe Bowie. Bowie's buds with everybody."

"Flash has a gambling problem. Did you know anything about that?"

"Yeah. I knew."

Hawk focused on him and shook his head. What else had his men kept from him?

He shook off the sense of betrayal and continued. "All right. What I want you to do is spend some time thinking about what could have triggered the attack. If you think of anything, call me."

"Yeah. You'll look after Zoe."

Hawk flinched. How was he supposed to do that now? "I'll look after her. You can count on it." He'd find a way.

CHAPTER 24

Just as Zoe lowered the lid on the washer, a knock sounded on the apartment door. She glanced at her watch. It had to be Bowie. He stopped by every day to check on her when he returned home from the base. She adjusted the crutches under her arms and made her way down the hall to the front door.

Had she not already lost her heart to Hawk, she would have certainly lost it to Bowie. She'd been unable to stay perturbed with him for long. His support had eased some of her anxiety. She felt safer with him next door.

A greeting hovered on her lips as she opened the door. It died as Flash's lean form and smiling face came into view.

"Hey," he said. Dressed in a desert camouflage print with his bonnet under his arm, he looked pure SEAL, until he smiled.

"Hello."

"I came by to see Bowie and thought I'd stop by and see how you were doing." He eyed the crutches with a frown. "Bowie told us what happened. How *are* you doing?"

"I'm all right."

At his expectant look past her into the apartment, Zoe eyed him for a moment. Was he the one who had attacked her? Had he slapped her brother? She'd never know if she didn't talk to him. Her breathing quickened and her throat felt tight as though something were pushing against the base of it holding back both her breath and the blood. Without the crutches her legs would have wobbled like rubber. She forced herself to move back. "Would you like to come in?"

"Sure." Flash stepped into the apartment and waited for her to lead the way into the living room.

"How long are you going to be on those?" he asked.

"About two weeks." She set aside the crutches, leaned them against the table next to her within easy reach, and lowered herself into a chair. Her mouth was dry as she continued, her breathing still labored. She had to calm down. "The bone wasn't broken. I have a titanium rod imbedded in it so I'm part bionic woman. But the muscle was bruised, and since I don't have the whole thing, I have to rest it until it's healed."

Flash sat down on the couch, his expression grave. He shaped the bill of his hat with his hands in a gesture of nervous energy. "I heard Cutter was going to be released."

"Yes, on Wednesday."

His smile held a charm she was afraid to believe in.

"That's great." He leaned forward to toss the hat on the coffee table and rested his elbows on his knees. "You haven't had a very good experience here in California. With Cutter being in the hospital the whole time and—everything else."

So he knew about Hawk breaking it off. "I won't hold it against the state. I'll come back again when I can visit just for fun."

"Does that mean you'll be leaving soon?"

"As soon as Brett can drive again, and I'm sure he's on the road to recovery. So, it will be another couple of months at least."

"You've been great about putting your life on hold to come out here and support him."

"Isn't that what families do?"

"Not always. My own—" Flash gave a shrug, and his Boston accent thickened. "That's another story I'll share with you some other time." He slid to the edge of the couch and leaned forward. "You haven't had much time to enjoy anything but the beach that one time and a few barbeques. I came by with an invite. There's been some rumblings that we may be shipping out again."

A dropping sensation hit Zoe's stomach and she placed a hand against her midriff. Had Hawk known this when he pushed her away?

"I thought you were on a six month rotation then had eighteen months off to train."

"In a perfect world, that's the way things would go. But we're not living in a perfect world right now. We won't know until the orders come down twenty-four hours before." He cleared his throat. "While Cutter's surrounded by medical personnel, he'll be taken care of. I wanted to invite you to go to Vegas for a day before he's released. We could fly up or drive either one. Flying might be more comfortable for you."

Zoe tried to shake free of the shocking news of their going wheels up and his invitation. "What if they page you to report for duty?"

"My gear's already packed and I know a guy in Vegas who can fly us back. It'll be my last opportunity to go and yours too, unless Cutter feels up to it later." He shifted. His blue eyes held an earnest expression. "Look, I know you had—have a thing for Hawk. So, it wouldn't be a romantic thing. I know you're not ready for that so soon after—" He cleared his throat. "I just thought it might give you a change of scenery for a day. And everyone needs to go to Vegas at least one time in their lives. There's no other place on earth like it."

"So, I've heard." Why was he doing this? Was it pity? She studied his even features and sun-streaked hair and felt no tug of attraction. Even the affection she held for Bowie wasn't sexual attraction, but just—a liking.

Flash had remained a stranger to her. For all his flirting, and teasing, he kept himself distant. Was it true he had a gambling problem? And would she just be a cover for that, if she went? And why was he inviting her to begin with? A guilty conscience? It would be impossible for her to relax with him. They hadn't had time to cultivate feelings of trust between them. And as long as there was a shadow of suspicion in her mind concerning him, there couldn't be.

"I don't think I can go, Flash. I appreciate your trying to take my mind off of things. It's a generous offer. But I'm still anxious about Brett and don't want to get too far away from the hospital—just in case."

After a brief pause, he nodded. "I understand." He rose to his feet.

Sudden anxiety sliced through her with his six-foot frame towering above her, and Zoe rose from her seat to position the crutches beneath her arms. When all he did was stride down the hall to the door, she breathed a sigh of relief.

He turned to look at her as they reached the door. "Maybe, Hawk will come around. I wouldn't give up just yet."

Trish had spent an hour telling her the same thing, the night she'd spent with them. Langley hadn't stated an opinion one way or another. Had he held any hope Hawk would change his mind about them, surely he'd have said so.

"The thing with his mother a few years back, really tore him up. I'm sure he's carrying around a lot of guilt because of that and with your—" His voice drifted off.

What was he talking about? Was there some reason behind Hawk's pulling back? If there was, she at least deserved to know about it.

"With my leg?" Zoe encouraged.

"Yeah. He'd be worried the same thing might happen while he was gone."

"He told me his mother died of breast cancer."

"Yeah. It was before my time, before I became a member of the team. He was in—the real world—and no one could reach him when she went into the hospital." Flashes pale brows drew together in a frown. "He didn't tell you about this?"

"No."

"I shouldn't have said anything then. I just assumed he'd—"

Zoe caught his arm as he reached for the doorknob. For a moment she struggled to maintain her composure. If there was a chance they could work through what had caused Hawk to draw back, she had to know. "Will you tell me what happened?"

He studied her expression for a moment. His gaze dropped to the leg she held suspended. "He was out of reach and she died alone at the hospital. When he came in from the mission they told him. From what I heard, she was the only close family he had. They gave him hardship leave. Veronica—" He glanced up.

"She's the woman Hawk was going to move in with before his last rotation." Zoe guessed.

"Yeah. She accused him of using his guilt over his mother to get out of their relationship." He shifted as though uncomfortable. "I wouldn't have known any of this, but I saw them fighting in the parking lot before we were shipped out and it was pretty intense, so I asked around." He shrugged. "This time, I really thought he was hooked. I still do."

"Thanks, Flash." Her throat, clogged with emotion, strangled her voice to a whisper. "Thanks for telling me."

"Guess, that knocks me out of the running completely doesn't it," he said with a lopsided grin.

Zoe dragged a smile to her lips. "No one else even had a chance from the first moment we met."

"Ouch!" Flash grabbed his chest. "Don't let me down easy, now."

Zoe smiled with a little less effort. "I thought you'd appreciate my honesty."

"I do." The teasing light in his eyes died, and his expression grew serious. "I'm really sorry things haven't panned out better."

He opened the door and stepped out into the hall. "I'm sorry about the leg too, Zoe."

She searched his expression. Was there a deeper meaning behind the apology than just sympathy? "It'll be fine."

"If you change your mind about the trip, I won't be leaving until tomorrow and there's always a seat available. They want to pack those tables in the casinos."

"Thanks."

She watched him stride down the hall, his heavy boots loud in the hallway. Could he really be that good an actor? Yeah, he could, the Navy had trained him to be.

****

Hawk settled back against the car seat with a sigh. Damn it! Why couldn't he get his butt out of the car and just go knock on her door? Instead of sitting here hoping to catch a glimpse of her.

Because things hadn't changed. He was still going wheels up with his team and he still wouldn't be there for her. But he wanted to be. Badly. He squeezed the steering wheel hard and with a sigh reached for the key in the ignition.

From next door, a bright red sports car shot free of the connected parking structure like a bullet and sped down the street. Flash.

Hawk started the car and pulled out into the flow of traffic. Flash wove through the streets like a stunt car driver in a car chase. Hawk followed him from a cautious distance. When he pulled into the parking lot next to his apartment, Hawk pulled in right behind him.

Flash had exited his car when Hawk pulled in and cut the engine. Flash paused as Hawk got out of the car. "Hey, LT. What's up?"

"I thought you might have time to show me the CD of images you've pulled off the video I gave you from the hospital."

"Sure, come on up."

The apartment looked like a show place for chrome and glass. The modern furnishings looked expensive but dust coated the glass-topped tables and where a flat-screened TV used to hang was an empty spot. A tall entertainment center took over one wall. The shelves that had contained electronic equipment, a DVD burner and recorder, VCR-DVD combo, and an expensive stereo system, stood empty.

"What happened to all your stuff, Flash?"

"I've put everything but my computer in storage, for when we go wheels up. If someone breaks in they won't have anything portable to steal, but the microwave."

Flash led the way into a bedroom converted into an office. His duffle bag with all his equipment sat in one corner already packed. The wide, flat computer screen nearly took up the top of the desk. He popped in a CD and waited for the images to come up. "I got quite a few stills of the top of the guy's head. He knew the cameras were there so he kept his head turned. But I caught a glimpse of his mouth and chin on one slide." He clicked through the images one at a time then paused on one. He looked up at Hawk. "What do you think?"

Hawk studied the curve of the man's jaw and the thin set of his lips. It looked like Derrick Armstrong. A sinking feeling hit the pit of Hawk's stomach and he drew a deep breath. He'd known all along that it had to be one of them, but affirmation dealt a blow that hurt.

Flash leaned back in his seat. "I've been sitting on this. I didn't want to bring it to you, LT. We've been in the same team since BUDs and I didn't want to believe Strong man capable of turning on one of us, but—if it isn't him it looks a lot like him."

Hawk nodded. "Burn me a copy of the images you have. I'll need to turn it in to Captain Jackson."

Flash unscrewed the lid on a canister of blank CD's and popped one into a drive. "I invited Zoe to fly to Vegas with me. I thought she might enjoy checking it out."

A rush of pain caught Hawk unaware and his face grew hot. "When do you plan to go?"

"Tomorrow. They haven't canceled leave yet and I have a buddy who can fly me back if we get called in."

Silence stretched between them. Flash continued to monitor the progress of the disk. Hawk nursed his pain and the sudden flare of resentment. She hadn't wasted any time moving on.

It was his own fault. He'd had his chance and he'd thrown it away.

Flash popped the disk out, labeled it and handed it to him.

"Thanks." Hawk swallowed against the knot in his throat.

As he walked back to the car, he drew deep breaths to contain the pain.

He sat in the car for several minutes, the silence beating at his ears as heavy as his heartbeat. He'd been going through old letters from his mother, trying to get a handle on his guilt. Trying to understand why she hadn't sent for him. Something his mother had written to him played through his thoughts.

Every day we have together is a gift. Every experience we share another gem to cherish. As a son, you've filled my heart with pride and love, always. But I worry that you're waiting to live your life after you've served your country, instead of living it while you're serving it. You've chosen a difficult path, but you don't have to be alone to follow it.

Had she known she was dying even then? Had she been trying to prepare him for it? Saying good-bye? And trying to tell him other things as well?

She had faced his decision to be a SEAL with pride, though he knew she'd worried for his safety, just as Zoe worried.

The jealousy and pain he'd been feeling eased. Zoe loved him, and she didn't take that love lightly. She wouldn't throw herself into someone else's arms hoping to fill his place.

She'd been offering him a gift, a gift that had cost her dearly to give him. She'd known what she was taking on, had seen it first hand with her father, her brother, and still she'd been brave enough to do it.

And he'd shoved it aside. And the words he had spoken to her—He flinched.

He'd been without her for nearly a week. A week of pure hell. At least together they'd see each other, share things. If she'd let him make it up to her. But first, he'd have to get her to talk to him.

Hawk reached for his cell phone, flipped it open, and selected the number. "Hey, Trish. I have a favor to ask."

When he shut the cell phone a moment later, he looked down at the CD he still held. Lang hadn't found an image like Flash had and he'd been all over the footage. He'd compare the footage himself with both CD's before he took everything to Jackson.

A guy who had bashed in his teammates head wouldn't think twice about framing someone for it. He had to know he wasn't helping him do it.

CHAPTER 25

Zoe grabbed the beach bag containing her clothes and scrambled out of the Mustang's bucket seat as fast as her sore leg would allow. She rushed around the car to help Brett out of the vehicle. Her brace made a clicking sound on the concrete driveway, but it allowed her to move more quickly than crutches, despite the discomfort.

Brett waved her off as he shut the car door. "I'm all right, Zo. You don't have to hover."

He looked pale and thin, but just walking from the car to the gate under his own steam brought color to his cheeks. It was such a triumph. His triumph. Zoe fought hard to suppress the urge to grow teary.

"Are you sure you're ready for this?" she asked.

"Yeah. More than ready." He paused with his hand on the privacy fence and drew a deep breath. "God, can you smell that? Grilled food. Manna. I'm telling you if I never have to eat another instant potato it will be too soon. And if I never have to breathe the scent of hospital air again it will be just fine with me, too."

"Ditto," she said with feeling.

He grinned at her, his teeth white, his jaw sharper than it had been a few months before. His gaze traced her features. "You and Mom are unbelievable. She's like Atlas. She's held up the weight of the world and kept right on going. With you, then Dad, then me and Sharon. And you're like her sidekick. Did Atlas have a side-kick?"

"Not that I know of."

"Well, if he had, it would be you."

Zoe smiled. Typical. He was trying to thank her without just coming out with it.

"Do you think, maybe we were born under an unlucky star."

Zoe caught her breath. "No. I don't believe that, and you shouldn't either. I believe in the old adage, *shit happens*. And we're a strong family. We've come through all of it better, stronger people." And somehow she'd survive her break with Hawk in the same manner. He'd given her no other choice.

Brett grinned again and opened the gate. "I'm starving."

"Good. You need to put some meat on your skinny bones, Mr. Q-tip man," she said as she switched the beach bag she carried from one hand to the other.

They stepped into the Marks' yard. A banner that read *Welcome Back Cutter* stretched across the eave of the house. A shout went out and the team converged on Brett with their girlfriends and wives. Zoe slipped around the group and stood to one side.

"Man you are one tough hombre!" Bowie said.

"A walking miracle," Langley added.

"I'd say one lucky mother- " Derrick shot a look Zoe's way and cut off the expletive. "Can't say what I was thinking in mixed company. "I'm damn glad you're back, Cutter." He slapped Brett's back.

Flash clasped his hand and shook it hard. "Glad you're over the hump, Cutter."

Oliver Shaker, stood to one side and stepped forward as soon as Flash moved aside. "Good to see you mobile, man."

Zoe paused to watch the men. Which one of them could have hurt Brett? And how could they shake his hand and wish him well after trying to kill him?

Hawk stepped through the sliding glass doors, a platter of raw hamburgers in his hand. He set the tray aside on a table and walked down the deck. His gray gaze locked on her first, pausing for a painful eternity before moving on to Brett and the group surrounding him.

Longing punched Zoe in the solar plexus with the impact of a medicine ball and she turned aside to hide her reaction. Even as her vision blurred, she repeated a mental mantra over and over, *I will not cry, I will not cry.*

She limped toward the pool where Trish Marks stood keeping an eye on the children in the water. "Hey, is there anything I can do to help?" Zoe asked.

"No, everything's done. How's Brett doing?" Trish asked.

"He's weak, but doing well. The aphasia he's experiencing seems very slight. It's going to take him some time to get back a hundred percent."

"So, they think he'll be able to return to his unit?"

"Yeah. The doctor thinks he's going to be fine." With a lot of work and speech therapy.

"Good. I'll go do my Mother Trish thing after the herd thins."

Trish ran her eyes down the slacks and camp shirt Zoe wore. "It's hotter than Hades out here, tell me you brought your bathing suit."

"Yeah, I did." Anxiety pinched Zoe's stomach. If she was going to show Hawk she was moving on, that would have to be part of it. But she dreaded seeing the other team members' reactions to her scars. The children's response concerned her the most. "You've told the kids about my scars, haven't you? I don't want to frighten them."

Trish placed a hand on her arm. "They know you were in a terrible accident when you were just a little older than they are now. They're curious more than anything. But they may ask questions."

"I don't mind that. In a way it makes things easier when someone does. It takes the elephant out of the room."

Trish's smile was half hearted. "And what about the other one that will be sitting by the pool?"

Zoe resisted the urge to look over her shoulder toward Hawk. "I can take it if he can."

"If it makes any difference, I don't think he's taking it well at all," Trish said.

"Good."

Trish laughed. "Do I hear just a tad of satisfaction?"

"Yeah, you probably do." She didn't want to hurt Hawk, but to deliver him a slap upside the head might make her feel better. Then again, it would probably make her cry, as so many things did lately.

"I think I'll rescue Brett before they drag him into the middle of a volleyball game he's not ready for," Trish said. "Why don't you go change and join the rest of us girls next to the pool while the guys play. I'll get Cutter settled in the shade with a glass of ice tea and something to snack on until the burgers are ready."

"All right. Thanks."

Zoe slipped into the house with her bag and went into the bathroom. She locked the door and removed her clothes and the brace. Nervous nausea cramped her stomach. She drew several deep breaths and slipped on her bathing suit.

As she wrapped the matching skirt around her hips, she looked up at the full- length mirror hung on the door.

This was a mistake. The men would be grossed out and the women would look at her with pity. She looked like a monster. The only one who hadn't looked at her that way, had dumped her. She fought against the wave of tears that burned her eyes. Had he thought her disability would make her too dependent, as she grew older? Did he think he couldn't live with her scars the rest of his life? If that were the case, she didn't want to hear it.

For several moments, she breathed in and out, to regain control. She prayed for the return of the anger that had helped her stay in one piece for the last week.

"Screw it." If he didn't have the balls to stick it out, he didn't deserve her.

Zoe grabbed the doorknob and jerked it open.

Hawk's large shape blocked the door. His t-shirt hugged his well-defined chest, the sleeves banding his arms.

For a long slow moment his gaze raked downward over her breasts, her hips to her feet and back up.

At the look that flickered across his face, heat trailed over her skin, and her nipples peaked beneath her bathing suit bra.

In a blink of an eye, his expression blanked. "We need to talk, Zoe."

She forced herself to meet his gaze. "About?"

"I think I've found out what happened to Cutter, or at least who's responsible. But I need your help to prove it."

Surprise held her frozen. "Who was it?"

Stress lines etched the skin around his mouth and eyes. Zoe ached to touch him.

"We'll talk about that on the way. I need you to go with me to Brett's apartment and see if what he was looking for is still there, or if he found them the night of the break-in and took them."

"I can't leave Brett. He just got out of the hospital."

"Trish has promised to look out for him while we're gone."

This might be the last time she could be with Hawk, talk to him. Only he could fill the emptiness inside her—An almost physical pain struck her. She couldn't let him go without trying one last time to reach out to him. "I'll need to change again."

He nodded. "I'll wait."

She fastened the brace back around her leg, put clothes on over her bathing suit, and stuffed the cover up into her bag. Slinging it over her shoulder, she followed the hallway to the kitchen where Hawk waited for her.

"I told Brett we needed to pick something up and we'd be back in just a few minutes," he said.

She nodded.

When he rested his hand against her back to guide her out the back door, her heart leapt into the same fast rhythm it always did. Would she ever experience that with anyone else?

"I called your mother last night," Hawk said as he fastened his seat belt.

Intent on fastening her own belt, Zoe raised her head in surprise. "What about?"

"I wanted to know which one of you unpacked Brett's stuff and you wouldn't answer my calls."

She looked away as pain constricted her throat. "What did you expect?"

"I didn't expect for it to hurt like this, Zoe."

Her breath caught in her throat and hope leapt inside her like a living thing. Zoe bit her lip to keep it from trembling.

Hawk rubbed his jaw and pressed the heel of his hand against his forehead. "I want what's best for you. You deserve some regular guy who'll be there for you when you need him."

"There's more to a relationship than that." Her voice sounded rusty. "I thought I'd found what I needed, not someone determined to hold himself at an emotional distance. Is that what you did, Hawk?"

"No, I didn't do that. I just thought—." He drew a deep breath. "I kept telling myself the whole time, you'd be going back home after Cutter got better. I convinced myself that we were just having a fling."

"Can you really compartmentalize your life like that?"

"I thought I could. I've always been able to do it before." He reached for the ignition.

Zoe grasped his arm. How could he have held her, made love to her with such tenderness, such intensity, and not be connected emotionally? "I never held anything back from you, Hawk. I tried to when we first met, but—I gave you everything there was in me to give. I thought you did, too. Was I wrong? Were you playing me the whole time?"

"No!" His voice sharp with emotion filled the inside of the car. "I never played you."

The ache she'd carried around for days eased some. "Then why did you push me away?"

He rubbed his palm over the steering wheel. "There are some things I've been carrying around with me for a long time. Some things that have been eating at me. When you do this job, it takes over your life, and the lives of the people you love. It's a job probably better for men who aren't married, who don't have families, because there's so much your loved ones have to sacrifice to it right along with you."

"I knew what I'd be taking on," she said.

"You don't know the half of it, Zo." He raised his head to look at her.

"You never gave me the chance."

Hawk reached for the key, started the car, and pulled out of the driveway.

Zoe turned away to look out the window at the houses on the street as they passed. Her pulsed skipped when Hawk's hand grasped hers, and it was a natural thing for her fingers to close around his.

"When my mother died, I was out of touch, out of the country. She died alone. I wasn't there for her."

The staccato sound of his words, stark, succinct, gave the impression he was ripping a bandage off a wound.

Zoe's fingers tightened around his hand and she grasped his wrist as well. "You couldn't control her cancer any more than she could control the danger you were in. She wouldn't have blamed you for not being there, any more than you would have her."

"I've told myself that—But she was my mother. My mother—" His throat worked as he swallowed.

"I know." She rubbed the taut muscle of his forearm.

"I can't be depended on to be there."

He had said that repeatedly in one way or another ever since she'd known him. How hard would it be for a man used to being there for everyone else, to know he'd failed the one person who meant the most to him? The guilt and pain would be crushing. No wonder he held women at an emotional distance.

But she'd never felt that from him.

She didn't even now.

"Do you want to be there, Adam?"

He glanced at her and his jaw worked. "Yeah, I want to be."

Fresh hope surged up to drain the strength from her limbs. Her heartbeat thundered in her ears. "Then, that's enough."

"Just like that?"

"Yes, just like that."

He fell silent. They pulled into the parking garage next to Brett's apartment and Hawk parked the car.

As they walked to the elevator, once again he reached out and grasped her hand. With an effort, Zoe controlled the need to lean into him. She had to be more certain of what he intended.

Hawk pushed the elevator button.

"You remember when I had the video images enhanced so we could see who was on the tape at the hospital?"

His change of subject drained her optimism and she sighed. "Yes."

"Well, I had the tape transposed to a DVD and gave copies to Flash and Lang. They both worked on them. But Flash found an image Lang didn't. So, I went back over the footage myself. The problem is there's no such image in the footage."

"You're sure?"

The elevator doors opened and they got in. The doors slid shut.

"Yeah. I even took it to Lang and we went over it together."

"So, he created the image himself."

"Yeah." Hawk drew a breath. "I went back to the hospital and got a copy of the footage where Derrick arrived at the hospital. The time he walked through the doors was twelve thirty-five. The time the guy walked out of Brett's room was twelve-forty."

"He couldn't have changed clothes and gotten upstairs to slap Brett."

"No."

Zoe experienced a quick twinge of guilt. She had lain it all at Derrick Armstrong's feet, blamed him for everything because of his treatment of Marjorie.

The elevator doors opened and they stepped off into the hallway. Zoe rummaged in her purse for her keys.

"Then it was Flash who slapped my brother," she said as they entered the apartment. She closed the door behind them.

"I think it was, but the only proof I have is that he created an image to try and frame Strong Man."

"He had no other reason to do it?"

"No. Not that I know of."

Flash had tried to kill Brett in Iraq.

The night the team had set up her bedroom raced through her mind. He had teased her and asked her out for ice cream—How could he do that?

Nausea struck her and she leaned back against the chair she'd flipped over during the attack.

"He betrayed Brett and you—your whole team. He tried to kill my brother." He grabbed me that night and terrified me.

Hawk ran a hand over his eyes, the gesture weary. "I'm a little numb about it now, Zo. I'm sure it will hit me later. But right now—I have to stay focused. I have to finish this before we're called up."

She nodded.

Hawk cleared his throat and swallowed as though it were painful. "Last night when I talked to your mom, she said you both unpacked Brett's gear. She said there were some cylindrical shaped stones stuffed into Brett's socks. She assumed they were just souvenirs. She said she left them with you."

"I think Flash used Brett's gear to smuggle something out of Iraq. There's a lot of looting going on there. I'm not sure what they might be, but there's a market for archaeological treasures on the black market. If they're the real deal, they could be worth a small fortune."

Zoe's lips parted in surprise. "We thought they were just souvenirs. If we'd known what they were—" She shook her head. "The day Flash bought the car, he helped me unload groceries out of Bowie's trunk for the cookout at the Marks. He dropped a small stone object out of his pocket. He said it was his good luck charm."

"What did it look like?"

"Just like the ones we found in Brett's duffle. It was about the size of my thumb, cylindrical in shape, and had a face carved on one side. I took the ones that were in Brett's stuff and put them in a frame for him. It was going to be a housewarming gift from me and mom."

She motioned for Hawk to follow her down the short hallway. Decorated in cream and brown, the small bedroom held a dresser, a chest of drawers, a bed and a nightstand.

She went to the chest and opened one of the drawers to find it a jumble of unpaired socks. She ran her hands under the socks but felt nothing but the lining of the drawer. She pulled open the next drawer, and the next, searching each one. "It's not here. And I know I put it in here."

Hawk opened a dresser drawer and looked through it. She crossed the room to search the drawers on the other end.

"If Flash needs money, why would he buy a car worth sixty thousand dollars?" she asked.

"You missed his news earlier. His car was stolen a few days ago, right after I saw him driving it last."

"But you don't think it was."

"No." He turned to search the dresser drawers. "If he set it up, the insurance will pay off the lien, return the money he paid down and whoever stole the car would pay him what they've settled on between them."

"It's because of his gambling isn't it?"

"I think so. I think he's in over his head and he's desperate. When I went by his apartment last, all his electronic gear, except his computer, was gone. He said he'd put it in storage, but—" He shook his head.

"There's nothing here," Zoe said as she stepped back from the dresser.

"Nothing here, either. God damn it!" He shoved the drawer closed with enough force the dresser moved. He rubbed a hand over his hair making it stick up. "Without the stones, I don't know how we'll prove any of this."

"You could turn it over to NCIS and let them follow the insurance fraud trail. There has to be a trail of some kind."

"Greenback said he and Brett were arguing about something and Flash told him to mind his own business. I think Brett was trying to talk to him about this. That's complete conjecture on my part, but the whole thing fits."

Flash was the one who'd attacked her that night. She flinched away from the thought. "He invited me to go to Vegas with him after the break in. Why would he do that?"

Hawk froze and his gaze searched her face. "A guilty conscience. He probably never expected you to show up here. What were the odds?"

Was that why he had told her about Hawk's mother as well? She looked up to find Hawk watching her.

"You didn't go?" he asked.

"No. Of course not. Brett was waiting for his release from the hospital and they hadn't settled on the exact day. I didn't want to leave him." And she hadn't wanted to leave in case Hawk came to her.

"Was that the only reason?"

Zoe slid one of the drawers more firmly shut. "No, you know it wasn't." Her voice dwindled away.

When he reached for her, she hadn't the will or the desire to resist. For countless moments, Hawk studied her features one-by-one with a look of such raw desire it stole her breath.

"What we have isn't a fling, Zoe."

"No." She couldn't bear it. She had to touch him. She cupped his face in her hands.

His pale gray eyes took on a feverish hue. He pulled her close and buried his face against her throat. "After the way I treated you—I don't deserve another chance."

"You can't keep punishing yourself for what happened with your mother." She breathed in the scent of his skin and smoothed the thick hair at the back of his head. "You taught me how to break free of the past and reach for the things I want. Now it's time you allowed yourself to do the same."

His arms tightened around her almost painfully. "I want you, Zoe."

Emotions coiled tight inside her released.

He pressed his lips to hers, their pressure harsh with need. His arms loosened, and as his tongue found hers, the kiss became, by degrees, more tender. Zoe ran her hands beneath the t-shirt he wore to stroke his back. The thrusting pressure of his arousal pushed against her.

A high-pitched ring tone cut through her desire laden concentration. Breathing hard, Hawk drew back to remove the cell phone hooked to the waistband of his cut offs. He flipped the phone open and identified himself in a brusque tone. The look on his face triggered knots of anxious tension along her shoulders, and her arms tightened.

"What is it?" she asked as soon as he hung up.

"We've been called up. I have to report to duty right away."

****

How did the married members of the teams do this? Five years had dulled the memory of what it was like to walk away from a loved one for him. A week without seeing Zoe had seemed an eternity. How was he supposed to endure six months, or longer?

The other members of his team, including Flash, had already bugged out. Weighted down with gear, Langley strode through the living room and out the front door. Trish and his three children followed close behind. Cutter slapped Hawk's back as he meandered through in their wake and walked outside.

Hawk pressed a house key into Zoe's hand. "Try and convince Cutter to move into the house with you. There's more room there and I'd feel better knowing you were sleeping in a bed rather than on his couch. The utilities and things come out of the bank at the first of each month. And the car will be there in case you need it."

"Brett may not agree to that." Her eyes looked dark against a face pale with stress, but she hadn't cried.

"Sleep in my room. If I can think of you there, it will make me feel closer to you." He swallowed though he hadn't enough saliva in his mouth to do so.

She nodded. "I will."

Jesus. Why hadn't he fallen at her feet and told her what a fool he'd been? "There's not enough time for me to say the things I want to, Zoe."

"I know."

"I'll email or call as soon as I can. If you don't hear from me right away, don't worry."

She nodded.

He grasped her hands and bent his head to kiss each one. His throat ached. "You'll be careful."

"I'll be fine." Her arms went around his neck. "Do whatever you have to to come home, Adam. No matter what it takes. Okay?"

"No matter what it takes." His arms tightened. The curve of her breasts pushed into his ribs, as she tiptoed to align her body with his. He breathed in the vanilla scent of her shampoo then drew back to look down at her. She shed no tears, but the struggle to suppress them showed in the careful composure of her features.

"It's only six months, maybe less." Was he reassuring her or himself? "We can call, email. Hell, I'll even write."

She nodded again.

He kissed her once, twice. His chest tightened painfully, his gut tangled with emotions stronger than any he'd ever known.

"Will you wait for me, Zoe?"

"You know I will." Her voice sounded choked.

"Hawk, man, we got to go," Langley spoke from the door.

"I'm coming." God, he didn't want to. He pressed his lips against her forehead then drew away. "I love you." The words sounded as choked as hers. He swallowed in an effort to clear his throat of the softball size knot there.

Her composure slipped, and her eyes grew glazed with tears. "I love you, too."

"You don't have to come outside."

"I'm coming."

Trish and the children huddled in a tight knot close to Langley's car. The girls, Anna and Jessica, clung to Trish. Tad stood a little apart, his thin shoulders hunched.

Hawk waited until Lang had embraced Trish and the children before doing so himself.

Brett shook the hand he extended, his features taut. "Watch your six, LT."

"Roger that. Watch over your sister for me."

"Consider it done."

Zoe stood at the car. Once again she'd managed to compose herself. "I can take care of myself."

Her tone brought a smile to his lips. "I know. He's going to have a hard time adjusting to not being with his unit, Zoe."

She gave a brief nod. "I know. He'll be back soon."

Hawk embraced her one last time. "I'll call as soon as I can."

"I'll be waiting."

His lips clung to hers. If only this kiss didn't have to end—If he didn't have to quit holding her— He got into the car and started it. Putting it in gear and pulling away was one of the hardest things he'd ever done.

CHAPTER 26

Brett tossed the remote control onto the coffee table. "I can't stand this one minute longer, Zoe."

Zoe drew a deep breath. She didn't want to go where he was leading the conversation. She had to get him out of the house or he'd explode and she'd have to respond to that and she'd end up in tears. They'd both end up feeling bad. "Why don't we go for a drive? We'll go to the beach and you can get some sun."

"God damn it! It's been two days, Zo." He rubbed his hand over his head, roughing up his fine blond hair and then fingering the scar on his scalp left from the surgery.

"Tell me where you want to go, Brett, and I'll drive you."

"It isn't that. It isn't about that. It's about you. I love you. You know I do. And Hawk is one of the best friends I've ever had. But seeing you like this, watching you pace the floors and—grieve—"

Zoe slumped into one of the dark blue chairs. Worry weighed on her like an anchor, dragging her down, and draining her reserves. She'd tried to hide the worst of it from him, but evidently she'd wasted her time, he knew her too well.

"Do you think it's any easier when it's you, Brett?"

"Jesus, Zo. I don't want to hear about it. If you tell me, I'll think about it and it will make it—We try not to think about how you guys feel. Hell, how we feel. If we did, we wouldn't be able to do what we do."

"Compartmentalize." The word sounded so cold. Hawk and her brother were anything but that.

"Yeah. Thinking too much can get you killed."

Doc's agony over his girlfriend and what he'd viewed as his failure came to mind. "I hope Hawk doesn't think of me for even a moment then."

A frown creased his forehead and bracketed his mouth. "You always said you'd never marry a guy in uniform."

"Things change when you care about someone."

"Jesus, it's weird. You slept with my boss. What were you thinking, Zoe?"

That I'd finally found someone who could love me despite my flaws and imperfections. Brett's deprecating tone made what they'd had sound cheap. Hot color stormed her cheeks and her anger ignited. "Are you being an asshole because you're upset about that, or because you're bored and just want a fight?"

His mouth fell open then he laughed. He leaned back and tilted his head back against the top of the chair. "All right-all right. I'm bored out of my skull." He rubbed the top of his head again, making his hair stand up. "But it's more than that and you know it." His brows furrowed. "I should be with them, Zo."

"You will be soon." She picked up the stack of photos with labels stuck to the back. "Let's work on your cards," she suggested. She had been over the photos so many times she could recite the names of the weapons in the pictures herself. Learning about the weapons and equipment had helped alleviate some of her anxiety.

She held up the first one.

"Nine millimeter Sig Sauer handgun," Brett said.

She raised the next one.

"Closed Circuit Daegar UBA."

Reaching the twenty-fifth card she paused as he hit a blank spot. Zoe watched as his eyes narrowed in concentration.

"M-m-m 88 sniper rifle," he said. He looked away but not before she saw the fear in his eyes.

"What does UBA stand for?" she asked so he wouldn't have time to dwell on the stumble.

"Underwater Breathing Apparatus." He shot her an impatient look. "Don't humor me, Zo."

"I'm not. I just think you should concentrate on how much you've accomplished in the three weeks you've been out of the coma and not dwell on these little glitches. Think of your brain as a computer. And you're running a program that still has a few bugs to work out."

His jaw tightened. "Bugs huh?"

"That sounds creepy, doesn't it? Bugs in your brain," Zoe wrinkled her nose. "Ewww—"

Brett rose and moved to the couch to sit next to her. "I know I'm being a pain the ass. I just can't seem to get past this. And not being able to remember what happened doesn't help any."

From her own experience, it was better that he couldn't remember. Especially if it had been, in some part, caused by one of his teammates. "Lots of people don't remember the moment they suffer a trauma, Brett. It wouldn't help you heal any faster even if you could." She stacked up the cards and set them aside.

Brett laid a hand on her arm, and she glanced up. A look passed between them and she knew he was remembering the flashbacks and nightmares she had suffered. She returned to their conversation. "Maybe the doctor will release you to take a class on post. You could take one you've already aced and review, and test yourself. You only seem to have problems with picture identification. You know what each thing is used for and how to use it. You just stumble over the name. That will come back once you've imprinted that information back into your memory."

"I suppose so. I just can't afford for this thing to linger on, Zo. I need to be on top of things so I can return to my unit."

He put his arm around her shoulders. She leaned into him and hugged him tight.

Even after being in a coma, he wanted to go back. Why? Why would he want to put himself in harm's way again?

She wanted him to get better, but if he got better he'd be sent back overseas. If he didn't get better he'd lose a part of himself, a sense of his worth. She'd felt less than worthy for so long. She didn't want that for her brother.

He had to make his own way, whether it put him in danger or not. She had to accept his decisions, just as she had to accept Hawk's. "I understand," she murmured her arms tightening around him. Pain sparked a need for Brett's comfort, as much as he needed hers.

"I know you do. I'm sorry I'm being a pain in the ass." Brett brushed her forehead with a brotherly kiss and gave her a squeeze. "How about you take me to the base so I can do some target practice? Maybe I'll work off some of the mad I've got going if I shoot something."

There was only so much she could do for him. He had to work things out for himself. And shooting wasn't so physically taxing he'd wear himself out. "All right. Call the base and schedule it and I'll take you."

An hour later, Zoe pulled into the parking lot he directed her to in front of the shooting range. Brett got out and she dipped her head to watch him as he walked around the car and paused at the driver's window.

"I'm trusting you with my baby," he teased as he patted the side of the candy apple red Mustang.

Zoe rolled her eyes. "Men and their toys. Call me when you need a ride home."

"I may be able to catch a ride. I'll call you and let you know."

"I'd rather you called me, Brett."

A smile crept across his face. "All right, Mom." Shaking his head he turned and walked down the concrete sidewalk toward a group of buildings, a navy blue gym bag swinging in his grip.

Zoe turned to back the car out and her cell phone rang. She put the car back in park and rifled through her purse for the phone.

"Hey, Zoe," Marjorie's voice came across sounding strained. "Would you have time to meet me for lunch?"

"Sure, I can do that. I'm on North Island and it might take a few minutes. Where would you like to eat?"

"I'll meet you half way." Marjorie named a seafood restaurant close by. Zoe grabbed a notepad from her purse and wrote down the directions.

It took only fifteen minutes to reach the place. It was early and the restaurant had plenty of empty tables. Zoe paused at the hostess's desk to allow her eyes to adjust to the change in light. Marjorie, her face partially obscured by sunglasses, rose from her seat in the corner and motioned to her.

A sinking sensation struck her midriff. Something had happened.

A waitress preceded Zoe to the table and, after she was seated, gave her a menu.

"Thank you for coming, Zoe." Marjorie's hands shook as she rearranged the candle, a glass dish lined with packets of sweetener, and the salt and pepper shakers.

"I just dropped Brett off at the base, so I was free."

"I'm leaving Derrick."

Relief and sadness tangled together inside Zoe and she reached for Marjorie's hand. "He's hit you again, hasn't he?"

"Yes." Marjorie's hands clenched into fists on the tabletop.

"I'm so sorry. Do you need me to take you to a doctor?"

"No, I just—I need—" Her lips trembled and it was several moment before she regained her composure. She clung to Zoe's hand, her grip almost painful.

"I'm afraid to go home and get my things," she said.

Why would she be afraid, he was gone wasn't he? "He shipped out yesterday with his unit, didn't he?"

"Yes, but he came home sometime this morning. It was some kind of homeland security thing he couldn't tell me about. They flew back this morning."

Why hadn't Hawk called her? Was something wrong? Zoe's anxiety spiked and she bit her lip. She dragged her attention back to Marjorie when she spoke.

"I went over to a girlfriend's house to spend the night. I was upset about him going wheels up." Marjorie's lips quivered. "When he came home and I wasn't there—He met me at the door when I came in at eight to get ready for work—"

"You don't need to go back to the apartment without police protection. I know you don't want to report this, but you really need to take out a restraining order and have him picked up, just to be sure. The police will call Derrick's commanding officer and have him detained there if he's on post."

Marjorie nodded. "Will you come with me?"

"Yes, of course."

"I love him so much, Zoe. But I've been so afraid."

Zoe moved to sit next to Marjorie and placed an arm around her. Marjorie trembled against her. Anger built inside Zoe in a wave. Damn Derrick Armstrong for doing this. "You don't have to be afraid anymore. Do you think you can eat something, or would you rather go to the police station now?"

"I don't think I could eat anything. You'll stay with me, won't you?"

The fear in the woman's voice, the way she trembled, triggered feelings of pity and protectiveness. "Yes, I will."

The waitress returned with filled water glasses to take their order just as she and Marjorie got to their feet.

"My friend is feeling ill and we're going to have to leave," Zoe said.

"Oh. I'm sorry. Is there anything I can do to help?"

"No, we'll be okay."

Zoe gathered her purse from the back of her chair and slung it over her shoulder. She looped her arm through Marjorie's and guided her out of the restaurant. "You can leave your car here in the parking lot. We'll come back for it after we go to the police station."

"All right." Marjorie began to cry. Zoe hunted for some tissue in her purse and handed it to her. She got Marjorie settled in the car and went around and got in. Murmuring words of encouragement and comfort, she pulled into traffic and turned onto Broadway where she knew police headquarters was located.

*****

Hawk swore beneath his breath as he hung up the phone. Damn, Flash. He'd gone AWOL before they'd reported for the shortest deployment on record. He'd either known he was suspicious, or something had happened to him.

Captain Jackson strode out of his office and Hawk rose to his feet. "I need to speak with you, sir."

"Has he been found?"

"No, sir. I've sent MPs to his apartment and he's not there. My guess is he's in the wind."

"God damn it." Jackson's brows slammed together and he scowled. "Come into my office Lieutenant."

"Did you see this coming?" Jackson asked as soon as the door shut behind them.

Hawk clenched his teeth in frustration. He'd thought of the possibility but without proof he couldn't have had Flash picked up or held. And when he hadn't reported to duty after the call had come in, he'd sent a detail out to find him, while the rest of the team caught a plane for Houston Texas.

"Sir, all I had was circumstantial evidence and speculation. It's in my report. There's no hard evidence that he attempted to kill Ensign Weaver or that he smuggled archaeological artifacts into the country. But Weaver's mother saw the cylinders when she unpacked his belongings. Weaver's sister, Zoe, was attacked by someone who broke into the apartment and took the artifacts, without leaving any trace. A flash bang was set up to go off in my house and a warning left for me to back off. All those things fall within our skill levels."

"You don't think Weaver was involved in this?"

"I've looked into all the men's finances, sir. There's been no unusual movement in anyone's accounts but Ensign Carney's. Carney and Ensign Armstrong packed Weaver's belongings. I believe that offered him the opportunity to slip the cylinders into Weaver's bag."

"Before the last mission, another team member heard them arguing. He said Carney told Weaver to mind his own business. I believe Weaver was trying to council Lieutenant Carney and get him to reconsider his course of action. Weaver knew about the gambling problem and suspected the money problems."

"So where do you think Carney is now?"

"He's painted himself into a corner. He'll be somewhere close to a casino trying to recoup his loses. I don't think he'll go to Vegas. He'll know we'll be looking for him. Atlantic City possibly."

Jackson rubbed his jaw and moved around the desk to sit down.

"I had hoped to settle this in house. It looks like we'll have to go outside and turn this over to the criminal division."

Hawk nodded, relieved. He hadn't relished the idea of bringing Flash in to face charges. By taking the investigation out of his hands, Jackson had also removed the probability of his men thinking him a snitch for turning in one of his own men. The investigators would follow the trail of insurance fraud, and other things, and draw their own conclusions.

"I'll take care of it, Lieutenant. You're dismissed."

"Aye, sir." Hawk saluted, turned and left the office.

Hawk drew a deep breath and returned to his office to complete another report. "There's a phone call for you, Hawk," Lang said as he passed him in the hall. "I think it's Zoe."

He'd attempted to call Zoe and tell her they were back several times and each time he'd been interrupted. God, he wanted to hear her voice. He'd wasted so much time sitting outside the apartment complex keeping an eye on her. He could have been *with* her instead.

He jerked up the receiver and pushed the button to connect him. "Yes."

A silent pause had him drawing a breath. Had she hung up?

"Hawk, it's Zoe."

Something in her tone sounded—Concern pumped up his heart rate and he frowned. "Are you all right, Zoe?"

"I'm at the police station with Marjorie."

Those few words kicked him in the gut. Jesus they'd barely landed five hours ago. What the hell had happened? "How bad is it?"

"She wouldn't let me take her to the hospital. A policewoman is taking photos of her injuries now. It looks as though she has some bruised ribs and a black eye. He punched her in the face first, and when she was down, he kicked her."

Bile rose in Hawk's throat. "Jesus." He took several breaths. "I'll call the MPs right now to alert them and have him brought in if he comes on post."

He flinched. Could he have done more? He'd queried Derrick weekly on his progress with the shrink. And kept an eye out for any sign he was getting stressed.

But Jesus, they were all stressed. He'd been working hard to get back to a hundred percent himself before deployment. And nursing his own pain over the break-up. Had that caused him to miss something?

"You couldn't have seen this coming," Zoe said.

"How did you know what I was thinking?" Stupid question. She knew because she knew him. At times, they were so in tune with one another, all it took was a look or a touch to know what the other person needed. God, how he'd missed that. Could they get it back?

"Marjorie didn't even see it coming," Zoe continued. "For the last month he's been doing great. No blow-ups, no mood swings. He's had insomnia for the last few weeks."

Hadn't they all? Hawk rubbed his hand over his face and got to his feet to pace the office as far as the line would allow. "Are you going to stay with her?"

"Yes. She doesn't have any family close-by. I convinced her to call her mom and she's on her way from New Mexico, but it will take a while for her to get here. I've told her she can come home with me after we're done here."

His gut tightened. What if Derrick showed up at Brett's apartment?

Brett was there, he'd watch out for Zoe and Marjorie. He had to talk to Jackson again. He was going to go ape shit over this. "She'll need to come here first to take out an MPO. That way the MPs can pick him up for assault."

"She isn't his wife. Will a military protective order still apply?"

"I don't know. I'll check with my commander."

"She's pretty shaky. Just going to the police was a huge step for her. She may not want to do that today."

"If you go back to the apartment, be careful. Lock up tight and stay there with Brett until I can get there."

"Brett's at the shooting range."

Shit. Anxiety hugged his ribs like a tight band. He sat down behind the desk again and leaned forward to place his elbows on the blotter.

"He was going to do some target practice. I'll call him and tell him I'm coming to get him," Zoe said.

"I'll send someone to the range to pick him up. You come here and get him before you go home, Zoe. Don't go to the apartment alone, okay?"

"All right."

"Be careful, baby. Stay alert."

She'd be all right. She'd come and get Brett and they'd hole-up at the apartment until they could find Derrick.

God, he was thinking of one of his own men as the enemy. As SEALS, they swore to defend and protect those weaker than themselves. Derrick had broken the code. As had Flash. His whole team was imploding.

"I have to go, Marjorie's coming out."

"Call me on my cell and keep me posted. Try and convince her to come here and do the paperwork for the MPO."

"I'll call if there's a problem. We'll be there to get Brett in a little while."

When they got to the base, he'd insist they stay until he could leave.

I love you was right there on the tip of his tongue when she said bye and hung up. Hawk swore. Why was that so fucking hard for him? Because every time he said it, it made him more and more vulnerable. Why was it he could deal with people shooting at him, trying to kill him, with a sort of controlled distance, and Zoe could twist him up inside with just a word or a look?

His finger was poised over the button to call her back when someone tapped on the door.

Langley poked his head in. "Captain Jackson wants us in his office ASAP."

Hawk rose to his feet and strode around the desk. "He's just the man I need to speak to. We have a problem."

****

Hawk paced the outer office as he waited for Zoe and Marjorie to arrive. He turned as Brett entered the office, a gym bag slung over his shoulder. "That was a short ride, wasn't it?"

"Yeah, there and back in twenty-four hours."

"Good. Zoe's been driving me crazy pacing the floors waiting for you to call. You did call?"

The big brother protective vibe Cutter was putting off brought the first smile in days to Hawk's lips. "I've spoken to her, but not about being back. I've been tied up here dealing with this thing about Flash."

Hawk scrubbed a hand over his face. He wasn't about to air team business in front of the office staff. "Come into my office." He turned and led the way and closed the door behind them.

"Marjorie called her, Derrick beat her up," he said.

"Jesus." Brett shook his head.

"They haven't found him, yet. I have men out checking all the bars and any other hangouts where they might find him. No luck so far."

Brett's frown deepened.

"You don't know of any place he might go, do you?"

"No. Is he in his car or on his motorcycle?"

"His bike is in the garage at the apartment complex. He's in his car."

"You've alerted the civilian police?"

"Marjorie has."

Brett nodded. "Good. Enough is enough. I tried to talk to him, convince him to see someone the whole time we were in the real world'." Brett's eyes narrowed in thought. He rubbed his forehead, the gesture at odds with the frozen stillness of the rest of him.

"What is it?" Hawk asked. Was he remembering something?

"There was something—" Pain flickered across his face. "I can't get it to come. It's like chasing shadows. I get a glimpse of something, it's like an impression or a feeling, then it dissolves."

Hawk hid his disappointment and slapped him on the back. "It'll come, Brett."

Brett shook his head. "Fuck! I hope so. It's fucking driving me crazy." He drew a deep breath. "What about Flash?"

"They haven't found him. Either he's in the wind or something's happened to him."

Brett slumped into a seat in front of Hawk's desk.

"Well, with me out on medical, and Flash and Derrick gone, it may take a few weeks for them to transfer in replacements," Brett said.

"Yeah, I've thought of that, too." Hawk's smile was grim. It might give him time to get things squared away with Zoe. Which was the one positive thing he had to hold on to in an otherwise fucked up situation.

But how many months would it take of evaluating his command skills before they dumped him into some shit detail? The men in a team were only as good as the commanding officer they followed. If he set the bar high enough. It had been his responsibility to keep these guys in line. To make sure they were the best they could be in every way. What did it say about his command skills that he'd been in the dark about so many things?

"Well this is a real cluster fuck," Brett said after a long silence.

"Pretty well sums it up from my perspective, too."

CHAPTER 27

Zoe eyed the front of the building housing Hawk's office. She had bats in her belly just as Bowie had described, but not because she was going to jump out of a plane. Hawk was here instead of off somewhere getting shot at. Thank God.

Marjorie moved restlessly beside her. "Are you sure this is the right thing to do?"

"Yes, I am, Marjorie. Derrick is here on post more than he's out in the civilian world. They have as good a chance of finding him as the police. Hawk said they'd look for him if you file an MPO."

Marjorie nodded.

"Let's get this done and go home. Okay?" Zoe urged.

With another nod Marjorie reached for the door handle.

Zoe followed suit. The woman needed her support but the anxiety she experienced just driving around with her had kept her nerves stretched taut as an exercise band. She'd been looking in her rearview mirror expecting to see Derrick behind them all day. She'd even thought she'd caught a glimpse of his vehicle two or three times.

As they got out of the car, Hawk and Brett exited the building with several other men and strode their way.

Hawk strode toward her, his normal fluid movements quick and purposeful. Zoe noticed the lines of tiredness around his eyes and mouth. Concern had her clenching her hands, but she held off touching him. Would he want her to show any open affection in front of the men?

"I have to leave," Hawk said as he reached them. "Something's come up."

Zoe's rapid build toward joy at seeing him snapped back to disappointment with the velocity of a bungee cord. Were they going wheels up again?

"Marjorie, Brett will escort you to Ensign James. He'll help you fill out the MPO." His gaze shifted to Zoe. "Zoe—" Hawk's voice sounded husky. His hand brushed down the back of her arm to her elbow. Her pulse leapt at her throat and wrists as he snagged her arm and pulled her aside. "It's just for a few hours," he said. "Brett will fill you in on everything. He'll stay at the house with you both until I get there. I emptied the refrigerator before I left, but there's stuff in the freezer to eat."

She nodded.

"I'm sorry, babe. I'll be there as soon as I can."

The look of genuine caring in his eyes, being close to him, eased her anxiety and loosened the knot of tension in her stomach. "It's all right. As long as you're safe that's all that matters."

Hawk brushed her lips with a quick kiss. "This isn't anything dangerous."

She offered him a smile.

He climbed into a Humvee with four other men and they drove off.

"What happened?" she asked Brett as the vehicle turned a curve and was lost from sight.

"They found Flash's car. The one he reported stolen. The front seat was covered in blood."

Zoe bit her lip. "Are you sure it was his?"

"Yeah. He may have found the guys who took it." Brett caught her arm and offered his other to Marjorie.

She slipped a tentative hand through his elbow.

He continued as he ushered them down the sidewalk to the front door. "Either way they're going to do DNA and see if it matches his."

"So he might not have gone AWOL," Zoe said.

"Maybe not. He may have run into some trouble instead."

Zoe drew a deep breath her thoughts spinning with possibilities. Would they ever know anything for certain?

****

In the restaurant parking lot, Zoe pulled next to Marjorie's car.

"Are you sure you'll be all right to drive, Brett?" she asked as she turned to look over her shoulder at her brother. He wasn't supposed to be behind the wheel, for at least another five weeks, if then. Marjorie, sitting silently beside her, was in no shape to drive. Short of making another trip to pick up the car later, to keep it from being towed, Zoe didn't know what else to do.

"Yeah, I'll be fine. There's no sense in Marjorie worrying about her car and it'll save time if we go ahead and pick it up right now."

"Be careful," Zoe warned as he got out of the car. He waved her off, and with Marjorie's keys in hand, walked to her vehicle.

Sometime later as Zoe turned onto the street to Hawk's house, Marjorie broke the lengthy silence. "I appreciate your helping me." Even with the sunglasses obscuring part of her face, Zoe could see the bruises growing more pronounced by the hour. The woman looked exhausted.

"You're welcome." Zoe sought something encouraging to add. "I know it doesn't seem like it right now, but things will get better. Once you feel better physically you'll be able to deal with the emotional things, too. Just take it moment to moment right now."

Marjorie nodded.

Brett pulled up behind them in the driveway. He held up a hand to stop them at the porch and took the key Hawk had given her. "Let me go in first, Zoe."

He opened the front door and slipped inside to disarm the alarm. She paused there with Marjorie at the threshold and looked around the living room. It appeared the same but harbored an empty air, as though no one lived there. Brett made a motion with his hand, meaning stay here. He disappeared down the hall.

He returned after only a moment. "Everything looks secure up here. I'll check Hawk's weight room under the sun room."

Zoe followed him through the kitchen. "I'll fix us something to eat." Perhaps food would distract Marjorie while they waited. She'd had nothing to eat all afternoon. Zoe's stomach growled. Neither of them had. "Would you like to lie down until it's ready?" she asked.

Marjorie took off her sunglasses and tentatively touched the bruised area along her cheekbone. "Yeah, I think I would. I'm a little tired." Her eyelid and the tissue around it was purple, the eye itself nearly swollen shut.

Zoe suppressed the urge to flinch and put an arm around Marjorie's waist. "I'll get you some ice. It will help with the swelling."

Brett returned from the sunroom and Marjorie held a hand up to shield that side of her face from him.

His gaze skimmed over her, then away, his mouth tightening. "All clear."

"Come on. I'll show you to a room," Zoe said.

She got Marjorie settled on the bed in her old room and went to the kitchen to get some ice.

Brett leaned against the counter and folded his arms across his chest. "You know, what we do—who we are, is about saving as many lives as we can. It has nothing to do with senseless violence against innocent people."

"I know." Zoe plucked a quart sized plastic bag from a box in one of the cabinets and filled it with ice. She wrapped it in a lightweight dishtowel. "Derrick has had some issues since your unit came back from Iraq."

"Derrick had issues before we left for Iraq. If he tries to use what happened over there as an excuse—"

Zoe glanced up as he trailed off.

"Did you know he was abusive, Brett?" she asked.

"I suspected something with his last girlfriend. I tried to talk him into some counseling. Then there was something—" His gaze shifted away from Zoe and he grew silent. A familiar look of concentration settled on his face as he grappled with a memory. "Something happened over there I was going to talk to Hawk about. It'll come back to me." He swore, a frustrated scowl marring his features.

He straightened and reached for the makeshift icepack. "I'll take this to Marjorie for you. She needs to know not all of us are like that."

It was going to take more than a few acts of kindness for Marjorie to regain what Derrick Armstrong had taken from her. But she'd have to start somewhere. "Take her some

Ibuprofen too, it will take down some of the swelling." He filled a glass of water, found the tablets and left the room.

Zoe opened the freezer door and rummaged through for something to thaw in the microwave and fix. A package of chicken breasts lay on top of a bag of rice. She took both out and placed them on the counter.

A puddle of water on the floor had her frowning. Had the line for the icemaker sprung a leak? Or had something tipped over and spilled as she opened the door? She closed the freezer door to peer closer. She caught a whiff of chlorine as the toe of a man's shoe came into sight next to her own. Shock like an electric jolt flashed through her. She grabbed the package of chicken breasts from the counter and swung them. Derrick blocked the blow with his forearm and the package went flying.

Zoe's startled squeak cut off as he covered her mouth with a hand that easily obscured the lower half of her face. Something hard dug into her side and she glimpsed the grip of a gun he thrust into her. Her insides turned to liquid. She bent away from him bowing her back against the counter.

The hot tub. He'd hidden in the hot tub. Had he been there all the time?

His wet clothes pressed against hers. Her blouse and pants absorbed the clammy moisture and she shivered. He raised a gun that looked like a cannon and rested the barrel against her temple. His body pushed against hers, hard and unyielding, pinning her to the counter.

"You know that little surprise I left for you in the living room a couple of weeks ago?"

The flash-bang. It was Derrick. Zoe nodded tentatively.

"That's nothing compared to what I can do. Make one peep and I'll snap your neck like a twig, you nosy bitch. I heard Marjorie's voice. Where is she?" Derrick Armstrong's voice was barely a rumble of sound.

Fear, icy cold raced through her, numbing her limbs and stealing their strength. If she told him, what would he do to Marjorie?

His hand tightened against her face, mashing her lips hard against her teeth and squeezing her jaw until she thought he might break it. Zoe squeaked in pain and clawed at his fingers.

"I could kill you, you know. And I'll still find her."

****

Hawk placed the duffle bag, he'd carefully packed with all his gear, in the Saturn's trunk. He should have insisted Zoe and Marjorie stay on post until he'd finished his meetings with the NCIS and the FBI. But it was good they hadn't. It was nearly seven o'clock and he was just leaving.

They'd be safe with Brett at the house.

He'd been telling himself that for the last hour and still anxiety nagged at him.

As he drove off the base, he looked northeast toward Mission Beach where he and Zoe had spent the day only weeks before. The gold ribbon of sand stretched down the coast against the backdrop of buildings that sprawled behind it. The azure blue sky extended along the horizon wisped with a scattering of clouds.

The two months they'd known one another was not enough time for him to ask Zoe to marry him. After their recent break up, she'd want him to woo her a little, and he'd have to regain her trust before he asked her for anything permanent.

Hawk rubbed a hand over his face. Damn, he was pathetic. Why would any woman in her right mind want to carry on a long distance relationship with a man who had withheld his love from her? He'd really screwed things up.

And now they had to deal with the debris left behind from Derrick Armstrong's behavior.

Damn him!

The team members he'd sent out to hunt for him hadn't had any luck finding him. As long as he was out there, he was a danger to himself, to Marjorie, and to anyone close to her. His stomach hollowed with anxiety every time he thought of Zoe driving around town with Marjorie while Derrick ran loose. Helping Marjorie was Zoe's MO. And the woman had to be protected.

Hawk wove his way down several streets toward home. A block from the house, he saw a canary yellow Jeep parked on the street and slowed. He whipped into a parking space down the street from it, and leaving his car running, walked back to the vehicle. A Trident symbol on the window had his heart racing. He looked inside on the passenger side of the car. A belt and empty holster lay on the seat.

Hawk's heart kicked into a sickening rhythm. He ran to his car and drove the vehicle around the corner and parked it three houses down from his drive. He exited the car and retrieved his duffle bag, then walked through the neighbor's yard to the back of his house.

The lock on the rec room sliding glass door appeared intact. He leaned forward to look through the window at the attached wiring to the alarm system. Fuck! It had been cut.

He withdrew a key from his pocket and unlocked the door. Scanning the room, he eased the entrance open. The alarm system didn't make a peep. Son-of-a-bitch. What if Derrick had already hurt someone? Cutter wouldn't take any shit from him unless Derrick had snuck up on them and was armed.

From the duffle bag, he retrieved his Sig and a clip of ammo and loaded the gun. His movements slow and cautious, he eased up the stairs to the back porch sunroom. The cover on the hot tub was shoved to one side. A trail of wet footprints led to the glider and then to the back door. His gun up and ready, he followed them to the entrance and peered through the window.

The kitchen appeared empty until he shifted to one side to get a better view of the entire room. Derrick stood to one side, his arm around Zoe's waist, his hand over her mouth. The barrel of a gun rested against her side.

A wave of rage and fear tore up through Hawk's chest to his throat and for a moment it was hard for him to breath. Shit-shit-shit- If he attempted to enter the house, the fucker might shoot first and ask questions later. He couldn't take any chances with Zoe's safety. Oh God, please don't let him hurt her.

Hawk's stomach lurched, and his temples pounded. He fell back to the rec room and took out his cell phone. His hands were shaking as he flipped it open and pushed a button. Langley's voice had him drawing a deep breath of relief. He spoke in a hushed tone. "There's a problem at my house. Derrick's broken in and he's armed. He's got Zoe. I know Brett and Marjorie are somewhere in the house. I can't enter the premises. It might cause him to do something stupid."

Langley swore. "Have you called the cops, yet?"

"No. If we alert them they'll call in SWAT and somebody will get killed. We need to handle this ourselves. I need you to call Bowie and get over here. I'll call Doc. Bring your gear."

"I'm on my way."

Hawk stared at the phone. If Derrick hurt her he'd kill him. But it wouldn't bring her back. His life would be empty—empty. He had finally tasted real love, and he'd nearly blown it. He'd only had a taste of the second chance Zoe seemed to be willing to give him. He wanted more.

Stay strong, Zoe. I'm coming. I'm coming.

****

Fear poured through Zoe stealing her strength and making her limbs rubbery, her breathing harsh. Please, don't let Brett come in here. Derrick's grip on her jaw tightened. Though her mouth was uncovered she couldn't utter a sound. Tears stung her eyes and her vision blurred.

"Damn you, tell me," Derrick said and turned the barrel of the .357 Magnum against her side. All the facts about the gun Brett had recited day after day flashed through her thoughts. If he pulled the trigger there was no way she would survive. Zoe raised a trembling hand and pointed toward the hall. Derrick twisted her around, his arm around her neck holding her back against him. He forced her forward.

Brett came out of the bedroom down the hall. He jerked to a stop when he saw them, his lips parted in shock. He recovered quickly and his eyes went flat and hard. "Let my sister go, Derrick."

"Not until I've seen Marjorie."

Zoe tried to shake her head, but Derrick dug the gun into her waist and gave her jaw a painful warning squeeze.

"Don't do this, man. You're just digging yourself a hole you'll never be able to climb out of."

Derrick's muscles bunched. "Shut up, Cutter. Get Marjorie, or I'll twist your sister's head off." His voice sounded hoarse.

"I'm here, Derrick," Marjorie appeared in the doorway. Her eye looked grotesquely swollen, her cheekbone, eye, and temple purple. The rest of her face looked paper white. "Let Zoe go. I'm here."

Where Derrick's brutal grip hadn't rung tears from her, the weary acceptance in Marjorie's features had them welling up and sliding down Zoe's cheeks.

"I didn't mean to hurt you, baby. I swear I didn't."

"I know, Derrick. But you did." Her voice sounded weary. "Let Zoe go. This isn't between you and her, it's between you and me."

Derrick released Zoe and shoved her forward. Her legs unsteady, she staggered and would have fallen had Brett not caught her.

Brett scowled. "God Damn it, Derrick. What is wrong with you?"

"She should have kept her nose where it belongs, just like you should have."

Brett's eyes narrowed and he pushed Zoe behind him. "You want to put that gun down and come over here and shove me around?"

Fear, abrasive as steel wool, scratched its way up along Zoe's nerves. From behind, she grasped Brett's arm and squeezed it tight. Didn't he know better than to bait an unstable man?

Looking over Brett's shoulder she noticed how haggard Derrick appeared. His eyes were red-rimmed and bloodshot, his jaw shadowed with beard stubble. He held the gun next to his side yet didn't take his finger off the trigger. All he'd have to do was raise it and fire and one of them would be dead.

"Come out from behind, Cutter so I can talk to you." Derrick motioned at Marjorie with the gun.

Marjorie shook her head and her body trembled visibly. "Not until you put the gun away. I'm afraid of guns, you know that."

Zoe laid a hand on her arm, offering her what comfort she could.

Derrick focused on Marjorie, intent, unblinking. "You went to the police today, didn't you?"

She hesitated, her eyes straying to the gun. "Yes."

"You didn't have to do that." There was accusation in his tone.

"Please put the gun away, Derrick."

"You didn't have to do it," he shouted, his voice cracking. The sound thrummed through the narrow hall making both Zoe and Marjorie jerk as though a jolt of electricity had leapt through them.

Brett reached out a hand to ease Marjorie further behind him.

"Get out from behind Brett and face me, damn it."

"No—No," Marjorie started crying in earnest. "You're going to hurt me again. You're going to kill me. I'm afraid— I'm afraid." She clenched part of Brett's shirt and cowered against his side as close as she could get.

"I'm not going to hurt you, but if I have to go through him to get to you, I will, Marjorie." Derrick cocked the gun at his side. The soft snick echoed over and over in Zoe's head growing louder and louder. The hallway seemed to shrink and become claustrophobic.

"I wouldn't have hurt you but—You won't be here when I get back. You won't stick it out. You'll be with some other guy, laughing with him, touching him, sleeping with him. Doing things with him you're only supposed to do with me. I thought you were already."

"You didn't go to Jessica's, did you? You didn't hurt her did you?" Marjorie asked a note of panic in her tone.

"Fuck her. Why did you go running off to her the minute I was gone?"

"Because I missed *you*, Derrick. I needed to have someone with me."

The open pain in Marjorie's voice punched through Zoe making her chest ache and her throat tighten. With Derrick standing just a few feet away, threatening and unstable, the words she and Hawk spoke outside his office seemed mundane and useless. Why couldn't they have said something important to one another? Why hadn't she told him she loved him?

Brett's muscles grew taut as he tried to cover them both with his body. "She's terrified, Derrick. Put the gun down and we'll all sit down and talk," he said, his tone soothing.

Derrick's face grew flushed and he scowled. He took two strides toward them, raising the gun as he came. He pressed the barrel of the weapon against Brett's forehead with enough force that he had to tilt his head back. "Shut the fuck up, Cutter. If I wanted your advice, I'd ask for it. Stay the fuck out of my business or I might just finish what I started in Iraq. You should have never put that kid between us, Cutter."

Brett braced his feet apart to maintain his balance. "What kid, Strong Man?" Brett's conversational tone belied the fact he had a gun pointed at his head.

Derrick's eyes narrowed. His tone grew scoffing. "Always the hero. That can get you killed real quick, you know."

Derrick reached for Marjorie's arm and Brett blocked the attempt with his own. "What do you mean, Derrick?"

Distracted, Derrick's aim wandered away from Brett's head and Zoe drew a shaky breath as the gun pointed at the ceiling.

"That kid would have just as soon killed you as looked at you."

"What kid?"

Derrick's gaze grew steady and dark as though he were focusing on some distant place inside his own head. "It doesn't matter now, you don't remember, and I'm never going to tell you. You'll just have to figure it out for yourself."

He lunged at Marjorie grabbing her arm. She squealed in protest and tried to pull away. Brett knocked the gun aside and twisted to one side in an attempt to shove Derrick back.

Zoe staggered back against the wall. Brett struggled to gain control of the gun. The barrel of the 357 swung toward Zoe's face. With a frightened cry, she grabbed both Derrick's wrist and the barrel of the gun. She tried to twist it from his grasp.

The front door crashed inward and Langley appeared in full body armor as Hawk stepped in from the kitchen doorway, a taser raised and ready. He fired and almost simultaneously the Magnum leaped in her hand as it discharged blowing a hole in the wall next to her. The magnitude of the sound jerked a startled yelp from Zoe. Sheetrock dust and insulation flew through the air. Derrick screamed and fell to the floor his body jerking from the electrical current as though he were having a seizure.

Doc, Bowie, and Langley, battle ready and armed, rushed into the hall. As a unit, they pointed their guns at Derrick. After holstering his weapon, Bowie whipped out plastic handcuffs, rolled him over and secured his hands behind his back. Langley retrieved the Magnum from the floor, while Doc bent to check Derrick's pulse. The only sounds in the hall were the dispassionate, well-trained replies of "target is secure" and "clear".

Hawk shoved the taser into Brett's hand as he pushed passed him and Marjorie. He reached for Zoe.

With a sob, she went into his arms. His Kevlar vest, stiff and rough, pressed into her breasts and his utility belt dug into her stomach. She didn't care. They were all safe and his arms held her close.

She drew back to look up at him, her vision blurred, and blinked away the tears that continued to fall. His gaze had never been more intent. His hands trembled as he ran them over her shoulders and arms as though checking for injuries and brushing the tufts of insulation away. "I love you, Zoe. I love you."

His voice sounded muffled beneath the ringing in her ears, but she heard him. A sweet tangle of emotion rushed through her, and she smiled through her tears. "I love you, too."

When Hawk bent his head to kiss her, her arms went around his neck and she rose on tiptoe to meet him halfway.

As their lips met, one word rang out behind them in a masculine chorus.

"Hooyah."

CHAPTER 28

"Come on, Ensign Clark. I know you can do it," Zoe said as she watched the young sailor struggle to maintain his balance between the parallel bars. She gripped the gate belt around his waist to steady him as he lifted his foot just enough to slide it over the floor, lay it down, and then shift his weight. His breath came in quick gasps. Sweat beaded his forehead dampening his blond hair in front and darkening it. He paused a moment before raising the other foot.

"Jesus, this hurts like a son-of-a-bitch," he said as he got the other foot going.

She grimaced in sympathy. "After having both legs nearly crushed, you didn't expect they'd work just like new the first time out, did you?"

"Well, a guy can hope can't he?"

"We certainly don't dissuade hope around here. Isn't that right, Tank?" She shot a look at the man standing directly behind Ensign Clark. He stood eight inches taller than the young serviceman and looked as though he could bench press a truck.

"Yes, ma'am." Tank retrieved the wheelchair, ran it between the parallel bars and lined it up behind Clark. He set the brake.

Zoe gripped the gate belt harder. "Just ease yourself down now. Tank will help you. Take it slow."

Once seated, Clark took several cleansing breaths. Zoe grasped one rail of the parallel bars to maintain her balance and bent to pick up the paper towels she had left lying on the exercise mat close by with a bottle of water. She offered them both to Clark and he grinned.

Another PT called to Tank for some help. After unbuckling the gate belt and removing it, Zoe leaned back against the parallel bars to wait for Tank's return. He'd take Ensign Clark back to his room as soon as he was finished with the other patient.

Clark tucked the water bottle between his thighs and wiped his face. "How long have you been a physical therapist?"

"Here in California, almost six months. I practiced two years in Kentucky."

He pointed the water bottle at her left calf encased in a brace. "How long since that happened?"

Her capris pants hid the scars on her thighs and buttocks but the more sever ones on her lower half of her leg were completely visible. She'd soon found showing her own scars encouraged the men not to be so conscious of theirs. "Since I was seven. Both my legs were involved too. It took me nearly a year to learn to walk again."

"Shit!"

"You'll get there Ensign Clark." She patted his arm.

"Aren't you going to give me a pep talk and tell me, if you can do it, I can, too?"

"Do you need me to?"

He grinned again. "Yeah, I think I could use a little moral support. You could come eat dinner with me when you get off."

Zoe rested her hand on her protruding stomach and shook her head, amazed. When she had first started the job every new patient started out this way. Flirting came as natural to these guys as breathing. Now that her pregnancy was so pronounced, she couldn't believe he was serious. "I have a boyfriend."

"I heard. He's in Iraq. It would just be dinner and he'd never know."

Zoe studied Ensign Clark's face. Young, handsome, and despite his current mobility problem, he'd be up and going again, as long as he did his therapy and kept a good attitude. She experienced not a single spark of interest. "I'd know, Ensign. I love my boyfriend."

"So it's the real deal, huh?"

"Yes, it is."

There was just enough regret in the young soldier's face for Zoe to feel flattered.

"He's a lucky man."

Thinking about the loving message Hawk had sent her that morning via e-mail brought a smile to her lips. "I'm a lucky woman, too."

Tank returned just then and grasped the handles of the wheelchair.

"See you tomorrow, Ensign." Zoe waved briefly as she moved out of the way so Tank could push the chair through. She scanned the room on the lookout for her next patient.

Exercise mats covered several areas of the floor. Padded benches lined the walls at equal intervals. Three sets of parallel bars stationed in each corner of the room were in use, the fourth, where she stood, was the only one free. The injuries they saw each day ranged from accidental injuries like Ensign Clarks, to amputations suffered in battle.

Knowing she was needed and appreciated by the men, helped her continue to get up each day. And it helped pass the time until Hawk returned from Iraq. The baby moved and she rubbed the spot where a tiny limb protruded. "Please let him come home before the baby's born. I don't want to go through this alone," she murmured beneath her breath.

"Zoe," Brett's voice came from a door to the left. She turned to face him. His intent expression had anxiety slicing through her. His long stride ate up the distance between them.

"What is it?" she asked her tone high-pitched with fear.

"Easy, Sis." Brett reached for her and gave her a squeeze. "It's nothing bad."

She drew a deep breath as her heart thundered against her ribs. "You never come here. I just thought—" She turned her face against his shirt as quick tears burnt her eyes.

"Shh—" Brett gave her another squeeze. "I should have called before I came. I just wanted to surprise you."

Zoe rested against him until the rush of emotion subsided. She drew back to look up at him. "It is a surprise. You never willingly show up here."

"I need you to go somewhere with me."

"I have one more patient, then I'll be free."

"Tank has agreed to take him for you."

"Tank isn't qualified to take him for me."

"Lt. Cameron said she'd supervise for you. It's important, Zo."

She studied him for a moment. Now that the fear had passed she grew more curious. "Where is it you want me to go?"

"If I told you, it wouldn't be a surprise anymore, now would it?"

She grimaced in agreement. "All right. Let me get my purse from my locker."

Brett grinned. "Good."

"Have you heard from Hawk today?" Brett asked as they got into the car.

"Yes. He emailed me early this morning. I know he tries to paint a rosy picture to keep me from worrying." She buckled the seat belt as he backed out of the parking slot.

"You do the same for him," he said accusation in his tone.

Zoe ran a hand over her stomach. "The only thing I want him thinking about is coming home. I'm not going to cause him any distractions."

"For someone who used to be determined never to get involved with a man in uniform, you've turned into the perfect military spouse."

"I'm not a spouse, just a girlfriend."

"Hawk will want to get married as soon as he finds out about the baby. Hell, if there'd been time he'd have married you before he left."

If she'd known she was pregnant then, she might have been in a little more of a rush. Zoe brushed at the soft curls that feathered around her face. "We'll deal with everything when he comes home." When he comes home. He had to come home.

"Where are we going?" Zoe asked as a guard waved them through the gates at the base.

"We'll be there in a minute."

"How is the class going?" she asked.

"Fine. I only draw a blank now and then."

Zoe's throat grew tight. She knew he was making light of things so she wouldn't worry. "Brett, please don't sugar coat things. I want to share things with you. I need to know you can talk to me so I won't feel I can't talk to you."

Brett glanced in her direction then reached for her hand. He gave it a squeeze. "I really am doing okay, sis."

"Good, I'm glad." She paused. "And how did your visit with Derrick go?"

"He finally admitted he knocked me out and left me to die."

His tone sounded so subdued, so weary, Zoe laid a hand on his arm in comfort. "I'm sorry."

He nodded. "He still won't explain what all that stuff was about the kid." Pain flickered across his features. "I thought we were buds as well as teammates."

"Is he getting counseling while he's in prison?"

"Yeah."

Zoe shifted the conversation. "Wonder who it was that slapped you in the hospital?"

"Since it wasn't Derrick, it had to be Flash. I don't suppose we'll ever know why since he's probably dead."

He turned into the fenced in area of the North Island Air Base and parked the car. He glanced at his watch. "We're here."

Suspicious she asked, "What are we doing here at the air field?"

"Hawk's plane will be touching down here in a few minutes."

"Oh, my God! Oh, my God! Why didn't you tell me?" She looked down at the rounded curve of her stomach. The instant joy, followed by panic, set her heart to flight. "He doesn't know. I've been waiting to tell him."

"Well, it's too late to do anything about it now."

"But I was holding off because I was hoping he'd propose before he knew about the baby."

Brett rolled his eyes. "You know he loves you, Zo. He damn well better propose now that he's knocked you up."

Zoe narrowed her eyes. "You have no romance in your soul Brett."

"There's Trish," He pointed at the woman as she got out of her car and walked toward them.

Zoe got out of the car and moved to meet her halfway. Trish gave her a hug and looped her arm through hers.

"Hawk wanted to surprise you. He asked Langley to tell me to hold off telling you."

Zoe blinked as she fought back tears and ran a trembling hand over her abdomen. "It's going to be a surprise for the both of us."

Trish gave her arm a squeeze. "A good one, huh?"

"Oh, God. I've been working all morning. I didn't have time to brush my hair or freshen my make-up."

"Too late for that now. Come on." Trish tugged her toward the gate. Brett fell into step with them.

The guard at the gate waved them through after looking at their IDs. The other girlfriends and wives clustered together before the terminal. Several called out greetings to Trish and to her.

Zoe's emotions seesawed back and forth between joy and anxiety. By the time the plane came into sight, she reached out and gripped Trish's arm hard. Brett rested soothing hands on her shoulders.

The huge transport touched down with a scuff of its tires and taxied to the terminal. A truck towed out the stairs as the door opened. Men loaded down with duffle bags filed down the stairs. Cries of pleasure broke out as women recognized their loved ones and raced forward to meet them. Langley appeared and Trish pulled away and ran to him. He caught her to him and kissed her.

Zoe looked back at the plane. Hawk's tall form came into view. His hair was long and shaggy and hung around his lean face glossy and dark. His Indian heritage had never seemed more apparent. For a brief moment he looked like a stranger.

His eyes scanned the crowd as he came down the steps. He spied Brett then wove his way toward him his gaze still searching. He finally saw her and her stomach plunged and her heart raced as the familiar punch of love and longing coursed through her. Tears welled up and she limped forward. Hawk dumped the duffle onto the ground and his long strides covered the distance.

He was there before she could catch her breath. His attention homed in on the rounded bulge beneath her loose top. His eyes widened in surprise. He faltered a moment, and then a smile split his lips wide.

Relief had tears blurring her vision.

"I didn't want to worry you," she said as she went into his arms.

"I love you, Zoe."

Hawk curved her closer and she rose on tiptoe to press tight against him. He kissed her with all the pent up emotion of a six-month separation. When he drew back, he didn't release her, but palmed the rounded curve of her belly. "God, Zo. What a homecoming gift."

She laughed in relief. "I love you so much."

"Are you, both of you, all right?" he asked, a touch of anxiety shadowing his face.

"Yes." She covered his hand with her own. "We're wonderful now that your home."

"I'm a little late from the look of things, but I have something for you." He reached into his jacket pocket. He popped open a wide jewelry box. Inside nestled a set of three rings fashioned from white gold with turquoise stones imbedded. Arabic words etched into the face of the wedding bands, foreign and beautiful.

"They say forever in Arabic, Zoe. I took a chance and bought wedding bands to match hoping you'd make an honest man of me? Will you marry me?"

His pale gray gaze was so intent, his expression so eager, she started to tear up again but laughed instead.

No matter how far away he was, her love would follow him, as his would rest inside her—deeper than the child she carried. She had no doubts. She was right where she was supposed to be. "Yes. Oh, yes."

Hawk kissed her again, his lips clinging to hers, his tongue tangling with hers so thoroughly they were both breathless when he raised his head. He removed the engagement ring from the box and slipped it on her finger. "What do you think?"

Zoe said the only thing she had breath left to murmur. "Hooyah."

11025918R0

Made in the USA
Lexington, KY
04 September 2011